THE STAR-CROSSED
SISTERS OF TUSCANY

THE STAR-CROSSED SISTERS OF TUSCANY

LORI NELSON SPIELMAN

THORNDIKE PRESS
A part of Gale, a Cengage Company

LIBRARY OF CONGRESS CIP DATA ON FILE.
CATALOGUING IN PUBLICATION FOR THIS BOOK
IS AVAILABLE FROM THE LIBRARY OF CONGRESS

ISBN-13: 978-1-4328-7282-3 (hardcover alk. paper)

Published in 2020 by arrangement with Berkley, an imprint of Penguin Publishing Group, a division of Penguin Random House, LLC

Printed in Mexico
Print Number: 01   Print Year: 2020

For Dieter and Johanna

AUNT POPPY'S ITINERARY

Day 1
Monday, October 15
Venice

Day 2
Tuesday, October 16
Venice

Day 3
Wednesday, October 17
Venice

Day 4
Thursday, October 18
Tuscany

Day 5
Friday, October 19
Tuscany

Day 6
Saturday, October 20
Tuscany

Day 7
Sunday, October 21
Amalfi Coast

Day 8
Monday, October 22
Amalfi Coast
Aunt Poppy's 80th Birthday

PROLOGUE

Many years ago, in Trespiano, Italy, Filomena Fontana, a plain, bitter girl whose younger sister was blessed with beauty, cursed all second-born Fontana daughters to a life without love. Filomena resented her sister, Maria, from the first time she cast eyes on her, sweetly cradled in their mother's arms.

And her childhood jealousy only festered as the two blossomed into teens. Filomena's sweetheart, Cosimo, a young man with a wandering eye, took a shine to the younger Maria. Though Maria tried to ward off Cosimo's unwanted advances, Cosimo persisted. Filomena warned Maria, "If you steal my Cosimo, you will be forever cursed, along with all second-born daughters."

Not long afterward, while Cosimo was picnicking with the Fontana family, Cosimo trapped Maria down by the river, where he thought they wouldn't be seen. He grabbed

Maria, forcing a kiss from her. Before Maria could shove Cosimo away, Filomena arrived. Seeing only the kiss, Filomena became incensed. She grabbed a river rock and threw it at her sister. It struck Maria in the eye. She lost her sight in that eye, which forever drooped. Maria was no longer a beauty, and she never married.

Some say it's a coincidence. Others insist it's a self-fulfilling prophecy. But no one can dispute the facts. Since the day Filomena issued the curse, more than two hundred years ago, not a single second-born Fontana daughter has found lasting love.

CHAPTER 1

EMILIA

Present Day
Brooklyn

Seventy-two cannoli shells cool on a baking rack in front of me. I squeeze juice from diced maraschino cherries and carefully fold them into a mixture of cream and ricotta cheese and powdered sugar. Through a cloudy rectangular window in the back kitchen, I peer into the store. Lucchesi Bakery and Delicatessen is quiet this morning, typical for a Tuesday. My grandmother, Nonna Rosa Fontana Lucchesi, stands behind the deli counter, rearranging the olives, stirring stainless steel containers of roasted peppers and feta cheeses. My father pushes through the double doors, balancing a tray heaped with sliced prosciutto. With tongs, he transfers it into the refrigerated meat case, creating a stack between the pan-

11

cetta and capicola.

At the front of the store, behind the cash register, my older sister, Daria, rests her backside against the candy counter, her thumbs tapping her phone. No doubt she's texting one of her girlfriends, probably complaining about Donnie or the girls. Dean Martin's "That's Amore" streams through the speakers — a final reminder of my late grandfather, who insisted Italian music created an aura of authenticity in his bakery and delicatessen — never mind that this one's an American song sung by an American singer. And I have nothing against my deceased grandfather's musical taste except that our entire repertoire of Italian music spans thirty-three songs. Thirty-three songs I can — and sometimes do — sing, word for word, in my sleep.

I turn my attention to the cannoli, piping cream into the six dozen hollow shells. Soon, the music fades, the smell of pastry vanishes. I'm far away, in Somerset, England, lost in my story . . .

She waits on the Clevedon Pier, gazing out to sea, where the setting sun glitters upon the rippling waters. A voice calls. She spins around, hoping to find her lover. But there, lurking in the shadows, her ex —

I jump when the bell on the wall beside me chimes. I hitch up my glasses and peer through the window.

It's Mrs. Fortino, bearing a bouquet of orange and yellow gerbera daisies. Her silver hair is pulled into a sleek chignon, and a pair of beige slacks shows off her slim figure. From behind the meat counter, my father straightens to his full five-foot, ten-inch frame and sucks in the belly protruding from his apron. Nonna watches, her face puckered, as if she's just downed a shot of vinegar.

"*Buongiorno,* Rosa," Mrs. Fortino chirps as she strides past the deli counter.

Nonna turns away, muttering, *"Puttana,"* the Italian word for floozy.

Mrs. Fortino makes her way to the mirror, as she always does, before approaching my father's meat counter. The mirror doubles as a window, which means that unbeknownst to her, Mrs. Fortino is gazing into the same window I'm peering out of from the kitchen. I step back while she checks her lipstick — the same shade of pink as her blouse — and smooths her hair. Satisfied, she wheels around to where my dad stands behind the meat counter.

"For you, Leo." She smiles and holds the daisies in front of her.

13

My grandmother gives a little huff, like a territorial goose, hissing at anyone who so much as glances at her baby gosling. Never mind that the "gosling" is her sixty-six-year-old son-in-law who's been widowed for almost three decades.

My balding father takes the daisies, his cheeks flaming. He thanks Mrs. Fortino, as he does every week, and sneaks a peek at my nonna. Nonna stirs the marinated mushrooms, making believe she's paying no attention whatsoever.

"Have a nice day, Leo," Mrs. Fortino says and gives him a pretty little wave.

"Same to you, Virginia." My father's hand searches for a vase beneath the counter, but his eyes follow Mrs. Fortino down the aisle. My heart aches for them both.

The bell chimes again and a tall man saunters into the store. It's the guy who came in last week and bought a dozen of my cannoli, the elegant stranger who looks like he belongs in Beverly Hills, not Brooklyn. He's talking to my dad and Nonna. I huddle near the door, catching snippets of their conversation.

"Hands down, best cannoli in New York."

A tiny chirp of laughter escapes me. I tip my head closer to the wall.

"I took a dozen to a meeting last week.

My team devoured them. I've become the most popular account manager at Morgan Stanley."

"This is what we like to hear," my father says. "Lucchesi Bakery and Delicatessen has been around since 1959. Everything is homemade."

"Really? Any chance I can thank the baker personally?"

I straighten. In the past decade, not one person has asked to meet me, let alone thank me.

"Rosa," my father says to Nonna. "Could you get Emilia, please?"

"Oh, my god," I whisper. I yank the net from my hair, releasing a thick brown ponytail that I instantly regret not washing this morning. My hands fumble as I untie my apron and straighten my glasses. Instinctively, I put a finger to my bottom lip.

The scar, no thicker than a strand of thread, is smooth after nearly two decades, and faded to a pale shade of blue. But it's there, just below my lip. I know it's there.

The stainless double doors push open and Nonna Rosa appears, her short, stout frame intimidating and officious. "One box of cannoli," she says, her lips tight. *"Presto."*

"Sì, Nonna. Good thinking." I grab three freshly filled cannoli and slip them into a

15

box. As I head for the double doors, she grabs the box from my hands.

"Get back to work. You have orders to fill."

"But, Nonna, he —"

"He is a busy man," she says. "No reason to waste his time." She disappears from the kitchen.

I stare after her, my mouth agape, until the swinging doors slow to a stop. "I am sorry," I hear her announce. "The baker has left early today."

I rear back. "What the hell?" I didn't expect romance. I know better than that. I simply wanted to hear someone gush about my pastries. How dare Nonna rob me of that!

Through the back-kitchen window, I watch the man chat with Daria as he pays for a bottle of Bravazzi Italian soda. He lifts the little white box that I — *Nonna* — gave him, and I get the feeling he's praising my cannoli again.

That's it. I don't care what Nonna says, or how narcissistic it seems, I'm going out there.

Just as I remove my apron, my sister's eyes dart to the window. She can't see me, but I can tell she knows I'm watching. Our eyes meet. Slowly, almost imperceptibly, she shakes her head no.

16

I step back, the breath knocked from me. I lean against the wall and close my eyes. She's only trying to protect me from Nonna's wrath. I'm the second-born Fontana daughter. Why would Nonna waste this decent, cannoli-loving man's time on me, a woman my entire family is certain will never find love?

CHAPTER 2

EMILIA

It's a four-block walk from the store on Twentieth Avenue to my tiny third-floor apartment on Seventy-Second Street, which I call Emville. As usual, I'm clutching a bag of pastries today. The late August sun has softened, and the breeze carries the first hint of summer's end.

Located on its southern edge, Bensonhurst is Brooklyn's stepchild — a modest neighborhood wedged between the more gentrified communities of Coney Island and Bay Ridge. As a kid, I dreamed of leaving, setting out for somewhere more glamorous than this tired ethnic community. But Bensonhurst — the place where my grandparents, along with thousands of other Italians, settled in the twentieth century — is home. It was once called the Little Italy of Brooklyn. They actually filmed the movie *Saturday Night Fever* on our sidewalks.

Today, things have changed. For every Italian shop or restaurant, you'll find a Russian bakery, a Jewish deli, or a Chinese restaurant — additions my nonna calls *invadente* — intrusive.

I spy our old brick row house — the only house I've ever known. While my parents honeymooned in Niagara Falls back in the 1980s, Nonna Rosa and Nonno Alberto moved all of their belongings down to the first level, allowing my parents to make their home on the second floor. My dad has lived there ever since. I wonder sometimes what my father, who was over a decade older than my mother, thought of his in-laws' arrangement. Did he have any choice? Was my mother just as strong willed as her mother, my nonna Rosa?

I have only faint memories of Josephina Fontana Lucchesi Antonelli, standing at the stove, smiling and telling me stories while she stirred bubbling pots that smelled of apples and cinnamon. But Daria says it's my imagination, and she's probably right. Daria was four and I was only two when our mother died from acute myelogenous leukemia — what I've since learned is the deadliest form of the disease. My memory surely was of her mother, my nonna Rosa, at the stove. But the smiling storyteller doesn't jibe with the reality of my surly nonna, the woman who, for as long as I can remember, has seemed perpetually irritated with me. And why wouldn't she be? Her daughter's illness coincided perfectly with her pregnancy with me.

"Afternoon, Emmie." Mr. Copetti, dressed in his blue and gray uniform, stops before turning up the sidewalk. "Want your mail now, or should I put it in your box?"

I trot over to him. "I'll take the Publishers Clearing House winner's notification. You keep the bills."

He chuckles and sorts through his canvas bag, then hands me a taco-like bundle, a glossy flyer serving as its shell.

"Just what I was hoping for," I say, giving it a cursory glance. "Credit card applications and Key Food coupons I'll never remember to use."

He smiles and lifts a hand. "Have a nice day, Emmie."

"You, too, Mr. Copetti."

I move next door to another brick building, this one beige, and step into the entryway. Patrizia Ciofi belts out an aria from *La Traviata.* I peer through the glass door. Despite the opera thundering from his 1990s CD player — the newest item in his shop — Uncle Dolphie is sound asleep in one of his barber chairs. Strangely, it's the jingling of the bells when I open the door that always startles him. I pull the handle and, as expected, he jumps to life, swiping at the drool on his chin and straightening his glasses.

"Emilia!" he cries, with such gusto you'd swear he hadn't seen me in weeks. My uncle is more cute than handsome, with a head full of downy white curls and cheeks so full you'd swear he'd just had his wisdom teeth extracted. He's wearing his usual barber smock, solid black with three diagonal snaps on the right collar, and *Dolphie* embroidered on the pocket.

"Hi, Uncle Dolphie," I shout over the music. The younger brother of Nonna Rosa, Dolphie is technically my great-uncle. But Fontanas don't bother with these kinds of distinctions. I hold out the bag to him. "Pistachio biscotti and a slice of panforte today."

"Grazie." He teeters as he snags the bag, and I resist the urge to steady him. At age seventy-eight, my uncle is still a proud man. "Shall I get a knife?" he asks.

I give my usual reply. "It's all yours, thanks."

He makes his way over to his CD player, perched on the ledge of a mirror. With a hand peppered in age spots, he lowers the volume. The opera quiets. I set my mail beside the cash register and step over to an old metal cart, littered with magazines and advertising leaflets, and pour myself a cup of coffee with cream.

We sit side by side in the empty barber chairs. His rectangular wire-framed glasses, similar to mine but twice as large, slide down his nose as he eats his treat.

"Busy day?" I ask.

"Sì," he says, though the tiny shop is empty, as always. "Extremely."

When I was a little girl, my uncle would have three men waiting for cuts, another for a hot shave, and two more drinking grappa and playing Scopa in the back room. Dolphie's barbershop was the neighborhood hub, the place to come for opera and boisterous debate and local gossip. But these days, the shop is as vacant as a telephone booth. I guess I can't blame anyone for no longer trusting a shaky old man to hold a razor to his neck.

"Your cousin Luciana scheduled a haircut today. I promised to fit her in." He glances at his watch. "She is late, as usual."

"She's probably tied up at work," I say, instantly regretting my choice of words. My impetuous cousin Lucy — *second* cousin, if

I were being precise — makes no pretense of her active "social life." This, together with the fact that her boyfriend du jour is her co-worker, makes it entirely possible that Lucy really is tied up at work. "How's Aunt Ethel?" I say, changing the subject.

Uncle Dolphie raises his brows. "Last night she saw her sister. She's always happy when she sees Adriana." He chuckles and dabs his mouth with his napkin. "If only I could get that woman to appear more often."

My aunt Ethel and uncle Dolphie live above the barbershop in a two-bedroom apartment my aunt has always believed is haunted. Sweet Ethel claims she sees the ghosts of her relatives from the old country, which, I suspect, is one of the reasons my uncle continues to keep regular hours at the empty barbershop. Everyone needs an escape, I suppose. I used to ask my aunt if she ever saw my mother. She always said no. A few years ago, I finally stopped asking.

Uncle Dolphie drops one last bite into his mouth and brushes the crumbs from his hands. *"Delizioso,"* he says and shuffles over to his barber station. He returns with the pages I gave him yesterday.

23

"I am liking this story, *la mia nipote talentata.*"

My talented niece? I bite my lip to hide my glee. "Grazie."

"You are building momentum. I sense conflict coming."

"You're right," I say, remembering the plotline I imagined today at work. I pull last night's pages from my satchel and hand them to him. "I'll bring the next installment on Thursday."

He scowls. "Nothing tomorrow?"

I can't help but smile. It's our secret, my little writing hobby. "Never underestimate the blueprint for a dream," he likes to say. Uncle Dolphie once told me he had a dream of writing an opera when he was young, though he refuses to share his notes with me, or even his ideas. "Silliness," he always says, and he turns fifty shades of red. But I love that he once had the blueprint for a dream. I only wish he hadn't underestimated it.

"Sorry," I say. "No time to write tonight. Daria is hosting her book club. She invited me to come." My tone is nonchalant, as if being invited to hang out with my sister and her friends were an everyday event for me. "She asked me to bring dolce pizza." I peek at the clock — half past three — and make

24

my way to the sink.

"According to Dar," I say, rinsing my cup, "the book club's main objective is eating, followed by drinking and talking. If they find time, they discuss the book."

His dark eyes twinkle. "This is wonderful news, your sister inviting you into her club. I remember when the two of you were insep-arable."

Without warning, I choke up. Horrified, I open a cupboard and pretend to search for a towel. "Well, I'm not a permanent member yet," I say, blinking furiously. "But I'm hop-ing that if her friends like me — or at least the pizza di crema — she'll ask me to join."

"Pizza di crema?" Uncle Dolphie gives a sidelong glance. "Do not let her take advan-tage of you."

"It's not that complicated. Besides, I love helping her." He raises his brows skeptically, and I pretend not to notice.

He checks his watch and scowls. "Luciana said she would be in for a trim at two. And I hear nothing. Not a word. I fear that one is too big for her britches."

I picture my cousin Lucy, with her curvy size 12 booty squeezed into size 8 jeans, and wonder if her grandpa is being literal or figurative.

"She's just a kid," I say. "She'll be fine."

He harrumphs. "A kid? Since when is twenty-one a kid?" He lowers his voice, as if the empty shop might hear. "Have you heard? Luciana has a new boyfriend — someone she met at that new job of hers. Ethel thinks this may be the one." He wiggles his wiry brows.

"Huh," I say. "Didn't Aunt Ethel say the same thing about Derek . . . and that drummer named Nick . . . and that other guy — what was his name — the one with the cobra tattoo?" I shrug my shoulders. "Lucy's young. She's got her whole life in front of her. What's the rush?"

He gives me a look, silently reminding me that Lucy is a second-born daughter, like me.

"Boyfriend or not," I say, wiping down the counter, "Luce seems to like her new job."

"Waiting tables in that slinky getup?" He shakes his head. "Tell me, Emilia, why would a smart girl like Luciana choose to work at this place — Rudy's?"

"Rulli's," I say. "It's the hottest bar in town."

"Something wrong with Homestretch? Irene and Matilde have worked there for years — wearing respectable blouses and sensible shoes, mind you."

My great-uncle, who emigrated from Italy a year after my nonna and great-aunt Poppy, is a traditionalist. The Homestretch was already two decades old when Dolphie arrived in Bensonhurst at the age of twenty-one. Fifty-seven years later, he's still loyal to the old pub.

"Uncle Dolphie," I say, "sometimes new is good."

He lifts his chin. "New cheese? No. New wine? No. New art? No." He takes my face in his hands. "*Dolce nipotina mia,* new is not good. Old is good. And you, of all people, should understand." He lifts my thick ponytail. "We have kept this same haircut for what? Twenty years now? And these glasses, they are the same spectacles you wore in your senior photograph, sì?"

"I wish," I say. "My prescription has changed three times." I whip off my small wire-rimmed glasses and bend them backward. "But luckily, these frames are pretty much indestructible, just like the optician claimed."

"Good for you, *cara mia,*" my uncle says. "Why change the tires if they are still rolling, sì?"

"Exactly." I plant my glasses on my face and kiss his cheek. "See you tomorrow with another pastry delivery."

"Grazie," he says. He shuffles over to the cash register. "Do not forget *la posta.*" As he lifts my mail, a purple envelope spills from the bundle, one I somehow missed earlier. He captures it beneath his suede Hush Puppy.

"A letter," he says, staring down at it. "The real kind."

I squat down to retrieve the mysterious envelope, but my uncle's foot doesn't budge. He bends down for a closer inspection. His eyes narrow. Then they widen. Finally, they cloud. He lifts his trembling fingers to his lips.

The hand-addressed envelope stares up at us, postmarked Philadelphia, Pennsylvania. My smile vanishes and I freeze. In flamboyant script, her name and address are splashed in the upper left corner. Poppy Fontana. Nonna and Uncle Dolphie's estranged sister, Paolina. The enigmatic great-aunt who has always fascinated me from afar. The curious woman Nonna insists is *un problema* — trouble. The only living relative I'm forbidden to see.

CHAPTER 3

EMILIA

I clutch my satchel protectively, as if it holds a concealed weapon rather than a simple letter, and force myself to slow down when I reach the sidewalk. Nonna Rosa stands at her bay window, peering past the heavy damask curtains. Though her eyes are small, Nonna boasts of 20/20 vision, something that comes in handy for a woman who, I'm convinced, can see around corners. I wave, hoping to appear nonchalant. With her typical flush of annoyance, she turns away. It's horrible for me to say, but I often wish she were the one who lived in the cozy space beneath the eaves. Or even in my dad's apartment on the second floor. That way she wouldn't hear my steps each time I cross the porch; she wouldn't be able to peek from the bay window and keep tabs on me, a woman of twenty-nine. But I'm not giving her enough credit. My nonna would naturally find a different window from which to spy.

I step through the beveled glass door and cross the terrazzo-tiled foyer, peeking into my satchel to make sure it's still there. A rebellious thrill shimmies up my spine.

I take the walnut stairs two at a time and throw open the unlocked door to my apartment. My tiny kitchen — basically a trio of cupboards and a small fridge covered in photos of my nieces — is dappled with afternoon sunlight. I dump the contents of my satchel onto the counter and snap up Aunt Poppy's letter.

Savoring the anticipation, I study the purple envelope, trying to guess the occasion. It's not my birthday. Christmas is four months away. My great-aunt Poppy — a woman I've met only once but who never misses a holiday — is getting older, after all, and must be confused.

Claws, my long-haired tuxedo cat, rounds the corner. I scoop him up and kiss his adorable grumpy face. "Shall we see what Aunt Poppy has to say? You must promise not to tell Nonna."

I position him over my shoulder and slash a finger through the seal. My heart thrums as I remove a sheet of linen stationery the color of lime sorbet. I smile at Poppy's purple ink, the whimsical sketches in the margin — a little girl wishing on a star . . . a bouquet of daisies . . . a map of Italy.

My dearest Emilia,

I'm writing this letter to ask a favor. No, not a favor, exactly. In fact, I will be doing you the favor. You see, what I'm proposing will change your life.

I drop into a kitchen chair and rub Claws's ears while I continue reading.

I will return to my homeland of Italy this fall to celebrate my eightieth birthday. I want you to join me.

I gasp. Italy? Me? I barely know my great-aunt. Still, images of sprawling vineyards and fields of sunflowers fill my head.

What fun we will have! You do like to have fun, don't you? I suspect your life may be lacking joy, working in that dreadful store with my sister and your father. No. I cannot imagine that is much fun at all.

I huff. My life is perfectly fine — fun. I get to work with my family and live here in Bensonhurst, the very town where I was

31

raised. And though it's less than an hour's train ride from Manhattan, it has a small-town feel. We still hang laundry on clothes-lines; we know our neighbors. I have Matt, a loyal, lifelong pal I see almost every day. How many people can say that? Paolina Fontana is way off base.

We'll leave in mid-October — a mere six weeks from now. I presume you've maintained your Italian passport. We'll arrive in Venice, cross the country via train to Florence, and end the trip on the Amalfi Coast, where I must be on the steps of the Ravello Cathedral on my eightieth birthday.

The Ravello Cathedral? What is she plan-ning?

Please call so we can make final ar-rangements. Until then, wishing you bouquets of four-leaf clovers and double rainbows.

With love,
Aunt Poppy

My stomach flutters with excitement before I catch myself. I can't afford a trip to Italy. Not on my meager salary. And even if

I could, Nonna would forbid it. I lean my head against the back of the oak chair and groan. Aunt Poppy will have to find another travel companion, another family member, perhaps.

But no, Aunt Poppy has no relationship with anyone in our family.

So she'll travel with friends. She must have friends.

Or does she?

An unexpected softness for the aunt I was never allowed to know comes over me. How lonely she seems to me now, the old woman who writes without fail each year on my birthday, who reaches out to me on every conceivable holiday, including Flag Day.

There was a time, when I was maybe nine or ten, that Poppy and I exchanged a handful of letters. It was thrilling to me, opening the mailbox and finding a letter from my great-aunt. She wanted to know which of my friends made me laugh hardest; whether I preferred laces or Velcro, dill pickles or sweet; which season of the year "made me bloom." No grown-up had ever shown such interest in me. Until one Saturday afternoon when Nonna caught me pacing the foyer.

"What are you doing, wasting time when you should be cleaning your room?"

"I'm waiting for the mail," I told her,

anticipation bubbling anew. "I have a pen friend." Aunt Poppy had used the phrase in one of her letters, and I loved the sound of it on my tongue.

Nonna frowned. "Pen friend? What is a pen friend?"

I grinned. "I'm writing to your sister, Great-Aunt Poppy!"

Without a word, she retreated to her apartment. Ten minutes later, just as our new mail carrier, Mr. Copetti, stepped into the foyer, Nonna emerged. She held out her hand for the day's delivery.

"Here you go," he said to Nonna. He winked at me. "Looks like a card today."

I smiled and peered over Nonna's shoulder. Mr. Copetti turned to leave, but Nonna lifted a hand. "Wait." She quickly perused our mail until she landed on a tangerine-tinted envelope.

"That's for me," I said, reaching for it.

Nonna pulled a pen from behind her ear. She slashed a red line through the address and wrote, *Return to Sender.*

"Nonna!" I cried. "What are you doing?"

She thrust the letter at Mr. Copetti. "Go."

His eyes bore the look of a milquetoast grasping for courage. Nonna took a step forward, aiming her finger at the door. "Out! Now!"

34

He practically charged from the house. I was grounded for a week, and all "frivolous" communication with Aunt Poppy was forbidden.

I waited a full ten days before secretly penning another letter to my great-aunt. I hid it inside my math book, planning to drop it in the mailbox on my way to school. My heart hammered as I sat down at Nonna's breakfast table that morning. All the while I ate, I kept a protective hand on the book.

Nonna eyed me suspiciously. I nearly passed out when she came up beside me, peering down at the textbook. I continued sipping my cocoa, keeping my hand fixed on the cover, praying to the Blessed Mother that I wouldn't be found out. But when I stood to leave, my sweater caught on the chair's arm. The book jostled. As if in slow motion, the letter drifted from the pages like a paper airplane, descending gracefully onto the toe of Nonna's Orthaheel slipper.

Needless to say, Nonna showed no mercy. Aside from the generic Christmas cards, the halfhearted thank-you notes, and the hit-or-miss birthday cards, I never reached out to my great-aunt again.

I turn to the window, an urban patchwork of rooftops and utility wires and ancient antennae, and absently rub the scar beneath my lip. What did Aunt Poppy think when my letters stopped coming? Was she hurt? Disappointed? Did she realize it was because of Nonna, not me? Or was it? Why hadn't I pleaded my case, convinced my dad to let me continue my friendship? The answer comes easily. My dad would never defy his mother-in-law. He's far too timid. And the shameful truth is, I'm not so different. When it comes to Nonna Rosa, the fierce little woman who signs our paychecks and holds the title to the apartments we rent, we're both cowards.

My stomach clenches and I drop my head into my hands, trying to silence the question that's calling to me. *Do you have the courage now, almost two decades later, to redeem yourself?*

CHAPTER 4

EMILIA

I don an apron, determined to put all thoughts of Italy and poor Aunt Poppy out of my mind. With my favorite possession — my mom's old cookbook — splayed on the Formica counter, I set to work.

In Italy, where Nonna and Uncle Dolphie and Aunt Poppy were raised, cake is called *dolce pizza,* or sweet pizza. I mix a teaspoon of soda into sugar and flour while Claws does circle eights around my ankles. My big sis, who has never learned to bake (and why would she, when she has a sister to do it for her?), has no idea that this sweet pizza, filled with a cinnamon–orange zest custard and Amarena Fabbri cherries, takes longer to make than the time we'll spend at book club tonight.

Forty minutes later, my phone rings. I catch my sister's name and punch the speaker button so I can stir while I talk.

37

"Hey, Daria. I'm making the pizza di crema now."

"Oh, good. Listen, Emmie, I just saw this Groupon — half off at Atlantic City's Tropicana. It'd be a nice getaway for Donnie and me, right? If I get it, will you watch the girls for a weekend, maybe sometime this fall?"

I pour the batter into the cake pans, not bothering to scrape down the bowl. "Uh, yeah, sure."

"Great. You're the best, Emmie."

I smile. "You're better."

Instead of our childhood ritual where she declares, "You're the bestest," she changes the subject. "So book club doesn't start until seven, but I need you here ASAP." She lets out a sigh. "Of course Donnie picks the first week of school to start an out-of-town job. You won't believe all the homework Natalie has. And Mimi's supposed to bring cupcakes tomorrow." She raises her voice. "And *someone* forgot to tell me!"

Poor Mimi. She's absentminded, like I was when I was seven. "I'm sliding the cake in the oven now. I'll be there as soon as it's done."

"Awesome."

She's about to hang up when I blurt out my news. "I got a letter today. From Great-Aunt Poppy."

"Oh, God. What did she want?"

I run my spatula down the bowl and stick it in my mouth, grateful we're not on Face-Time. "She wants to take me on a holiday." An unfamiliar sensation brews and a smile takes over my face. I go in for another scoop of batter. "To Italy."

"Oh, well, you can't go. Nonna will never allow it. She'll have to take another niece. Carmella, maybe. Definitely not Lucy." She laughs. "Nobody in her right mind would set that girl loose in a foreign country."

I suck on the spatula. "That's Poppy's decision, not Nonna's."

"Nonna hates Poppy," Daria says, ignoring my statement. "You know that."

"But why, Dar? Poppy's her sister."

"She has her reasons. We need to respect that."

"I'm going to talk to Nonna."

"Don't!"

"I have a chance to go to Italy, Dar. I'm not going to blow it just because Nonna has issues."

"Issues?" My sister's voice rises, and I brace myself, knowing what's coming next. "Nonna may not be perfect, but she sacrificed her entire life for us, Emmie. She's been like a mother to you."

It's her trump card, the one that always

stops me cold. A heaviness takes hold of me and I hang up the phone. I plug the sink and turn on the faucet, rubbing my scar as I wait for the sink to fill. My sister has confirmed it. I can't go to Italy. Doing so would be an unforgivable breach of loyalty to the woman who raised me. Poppy will need to find another travel companion, maybe someone on the other side of her family. But again, I'm reminded, my great-aunt has no other family. She never did. She never will. Like me, she's single . . . and the second daughter.

I was seven when I first caught wind of the Fontana Second-Daughter Curse. We'd constructed family trees for social studies class, and I chose my mother's side of the family — the Fontanas. After studying my lineage for all of three seconds, my teacher, Sister Regina, blurted out a fact I hadn't seen — or perhaps hadn't wanted to see. "Look at all the women on your family tree who never married." She scowled and looked more closely. "That's peculiar. They're all second-born daughters."

I pushed up my glasses and peered at the felt-penned branches, where I'd carefully written my ancestors' names on the leaves. I'd always known Nonna's aunt Blanca was single. She was the reason my great-grandparents couldn't come to America. And I knew my nonna's sister, my great-aunt Poppy, hadn't married, either — an old maid, Nonna Rosa called her. But tracing the branches with my finger, I found that Nonna's cousins Apollonia, Silvia, Evangelina, Martina, and Livia were also single . . . and also the second daughters.

My eyes drifted downward, like a falling leaf. And there it was, plain as the white posterboard it was drawn on: my branch of the Fontana family tree.

Beneath my mother, Josephina Fontana Lucchesi Antonelli, and my father, Leonardo Phillip Antonelli, I placed a finger on my sister Daria's name. I slid it to the right and found my name, Emilia Josephina Fontana Lucchesi Antonelli. The second daughter.

CHAPTER 5

EMILIA

Clutching the box with both hands, I trot down the sidewalk toward Sixty-Seventh Street, my temporary fit of melancholy replaced with excitement now. I imagine Daria and me bustling around her kitchen, chatting as we set out the snacks and drinks for book club. I cross Bay Ridge Avenue, watching my step as I approach the curb, taking care that the box doesn't shift. The pizza di crema is a masterpiece, if I may say so myself.

Please let Daria like it, I chant silently. Moments later, I realize my mental chant has become, *Please let Daria like me.*

A horn blares and I lunge onto the sidewalk, my heart racing. Then I spot the shiny black truck with *Cusumano Electric* splashed on the side door. The vehicle slows and the window lowers. Matteo Cusumano lifts his aviator sunglasses.

"Hey, gorgeous. Need a lift?"

I smile at my dearest friend — one I've never not known. Cradling the cake, I lean into his truck. "You sure know how to spoil a girl, showing up when she's two blocks from her destination."

"Hey, I'm that kind of guy." Matt laughs. "Hop in. Let's grab a beer."

"Don't you have electricity to restore? Wires to cross?"

He grins. "Just finished my last job for the day — the exhausting task of changing a lightbulb in Mrs. Fata's kitchen."

"Wow. That electrician's license is really paying off."

"Smart-ass."

I climb into the cab of his truck, holding tight to the box as I fasten my seat belt. "You do realize Mrs. Fata is hoping you'll change more than her lightbulbs, don't you?"

"Women in their sixties love me," he says. And it's probably true. Matteo is lean and lanky, with a beautiful head of curly dark hair, front teeth that overlap slightly, and an infectious laugh that's been known to tease a smile from Nonna Rosa herself. He elbows me. "It's those twenty-nine-year-olds I can't seem to charm."

I stifle a groan and turn to the window,

43

where a young mother pushes a stroller down the sidewalk. Though Matt is ten months older than I am, he's always felt like my kid brother. He's the scrawny boy who walked me to Saint Athanasius on the first day of kindergarten, the one who bloodied Joey Bonofiglio's nose when he called me "fish lips" in the fifth grade, the brainiac who let me copy his chemistry homework our entire sophomore year, the sweetheart who took me to prom and later accompanied me to Daria's wedding and every other event that required a date. Matteo Silvano Cusumano is my plus-one, times a hundred. Nobody could hope for a better friend. And that's exactly how I want to keep it.

"Can you drop me at Daria's, please?"

"No time for a beer?"

"It's book club tonight, remember?"

"Right. All the more reason for alcohol."

I shoot him a look. Matt isn't a fan of Daria. "A raving bitch," he once dubbed her, before I called him out on it. Nobody talks about my sister like that.

The truck slows to a stop in front of her house. "Thanks for the ride, MC."

"What time does this shindig end? I'll pick you up."

"It's okay." I open the door. "I can walk home."

"Seriously. It'll be the highlight of my night."

His eyes are as tender as a lover's. I cringe, hating the awkward moments that seem to be creeping into our conversations more and more frequently. Our relationship shifted last May, when Matt broke up with Leah, his girlfriend of eight months. It's always easier when Matt's in a relationship. But our friendship reached an unspoken tipping point last month, when we attended his best friend's wedding. Afterward, when we were walking through the parking lot, still howling over the father-of-the-groom's attempt to moonwalk, Matt grabbed hold of my hand. Naturally, I let out a crack of laughter, slugged him in the arm, and stuffed my hand into my coat pocket. Matt and I hug. Sometimes I kiss his cheek. We high-five and fist-bump. We don't hold hands. Ever. But I hurt his feelings and I feel awful, and there's no way to apologize without bringing up the mortifying event — or worse, having to talk about "us." So I pretend it didn't happen.

I step out of the truck. "You're pathetic, Cusumano. Thanks anyway. Really."

I wave good-bye and turn up the sidewalk to the 1940s row house Donnie and Daria bought after Donnie's dad passed. Their plan was that Donnie, who lays brick and claims to know a "shitload" about construction, would fix up the dated interior. Two years later, aside from a coat of paint in the bathroom and new carpet in the girls' room, the place still looks like a set from *I Love Lucy.* It's retro-cool, I tell Daria. A classic.

Laughter rises from the backyard. I round the corner and step up to the chain-link fence, where my nieces are practicing gymnastics in a yard not much bigger than a collapsed refrigerator box. Already they're so different, Natalie and Mimi, the firstborn daughter and the second. Just as my great-great-great-great-great-great-aunt Filomena predicted when she cast the Fontana Second-Daughter Curse — not that I believe the old myth.

I watch as nine-year-old Natalie does a perfect handspring. She lifts her arms triumphantly, then brushes back loose strands of shiny brown hair from her angelic face. Today, my sister has styled it into a French braid, entwined with a pretty red ribbon. Her turquoise leggings show off her lean, muscular frame, and she's wearing a T-shirt that says *Future President,* which might actually be true.

"And that's the way you do a handspring," she tells Mimi. Yup, the girl is as self-assured and borderline bossy as a young Hillary Clinton.

Seven-year-old Mimi gazes at her big sister with awe. As usual, Mimi looks a bit rumpled today. She's wearing a wrinkled, hand-me-down dress that hangs from her bony frame. Her long legs are grass stained and her toenails, unlike her sister's purple ones, are bare. Her dark hair is clipped short, slashing twenty minutes of bickering from their morning ritual, according to my sister.

"Auntie Em!" Mimi cries when she sees me. She runs full force to me, her arms outstretched. I place the cake on the lawn and squat down, pulling her into my arms.

"Hey, sweet pea!" I close my eyes and breathe in her slightly sour smell. "How are my girls?" I rise and open my arms to Natalie. "Nice handspring, kiddo."

She gives me a quick hug. "Thanks."

"Swing me!" Mimi says.

I smile and tousle her hair. "Just once. I'm helping your mom get ready for book club."

I take her hands and turn in fast, tight circles. Mimi, airborne, screams with laughter. I'm laughing, too. Somewhere behind us, the back door opens.

"Em? What are you doing?"

I slow to a dizzying stop. "Hey, Dar." I drop Mimi's hands, trying to orient myself as the yard spins. "I'll be right in."

"Where's the cake?"

I laugh and stagger backward, accidentally poking my cheek as I go to straighten my glasses. "Don't worry, I've got it."

"Auntie Em!" Mimi cries. "Watch out!"

My heel hits against something hard. I try to avoid it, but the earth is still spiraling. I'm stumbling now.

"Emmie!" Daria yells as I tumble backward.

My hip hits the ground. Hard. I hear the door slam shut. Instantly, Daria's at my side.

"I'm okay," I assure her, rubbing my side.

"Damn it!" she says, wedging the crushed box from beneath my feet. "The cake is ruined!"

She rushes off to the house. I push myself onto my elbows, the earlier excitement draining from me. "I'm so sorry," I call to her.

"You're in trouble," Natalie tells me.

"I know." I scramble to my feet and quickly kiss both their cheeks. "I better go see if I can salvage the cake before Nonna goes ballistic."

It isn't until I see their puzzled faces that I realize I misspoke.

Twenty minutes later, I've managed to prop the cake back up with the help of toothpicks and a second layer of icing. "Ta-da!" I say, holding it up for Daria.

She stands on a stool with her back to me, pulling wineglasses from her metal kitchen cupboard. She's wearing a cute floral sundress that shows off her long, tanned legs.

I slide the cake onto her kitchen table, already filled with cheeses and crackers and tiny sandwiches. "Nobody will be the wiser," I say.

She finally turns around. She zeros in on the cake. I wait, holding my breath.

"Good work, Emmie."

I let out a breath. "Great. And, Dar, I really am sorry."

She hops off the stool and I catch a whiff of her floral perfume. Her brown hair, highlighted with shades of gold and perfectly ironed, falls softly at her shoulders.

I pull my concealer stick from my pocket. "By the way," I say, dabbing flesh-colored putty on the scar beneath my lip, "you look gorgeous."

"Thanks. Hey, where's Natalie? I told you, she needs help with her homework."

"Oh." I peek at my watch. "Right. I'll get her." I stop halfway to the door. It's almost seven. A sinking feeling comes over me.

"And those cupcakes Mimi has to take to school?"

"Thanks for remembering." She tips her head toward a Duncan Hines cake mix sitting on the counter. "I owe you one, Emmie."

I gaze out the rain-spattered kitchen window, my sister's backyard shrouded in darkness now, and fill the sink. Daria's voice drifts in from the living room, saying her good-byes to the last guest.

"Tell your sister her cake was amazing," the woman says. "Invite her next month when I host. But warn her, I chose nonfiction. Probably too heavy for her."

I scowl. What does that mean? I quickly dry my hands, ready to go defend myself, but Daria's words pin me in place.

"Emmie's got a degree in English lit. Trust me, she can handle it." There's no mistaking the edge in her voice.

I grin. Though it's been years since she told me herself, my big sis is proud of me.

Ten minutes later, I place the last wineglass in the cupboard and fold the dish towel over the oven door handle. After surveying the spotless kitchen one last time, I grab my cake plate and turn out the kitchen light.

50

"I'm leaving," I call down the hall.

Daria steps from her bedroom, already changed into her baby blue nightshirt. Memories rush in. My big sister in her pj's, sitting cross-legged on the bed, polishing my nails. The two of us in matching night-gowns, singing into our hairbrushes to the Spice Girls' "Wannabe." Her hand rubbing circles on my back after I'd had a nightmare.

"Thanks, Emmie," she says.

"And thank you. I heard what you said to your friend, the one who didn't think I could handle nonfiction."

She shrugs. "I'd say anything to shut Lauren down. That woman can be such a bitch."

"Oh. Still, thanks." An awkward silence settles. I hitch up my glasses. "Mimi's cupcakes are on the counter."

"Great." She moves down the hallway, stopping an arm's length from me.

"How was the book discussion?"

She looks away. "Fine. Boring. You didn't miss a thing."

"Really? Sounded like you guys were having fun."

She sighs. "I'm sorry, Emmie. I didn't realize Natalie's homework would take so much time."

What happened to us? I want to ask. My heart pummels against my rib cage. I muster all my courage and blurt out, "What did I do wrong, Dar?"

She crosses her arms and shifts uncomfortably before letting out a nervous chortle. "You should have let her use a calculator. I don't care what the instructions say, it saves hours."

She's deflecting, as she always does, and we both know it. I drop it.

"I guess I'll take off."

"Okay. Be safe."

I stare at the plate in my hand and wait, willing her to say something . . . *anything.* Finally I say, "You haven't mentioned my cake, the one you asked me to make." I hear the snark in my voice, but I can't help myself. I'm too hurt. "How was it?"

She bats her forehead. "The pizza di crema! It was a huge hit. Nobody suspected that just an hour earlier, it was in pieces. Honest to God, Emmie, you should be a baker or something." She tips her head back, and I'm enveloped in my sister's rich, lilting laughter, a magical sound I once took for granted. "What would I do without you?" she says.

And just like that, all is forgiven.

CHAPTER 6

EMILIA

I'm one block from Daria's house and my hair's already drenched. The winds have picked up, and the temperature has dropped a good twenty degrees since this afternoon. I trot down the street, cursing myself for not wearing a raincoat. Ahead, a man strolls toward me, nearly hidden beneath a gigantic golf umbrella. Headlights from an oncoming car illuminate his smiling face. A well of gratitude rises in me.

"MC!"

"Hey," Matt says, shepherding me beneath his umbrella and handing me his Nike hoodie. "I know you said you would walk, but since it's raining . . ."

I wriggle into his jacket. "Thanks."

He lifts the hood over my head. "That hoodie's never looked better."

I ignore the compliment, and together, we set off walking.

"How was book club?"

"Fun," I say, concentrating on the rain reflecting the streetlights.

"Yeah?" The air fills with silence — the pause of a lifelong friend who knows when I'm lying.

"I meant to tell you earlier," I say, shifting the conversation. "My great-aunt Poppy invited me to Italy."

"What? That's awesome. You'll finally have that adventure you've always wanted."

Matt's one of the few people who know about the travel magazines I borrow from the library and the dream board I concocted back in high school, per Oprah's instructions, foolishly thinking mental images of far-off cities might make my dreams come true. I settle my eyes on the wet sidewalk.

"Uh-huh."

"Aunt Poppy . . . she's the one nobody talks to, right?"

"Yes. I have no idea why she's chosen me as her travel companion."

"Smart woman. When do you leave?"

"Oh, I'm not going. Nonna would have a stroke. She despises Poppy."

"What does that have to do with you and your aunt?"

"Befriending Poppy would be the ultimate act of betrayal. Daria was the first to point this out."

Raindrops pelt the umbrella. We walk in silence another block before he speaks again.

"Why do you let your family do this to you?"

I look over at him. The little muscle in his jaw twitches and he shakes his head. I let out a sigh.

"Look, I know what you're thinking. But this is different, Matt. This is about loyalty and —"

"Bullshit." He holds up a hand, blocking my rebuttal. "God, Em, you have no problem speaking your mind. Just last week, when we were in line at Da Vinci's, you reamed the guy behind the counter for ignoring that Middle Eastern couple. And Fourth of July, when it was ninety degrees and you saw that collie trapped in a car? You waited thirty minutes for its owner to return, just so you could let her have it." He gives me a lopsided grin and softens his voice. "I love that about you. So why the hell do you let your nonna — and your sister — push you around?"

I shake my head. Matt has never understood my family. He and his three younger brothers are best buds. Nobody in the Cusumano family ends a phone call without

55

saying "I love you."

"My family shows love differently than yours," I say, already weary of this tired conversation. "But that doesn't mean they don't care. You remember when my uncle Vinnie had that scare with his heart eight years ago?"

He rolls his eyes. "Your entire family rallied."

"That's right. They did, Matt, so don't give me that look. Every night, Nonna delivered dinner to Aunt Carol. Carmella and Lucy stayed with my dad and me for an entire month. And they've been there for me, too — especially Nonna. She dedicated her entire adult life to helping raise Dar and me. She's never asked for a thing in return."

"Except your complete obedience," he mumbles.

I skate right over his sarcasm. "And when I was in the accident back in college, Nonna closed the store for three days so they could be by my side. That," I say, "is what family is all about. So please, don't act like my family has no soul. They're good people."

"To everyone but you and your aunt Poppy."

Mercifully, my house comes into view. "Thanks for the umbrella and the hoodie."

He turns to me. "You know, it just hit me.

I think I finally realize why you put up with their abuse." He chews his lip and studies me. "You're scared."

I laugh. "Scared? Whatever, Cusumano." I step into the rain. "I'll talk to you tomorrow."

He grabs hold of my — *his* — coat sleeve. "C'mon, Ems. Think about it. You've seen firsthand what happens to people in your family who don't conform."

Rain speckles my glasses and drips from my nose. "What are you talking about?"

"I'm talking about Poppy. And the fact that you're both treated like shit, like you're somehow less worthy, all because of that fucking lie."

My heart trips. He's talking about the curse.

"It's not natural, the way your nonna cut off all ties with her sister. I've always thought it was weird. And you . . . you tiptoe around her and Daria, bowing to their every need — even forfeiting a trip to Italy that I know damn well you want to go on — just so they'll love you. Because if you don't, you're afraid one day you could end up alone and abandoned, just like your aunt Poppy."

I want to argue, but I don't trust my voice. I cover my chin. Matt's eyes go soft.

"Hey, I didn't mean to upset you." Without warning, he leans in and kisses my cheek. Instinctively, I flinch. Then, as if he needed further humiliation, I swipe the spot where his lips were. Even in the dim streetlight, I can see I've hurt his feelings.

"I'm sorry, MC. I didn't mean —"

He lifts a hand to silence me. For a moment, he just stares at me, shaking his head. "Can't you see, you've got a chance of a lifetime here? And you're about to lose it. You're about to throw it away, because you're too damned scared to move forward." His voice is picking up steam, the way it does when he's frustrated. "You're twenty-nine years old, Em. You're not a kid anymore. Stop pretending you don't see what's right in front of your nose. You've got an opportunity. Grab it. Because one day, mark my words, you're going to regret losing the best thing that's ever happened to you."

I swallow hard, my mouth suddenly dry. There's not a doubt in my mind, this conversation has nothing to do with Italy.

He places a hand on my wet cheek. This time, I make sure I don't recoil. "Do you understand where I'm coming from?"

"Yes," I whisper, my heart pounding in my chest.

This is a pivotal moment. He's waiting for

me to elaborate, to say something that gives him hope. My lifelong friend, my easiest companion, the man I'd step in front of a train for, wants more than my friendship. I close my eyes, intoxicated with terror and rebellion and guilt.

"I know exactly where you're coming from," I say. "And you're right." I smile and slug his arm. "I *do* want to go to Italy."

I wave good-bye and turn up the sidewalk. God help me, I've become just as good as my sister at deflecting.

I nudge the front door open ever so slowly, and I'm assaulted by a blast of heat, the one indulgence Nonna, who's never gotten acclimated to New York winters — or even summers — allows. My mind whirls. Matt is flat-out wrong. My family would never cut ties with me, the way they did with my great-aunt. With the slightest whisper of a click, I lock the door behind me. In the darkness, I navigate the terrazzo foyer. I'm almost to the staircase when I stumble over a pair of shoes.

"Damn!" I cry, and immediately I slap a hand over my mouth. But it's too late. The hallway light flickers on. In an instant, Nonna Rosa's butterball frame appears at the door to her first-floor apartment, her faded green robe zipped knees to chin.

"Silenzio!" she hisses, knuckles planted on her wide hips. "You will wake your father." She speaks with a heavy accent, using broken English sprinkled with her native Italian. After fifty-eight years of living in the United States, my grandmother, whose world is largely made up of Italian immigrants like herself, is only moderately fluent in English. She's a woman who chooses seclusion over inclusion and then complains about not fitting in.

I bend down. A pair of black orthopedic shoes lay haphazardly in the foyer. "Your shoes, Nonna," I say, and hand them to her.

She snatches them from me as if she's peeved. But I know my nonna. She left her shoes out on purpose so she would hear me when I came in.

"Mi dispiace," I say, offering an apology, never mind that I nearly broke my neck.

I turn and make my way to the staircase, hoping for a quick escape to Emville.

"You received a letter?"

I close my eyes. Is there nothing Dar doesn't share with Nonna?

She crosses her arms, settling them atop her round belly like it's her personal countertop. "How does my sister get the idea that you would go with her to Italy? You have been corresponding with her, Emilia

60

Josephina?"

"Only on holidays, Nonna. She still sends cards. I haven't seen Poppy in a decade, not since Uncle Bruno's funeral. I swear. We're friends on Facebook, but she hardly ever posts."

Nonna bats a hand and harrumphs. "Facebook. Who does she think she is, doing the Facebook? I tell you, Emilia, the woman is *indecente.* You must stay away from her. *Capisci?* Stay away!"

I stare at my grandmother's pinched face, her glowering eyes. If her teeth were visible, I'm certain they would be gnashing. She glares at me, waiting for my assurance. It takes all my strength, but tonight I refuse to acquiesce or even blink. She lifts her chin.

"In the morning, you will give me the letter. *I* will reply. I will tell my sister you want nothing to do with her and her tricks."

I clench my jaw, Matt's words shouting to me as I march up the steps. *You're scared. You tiptoe around her . . .* I'm almost to the landing when I stop. I look down at my grandmother shuffling back into her apartment, her shoes dangling at her side.

"Nonna?" She turns and looks up at me, her brows creased. My pulse speeds. "*I'll* reply to Poppy."

She blinks several times. "You will tell her

61

you do not wish to travel with her to Italy?"

But that would be a lie. I do want to go to Italy. *Indecente* or not, I want to know Paolina Fontana, the enigmatic woman who annotates her letters with silly little drawings, the spunky old gal who's ready to travel the world.

"You will do this, Emilia?" Nonna continues, her eyes narrowed.

I turn away and continue up the stairs, knowing that tomorrow, the dutiful granddaughter that I am will comply with her wishes. Nonna will be satisfied. Daria will be relieved. But tonight, it gives me a perverse charge of pleasure having not agreed to it.

Young girls often dream of a white dress and a diamond ring. I suppose I had that dream, too, when I was younger. But I'm over it now. I've learned to accept single life — in fact, I embrace it. Unlike most women approaching thirty, I can enjoy a night with my friends without the anxiety of wondering whether I'm going to meet "the one." With the exception of my concealer stick, I save a fortune on makeup and skin care. I get to wear practical shoes and comfy glasses. I'm spared from awkward first dates and the heartbreak that inevitably follows. I don't bother joining a gym, where I might meet other "active singles." I run outside in sloppy old sweats and do online yoga in my living room, sometimes in my pajamas. When I do meet the occasional guy who shows interest, my chest doesn't flood with butterflies. I don't imagine a flock of children with his nose and my eyes. I never make a show of being witty or clever. I'm simply myself — which generally stops potential suitors from continued pursuit.

It's a gorgeous Monday afternoon — my day off — and I'm jogging in Petrosino Park, lost in a new song by Lord Huron, when my phone chimes. I slow to a trot and glance at a text. Hey, Ems. Netflix tonight?

Matt and I are currently binge-watching reruns of *The Office*, providing the perfect excuse for hours of dormancy and gluttonous amounts of cheesy popcorn. I smile, happy to see he's using my old nickname. Maybe the weird vibe between us is finally waning. I reply with a thumbs-up. Immediately, he responds with a heart.

A heart? Seriously? I stuff my phone into my pocket and break into a sprint. A minute later, a call comes in. I double-tap my Air-Pod.

"What's up, Cusumano?"

"Well, hello, Emilia!"

I screech to a halt and pull out my phone. A pretty, olive-skinned woman smiles into the screen. Who FaceTimes without fore-warning? I rear back and remove the clip-on shades covering my glasses.

"Aunt Poppy?"

CHAPTER 7

EMILIA

A cobalt-blue scarf snakes around Aunt Poppy's head, corralling a mass of silver-threaded waves. I wipe my brow with my shirtsleeve.

"Aunt Poppy? Is that you?"

"Last I checked." She laughs, unleashing a magnificent display of lines from the corners of her dark eyes. "Look at that beautiful smile," she says, peering closely at the screen. "You've finally grown into your teeth!"

I laugh. "I guess I have," I say, and put a finger over the scar beneath my lip.

"And you're still wearing those vintage glasses."

"Oh," I say, "these aren't vintage."

"No, but one can pretend. Now, let's talk about our upcoming trip."

I bend over and grab my thighs, trying to catch my breath . . . and collect my thoughts. It's been almost a week since I received my aunt's invitation. As Nonna demanded, I replied the next day with a polite note of thanks-but-no-thanks. Did she not receive it?

"I'm sorry, Aunt Poppy. I can't go to Italy."

She taps a painted fingernail against her chin. "Please, my dear girl, avoid saying no so quickly. You'll find life is much more interesting when you learn to say 'It's possible.' "

In the background, her doorbell chimes.

"Look," I say, grateful for an excuse to end the call. "You're busy. We'll talk another time."

"Nonsense. We've got a trip to plan."

She scurries through a periwinkle-blue living room as she talks, the bobbing screen making me dizzy. I catch sight of a cluttered array of knickknacks — an old gas station clock mounted above a fireplace, mismatched pillows of every size and color, a zebra-print chair sitting on a purple shag rug. In a corner, an egg-shaped wicker chair hangs on a chain from the ceiling. Is that a carved monkey, dangling from her light fixture?

Suddenly a door bursts open and the screen erupts in sunlight.

"Brody!" She aims her phone at a tall, sixty-something man with shaggy blond hair, dressed in jeans and a flannel shirt. "Brody, meet Emilia. Emilia, meet Brody."

I chuckle awkwardly. "Oh. Well. Nice to meet you, Brody."

"Same to you," he says in a deep voice that matches his rugged exterior. "Your aunt is mighty excited about the trip."

I cringe. She's telling people I'm going to Italy? I listen as the man informs my aunt he's finished for the day. The phone wobbles, then I catch sight of a wrinkled hand. "For luck," Poppy says, placing a shiny penny in his palm. "So long for now, dear friend." Poppy's hand flutters in the screen as she waves good-bye. "Go spread your sunshine in the world!"

The phone finally returns to her face. "That man is a godsend," she says, closing the door behind her. "Lost his leg in Vietnam, but he's my right hand. He comes every day to help with Higgins — that's my twenty-year-old gelding."

I'm still trying to digest the fact that my aunt has a horse when she adds, "Brody's father was my man companion."

"Your man companion? You mean . . ."

"Yes, Emilia. My lover. Past tense, God bless his soul."

67

If Nonna is old Italy, heavy and drawn and dark, Poppy is cosmopolitan America, with a light and frivolous air that complements her bright, perky voice. She's kept just enough of her Italian accent to sound European and exotic.

I almost feel like I'm with her, in Devon, Pennsylvania, as she moves into a cluttered kitchen. When Poppy announces it's tea-time, I naturally assume she's talking Earl Grey or oolong. Instead, she lifts a bottle of Bombay gin from her teal-colored cabinet and grins. "Do you prefer your martini up or on the rocks?"

"Up and a little dirty," I say, playing along and sending Poppy on a riff of laughter.

"Oh, how I wish we were side by side right now, lost in day-drinks."

I settle onto a park bench, the sun warming my shoulders, and watch my aunt mix her martini. She has propped her phone against a bottle of wine, but it's off center, capturing only a slice of her left side. Most of the screen is aimed at a fridge covered in photos of babies and children and adults of every race and shape. A mass of pink-capped women carrying signs at a rally.

Poppy in full riding gear astride a beautiful black horse — Higgins, I presume. My aunt ankle-deep in the ocean, locking arms with a swarm of friends who look half her age.

She glances at the fridge behind her. My cheeks warm, as if I've been caught snooping. Her eyes twinkle. "Life is better measured in friendships than years, don't you think?" Without waiting for my answer, she grabs her drink, along with the martini shaker. The screen goes dark, and I imagine it's tucked under her arm. Next thing I know, she's standing on a shady terrace.

"My little heaven," she says as she slowly pans the area with her phone. Misshapen plants and unruly vines, pink hibiscus and bright orange poppies mingle haphazardly in clay pots, littered among ceramic fairies, colorful gnomes, a life-size alligator, a wooden peace sign, a tin rainbow. "Check out my latest project," she says and lowers herself next to a koi pond. "Come here, Nemo," she calls, making ripples in the pond. "Over here, Dory!"

I laugh out loud. "Your place is fascinating." It's the truth. Poppy's home looks stimulating and dizzying and strangely inviting, like a scene in a fantasy novel, where the character might be whimsical and young at heart . . . or batshit —

"Crazy as a crane fly," Poppy says, interrupting my thoughts.

"What?"

She rises to her feet. "That's what you were thinking, was it not?"

"No!" I give a nervous chuckle. "I, uh . . ."

She laughs and settles into a wicker chair with mismatched cushions. "It's okay, Emilia. You see, I adore crazy people. Those who are crazy to explore. Crazy to laugh. Crazy to create. The ones who embrace broken bones and broken hearts, who risk failure and welcome surprises. I suspect you're one of these people."

"Mmm," I murmur, hoping she interprets this as a yes.

She props her phone on a table in front of her. This time, it's pointed in the right direction, giving me my first chance to study my aunt. She's thin, with pretty olive skin and a wide, full mouth painted bright pink. She's wearing a white linen sundress, with a chunky orange necklace and a fuchsia belt.

"To Emilia," she says. She lifts her glass and a dozen colorful bangles clatter against her dainty wrist. From my park bench a hundred miles away, I pretend to raise a drink when she adds, "My fellow second daughter."

I choke on my make-believe martini,

thoughts of Filomena and Cosimo and poor Maria surfacing.

"Cheers," I say. "But I don't believe in that curse."

"Well, I should hope not!" She shakes her head. "I've always bristled at the injustice of that tale."

"Same here. A woman is sexually assaulted and, as a result, gets pummeled with a rock and slapped with a lifelong curse. Go figure."

"Shameful. Filomena and Maria should have locked arms and given Horny Toad Cosimo a boot in the balls."

I burst out laughing. "Amen!" I say, feeling a kinship with my fellow second daughter, never mind that we're two generations removed.

She tucks her legs beneath her, exposing bare brown feet tipped with tangerine toenails. "Tell me every good thing about you, Emilia."

I shift on the bench and try my best to make Daria and Matt, my cat and my job and my nieces, even my little apartment, sound fascinating.

"That about sums it up," I say. "My life isn't all that interesting."

She shrugs. "No matter. That will soon change. You're about to embark on an all-expenses-paid trip to Italy!"

All expenses paid? Last I knew, Poppy was some sort of teacher — art history, I think. How can she afford a European trip for two, along with a beautiful home and a horse and an employee? Is she spending her entire life savings on this trip?

I rise and meander over to the paved jogging path. "That's really generous," I say as I stroll. "But I can't get away from the store. I'm sorry."

"Ah," she says. "Making cannoli is certainly more memorable than a trip to Europe." Before I can reply to her sarcasm, she continues. "You're a young woman, Emilia. If you can't travel and see the world, you may as well jump in the box right now."

I think "box" means casket. To Poppy, a life like mine is akin to death.

I open my mouth to say something — what, exactly, I haven't decided — when a cyclist nearly swipes me. "Watch it!" he yells.

"Sorry," I call to him and scurry back to the park bench.

"Emilia, my child," Aunt Poppy says. "Do me one favor, please? Stop apologizing when you're not sorry."

I scowl. "What?"

"Back to the business at hand," she says. "I've got our itinerary all planned. Eight

72

days in Italy, with a travel day on each end. We'll see some sights first, but we must get to Ravello — a beautiful hillside town on the Amalfi Coast — by October twenty-second." She smiles into the camera. "The day I turn eighty."

"But, Aunt Poppy —"

"We'll leave in six weeks. I thought you could drive here, to Devon, and pick me up. I live twenty minutes from Philadelphia International Airport."

"I don't drive," I say.

"You New Yorkers," she says, tsking. "In that case, we'll meet at JFK. What a grand time we'll have. We'll begin our journey in Venezia — Venice — then —"

I absently massage my scar. "Aunt Poppy, please. I can't go to Italy. It's im—"

"It's possible." She stares at me with such force that I'm grateful she's only on-screen. "Despite your protests, you're dying to go. Isn't that why you included your phone number in your letter?"

I sigh. "Okay. Maybe I would like to go. The truth is, Nonna won't allow it. She wanted to write you back herself, but I insisted. For some reason I thought it was important to tell you myself."

Poppy grins. "Well, what do you know? You've got some spunk after all. Must drive

Rosa bananas. Your mother was made of honey water. I'm glad to see you're different."

My heartbeat quickens. All my life I've longed for details about my mother. I stopped asking my father about her years ago, after Nonna accused me of pulling scabs off wounds, something that sounded excruciating to my young ears. Aside from physical traits I've gleaned from photos, my father has shared exactly three things about my mother. She liked to dance. Her favorite color was blue. And she hated spiders. It saddens me to think perhaps this was all my father knew of his young wife.

"How well did you know my mom?"

"I saw her every Christmas and Easter. She'd leap from the porch and rush down the sidewalk when she saw me coming."

I picture my mother and her aunt, spinning in circles, giggling like Mimi and I do.

"Rosa resented our relationship. She was very controlling, as you well know, and sweet Josie was a pleaser."

I grip the phone. "Tell me more. Did she love books? Was she curious? Kind? Please, Aunt Poppy, tell me everything you know about my mom."

CHAPTER 8

POPPY

1959
Trespiano, Italy

The entire country of Italy, it seemed, was booming in the 1950s, especially those in the "Industrial Triangle" — Milan, Turin, and Genoa. Billions of dollars were streaming into our country, thanks to the Marshall Plan. But our small Tuscan village of Trespiano, just outside of Firenze — the Italian city of Florence — remained more or less untouched. My father, a hardworking farmer, was missing out on the windfall.

My oldest brother, Bruno, along with Rosa's handsome fiancé, Alberto, worked in the fields alongside Papà. Each week they took their crop to market, and returned with barely enough money to cover the rent and family expenses. Although he had toiled for years in these fields, Papà still leased his land. The wealthy landowner was the one who was making money.

Rosa's fiancé was the first to voice his frustration. In a few years, Dolphie, who was still too young, would join the trio. Alberto wondered how the farm could support four men and their families when it could not support three.

All the while Alberto hoed the land and tilled the soil he was planting seeds — literally and figuratively. He and my brother Bruno, both twenty-four at the time, would leave this place where they were not appreciated. They would go to America, where milk and honey flowed from the riverbanks.

Alberto had an uncle who had immigrated to the United States three years earlier. This uncle, Ignacio, wrote to Alberto, telling of the place he lived, New York, and the refrigerator in his apartment and the machine that washed his clothing. Ignacio had opened a little store called Lucchesi's in a Brooklyn neighborhood called Bensonhurst, where many of his fellow Italian immigrants made their homes. But Ignacio needed help slicing meats and preparing foods in the kitchen. If Alberto and his friend Bruno came to America, they would make more money in one month than in an entire year of farming.

My brother Bruno thought it was a grand idea. He and Alberto began saving their money. Alberto would marry Rosa before he left. Once he was settled in America, she would join him and they would start a new life in America. Dolphie would soon follow. "You will be welcome, too," Alberto told my parents. "Paolina as well."

The thought of going to America, a country brimming with modern ideas and freedom, a daring new Guggenheim museum that was said to look like a nautilus shell, and the handsome senator John Fitzgerald Kennedy, rumored to be a future presidential candidate, thrilled me. But not my sweet sister Rosa. At night, beneath the eaves in our tiny bedroom, she shared her fears with me. Though she was two years older than I, and sassier than most men, Rosa was timid, even cowardly at times. She craved security and safety and certainty. She wanted nothing more than to remain in Trespiano forever, surrounded by our family and Alberto and a flock of children.

Alberto and my father talked every night at the dinner table. Bruno and Alberto would leave for America. They would have no trouble getting visas. Uncle Ignacio would sponsor them, assuring the US government that the men would have jobs upon their arrival.

Behind his back, Rosa scoffed at the idea, claiming her fiancé was a dreamer, that they would never leave Trespiano and Mamma and Papà. But I knew her fate was sealed. She would soon be married to Alberto. Women in our family had no voice. Once her husband was in America, she would be expected to join him. Alberto wanted a strong, hardworking wife in his new homeland, a woman who would bear him many children. And if Rosa wasn't willing to travel to America, there were plenty of girls in the village who would.

Alberto Lucchesi was smooth as a swan on the dance floor, and when he laughed, you couldn't help but join in. Over six feet tall, he had a thick head of black hair and a twinkling gaze that seemed to mesmerize. I witnessed him charm more than one of my girlfriends, though I never told my sister. She was already insecure. And Papà was no help. He congratulated his eldest daughter on her prize fiancé, joked about her good fortune. "You, my dear daughter, are a simple fishing net. Yet somehow you have managed to catch the biggest fish in the sea."

Each time Papà made comments like these, Rosa seemed to shrink. And when

Alberto read books and newspapers or used words that Rosa could not pronounce, let alone define, Rosa's self-doubt grew.

"Alberto will soon be bored with me."

"The kindest girl in Italy?" I would say. "The most wonderful cook in Trespiano? The one who will make him a perfect wife? Nonsense."

"*And* mother," she added. "Alberto wants many children."

"Of course. You will make the best mother."

Rosa said nothing when Alberto began saving money for his voyage to America. She didn't want to think about what would come next — a trek across the Atlantic all by herself. Often she would wake with nightmares and cling to me, relaying the visions of the whirling waters, the tiny ship's cabin that she could not escape.

One day at dinner, Rosa announced that she had wonderful news. My father continued to roll his pasta onto his fork, uninterested in his daughter's silly thoughts, but I sat up, curious.

"Alberto has written to his uncle Ignacio," Rosa said.

My father's eyes lifted.

"Ignacio has agreed to marry Paolina."

I choked on my bread.

"They will marry as soon as Paolina and I arrive in Brooklyn."

My father's face lit up. He raised his glass of Chianti. "To Ignacio and Paolina. I never thought it would happen."

To my family, it was settled. I would go to New York and marry Ignacio, a hot-tempered forty-one-year-old who needed a young bride to cook and clean and wash his filthy clothes. I shuddered. "Never!"

"Please, Paolina," Rosa said, her hands folded in prayer. "You must accept his proposal. If you are engaged to a man in America, immigration into the United States will be easy. And best of all, we will travel together to America."

My fork clattered onto my plate. "I will never marry this man. He is too old. I do not even know him."

"Hush," my mother said. "You are the second daughter. Do you not realize how lucky you are that someone is willing? Think of all your cousins who would jump at this chance."

I threw my napkin on the table. "I do not believe in that curse. I never did."

But as I spoke, my thoughts drifted to my great-aunt Isabella, my aunt Blanca, my cousins Apollonia, Silvia, Evangelina, Martina, Livia. All second-born Fontana women. All single.

"And what about children?" my mother said. "You finally have a prayer."

I nearly upended my chair when I stood. "I no longer have an appetite."

I was halfway up the stairs when Rosa grabbed my arm.

"Paolina, please forgive me. I thought you would be happy about Ignacio. Now we can go to America together."

I felt trapped. Yes, I wanted to help my sister. And I longed to go to America. I yearned for the freedom and opportunities. Perhaps I could even go to college. But I would never marry a man I did not love.

"I do not need a husband. I am happy to be single forever."

"Do you not see? This is the easiest way for you to get into the country." She pulled me close and whispered, "Who is going to make you marry this man once we are in America?"

I looked into her mischievous eyes. She was right. Rosa and I would arrive in America at least a year before my parents. America was the land of the free. Women actually had a voice. They smoked and drove automobiles and some even took pills for menstrual cramps that were rumored to prevent pregnancy. Once there, I could do anything, be anyone I wanted. The idea left me breathless . . . and hopeful. I grabbed Rosa into a hug.

"I love you, my clever sister."

In late September, Rosa and Alberto were married in a sober ceremony that seemed, to my young heart, completely void of passion. But Rosa was deliriously happy. "I finally have him," she told me. "The man of my dreams is all mine, and nobody can take him away."

Two days later, she and I applied for visas to America, Rosa as a young wife whose husband would soon be living and working in the United States, me as a woman engaged to an Italian American who had already gained his citizenship. We were told it would take months, maybe over a year, to get approval. Until then, we would work and save our money for the passage — the ship's fare to America was expensive.

I was almost twenty years old, curious about everything — languages, history, science. But I had no skills or education. I found work as a laundress four days a week, a dreadful job steaming linens in the basement of a hotel in the neighboring town of Fiesole. When I wasn't at the hotel, I was home with Mamma, helping her prepare enormous meals and clean the house and take care of the chickens. She taught me to darn socks and mend clothing, so that I could assist with the sewing jobs she took in for extra money.

But sewing was a bore. I was a dreadful cook. And cleaning the house? Who wants to spend their days on hands and knees, half the time with your head in a bucket? I was restless in the home, so I lost myself in fantasies. I dreamed of going to the university, once I got to America, and becoming an architect one day. And a physicist the next day. And a professor the next. *La mia sognatrice* — my dreamer — my mother would call me.

Rosa, a married woman of twenty-two, had more options. Her new husband, Alberto, had a cousin whose friend worked at La Galleria degli Uffizi in Florence. If Rosa could pass the test, she would be hired as a tour guide at the famous gallery.

I was so envious! The Uffizi Gallery housed one of the finest collections of Renaissance art in the world. My lucky sister would have a prestigious job in the city, a job that was stimulating and exciting. But first, Rosa had to pass her examination, which was no small feat. Her eyes would glaze over each time she tried to study the sixty-page manual the museum's curator had given her. Poor Rosa had little curiosity and absolutely no interest in art.

Each night after my long day of work, she and I would sit on the little bed we used to share in the attic before Papà put up the partition creating a separate space for her and Alberto. I would quiz her, asking about Leonardo da Vinci's *Annunciation* and Michelangelo's *Doni Tondo,* the dates and history of every major piece in the museum. But Rosa never seemed to remember. Her mind was too fraught with worries. She fretted over Alberto's upcoming departure, bombarded me with questions that had no satisfying answers. Would her new husband forget about her once he left Trespiano? And what about the ship that would one day carry us to America? What if it sank? What if we arrived in New York and Alberto was not there to greet us?

Finally, the night before the exam arrived. But this time, I was the one with the knot in my stomach. My sister knew nothing. She confused her dates, couldn't distinguish the sculptors from the painters. I flung the book onto the bed and took Rosa by the arms. "Do you not understand how important this is? You must get this job, Rosa, so we can save money to get to America, and you can be with Alberto."

"La mia sorella testarda." It was her pet name for me, her stubborn sister. She fell back against the bed. "I cannot do this, Paolina! How would you like to have to learn all of these boring facts?"

"Boring? These artists are fascinating. And for your information, I do know it."

She sat up. I could see the balls in her head rolling. "You," she said, pointing a finger at me. "You take the exam. You work as the tour guide. I will take your job as the laundress and help Mamma with the house chores."

I couldn't believe it. She would rather work in a stifling laundry room than give tours at the famous gallery? Why?

"I need to stay close to home," she said, answering my unspoken question. "Here, I can learn of the local gossip, keep track of Alberto's comings and goings."

How do you reply to someone so fearful? My heart hurt for my sister.

"But, Rosa, I have not applied. The Uffizi is expecting you."

She turned and looked me directly in the eyes. "Then you will pretend to be me." Her eyes were absent any conflict or guilt.

I rubbed the gooseflesh from my arms. "Rosa, no. We cannot . . ." My voice trailed off.

Hidden within my fear, a tingling of excitement rose. Could we possibly get away with such a charade?

CHAPTER 9

EMILIA

Through the screen of my iPhone, Poppy shakes her head, as if she's coming out of a trance. I watch and wait, hoping she'll continue. But she's reaching for her martini shaker now.

"What a fascinating story," I say. "You and Nonna were close when you were young."

"We adored each other."

"I never knew my nonno Alberto. I had no idea he was a heartthrob, or that Rosa kept tabs on him."

"My sister treated love like a possession," Poppy says, pouring the last drops of gin from the shaker. "To me, love is more like a lending library. To keep it, we must continually renew it. Otherwise we pay a hefty fine."

I smile. "That's lovely. Did she ever grow confident in Alberto's love?"

"Things improved once they were in America. Parenthood created a bond, as it

87

often does."

I peel a flake of green paint from the park bench. "You honestly didn't believe in the curse, Aunt Poppy? Even when you were young?"

She laughs. "Never. You?"

"No," I say, and quickly change the subject. "Hey, you never got to the part of the story about my mom."

"In time, dear." She sips her drink and leans back in her chair. "Now, I'll purchase our tickets this week."

A secret yearning gathers in me. Like mist from a river, it begins to rise. What will Nonna do? What will Daria say? My temples throb as Matt's words echo in my head. *You tiptoe around them, bowing to their every need, so that they'll love you. Because if you don't, one day you could end up alone and abandoned, just like Poppy.*

If being ostracized once terrified me — and I'm not saying it did — it's not so scary anymore. In the course of an hour, I've come to know my aunt Poppy, the woman my family cast aside like an empty soup can. I've been given a snapshot of her rich, full life. I've seen photos of her friends and even met her lover's son. Today, the idea of being the rebel in the family doesn't frighten me. It inspires me.

"You do have your Italian passport, yes?" Poppy continues. "It's something your mother would have insisted on."

Because my mom was born in Italy, I have dual citizenship, and apparently this was important to her. "Really? What else do you know about my mom?"

"She loved this farm. She stayed here with me the summer she turned eighteen."

For a moment I wonder if she's lying, or simply delusional. Nonna would never have allowed that. But then she adds, "Of course Rosa was incensed. She ordered her home, and eventually Josie obeyed."

"I never knew that. What else?"

She gazes into her martini glass. "You come to Italy and I'll share everything I know about your mother. Everything."

A flurry sets off in my chest, like a collector awaiting the unveiling of a newly discovered masterpiece. I have a once-in-a-lifetime chance to get away, to travel to Italy with my free-spirited great-aunt, to hear stories of my mother. My heart batters. At this very moment, sitting in Petrosino Park, I make a decision.

"Aunt Poppy?" I take a deep breath. "It's possible." My eyes flood with emotions — freedom and excitement and independence and terror. "I'm coming with you to Italy."

89

"Yes!" Her face beams. "Emilia, my dear girl, you have inherited the Fontana gene of fortitude. You've kept it hidden, but there it is, shining from you like a pollia berry."

"A what?"

"Pollia berry. Shiniest living organism in the world."

I laugh, touched by an unfamiliar sense of pride. "Well, thanks."

"Now that you're on board, I can invite Luciana."

"Lucy?" I snicker. "You mean Carmella, your other niece, Lucy's older sister. My . . . quieter cousin."

"No. I mean Luciana, the twenty-one-year-old."

My smile fades. I feel like I've stepped into a sinkhole and it's too late to pull myself out. As second daughters, Lucy and I share an unspoken bond. And now that we're both in our twenties, we've grown even closer. But I can think of no more unlikely travel companions than Lucy and me.

"I — I didn't know she was coming with us."

"She doesn't know, either. Shall we call her now? You can put her on speaker. Ask her if she'd like to have a three-way."

I can only imagine my cousin's colorful

response to that proposition. "Uh, no," I say. "Lucy is not someone you put on speakerphone."

She claps her hands. "I like her already!"

"Aunt Poppy, Lucy's got a new job. And she just started seeing someone. I guarantee she won't leave now."

Poppy scowls. "She's afraid she might lose this new boyfriend if she's away from him?"

"Exactly."

"How positively dreadful, allowing someone such power."

"Lucy's a second daughter," I remind her. "Like us."

She gives me a sidelong glance. "You actually believe the myth."

"Me? I already told you, no. Absolutely not."

She stares at me. My heart stammers and I return to that day in Sister Regina's classroom, when my seven-year-old mind slowly digested the fact that Fontana second-born daughters once shared a strange coincidence — past tense. It would be another three years before Nonna Rosa marched into the room I shared with Daria and announced that the Fontana second-born daughters are cursed — present tense. On the very day she handed me my first training bra, she told us the legend of Filomena and Maria. Who was I, a girl of ten with mosquito-bite breasts, to argue with a centuries-old curse?

But Daria, who was twelve at the time and my biggest cheerleader, burst out laughing the minute Nonna left the room. "That's a load of bull crap, Emmie. Don't believe a word of it. You are not cursed. I swear to God." She snatched the garment from my hand. "You might have to accept this old hand-me-down," she said, stuffing her frayed and graying tee-bra into my drawer. "But you must never accept Nonna's ridiculous story."

That day — and, if I'm being perfectly honest, as recently as a dozen years ago — I believed my sister. What girl doesn't expect a conventional life with a husband and kids? But as I've grown older, I realize Filomena and the second daughters before me have given me a gift. I have a pass, a perfectly valid excuse, to turn my back on the wretched dating scene. Though I don't for a minute believe in that ridiculous curse, I am grateful nonetheless.

I smile at my aunt. "Of course I don't believe in the curse. It's just an old wives' tale, an old-world myth. But Lucy does believe. And she's determined to break it."

"Oh, for Goddess's sake! You tell Luciana

if she comes to Italy, we'll put that ridiculous Fontana second-daughter myth to bed once and for all."

I rub the back of my neck. "You can't promise that. Lucy takes the curse very seriously. You'd be setting her up for disappointment."

"Oh, but I can. Come with me to Italy, and you and Luciana will return freed from the curse. I swear on my life."

The hairs on my arms rise. "That's im—"

"It's possible," she says, finishing my sentence.

CHAPTER 10

EMILIA

When I described the supposed Fontana Second-Daughter Curse to Matt a decade ago, I compared it to a baseball team with a losing streak. The fans have no idea when, or even if, the losing streak will end. But the faithful crowd watches with wonder.

It's the same thing with the curse. Some in the Fontana family battle it head-on, like my aunt Carol. Others seem to accept it, like Nonna. Some, like me, swear the curse is an odd coincidence. But one common thread exists in our family's patchwork of personalities: everyone — from Nonna to my sister to Aunt Carol — finds the curse curious. Every generation wonders if theirs will be the one to finally see a second daughter marry. And if so, which second daughter will it be? And there have been some near misses, like a distant cousin of Nonna's who developed smallpox three days

94

before her wedding. Or Livia, the unfortunate second daughter whose betrothed turned out to be a married preacher with six children. Now it's up to my generation to break the curse. So far, Lucy is the crowd favorite.

The evening sun casts shadows over Uncle Dolphie's barbershop. I go around to the back and climb the familiar porch steps. Even though I visit my uncle's shop every afternoon, it's been three weeks since I've been to the adjoining apartment where his son, my uncle Vinnie, lives with his family. I knock on the metal screen door, hoping whoever's in there can hear me over the Ed Sheeran ballad coming from inside.

"Lucy?" I call through the open screen. "Aunt Carol? Carmella?"

I'm about to knock again when Lucy rounds the corner, adjusting her bra strap. Her long hair, a different color each time I see her, is platinum blond tonight, and she's wearing a half smile that can only be described as sultry. She sees me and her face falls.

"Emmie? What are you doing here?" She cranes her neck to look down the street. "Carmella's not here. My mom's out making deliveries. Come back tomorrow."

My aunt Carol, who sells Avon, doesn't

think it's professional to leave orders on customers' porches. Whether it's a complete facial regimen or a single bottle of nail polish, my aunt insists on a personal delivery, one that inevitably leads to a piece of cake or a cup of coffee. Since she started selling Avon, she's gained thirty pounds and all of the gossip from Coney Island to Bay Ridge.

"I'm here to see you, Lucy. Is now a good time?"

She checks the phone in her hand. "Um, I have a sec, I guess." She holds the door open. As I pass, she peers out at the street again, searching in both directions. "I'm having someone for dinner."

I bite back a smile. Decked out in a red spandex jumpsuit with smoky eyes rimmed in thick black liner, my cousin looks like she really could "have someone" for dinner. Or perhaps she's hoping someone has her.

The tiny living room that, for years, has served as our family's gathering place for baptisms and first communions and high school graduations is immaculate, as always. Aunt Carol claims that the only thing worse than a messy house is a woman without lipstick. The savory aroma of roast chicken wafts from the kitchen, making my mouth water. In the adjoining dining room, I notice the table set for two. A vase of hydrangeas rests in the center between two flickering candles.

"Are you here to gawk or talk, Emmie? Can't you see I'm in a hurry here?"

I smile. There was a time when my sharp-tongued cousin, who's eight years younger than I am, intimidated me. But I realize now, her sarcastic barbs are generally aimed at those she loves most dearly.

"I promise I'll vanish as soon as your friend arrives. But I have an offer for you." I take a deep breath. "How would you like to go to Italy, all expenses paid?"

She blinks. "Italy? With you?"

"And Aunt Poppy."

She chokes out a laugh. "That sounds like massive amounts of no fun." She spins around. "What do you think?" She puts a hand to her hair. "Marilyn Platinum."

"Nice," I say, hoping I don't get struck by lightning. Why she'd choose to disguise her naturally rich, dark hair is beyond me.

"We'll leave sometime in mid-October," I say, steering the conversation back to Italy. I quickly describe our aunt and relay her story of growing up in Trespiano.

Lucy pretends to snore. "Like I'd go to Italy with a boring lady who's got one foot in the grave."

An unexpected sense of protectiveness

takes hold of me. "Boring is the last adjective I'd use to describe Poppy."

"I wasn't talking about Aunt Poppy."

I shake my head. "Very funny, Luce. C'mon. It'll be an experience. And you'll love Poppy. She seems . . . extraordinary. Really."

"Extraordinarily nutso." She checks her phone again. "Nonna's good with this?"

I rub my scar. "She will be," I say, praying it's true. "Lucy, we're talking Europe. How cool is that?"

She gives a little huff. "It's not exactly Vegas." She glances at her phone again before plopping down on the sofa. "Go ahead. Sit."

I lower myself onto a brown sofa draped in one of Aunt Carol's crocheted blankets — this one in oranges and yellows — and explain my conversation with Aunt Poppy. "She insists we both come with her to celebrate her eightieth birthday. She doesn't have anyone else. Aunt Poppy is . . . a second daughter."

Lucy flinches. Always an undercurrent, the curse is something we Fontanas rarely mention aloud. "Thanks to her, we're left to break the curse — not that you're any help." She scowls and points at my sweater. "Don't tell me. Coldwater Creek clearance rack? Or have you been raiding Nonna's closet again?" She starts singing her own rendition of Right Said Fred's "I'm Too Sexy."

"I'm too sexy for my cardigan, too sexy for my cardigan, too sexy for my No-nna's cardigan."

I laugh. "Okay, okay. I get it. You don't like the sweater."

She checks her phone for at least the twelfth time. "Seriously. Tell Pops thanks anyway, but the timing's all wrong. I'm in a relationship."

"Yes. I know. That's great."

She scowls as she taps her keyboard. My eyes travel to the beautifully set dining room table. Wax pools at the base of the candles and I catch a faint whiff of charred meat. Lucy's date is late. Very late. My heart breaks for her. I rise and give what I hope is a reassuring smile.

"We can talk later. I'll get out of your hair."

She grabs my arm, her purple nails digging into my skin. "Don't do that, Em."

"What?"

"Don't give me that pitiful look!"

I sit back down, unsure what to do or say. "I'm sorry."

"He just texted. He's running late. But

he's coming. You'll see."

"I believe you, Luce. But, um, you might want to turn down the oven."

The final rays of sunlight fade and I click on a lamp. Lucy twists open a bottle of Budweiser. Then another. "He's coming," she tells me once more as she opens her third beer.

"I know."

"We've been out five times," she offers. "Well, four, actually. The first was just a hookup." She shoots me a look. "Got a problem with that?"

"No," I say, honestly. "I don't care."

She peels the label from her beer bottle. "Carmella thinks I'm a slut who dates pigs."

I rear back. "Your sister actually said that?"

Lucy shrugs. "May as well have. My mom thinks I'm a loser. She prays — literally prays on her knees — that I'll meet a nice boy and get married and have kids. My dad's no better. They're both terrified I'll be single forever."

I frown. "Why is being single terrifying?"

She gives me a look. "No grandchildren."

"Ah," I say. "My family's the opposite. They've given up on me. And I'm good with that."

"Yeah," Lucy says, "you're lucky." She

looks down at her cleavage. "When you look like I do, they think you might actually have a chance."

I picture adorable little Lucy, with big curious eyes and short chubby legs mapped with scrapes and bruises. Poor Luce. Aunt Carol, a pretty woman whose face I've yet to see without full-coverage foundation, didn't appreciate her little tomboy. She enrolled Lucy in dance classes and every princess contest in Brooklyn. But Lucy wasn't a dancer, and chubby girls didn't win beauty pageants.

Things changed when Lucy hit puberty. Her baby fat morphed into voluptuous curves, and her confidence seemed to grow with each cup size. I study her now and can't help but think my cousin looked more natural in her baggy shorts and Popsicle-stained T-shirt than she does in that ridiculous Spider-Woman jumpsuit.

"Tell me about him," I say. "Your friend — this guy you're seeing. I can't remember his name."

She lets out a breath. "Jack. As in beanstalk, if you get my drift." She grins. "He's gorgeous — even ol' Carol's hot for him. And he likes me, Em. He told me he's never met anyone like me." She checks the time again.

"Lucy," I say, taking advantage of her alcohol haze. "Come to Italy with Poppy and me. Get out of Bensonhurst for a while."

She gnaws on her thumbnail. "I can't. It's too new. You think Jack's going to stick around if I'm gone? Get real."

The guy is obviously a complete jerk, standing Lucy up. But still, she wants him. She's one determined second daughter, I'll give her that.

As she drones on about Jack, my thoughts spin. I could leave right now. I could call Poppy tonight and tell her that Lucy refused her offer. Poppy would find other travel companions, Lucy wouldn't be disappointed, and Nonna would never know I entertained the thought of going to Italy.

I jump when Lucy slams her phone on the table. "Check your messages, asshole!" She leans her head against the sofa and stares at the ceiling. "It's happening. It always happens. Jack's losing interest."

"Oh, Luce, I'm so sorry."

"We haven't hooked up in a week. And now the fuckwad's standing me up."

I long to wrap this desperately lonely girl in my arms, but I know better. "You don't deserve this."

"And neither do you. But we both have it,

102

don't we?"

She's talking about the curse. Do I owe it to Lucy to tell of Poppy's promise? No. If she's gullible enough to believe in the curse, she may be gullible enough to believe Poppy could break it. And of course that's . . .

Poppy's words call to me: *It's possible.*

With a nagging sense of foreboding and the utmost care, I open my mouth. "Luce, I need to tell you something." I turn to her, the knot in my belly tightening. "Poppy has some ridiculous notion that if we come with her to Italy . . ." I pause, caressing my scar. What if Lucy actually believes our crazy aunt? What if she agrees to go to Italy, expecting to return home no longer plagued by the centuries-old curse? She may never recover from the disappointment. I imagine Lucy an old woman, bitter and angry and frustrated, just like the second daughters in the old family photos.

"She swears the second-daughter curse will be lifted."

"What?"

"I know. Complete bullshit, right? I mean, first of all, there is no curse. Let's get that straight. But secondly, the idea of Poppy somehow breaking it . . ." My voice trails off and I laugh, as if the idea is absolutely ludicrous.

Lucy stares at me, her eyes brighter now. "I guess I could go, I mean, if it's so important to Poppy."

"O-kay," I say cautiously. "But, Luce, it's just a trip to Italy. That's it. Please don't expect Poppy's foolish promise to —"

"I know!" she snaps. "Jesus. Do you think I'm that desperate?"

I want to spare her some dignity, so I don't answer. My heart settles in the pit of my stomach. Aunt Poppy is setting Lucy up for the greatest disappointment of her life.

And I'm her accomplice.

CHAPTER 11

EMILIA

Every Sunday following mass at Saint Athanasius, our family gathers for dinner at Nonna's apartment. We sit around her custom-made, eighteen-foot walnut table, covered with a trio of ancient-looking cloths flaunting more wine stains than a vintner's apron. The arms of our chairs — all two dozen of them — overlap, just like our conversations. Most Sundays we fill the table, but sometimes Uncle Vinnie has to work at the dock, or Daria's husband, Donnie, has one of his Sunday head colds.

Today we have fourteen people, including Matt, who's here for moral support. Daria and the girls arrive with two loaves of bread and a jar of olives and garlic. They've dragged Donnie along today, too. He's in the living room, watching the Mets game with Matt, while Uncle Dolphie rants about the new development on Forty-Second

Street. "It is six stories high. Too big, I say. Does not fit with the old style."

I move from room to room, conversation to conversation, half listening, half fretting.

"Lucy's boyfriend is very handsome," Aunt Carol whispers to Aunt Ethel as they set the table. "I think this could be it."

My heart sinks. She's talking about the jerk who stood Lucy up. The odds that this could be "it" are about as remote as Uncle Dolphie switching from opera to Eminem.

"Eccellente!" Aunt Ethel cries. She leans in to Aunt Carol and lowers her voice. "The ghost told me, *un matrimonio presto."*

Aunt Carol laughs. "The ghost is right . . . there may be a wedding soon. But we must keep it secret. Let Lucy tell you about her new beau all by herself."

My niece Mimi looks up from the game she's playing on her iPad. "I love secrets!"

At two o'clock, Uncle Dolphie calls everyone to the table. *"Mangiamo!"* he cries, clapping his hands. "Let's eat!"

Matt settles into a chair beside Lucy's sister, Carmella. My twenty-four-year-old cousin looks especially cute today, sporting black Converse sneakers and bright red lipstick. She was laid off from her job at the bank last month and now starts regaling

Matt with stories of her "interviews from hell."

I help Nonna bring out our first course, antipasto, followed by steaming bowls of ravioli. My dad pours wine — just a shot glass for the kids. Voices merge and forks clatter. We clink glasses, tear bread, dip the crusts into oil and herbs. But I can barely swallow.

"Buona pasta, Rosa."

"Il migliore! The best," Uncle Vinnie agrees.

I leave the table at the first chance and clear plates. I pass my father as he's bringing out the next course, a rack of lamb. "Are you okay, Emilia? You look pale."

"I'm fine," I lie.

The lamb is delicious, but I can hardly get it down. I wait until the chocolate amaretto cake is served and the grappa has been poured. Voices lower, movements slow, postures slump with the sated satisfaction of the well-fed.

Catching my eye, Lucy taps her watch. Like me, she wants this to be over with. My heart thuds. I lean in and clear my throat. "I have some news," I say, careful not to look at Nonna.

Across the table, Daria shushes the girls. "Looks like Aunt Emmie has been keeping a secret."

Mimi's eyes go wide. "You have a boyfriend?"

Everyone laughs except Matt. He raises an eyebrow and I look away.

"No!" I say, and bat a hand at Mimi. I take a deep breath. "I'm going to Italy."

Daria's face falls. The table goes silent. From the corner of my eye, I see Nonna cross herself.

"That's right," Matt says, looking around the table. "She leaves next month. Eight days in Italy. Pretty cool, huh?"

Heads turn. Confused looks are exchanged. Slowly, my family members find their voices.

"Why is she going to Italy?"

"Is it safe?"

"Not for a young woman."

"Europe is teeming with crime these days."

"Yes," Aunt Carol agrees. "Terrorists."

"And gypsies. They'd steal the blood from your veins if you let them."

Matt rubs his forehead and steals a glance at me. I work my face into a smile, trying to lighten the mood.

"C'mon," I say. "It's Italy, our homeland."

"You are not traveling alone, are you, Emmie?"

Lucy closes her eyes, as if preparing for a hit. All eyes turn to me. "No," I say, and glance down the table. "I'm going with Lucy."

"Lucy?" Aunt Carol snaps her head toward Lucy. "You're not going to Italy. Are you?"

I twist the napkin in my lap. "We're going with Aunt Poppy."

A silence takes over the room, so profound you could hear dust drop. I run a finger over my scar. Finally, Nonna's chair scrapes against the wood floor. Wordlessly, she rises. Gripping her espresso cup, she moves into the living room, as if she hasn't heard a word I've said.

While my dad and Uncle Vinnie squat beside Nonna's chair, offering their comfort, Aunt Carol lobs questions at Lucy. I busy myself gathering dishes from the table, trying not to eavesdrop.

"What are you thinking, Luciana, leaving your new beau to go traveling? You'll ruin your chance."

As I stack plates, their exchange becomes heated. The vein in Lucy's forehead bulges. Finally, with her nose inches from her mom's, she whispers through clenched teeth, "The effing curse will be broken. In Italy. Aunt Poppy promised."

109

Aunt Carol's eyes become saucers. She leans in, clutching her chest. "The curse will be lifted?"

My heart sinks. I hang my head and curse myself . . . and Lucy . . . and Aunt Poppy.

My entire body shakes with frustration as I rinse glasses at the kitchen sink. Just one person with no ulterior motives. That's all I wanted. Just one person in my family to cheer for Lucy and me, to tell us they're happy for our adventure, to wish us a good trip. But no, they'd never voice their support aloud. Not one person dares to upset Nonna. She controls all of us . . . including me. Up until now.

My dad comes up beside me and sets his plate on the counter. "Eight days in Italy. That is a long time to be away from the store."

"Yup." I snatch his plate and blast it with spray. "And it's actually ten days, if you count the travel."

He does a quick perusal of the kitchen, then bends to my ear. "I'm happy to take care of Claws while you're gone."

I turn to look at my father, and see the twinkle in his eyes. My mouth falls open. I want to kiss him. I want to throw my arms around him and thank him and tell him I love him. But that would be too awkward.

Instead, I smile. "Thanks, Dad. I thought I'd ask Carmella if she'd like to stay at the apartment. It's easier on Claws." I don't mention the fact that my single cousin, who still lives with my aunt Carol and uncle Vinnie, would probably kill for her own space, if only for ten days.

"Sure," he says and turns to leave.

"But Dad?" He looks back. "Thank you."

He squeezes my shoulder and disappears from the kitchen.

I'm filling the kitchen sink when Matt appears. "You were amazing," he says, surprising me by bending down to kiss my cheek.

I twist away, uncomfortable. "Thanks. Hey, go back out there, will you? I need to know what they're saying about me."

He turns to leave, but not before I see the disappointment in his eyes. "Shit," I whisper. I plunge my hands into the sudsy water and I set about scouring a cast-iron pot. Suddenly, a cold hand grips my elbow. I jump, showering the counter with tiny bubbles. Through my steamy lenses, I see my nonna's pinched face. She leans in so closely I can smell the espresso on her breath.

"You went against my wishes. You made this decision without telling me."

Um, maybe because I'm twenty-nine years

old, and I'm long overdue to start thinking for myself. But I swallow the brazen words. "I didn't think you'd let me go," I say truthfully, and dry my hands.

"This is right. I would not have allowed it. Not now. Not ever." She turns away and covers her face, her way of displaying emotion without shedding a tear.

"I'm not doing this to hurt you, Nonna." I put a hand on her shoulder and she flinches.

"You have hurt me, Emilia. Very, very badly."

"I'm sorry. But I don't understand."

She looks away and swabs her dry eyes with a tea towel. "No, you do not understand. How could you? You do not know the story." Her eyes return to mine. "My sister is *il diavolo.*"

"The devil?" I chuckle. "No, Nonna. She's really nice now. You should call her, talk to her."

"You are a fool!" The vein in her forehead bulges, and I fear she's going to keel over with a stroke. "Paolina tried to take my child from me, my Josephina. She tried to snatch my baby girl right from my arms."

The kitchen goes cold. "Au-Aunt Poppy tried to kidnap my mother?"

"Sì."

I shake my head. "How? Why?"

She pats her heart, making a thumping sound. "I cannot talk about it."

"That was decades ago," I say, trying to convey a confidence that I'm not feeling. "Surely you believe in second chances. She's your sister."

"You listen to me, Emilia Josephina." Her eyes narrow and she points her arthritic finger at my chest. "No more talk of Italy, not with that woman. I forbid it."

I try to lose myself in cleanup and conversation and Chianti, but by afternoon's end, Nonna's words have sunk in, and with them, a fog of doubt. Poppy tried to steal my mother from Nonna's clutches. No wonder Nonna is so bitter. Just who is this woman I've agreed to travel halfway across the world with?

The five o'clock sun casts shadows on the small patch of grass out front. I wander onto the porch, where Uncle Dolphie sits smoking a cigar, gazing out at the passing cars.

"Uncle Dolphie," I say, perching beside him. "Is your sister evil?"

He taps his cigar, then shakes his head. "Nah. Not evil. Just mean."

I laugh. "No, not Rosa. I'm talking about Poppy."

"Paolina?" He lets loose a heavy sigh.

"That one broke my heart. She was sunshine in our home, my favorite sister. She loved to play tricks on me. Always she would find lucky coins. And her imagination!" He lifts his hands. "Endless! She would take me into the fields and we would pretend to be orphans, running away from an evil monster. I think it was our father she was imagining. You see, our papà, he was hard on Paolina."

"Was he hard on Nonna, too?"

"Yes. That was his nature. But everyone knew he favored Rosa, his firstborn daughter. She was a pretty girl before she came to this country, and she had a loving heart. It is as if America leached the kindness from her."

"You said Aunt Poppy — Paolina — broke your heart. How?"

He groans, as if a steel vest has been placed upon his shoulders. "When Paolina came to America, she lost her mind. I was back in Italy, still living in Trespiano with Mamma and Papà. Rosa and Bruno sent letters. It was very hard for my parents to learn that their daughter was so ill."

"Was this when she kidnapped Rosa and Alberto's baby?"

His head snaps to attention. "You know about this?"

"Nonna told me. Why would Aunt Poppy do such a horrible thing?"

He takes a puff of his cigar and stares off into the distance. "She was heartbroken when her baby died."

I gasp. "Aunt Poppy had a baby?"

"She was pregnant, sì. But of course, she was the second daughter. She should have known it would end badly."

I rub the gooseflesh from my arms. Dolphie shakes his head. "Poor Paolina . . . she was never the same. When Rosa delivered her own baby, it was too much for Paolina. She snapped like a twig. Paolina became attached — too attached — to baby Josephina."

"So she took the baby," I say. "But then she realized she was wrong and she gave Josephina back."

He nods. "And two days later, she left Bensonhurst for good, allowed to return only on holidays." He stubs out his cigar and plants it tip side up in the front pocket of his sports coat. "It was for the best. Being near Josephina was too tempting for Paolina. Rosa and Alberto no longer trusted her. Your nonna still thinks Paolina is *pericolosa.*"

My heart breaks for my young aunt. Did she ever recover from the loss? She seems

115

quite functional now. "What about you? Do you think she's dangerous?"

He smiles. "Only as dangerous as a kitten. Paolina's heart oozes honey, of that I am certain." He rests a hand on my knee. "You know, this trip to Italy could be fortuitous. My sisters are growing old. I am not saying it will happen, but if you were to get into Paolina's good graces, perhaps you could convince her to beg Rosa's forgiveness once more, before it is too late."

CHAPTER 12

EMILIA

It's been thirty-two days, and thanks to my preoccupation with the trip, I've managed to avoid another serious conversation with Matt. Now, as our taxi zips down the Belt Parkway Sunday afternoon and Lucy's busy painting her nails, I lift my phone to text him. I want to tell him good-bye, that I love him, that I'll miss him. But everything's become so complicated. What once would have been a completely natural message now feels unfair. I don't want to lead him on.

On way to JFK. I type. See you in ten days. Take care of yourself, MC.

As always, his reply pops up instantly. I'm proud of you, Ems. I'm here if you need anything. Oh, and have you seen my hoodie?

His Nike hoodie, the one he loaned me the night of Daria's book club. Sorry. On my coatrack. Carmella's staying at my place while

I'm gone. Knock first so you don't scare her.

Before I have time to turn off my phone, he replies. Can we talk when you get home? Please?

My stomach clenches. I take a deep breath. Sure.

I toss my phone into my purse. As I go to snap it shut, something in the bottom catches my eye. I freeze. The hairs on my arms stand erect. No. It can't be.

It's heavy and cool as I lift it, about the size of a silver dollar. Around its circumference it reads *Saint Christopher, Protect Us.* The bronze medallion that once belonged to our mother.

For years this medal was Daria's most prized possession. My dad gave it to her when she made her first communion. "The patron saint of travelers," he told her. "Your mother would want you to have it."

And now Dar wants me to have it. She must have slipped it into my purse, too embarrassed to give it to me personally.

A soft moan rises before I can catch it. I clutch the medal and hold it to my heart, filled with the comfort of Saint Christopher's protection . . . my mother's memory . . . my sister's love.

Lucy stops blowing on her nails and looks

over at me, her head cocked. "Jesus, Em. You having an orgasm over there, or what?"

As promised, Aunt Poppy is waiting just outside the Delta counter. Though it's been ten years since I've seen her in person, I recognize her instantly. In fact, she'd be hard to miss, dressed in bright green slacks, a patchwork blazer, and big round glasses that nearly swallow her tiny face.

"If it isn't Elton John–ette," Lucy mumbles.

Poppy's waving both hands at once. Beside her sit two wheelie bags splashed with purples and reds and yellows, as if someone — Poppy perhaps — took a brush dipped in paint and flicked it at a perfectly good set of white luggage.

"My sunshine!" she cries, trotting over to us. Her nails are painted a flaming coral to match her lips. "You're even lovelier in real life!"

I want to be angry with this woman who tried to steal my mother. But when I step into her open arms, all reservations vanish. Criminal or not, my aunt makes me feel loved, a feeling I'm growing to like. But just as quickly, guilt rises. I've lived my entire life with Nonna, and now I'm betraying her for an aunt I barely know.

"My heart is dancing!" she says, planting one last kiss on my cheek before turning to Lucy. "And you!" She goes to draw her other niece into a hug, but Lucy stands stiffly, her arms at her sides.

"It's wonderful to see you, Luciana," Aunt Poppy finally says, and she grins. "Though I may have preferred seeing a little less of you."

Lucy rears back. "What's that supposed to mean?"

I turn away, embarrassed for my poor cousin. What was I supposed to do when Lucy came wobbling down her porch steps, dressed in a clingy white cocktail dress and black open-toed ankle boots? Who, besides my cousin, ever thought open-toed boots were a good idea? But the cab was racking up a fortune, and we needed to get to the airport. Why start the trip with an argument?

Poppy pats her cheek. "That silly old curse has made fools of us all. Just look at you, my dear girl. So desperate for love. And this one" — she points at me — "shows up looking like a scuffed shoe."

I gasp. "Me?"

Lucy cracks up. "I know, right? But you're going to break it now? The curse?"

Poppy lifts her chin. "On my eightieth

120

birthday, I will meet the love of my life on the steps of the Ravello Cathedral."

Lucy's jaw drops. "That's your plan to break the curse?"

Poppy's face erupts in childlike joy, and she nods. Lucy grabs her by the shoulders.

"No. No! No! No! You can't be serious. What makes you think you're going to meet the love of your life at age eighty, when I can't find mine at twenty-one?"

"What Lucy means," I say, my heart in my stomach, "is that the odds of meeting someone at your . . . um . . . stage in life . . . is . . . well . . ."

Lucy interjects. "I hate to break it to you, Pops, but very few men are into windsock boobs and wrinkled asses."

I wince, and pray our aunt has a hearing problem.

"Tell me," Poppy says, looking from Lucy to me. "When was it that you stopped believing in magic?"

Her question catches me off guard. I'm tempted to tell her the truth, that I stopped believing sometime around the fourth grade, when, after years of wishing and praying, I still hadn't gotten a mother.

"The only reason I'm here," Lucy says, "is because you promised to break the curse. My mom's already blowing up my

121

phone, wondering when I'll be freed. Please tell me you have a plan B."

Poppy turns away and lifts the handles of her wheelie bags. "Forget about the curse, Luciana. We're off to Italy!"

I avoid Lucy's eyes, but I can feel them, shooting daggers at me. I want to assure her that, if there really is a curse (which of course there's not), Poppy will break it. She will keep her promise. But I can't. My great-aunt just may be the biggest manipulator since *Downton Abbey*'s old Lady Grantham.

I follow Poppy through security. Unlike my pristine passport, stamps from foreign countries fill every page of Poppy's book.

"How many countries have you visited?" I ask as she slips her passport back into her oversized orange purse.

"Thirty-four and counting. But Italy's special. I return every year."

"You travel to Italy each year, hoping to meet your true love?"

"Oh, goodness, no! Only this year. I haven't set foot in Ravello since 1961. I've been saving that town for next week."

We three sit at the gate, side by side on pleather sling chairs. Lucy turns her back to us, typing furiously into her phone. Poppy seems oblivious. She sits erect as a queen, smiling and nodding to the travelers as they scurry past.

"Airports are such fun, don't you think, Luciana?"

"Second only to Brazilian waxing," Lucy says, her eyes never leaving her phone.

Poppy tips her head back and laughs. "How clever you are, Luciana, for someone who chooses to wear stilettos for international travel."

Lucy looks over her shoulder. "Hey, they're better than Em's church lady shoes."

"What's wrong with my shoes? These Clarks are super comfy."

Poppy plants a hand on mine. "Once you start dressing for comfort, dear, it's all downhill. Ever visit a nursing home? Nothing but elastic and Velcro."

Ouch. She's managed to ding both Lucy and me in one conversation.

As Lucy taps her phone, Poppy tells me of her love for horses. "Bought Higgins on my sixtieth birthday." Her favorite music. "I just got wind of a terrific new indie band called Chastity Belt. Have you heard them yet?" And the yoga classes that keep her limber. "Do you know that seventy percent of adults cannot get up from the floor without using their hands? Imagine!"

As she talks, I study her, the way she emphasizes with hand gestures, furrows her brows, leans back and howls. She's wrinkled, no doubt about it. But her face isn't pinched, like Nonna's. And those eyes. They're the same oval shape as Nonna's, the same deep chocolate brown. But I'd bet my life savings the creases that sprout from Poppy's are etched from amusement, not animosity.

I startle, and realize Poppy has stopped talking. "I'm sorry. Go on."

She leans in. "You're looking at me as if you're seeing me for the first time, dear."

I smile, feeling heat rise to my cheeks. "I guess I never realized you were so beautiful."

"I was a plain child. But you see, planted in the right spot, we blossom. You'll find it happens to you, too, once you find your home."

"Bensonhurst is my home."

"Is it?" She holds my gaze. "What if, after nearly thirty years of life, you discover you've been planted in the wrong place?"

An inexplicable chill comes over me. At once I remember the medal in my purse. "Excuse me," I say. "I need to make a call."

I punch in my sister's number as I walk over to the window. She answers after three rings. "Thank you for the Saint Christopher medallion, Dar. I just found it."

"It's only on loan," she says. "Don't lose it."

"I won't, I promise. I'm here now, at the airport." A smile hijacks my face and I practically levitate.

"I can't believe you're actually doing this. Nonna is beside herself."

"She'll be fine," I say, wishing I believed it.

"So you'll be back Friday?"

"Friday? *This* Friday? Of course not. We'll be back a week from Tuesday — the twenty-third. Eight days in Italy, remember?"

Daria lets out an exaggerated groan. "But this weekend is our getaway to Atlantic City."

I slap a hand on my forehead. Oh, God! The Groupon deal. I'd agreed to watch the kids . . . but that was weeks ago. Why hadn't she reminded me? "I am so, so sorry. What can I do? I'll call Carmella. Maybe she can babysit."

"You think because she's my cousin she'll babysit for free? Forget it. She'd charge me a fortune."

"Look, I'll pay —"

"Never mind, Emmie, just go. Obviously, pleasing Poppy — someone who broke our nonna's heart — is more important than we are."

My fingers tremble as they trace the scar beneath my lower lip. "I'm sorry, Dar. We're about to leave. I can't abandon her now."

"You can't . . . or you won't?"

I look over at my aunt. She's playing peekaboo with a baby across the aisle. This peculiar old woman is ready to embark on yet another adventure, one that might lead to great joy . . . or bitter heartbreak. And something tells me that if I'm brave enough to join her, I might have an adventure, too.

My voice is soft when I finally speak. "Please understand —"

"No, Emmie, I don't understand. This isn't like you. Nonna's right. Poppy has brainwashed you."

"Daria, please —"

"I have to go," she says, interrupting me. "Have a great time."

Her sarcasm is punctuated by a *click*, disconnecting us.

I rush to the restroom. I fling my glasses onto the counter and blot my eyes with a paper towel. Daria is furious. Nonna is livid. Lucy is pissed. My father's probably a wreck. Is there anyone I haven't disappointed? And for what? An old woman's fantasy that she'll finally find true love? To end a curse that I don't even believe? To hear stories about my mother that may or may not be true?

Poppy rounds the corner, and skids to a stop when she sees me in the mirror. "Oh, heavens!" She takes me in her arms, and I'm enveloped in her citrusy perfume. "What's wrong, my girl?"

"Nothing," I say, pinching the rough paper towel to my nose. "Everything."

She rocks me against her bird-bone body. I swear I can feel her heart beat with mine. I close my eyes.

"Daria's upset. I was supposed to babysit Natalie and Mimi this weekend."

She pulls back. "You gave your word?"

I nod. "Back in August. We never confirmed a date. I forgot all about it." I toss the paper towel into the trash. "Maybe I should just forget this trip."

She takes me by the arms and spins me, so that my back is to her. I'm startled when she starts swiping at my shirt.

"What are you doing?" I ask, looking over my shoulder.

"Wiping the footprints off you."

"Footprints?"

"The ones your sister leaves when she walks all over you."

Poppy looks into my eyes and then bursts out laughing. Despite myself, so do I.

"Is there any feeling more sublime," she

says, lifting my glasses from the counter and settling them onto my face, "than laughing through tears?"

This, I realize. *This* is why I'm going to Italy.

Ten minutes later, I return to the gate, my eyes red rimmed but dry. Poppy is happily people-watching and Lucy's on her phone, uttering a series of curt, one-word responses. I'm guessing it's her mom, quizzing her about Aunt Poppy and the curse. I grab my notebook and pen, desperate for something to take my mind off all the family members I'm failing. I shield the page with my left hand as I write, but still Poppy zeroes in.

"You're a writer!"

I close my notebook. "Oh, no. Not even close. It's just a silly hobby."

"That which brings us joy should never be besmirched."

I let out a laugh. "Besmirched? Who even uses that word?"

"Writers, that's who. Now tell me, what is it you write?"

"Romance," I say. I quickly add, "But my stories have never been published."

"Romance. I'm impressed." She wiggles her brows mischievously. "You must have plenty of experience?"

"Um, well, not exactly. I did have a boy-friend in college, Liam. It lasted a few months." I laugh. "Lucky for me, I have a good imagination."

"I suspect we're alike that way. We prefer to see life as it should be, not as it is." She plucks a tube of lipstick from her purse. "This boyfriend . . . Liam. What happened? Were you in love?"

I'm caught off guard by her direct questions. Without warning, a lump rises in my throat. I work my mouth into a smile. "I think so. It ended before it got started, really. I left Barnard at winter break to fill in for Uncle Bruno at the store. I ended up transferring to Brooklyn College. Liam and I just . . . grew apart."

Poppy knits her brows. "That little fucker." She slaps her mouth, as if she, too, is surprised by the word. "Pardon me," she says, "but there are times when no other noun will suffice."

I can't help but laugh. "Liam was a good guy," I say, hoping to leave it at that.

"Sounds like my Thomas — another good guy." She runs the glossy coral tube over her lips. "It's time we found you someone with a more interesting description." She smacks her lips. "I'm thinking someone cerebral. A dreamer . . . a lover of books.

Someone with a sharp mind and a firm rear end."

She erupts in guffaws. Before I have time to tell her I'm not interested, she shifts the topic. "Do you play a musical instrument?"

"Oh, God, no."

"Your grandfather was a musician."

"He was?" I've seen pictures of Nonno Alberto, always with a cigar stub in his mouth, never a musical instrument. Surely she's mistaken, but I don't challenge her.

She extends her lipstick to me. I shake my head no. She stares at my scar before dropping the tube into her purse. "Do you paint? Draw?"

"Honestly, I've told you pretty much everything. My life isn't all that interesting."

"No matter," she says. "That will soon change."

"Tell me about you," I say, steering the conversation to safer topics. "You left Bensonhurst in 1961. What happened next?"

A shadow crosses her face, but she quickly recovers. "I moved to Hershey, Pennsylvania, and got a job at the chocolate factory." She puts both hands to her neck and crosses her eyes. "Assembly line. A nerve-twanging bore."

I laugh. "And then you got a degree in art

history?"

She nods. "I enrolled in night classes at Franklin and Marshall College. It took five years to earn my bachelor's degree. After graduation, the University of Pennsylvania offered me a rare fellowship in their master's program. That's when I quit the Hershey factory and moved to Philadelphia." She tells me about her job at the Shipley School in Bryn Mawr, teaching art appreciation to teens. "Forty-nine years and counting, though for the past decade, I've chosen to volunteer."

"That's so inspiring," I say, gazing at this educated, curious, independent woman, so unlike the other Fontana women I know. To think that I share her DNA. I glance at my watch. "We have an hour before we board. Would you tell me something about my mother?"

Lucy looks up from her phone. "How about we keep the convo in the present century, like, maybe who's our favorite pick on *The Bachelor,* or something remotely interesting."

It's odd to me that nobody in my family, including Lucy, seems to understand my curiosity about my mother. Do they not realize how someone could miss, so deeply and profoundly, a person they've never known?

"Of course," Poppy says, and I assume she's agreeing with Lucy. But then she laces her fingers with mine and lets out a sigh, as if she's about to embark on a difficult and daunting journey.

CHAPTER 13

POPPY

1959
Florence, Italy

Rosa insisted nobody would be the wiser. I scored ninety-eight percent on the Uffizi examination — or rather, Rosa did. Each morning I'd rise at five and walk two miles to the town of Fiesole. From there, bus number seven would pick up the village commuters. An hour later, we would be dropped off on Via Ricasoli, in the center of Firenze. Once I stepped off the bus, I would proudly pin my name tag to my uniform — Rosa Fontana Lucchesi.

It was December. I had been working at Florence's famous gallery for a month, pretending to be Rosa. I adored my job, though I detested the plain brown suit we guides were expected to wear. To brighten the drab uniform, I wore cheap jewelry I'd accumulated since I was a child — a strand of plastic beads one day, a feathered peacock pin the next. Each day, I wound a brightly colored scarf around my head. Every guide held a stick so we could be easily identified in the crowds. I tied a bright orange ribbon to the end of mine.

It was chilly that morning, and I shivered as I stood outside the entrance to the gallery, waiting for my tour group to gather. Soon, Italian tourists from around the country began swarming around me. And there, standing alone in the back, was a yellow-haired man. He looked to be in his twenties, with a fine chiseled face and piercing blue eyes. He was so tall and broad I assumed he was American, or maybe an Aussie.

I introduced myself to the group and flashed my broadest smile. "The collection is vast," I announced. "I am here to answer any questions you may have. Any questions whatsoever."

A middle-aged woman raised her hand.

I lifted my chin and straightened, grateful for the opportunity to demonstrate my knowledge. "Sì?"

"Dove sono i gabinetti?"

Where are the toilets? The yellow-haired man burst out laughing, and despite my embarrassment, I did, too.

For the next ninety minutes, I led the group through the exhibits. The dashing yellow-haired man never spoke. But all the while, I was aware of his presence, as if he radiated some secret energy only I could feel. I studied his strong jawline, the long lashes that fanned over his clear blue eyes. More than once, when he was pretending to admire the paintings, I caught him watching me, too.

When the tour ended, he slipped away, taking with him a sliver of my heart. That sounds trite, but it's true. We hadn't spoken a word, but something had passed between us. I felt it deep in my soul, the way one does when touched by magic.

The following day, I was back . . . and so was he, the gorgeous man from the day before. I couldn't believe my luck. I'd been a bit flustered by him the previous day, distracted by his presence. I wanted so badly for this tour to go perfectly. But then he smiled, and a dimple appeared in his cheek, and those blue eyes twinkled. I couldn't think straight.

Mercifully, the tour ended, and I answered a few last questions. I was anxious to get away, to find the yellow-haired man and properly introduce myself. But when I went

135

to find him, he was gone, *poof!* Vanished, once again.

I was so angry with myself. The goddesses had given me a second chance, and I'd squandered it. We hadn't spoken a word.

On the bus ride back to Fiesole that evening, I watched out the window. Each time we entered a village, I'd search the crowds, hoping to catch sight of the blue-eyed man. I do believe if I'd seen him, I would have charged from the bus.

Two days later, as my morning tour was about to begin, who did I see but Mister Blue Eyes. My heart nearly burst! He was in my group, waiting with the others for the tour to begin. This time I wouldn't blow my chance. I made my way through the gaggle of tourists and stepped up to the man. Oh, how my heart thundered! Up close, I could see his fine cheekbones, his even white teeth. He was so tall, so powerful, but at the same time, gentle. To me, he was as exquisite as any statue in the gallery.

"Buongiorno," I said to him. "Back for your third tour, I see. You must be a glutton for punishment."

He looked at me, confused. *"Non capisco. Es tut mir leid."*

His words were a concoction of both Italian and German.

"You're German?" I said to him in English. "No wonder you were so quiet." I pointed to the German guide. "You will want to be in Ingrid's group."

He smiled at me, and I will never forget the look on his face. Admiration, is what I call it. "Grazie," he said to me in Italian. "But I am where I want to be."

"So you do speak Italian."

"I know how to ask for the bathroom," he said, his eyes twinkling.

Together, we laughed at the memory.

"But twice you joined the Italian tour — and you paid money. Did you understand anything from these tours?"

"Not much," he said. "But I enjoyed them very much."

I felt suddenly hot. I looked around until I spotted Ingrid. "There," I said, pointing across the lobby. "The German tour is about to begin."

"I am where I want to be," he said in his broken Italian. "Hearing your voice is enough. I do not need to understand the words."

When my shift ended that day, the beautiful German with the yellow hair was waiting for me in the piazza with a cup of gelato. How could I say no to a man who had twice

— no, three times — spent money on a tour he didn't understand, just to be near me? It was the most romantic thing ever to happen to me, the second daughter.

We communicated using a medley of English and German and Italian, as well as hand gestures that made us both laugh. He was from Radebeul, a village in East Germany, outside of Dresden on the banks of the Elbe River. He'd left his home and family eighteen months earlier, desperate to escape the harsh rule of the Communists in the German Democratic Republic, or GDR. His name was Erich.

"Erich?" I asked, licking gelato from my spoon. "You must mean . . . Rico. You see, here in Italy, a man's name must end with a vowel."

His eyes crinkled at the edges. "Fine. To you, I will be Rico. And what shall I call you, Rosa?"

I'd almost forgotten. My name tag read Rosa. He heard me introduce myself as Rosa. If I told him I was pretending to be my sister, might he think badly of me? Might he report me to the Uffizi Gallery? I decided to take the chance.

"My name is Paolina. I — I only pretend to be Rosa at work."

He studied me, the corners of his lips

138

upturned. "You should have chosen a more fitting pseudonym. The rose is much too thorny. You are more like the beautiful *Mohn,* bold and radiant."

He pronounced it like the English word "moon," and I blanched. "Moon? I will not be called Moon. Who wants to be a ball of cheese in the sky?"

He laughed then, a sound so rich I wanted to marinate in it. "Not moon, *Mohn,* the vibrant orange flower. I believe here it is called the *papavero.*"

"I adore papaveri. But it is a dreadful nickname." I thought for a moment. "How about you call me Poppy, the English word for the flower?"

"Poppy," he repeated, and my name never sounded sweeter. "It suits you. Vibrant, colorful . . ." He leaned in and stroked my cheek, ever so gently. "And addictive."

I knew then, with the touch of his finger on my skin, that I would never be the same. And I was right. Fifty-nine years later, I can still feel the touch of the only man I've ever truly and completely loved.

CHAPTER 14

EMILIA

Everyone adores Poppy — everyone except Lucy, perhaps. I follow my aunt down the aisle of the plane, drawing back each time she calls out to our fellow passengers "Hello" and "Happy travels!" and "Off we go!" I sneak a peek at Lucy, behind me. Her jaw is clenched and she shakes her head.

"What the hell have you gotten me into? The woman is effing nuts."

I lift my shoulders as if to say, "It's too late now."

We settle into our seats — an upgrade, thanks to Aunt Poppy's new BFF at the check-in counter. Lucy insists on the aisle seat. Poppy slides into the window seat, leaving me in the middle of their growing tension.

"Spill it," Lucy says, yanking on her seat belt. "Did you and Herr Yellow-Hair hook up, or what?"

Poppy's dark eyes are soft and dreamy. "We did." She pats Lucy's cheek, seeming not to notice Lucy flinch. "Rico is the man I will meet on the steps of the Ravello Cathedral."

Lucy's eyes go wide. "You mean it's not some random dude you're hoping to meet? It's someone you actually know?"

"Of course I know him. I am not that naïve, Luciana."

I let out a sigh of relief. "So you fell in love with Rico. And the two of you have kept in touch all this time?"

She turns to me, her brows knitted. "Oh, no, dear. We haven't spoken in nearly sixty years."

Lucy groans. "For fuck's sake, tell me you're joking." She leans over me, getting as close to Poppy as she can. "You might have told us this little detail before we committed to the trip."

Poppy smiles sweetly. "What little detail, dear?"

Lucy's nostrils flare. "What makes you think a man you haven't spoken to in decades will suddenly appear at the Ravello Cathedral?"

She lifts her chin. "He promised."

Lucy closes her eyes. "Right," she mumbles. "Just like they all do."

As the plane prepares for takeoff, Poppy presses her face to the window, looking so childlike I half expect her to blow steam and draw stick figures. I lean in beside her. Below, the flight workers direct the plane from the tarmac, using arm signals.

"Look!" Poppy says. "He's waving at me!" She waves her hand furiously, as if the man might see her.

I can't tell if my aunt, who's smart and sophisticated and well traveled, is being funny or serious. Or maybe she really is crazy. I look over at Lucy, but she's busy texting. Jack's name shows on the header.

"You're still seeing Jack?" I squint at her screen, hoping to find something akin to *I regret ever hooking up with your sorry ass.*

She shields her phone from my view. "It's all good," she says, whatever that means.

Poppy leans in. "Better say good-bye now." She nabs Lucy's phone, turns it off, and stuffs it into the seat pocket.

Lucy's mouth falls open. "I wasn't finished!"

Poppy smiles. "Imagine how perplexed he'll be, wondering what in heavens happened to you."

Lucy starts to reach for her phone, stops, seems to digest the comment, then pulls her hand back. Score one for Aunt Poppy. It strikes me that my aunt and my cousin aren't really so different. Both are hoping against hope that one day, love will keep its promise.

The plane speeds down the runway and lifts. My stomach does a flip-flop. Poppy claps. "Isn't flight glorious?"

"Simmer down, Pops," Lucy says. But thankfully, her voice has lost its edge. She looks at me and shakes her head, like a secretly amused mother whose child said a bad word.

Once we're airborne and our meal has been served, Lucy swallows a pill. Minutes later, she's leaning on my shoulder, softly snoring. It's sweet having her snuggled beside me, like she's my little cousin again.

On my other side, Poppy's ears are covered with her headset, and she's laughing out loud at some Amy Poehler movie on the screen. I close my notebook and savor her laughter. I'm a bit miffed with her for manipulating us into traveling with her. But more than anything, I'm sad for her.

I silently study my aunt, the woman who couldn't let go after her child died, the woman who grew too attached to my mother and tried to take her as her own. Is she suffering from some sort of attachment disorder? I'd asked Poppy to tell me of my mother, like she promised. Once again, she spent nearly an hour talking about her young life in Florence. A shiver comes over me. Did Aunt Poppy even know my mother? Or was that just another ruse she concocted to get us to Italy?

The cabin lights flicker on. The intercom crackles and the captain announces our descent into Venice, the floating city. One by one, passengers lift their window shades. Sunlight bursts into the plane. I rub my eyes and turn to Poppy. She's perched upright in her seat, her lips and cheeks freshly painted, smelling of Chanel perfume.

"Did you sleep?"

She bats a hand at me. "Not a wink. I'm much too excited."

The plane tilts, providing a panoramic view from Poppy's window. Brilliant sunlight reflects off the green waters. And there, in the middle of the sparkling Adriatic Sea, sit two perfect puzzle pieces, separated by the graceful curve of the Grand Canal.

"Look!" Poppy cries. "The new Port of Venice! And there's Piazza San Marco!"

Beside me, Lucy comes alive. She stretches toward the window. Poppy grabs each of our hands and she raises them to her face. "Thank you," she says, her eyes bright.

Her voice breaks, and so does my heart. There's no turning back now. No excuses to be made, no rationalizing to take the sting out of it. We're here now, in Italy, the place where, in eight short days, Poppy's heart will be either filled with joy or completely pulverized.

CHAPTER 15

EMILIA

Day One

Venezia — Venice

Marco Polo Airport is bustling this Monday morning, and we make our way through customs. Aunt Poppy's gait isn't quite so sprightly, and under the airport's fluorescent lights, her olive skin reflects a grayish undertone. She looks every bit her seventy-nine years — or worse. Of course she's just made an eight-hour overnight flight without sleep. I wouldn't expect her to look youthful.

It's eleven in the morning when we step outside the airport. The sun spills over the Laguna Veneta — the enclosed bay of the Adriatic Sea — and at once, we all seem more vibrant.

"Hiraeth!" Poppy cries, and claps her hands. "Do you know this Welsh word? It's

146

a feeling not easily translated into words. A deep longing for home, a nostalgia — a yearning — for the place that calls to your soul."

"That's beautiful," I say, "though I've never actually experienced *hiraeth.*"

"I'm not surprised." She tips her head. "But one day you will."

Five minutes later, we board a water taxi, a small wooden craft Poppy arranged to deliver us to our hotel on Venice's Grand Canal. Taavi, our handsome driver, stands at the helm dressed in tight jeans with a scarf snaked around his neck. Lucy plants herself beside him, while Poppy and I claim a red vinyl bench.

Boats of every shape and size zip up and down the lagoon, ferrying passengers to and from the mainland. Ahead, Venice beckons us, a city of more than a hundred tiny islands stitched together by bridges and alleys and canal sidewalks.

"Once," Taavi tells us, the wind at his face, "the only way to reach the city of Venice was by boat. In 1846, the Ponte della Libertà was built — the Bridge of Liberty."

"Bridge of Liberty," I say. "I love the sound of that."

"It is our causeway," he continues, "the railway into the city."

"What about cars?" Lucy asks.

Taavi grins. "No automobiles in Venice. We use the vaporetti — much like the ferry boats — to get around the islands."

Lucy leans close, her jacket unzipped, and tells him about the ferry boats in New York. He listens politely, but he shifts away from her, keeping his eyes on the water instead of her cleavage.

The boat swerves and the salty brine trickles down on us like holy water. Poppy lifts her hands and cheers, her pink and orange silk scarf billowing in the wind. Taavi waves to his mates, the fellow water taxi drivers. *"Oi, oi,"* he calls, warning them as we pass.

Poppy waves, too. *"Oi, oi,"* she mimics.

The wind laps my face. Without warning, I begin to laugh. "I'm in Italy. *We're* in Italy. We're actually here!"

Lucy shakes her head. She doesn't understand that for twenty-nine years, I've longed for an adventure like this.

The lagoon curves, and we enter a wide swath of water lined with ancient Venetian palaces, domed cathedrals, and sumptuous hotels, all awash in peaches and pinks and yellows.

"Welcome to the Grand Canal," Taavi says, slowing the boat. "The Main Street of

Venezia."

Pilings of timber line the waterway, serving as markers for the myriad of water vessels.

"The city of Venice was built on a wooden platform," Taavi explains. "Back in the fifth century, after the fall of the Western Roman Empire, barbarians from the north raided the mainland. People escaped to the marshes. Later, many decided to make the wetlands their home. These early Venetians drove stakes into the sand and constructed wooden platforms atop the stakes. The beautiful buildings you see today are built upon those wooden platforms."

"It really is a floating city," I say, studying the ornate structures with even greater appreciation.

Taavi docks the boat in front of the Ca' Sagredo Hotel, an exquisite pink building dotted with white balustrades. He takes hold of each of our hands as we climb from the boat onto a concrete platform. Lucy steps off last.

"Do you have a business card?" she asks Taavi, her head tilted in what I'm sure is a calculated angle, ensuring that a lock of hair spills over one eye. "We're here for three days. I might need you again."

I cringe.

"Uh, sì." Taavi pulls a card from his shirt pocket. Before handing it to her, he scribbles something on it.

Lucy's mood seems to brighten three shades. She waves as Taavi speeds away. *"Arrivederci!"*

She glances at the business card as we move to the hotel, and stops in midstep. "Motherf—" She catches herself. "Motherducker." She tears the card in two, but not before I see *No, thank you* written on the back. "Don't you hate it when you're just being friendly, and guys think you're hitting on them?"

Poppy rests a hand on Lucy's back. "A pair of breasts in one's face is apt to imply the latter, dear."

Lucy gushes when she opens the door to our spacious suite. "Whoa. Someone's laying down some serious cash."

"It's gorgeous," I say, admiring the glossy wood floor and soft gray walls. Two gigantic beds take up the front of the room, with a comfortable sitting area toward the balcony. I peek my head into a white marble bathroom with double sinks. How can a retired art teacher afford this place?

"Apple stock," Poppy says.

"What?"

"That's how I made my money."

"Oh," I say, feeling heat rise to my cheeks. Is this equestrian-teacher-yogi also a mind reader?

She lifts her chin, her dark eyes dancing. "Invested ten thousand dollars in that little-known tech company the day it went public in 1980. Twenty-two dollars a share. By the time I sold it, it had gained over twenty-nine *thousand* percent. Can you imagine? And that doesn't include dividends." She tips her head back and laughs.

"Oh, hell yes!" Lucy says and holds out her fist for a bump.

"Well, thanks for being so generous," I say.

"Money is a tool, not a treasure." She opens a set of double doors, and we enter an equally pretty, completely separate bedroom.

"Nice," I say. "Your own private suite."

"You and Lucy don't mind sharing the other, do you?"

Behind me, Lucy lets out a screech. I shake my head.

"Oh, c'mon, Luce. It's only three nights."

"My phone!"

I rush to her side and help rummage through her bags. But she already knows, and so do I. Her phone is on Delta Flight

474 in her seat pocket, right where Poppy placed it. "I have to go back to the airport," she says, gathering her purse.

Poppy takes her by the arm. "It's too late. Surely they've cleared the plane. Let it go."

Lucy wriggles away. "Are you insane? I need my phone."

"I'll contact the airline." She takes Lucy's face in her wrinkled hands and stares directly into her eyes, like a female Svengali. "But in the meantime, let it go," she repeats, this time very slowly and with a gentle firmness. Lucy finally steps back, shaking her head.

"You owe me a new phone," she says.

"When we return, I'll buy you the very latest." Poppy pats her arm. "I'm sorry I was so careless, Luciana. But trust me, you'll find freedom from its absence, I promise."

Lucy continues to grouse, but she'll be okay, I can tell. I'm guessing Poppy's right. It can't be easy waiting for a lover's message that never comes, or being grilled by a mother who's been promised a miracle.

I cross the room and pull back sheer white curtains. Sunlight spills in. I step onto a balcony staged with a pair of chaise lounges and urns of red geraniums. I lean against the concrete balustrade, inhaling the salty sea air that tickles my nostrils. Three stories below, people mill about along the Grand Canal, taking photos and eating gelato. The water is rough today, and spray from the water taxis mists the air. I gather my sweater across my chest. Aunt Poppy comes up beside me and tucks her hand into the crook of my arm.

"My country," she says. "The land where I met my Rico."

I give a wan smile. "Maybe, just maybe, we really can find your old friend. What's his last name? I'll Google him. If he's on Facebook or Twitter, we'll send him a message and remind him —"

"Nonsense," she says, cutting me off. She plants both hands on the balcony ledge and closes her eyes. "Rico has not forgotten."

Poppy suggests a costume change before we set out to explore the "splendiferous sights of Venezia." I throw on a pair of jeans and a cotton sweater. Lucy wriggles into a short suede skirt and ankle boots. Poppy flaunts a red and purple knit cardigan, belted at the waist, and a giant firefly brooch nearly hidden beneath a necklace with turquoise beads the size of my fist. Up and down her arms she wears colorful bangles. They look like they're made of plastic, but I can't be sure. She catches me staring.

153

"You wear one, and they look cheap. You wear a dozen, and it's a style." She grabs a pair of gigantic red sunglasses and plants them on her tiny face. "We're off!"

On the street, Poppy doesn't seem to notice the conservatively clad Europeans staring at her flamboyant garb. She laughs and waves and calls out, *"Buongiorno!"* to puzzled passersby. I link arms with her. Back home, I might be embarrassed. But here in Italy, I'm strangely proud of this woman who displays her style — and her heart — so fearlessly.

Poppy darts into the first bakery she sees, Pasticceria Rizzardini. We each order a baba, an individual cake soaked in rum, filled with pastry cream.

"Here, we call it *fiamma,* or flame," the man behind the counter tells us, "because it is so richly drenched in alcohol."

I plunge a plastic forkful into my mouth. The cake's buttery sweetness collides with the sharp tang of alcohol. "Mmm," I murmur, wondering why my baba doesn't taste this good. Butter, I decide. Their butter is different here . . . fresher.

We nibble on our cake as we meander through Venice. The green waters of the canal follow alongside us, and we stroll the narrow streets — or *calli,* as they're called here in Venice. The entire city, it seems, is in a breathtaking state of opulent decay. Stucco peels from the sides of homes and buildings, revealing gaping chunks of exposed brick, a look urban designers at home try desperately to duplicate. We reach a spot where the street is so narrow I can almost touch the buildings on each side. Sunlight disappears, dropping the temperature ten degrees. For a moment, I feel claustrophobic. Ahead, I hear voices, laughter. The street widens, and light spills over us again.

Potted plants and stenciled house numbers tell me we're in a residential area. Black shutters adorn the homes, splayed like outstretched arms. Pink bougainvilleas cascade from second-story window boxes, and every now and then I spot a little cubby housing a statue of the Virgin Mother and Child.

"I love this place," I say, snapping a photo of creamy linen sheets, meticulously hung on a wire suspended between two houses. "I never realized laundry could be so pretty."

Poppy smiles. "For centuries, Venezia was one of the most powerful cities in Italy. Today, it's simply magical."

And it is. Every block, it seems, we climb another arched stone bridge, one of three hundred and forty in the city, Poppy tells us. A giggle escapes me. With each step, a strange sensation of lightness fills me, as if I've been freed from shackles and set aloft. I can't help but do a little dance when I reach the top. Poppy sees me and joins in, doing her own little two-step. Lucy shakes her head at us, and we all laugh.

We wander down a crowded cobblestone alley where tourists peer into shop windows, admiring colorful trinkets and mouthwatering pastries. A woman squeezes ahead of us, dressed in flat shoes and a fur coat, clutching a bag from the market. A merchant wearing a paper hat leans against his building, eyeing Lucy as we pass.

I'm smiling when the alley empties into yet another town square, or *campo,* as the locals refer to them. In the center stands an ancient cistern, ornately carved in stone. Children giggle as they squat beneath it, filling balloons with water. I snap a photo, then pull my map from my purse. We must be in Campo Santa Margherita. Or maybe it's Campo San Trovaso.

"Put that away," Poppy suggests. "Venice is a maze. You'll never find your bearings. I always say, when you feel lost or confused, consult your heart. It's your most reliable source of navigation."

Yeah, right. I smile and stuff the useless thing into my purse, charmed by the sound of a man on a balcony, singing in Italian. Pigeons swoop overhead. Wine bars and upscale restaurants sporting colorful awnings span the perimeter of the square, alongside jewelry stores and bakeries and pizzerias. At the far end stands a small but proud cathedral. People stroll and shop with their families, or sit in pairs at little iron tables.

We cross a longer bridge where a half dozen gondolas idle in the water. Poppy clasps her hands, and her entire body seems to tremble with glee.

"A gondola ride! Let's go!"

"Seriously?" Lucy asks. "A gondola?"

Poppy laughs. "Oh, Luciana, be on the lookout for childhood joy, won't you? I fear you have lost yours."

Italian men of various shapes and sizes stand at the helms of their Venetian flat-bottom boats, wearing black-and-white-striped shirts and red kerchiefs, a vision so corny that it's quaint. Lucy points a finger at a particularly good-looking gondolier.

"Quello!" she says.

The shiny black gondola rocks when we step into it, and I help Poppy move to the red upholstered seat. The handsome gondolier stands on the asymmetrical boat, using a single oar to push the gondola down the narrow canal.

Poppy drapes an arm around each of us, and I'm lulled by the relaxing gurgle of water. I breathe deeply of the canal, a unique smell that's dank and fishy and fresh all at once. We pass beneath old stone bridges so low I almost duck, and float alongside beautiful calli lined with fancy hotels. Flags hang suspended from an iron balcony, red with gold, blue, and green, their brilliance shimmering in the dappled sunlight. The gondola veers close to the canal wall, and our driver uses his oar to push off. Lucy eyes him like a T-bone steak.

"To symbolize their love for water," Poppy says, "Venetian mythology claims a gondolier is born with webbed feet."

"Who cares about webbed feet?" Lucy says in perfect Italian. She raises her eyebrows. "I prefer a very long oar."

My eyes go wide and I tip my head toward Aunt Poppy, hoping to remind Lucy that our eighty-year-old aunt can also speak the language. But Poppy only laughs.

"Luciana, you slay me!" She sits up straight. "I'm so pleased you're both fluent in Italian. Your mother would be proud, Emilia."

I perk up. "Really? She wanted me to speak Italian? Why?"

Poppy gazes out at the water, as if time is calling to her. "Rico struggled with Italian, but he eventually mastered it."

"And my mom?" I say, clutching her hand, trying to keep my frustration in check. "What else do you know about her?"

She looks up at us. "Have I gotten to the part of the story where Rico plays his violin?"

"Nope," Lucy says, and she gives an exaggerated yawn. "But feel free to skip ahead."

CHAPTER 16

POPPY

1959–60
Florence

Monday through Saturday, from eight until four, I worked at the Uffizi Gallery. But the bus back to Fiesole didn't leave until six thirty. Mr. Blue Eyes worked nights, stretching gloves at a leather factory from seven until four in the morning. Which meant that six days a week, for two and a half glorious hours, I was free, and so was Rico. We'd stroll the streets of Firenze, speaking in Italian and German, laughing at our silly mistakes, soaking in everything we could learn about each other.

One day, about a week after we'd met, he brought along a weathered leather case. We sat on a bench in front of the Duomo, and to my surprise, he lifted a violin from the case and began to play. It was thrilling,

160

watching the bow travel up and down the strings, creating the most beautiful sound I'd ever heard. I couldn't believe it! He was a violinist!

He explained that his father, who was a prisoner in a Russian war camp during World War II, learned to play music so he could be part of the troupe that entertained the Russian soldiers. When he returned home to Germany, he taught his young son to play the accordion, the guitar, and the violin. Young Erich was a natural, and soon he was teaching his father new songs.

Rico stood before me, his foot propped on the bench, his chin tucked into the violin's body. It was mesmerizing, the sound that he created, as if by magic. An old man passing by took notice. Then a smartly dressed couple.

In no time, we were surrounded by thirty, maybe forty people — local merchants and children and English tourists. The energy from the crowd seemed to ignite Rico. He walked among the people, the ballad merging into a chirpy melody. The bow swept over the strings, faster and faster at a dizzying speed. People cheered and laughed and clapped. Rico didn't miss a note! He finished with a flourish of the bow. The ap-

plause and whoops and whistles were deaf-
ening.

When the admirers finally disappeared,
we couldn't believe what they'd left behind.
Coins . . . so many of them! More than he
made in an entire day at the factory.

"You are a star!" I told him as I helped
gather the coins.

He gently closed my fist when I tried to
hand him the money. "It is all yours, Poppy.
I was only trying to impress you."

He leaned down and kissed me for the
first time. It was slow and gentle and ex-
ceedingly provocative. My heart erupted like
Mount Vesuvius. Make no mistake, I'd been
kissed by a boy before. But not by a man,
and never with love.

"You accomplished your goal," I told him,
my head still spinning. "I am impressed."

"All my life I've dreamed of being a musician. Thank you for making me feel like one
today."

"You must quit that job at the factory," I
said calmly. "You must spend your time
making music."

"People may grow tired of my violin. The
leather factory is solid work."

I shrugged. "Failure *is* an option. A far
better outcome than not trying at all. This
instrument, Rico, it is your gift, your pas-

sion. You must not deny the universe of your music."

And that was the start of his new career.

He carved out a little spot in Piazza della Signoria, in front of the Fountain of Neptune. And just as I predicted, he became quite a figure. The crowds went bananas over the happy yellow-haired man who could make his violin weep. He performed three, sometimes four times a day. But between the hours of four and six thirty, Rico was mine.

At this point, we'd been secretly meeting for four weeks. I knew all about my Rico, how he was a young boy at the time of the war and how his home on the edge of Dresden had been bombed beyond recognition. How his family escaped to another village, called Clausnitz, and found shelter in a sawmill. How memories of Jewish prisoners being marched down the icy road, and shot when they fell, still gave him nightmares. How he and his sister would sneak bread to the American soldiers who were imprisoned across the street. How he loved sausages and cheese.

It was Rico's father, the owner of a small auto repair shop, who encouraged Rico to leave the Communist-controlled German Democratic Republic. His older sister was in love with a man who worked at a waffle factory, and refused to leave. His mother would go nowhere without her daughter. The family was stuck . . . but not Rico.

"You must go," his father had told him eighteen months earlier. "Opportunities in East Germany will only get worse. Escape, without a word to anyone. Take three things: your temporary travel permit, your bicycle, and some marks to pay for the train. When you reach the station, purchase a round-trip ticket to Munich. The guards must think you are returning. But take nothing else, not even a change of clothing. If the guards catch you with so much as a toothbrush, they will know you are trying to escape.

"When you reach Munich, transfer trains to Mindelheim, a small Bavarian town in the Allgäu. Present yourself to the West German authorities. You will be welcomed and given a West German travel permit, along with voucher stamps to use for food and lodging at the youth hostels. The East German mark is nearly worthless. Then, with your bicycle, you will travel to Austria. From there, you will be free, Erich, free to go wherever you choose."

His father's eyes glistened with tears.

"Tell no one of your plan. When you fail to return to East Germany, the authorities will grow suspicious. They will come here and question us. You will be considered a *Republikflucht* — an escapee. The punishment would be brutal, should you be caught. Do you understand?"

Rico nodded, the gravity of his decision bearing down on him. "And what about Mother? And Karin? Surely I must tell them good-bye."

His father grabbed his face and held it in his calloused hands. "No, my boy. Not even them."

"But they will think I deserted them."

"I will take care of this."

Rico turned to me then, his beautiful eyes misty. "I pray one day my mother will understand." He looked down, hesitating a moment. "And Karin, too."

"Your sister?" I asked.

He shook his head. "My fiancée."

My heart plummeted. All spirit drained from me. The blessed curse had caught me at last. All along, I was certain the family myth was nonsense. But here I was, the second daughter, in love — yes, in love — with a man who was engaged to be married.

CHAPTER 17

EMILIA

I clutch Poppy's hand. "Oh, Aunt Poppy, I'm so sorry. Rico married someone else?"

She pats my knee. "I'll continue the story later."

"So we really are cursed," Lucy says. "But you're going to break it, right? Aside from your plan to meet this two-timing turd, you have some other way, right?"

"Curse?" Poppy says. "Don't be ridiculous."

I keep my gaze on her, hoping — *willing* — her to say something, something to ease Lucy's anxiety. Her thin face is drawn, and dark circles hollow out her eyes. Break the curse, damn it.

Poppy calls to the gondolier, "We're ready to get off now." The gondolier slows the boat, steering it toward a bridge. "It's time for me to lie down," she says. "Tonight at dinner, I will tell you more about Rico."

166

"No!" Lucy's voice is angry now, and I can't blame her. "We've heard enough of your sorry-ass story." She crosses her arms over her chest. "If you think your Rico is going to show up after all these years and marry you, you're as batshit crazy as everybody says."

"Lucy!" I say, but Poppy only shakes her head.

"It seems you take pleasure in painting storm clouds, Luciana."

"You promised you'd break the curse," I remind Poppy, emotion rising in my voice. "Lucy believed you. She's counting on you."

"Hello?" Lucy says. "It's the only reason I'm here!"

Aunt Poppy bats a hand. "*Pfft!* All this time you've been told what to believe. Imagine the power in deciding what it is *you* hold to be true."

"Easy for you to say," Lucy says, as the boat slows to a stop. "You're older than the pyramids. What about me? I've got a lifetime ahead of me being cursed."

Poppy places a hand on Lucy's cheek. "It's fascinating, isn't it, how, when someone tells us something about ourselves — good or bad — we try so desperately to prove them right."

Lucy drags me into the first trattoria along the calle. A group of old men sit at a table drinking Peroni beer, their eyes glued to a flat-screen television, where they cheer for the soccer players dressed in orange and black. *"Leoni Alati!"* they shout, declaring their loyalty for Venezia's Winged Lions.

We settle in at a table and my cousin orders a liter of wine. From our spot by the window, we watch Poppy's slim figure disappear down the cobblestone street. My good angel tells me I should get up, walk her back to the hotel, and tuck her into bed. This city is impossible to navigate and she may get lost. But my bad angel is too angry. She's been here before. She can manage.

"What the hell?" Lucy says. She plants her elbows on the table and rakes her fingers through her hair.

"I know," I say, shaking my head. "She's trying to weasel out of this deal. I'm losing faith, big-time. She just wants to relive old memories."

"Poppy has no pride. That little prick was engaged, and still she pines for him."

The waiter arrives with the wine. While he fills our glasses, I share the story Uncle Dolphie told me, about Poppy and the baby she lost and her mental breakdown.

"Jesus," she says, lifting her glass. "And she claims we're not cursed?"

I wait until Lucy takes a long drink before I ask, "When did you first start believing in it?"

Her eyes lock on the television behind the bar, where the Winged Lions have fallen behind. "I was eight," she says. The little muscle in her jaw twitches. "Eight fucking years old when my parents told me I was cursed." She shakes her head, still focused on the television. "The only curses I knew were in fairy tales, when some sorry-ass victim was sentenced to years of sleep, or death, or made to live as a beast. So that's what I thought — that I'd be forever ruined if I didn't marry." Finally, she turns and meets my eyes.

"I was down the block, playing in the street, kicking a soccer ball around with Giulia, my bestie." She smiles. "I pretended not to hear my mom when she called from the door, *'Lu-cy! Lu-cy!'*

"Even as an eight-year-old, I found that humiliating. I wasn't a goddamn cocker spaniel, was I? So I ignored her. And the longer I ignored her, the more pissed off she got.

169

" 'Luciana Maria Fontana, you get home now!'

"I figured she wanted me to come practice my piano, or the dance steps she was making me memorize. She hated it when I played ball with Giulia. But I couldn't give it up. I loved soccer.

"I whispered to Giulia to help me hide. She grabbed my sweaty hand and we ran behind her house.

"We giggled like, well, like little girls." She grins. "We found a kick-ass hiding place, in the shrubs by her back shed. We burrowed side by side, a couple of toads trying to blend into the green space.

"Sure enough, ol' Carol appeared in her floral skirt and pink pumps, searching for me. Giulia covered my mouth with her dirty hand to keep me from bursting into hysterics. We sat huddled together, trying not to laugh, watching my mother wander the yard, calling, 'Luciana? Lu-cy?'

"All at once, the bushes parted like a scene in a horror flick. Even though we knew it was coming, we screamed bloody murder and clung to each other. The afternoon sun practically blinded me. But then I saw it. My mom's red-blotched mug staring down at us. And I'll never forget. It wasn't anger, exactly. It was more like panic. She grabbed my arm and yanked me to my feet.

"As she dragged me from the yard, I looked back at Giulia. She sat there in the bushes, still as a stick. 'I'm sorry,' she mouthed.

" 'Me, too,' I mouthed back, though I wasn't sure why."

Lucy lifts her glass and takes a long drink.

"That night after my dad got home, he and my mom sat me on the couch. I could tell it was something serious because Dad made Carmella leave the room.

" 'Go on, tell her,' my mom said, her voice flat.

"I remember thinking that someone must have died. Or that maybe my mom and dad were getting a divorce, like Francie Falcone's parents.

" 'You have a curse,' my dad told me, cutting through the bullshit.

"My mom freaked. 'Vinnie! Be kind.' She looked at me. 'Your dad is right,' she said. 'But don't worry, *amore.* You are going to break the curse.'

"My heart was seriously banging against my ribs. *What kind of curse?*

"My dad stood up then. He went to the hallway and took an old family picture from the wall, taken eons ago back in Italy. I'd seen the ratty-ass photo a thousand and two

171

times, but I'd never really looked at it. He plopped down beside me.

" 'You see these women, Luciana?' One by one, he pointed to his great-aunts and great-great-aunts, a dozen or so leather-faced ol' bags I'd never met.

" 'Yes, Daddy.'

" 'Not one of them has married. Ever.'

"Well, no shit. Who'd want to hook up with these hairy-chinned biddies?" Lucy looks over at me. " 'Course, I didn't say this, but that's exactly what I thought — more or less." She looks down at the table and gives a sad little smile.

"My mom took over then. She placed her hands in mine, all serious-like. 'In your *dad's* family,' she said, shooting him a look of superiority, 'the second-born daughter does not marry. The women in this photo, these Fontana women, are all second-born daughters.' She paused for a sec, probably hoping I'd pick up on the gist of her message. But I didn't. I swear, I didn't have a damn clue what she was getting at. Finally she said, 'Just like you.' "

Lucy pinches the stem of her wineglass and shakes her head.

"I sat staring at the picture, taking in the ol' nanny goats, with their lifeless faces and hollow eyes. 'They don't look very happy,' I said.

" 'Oh, they're not,' my mom agreed. 'They're miserable. And eventually they become bitter and mean. They'll never know the joy of children, or a house of their own with a warm kitchen to cook in, or a man to love them.'

"I seriously thought I was going to puke. This really was a fairy tale — a bad fairy tale where the cursed second daughter turns into a wicked old witch. I swallowed hard. 'Am — am I going to be like them?'

"My mom smiled and smoothed my hair. 'No, *mia dolce.* You are beautiful. You will break the curse, and spare all of the future second daughters from this horrible fate.'

"I nodded. O-kay. Right. Sure. I would be the princess who saved the village. But c'mon, Carol, let's be real. How the hell could an eight-year-old kid possibly break the curse?

" 'How?' I croaked.

" 'Listen to your mamma. I will teach you. First rule. No balls.' "

Chapter 18

Emilia

"Another," Lucy calls to the waiter, pointing to our nearly empty carafe. Her hand trembles when she pours the last drops into her glass. I don't know what to say. My poor cousin has tried nearly her entire life to become someone she's not, so she doesn't turn into a wicked old witch — no, worse: a wicked old *single* witch.

Poppy's words return to me. *It's fascinating, isn't it, how, when someone tells us something about ourselves — good or bad — we try so desperately to prove them right.*

"I'm so sorry that happened to you." I take hold of her hand. "But Poppy's right. This Fontana curse is nothing more than a self-fulfilling prophecy, an old-world myth that's been perpetuated for years, devaluing us single women, making us feel subordinate. And you're just living up to your expectations."

Lucy scowls and pulls her hand from mine. "I haven't a fucking clue what you just said. All I know is that for generations, second daughters have been screwed."

"Or have *not* been screwed, as the case may be."

She grins. "Well, what do you know? The girl made a funny."

The waiter arrives with our second liter. Lucy goes to fill my glass, and I cover the rim with my hand. She shoots me a look.

"C'mon, Em. Can you, like, try to be cool for one afternoon?"

Like a wimpy teen caving to peer pressure, I remove my hand, allowing her to fill my glass.

"I'm sorry I got your hopes up, Luce. It's obvious Poppy only wants to talk about Rico."

"Right?" Lucy says. "It's like we're her captive audience. We're only here so she can relive the one and only love the old coot's ever had — and now we learn he was a player."

"It's so sad. He could be dead for all we know."

"Sad? It's pathetic. And manipulative." Lucy leans in. "She bribed us, Em. She lied to us. And we fell for it. How friggin' stupid were we? This trip is a total waste."

"Not necessarily." I run a finger over the rim of my glass. "Uncle Dolphie thought maybe we could help reunite Poppy and Nonna."

Lucy chokes. "Oh, please! Like that's going to happen. Coming here was a huge mistake."

"She promised to tell me about my mom."

"Well, that's not happening, either. Sorry, Em, but think about it. Poppy left Bensonhurst in the sixties. Your mom was just a baby. Sure, she visited on holidays, but that's, what — maybe sixty days with your mom, total? She doesn't know shit."

I rub my temples. I risked my family, my job, my life for this trip. My aunt lied. We've been set up.

I can't say I wasn't warned. Nonna's probably back home right now, ranting to Daria about how I betrayed her. My stomach churns. For the first time, I understand why Nonna has nothing to do with her sister.

"She sounded so sincere."

Lucy shakes her head. "They always do."

Forty minutes later, Lucy drains the last drop from the carafe and I collect the bill.

"So much for the all-expenses-paid trip." Lucy's words slur, like a record playing at the wrong speed.

I fish into my purse for my wallet. "It's

fine. I've got it."

"Stuck with the bill and stuck here for eight days." She stares at me with glassy eyes, and then her face changes shape. "Unless we leave."

"Yeah, right."

"Seriously. She knows her way around Italy. She doesn't need us. She's using us. I say we head back to the hotel and pack our bags."

"That's ridiculous. We've come all this way. We're in Italy."

"Yup." She rises, and her body sways. "And now we can say we've been here." She staggers toward the door. I grab my purse and follow.

"You're drunk, Luce. The trip will get better. We haven't even seen anything."

Lucy steps into the street and gazes in both directions. "Old buildings. Italian restaurants. Italian bakeries. Looks pretty much like Bensonhurst."

Nonna was right. This was a mistake. But leaving isn't an option. I know this. Still, I can almost understand Lucy's drunken stance. The floating city that delighted me this morning has lost its magic.

Lucy marches down the street and I struggle to keep pace with her. Twenty minutes later, we've miraculously found our way back to Ca' Sagredo Hotel. The filmy white curtains billow when we let ourselves into the room.

"I thought she wanted a nap," Lucy says, pointing to the balcony. Poppy stands with her hands on the balustrade, staring out at the canal, unaware that we're watching her. She's changed into a loose caftan, and her silver-threaded hair blows in the breeze.

Lucy charges into the room and grabs her suitcase. She throws open drawers and begins stuffing clothes into her bag. But I stand transfixed by the slip of a figure on the balcony, the tiny woman in the floral dress standing against a blue-gray sky.

"Get packing," Lucy whispers. "We'll call her from the airport. Or at least, you will. Someone poached my phone."

"I'm not leaving," I say. "She's lonely. Look at her, Luce."

Lucy rises. Together, we secretly watch our aunt as she savors the view of Venice. She turns in profile and smooths her salt-and-pepper hair. Then, without warning, she lifts the entire mop from her head like a lid from a pot.

I gasp and Lucy yelps. Poppy whirls around.

She stands facing us, wide-eyed and bald as a baby.

Chapter 19

Emilia

My feet seem to move of their own volition, ferrying me across the room, closer to this woman with the smooth oval head. How fragile she has become, without the cover of hair. As I draw closer, I notice a six-inch incision on the side of her head. She puts a hand to it.

"My battle scar," she says, her smile wavering. "Surgery helped, along with chemo and radiation. I was feeling quite chipper for a while. But those wily cells decided to check back in to the Poppy Hotel. I'd been warned they might. Seems I make it far too comfortable for them in my soft little head."

My heart races, and I pray she'll rebut my next question. "You . . . you're dying?"

"Aren't we all?" She offers a smile, as if I were the one who needed comfort.

"Yes, but, you . . . I . . ." I'm stammering

now, and my aunt reaches for my hand.

"I much prefer to say I'm living, don't you?"

I pull her into my arms and squeeze my eyes shut, suddenly aware of how much I love this crazy, frustrating little lady.

"You should have told us," Lucy says. She's sober now, and all fury seems to have vanished. "We get it now, why we're here. Your doctor wouldn't let you travel alone."

She rears back. "What? You think a doctor's order would stop me?"

My eyes sting and I give a wobbly smile. "Of course not," Lucy and I say at the same time.

Sure, she conned us, but still, I can't help but admire my feisty aunt. She wanted one final trip with her family, and settled for two nieces she barely knows.

She gives us a brief account of her illness. "Ependymoma — a tumor in the brain, in that little passageway where cerebrospinal fluid is stored. Mine is slow growing, but it's catching up to me now, the little stinker." She smiles, as if her deadly tumor were nothing more than a pesky bug.

I blink back tears. "What can we do for you?"

"Yeah," Lucy says. "Whatever you need. Say the word."

She gathers us to her sides. "This" — she kisses each of our foreheads — "is all I want. To be with my girls when I finally see my love."

I steal a glance at Lucy.

"Now go," Poppy says, flapping her hands to shoo us away. "I still need to catch a wink of sleep. I'll be fresh as a flamingo by evening, just you wait."

Lucy and I wander aimlessly alongside a narrow stretch of the canal, both lost in thought. We visit little shops, stop for a cup of gelato, step into cool cathedrals. But nothing feels right. Our aunt is dying.

"We have to make this trip special for her," Lucy says as we meander down Rio della Sensa.

"I know." A speedboat chugs as it makes its way past us. "Rico's not going to be in Ravello. You know that, right?"

"Yup." She gazes out at the canal as she walks. "I think the crazy old fool actually expected to marry the guy."

"No. She's not that unrealistic."

"I'm serious. Why else would she insist on meeting him at the cathedral?"

I stop and turn to her. "Oh, God. You might be right. What if she's thinking he'll show up after all this time, fall in love, and marry her?"

"And break the curse and fulfill her promise, all in one swell floop."

She means "fell swoop," but I don't correct her. "Oh, Lucy," I say, and rub my forehead. "I am so sorry. I should have pinned her down with details before I dragged you into this. I knew it was a long shot, but I was hoping she might actually have some way of helping you with this supposed curse."

She looks away. "It was stupid to believe. I should know that by now."

I think of little Lucy, being told she must give up her soccer ball. "You don't deserve this," I say.

"Neither do you."

We walk in silence. Couples pass, holding hands. A woman in sneakers talks on her phone, her child in a front-pack. Two rosy-cheeked kids shriek as they race past on scooters. Lucy gazes longingly, as if she wishes she could be riding alongside them.

"Luce," I say. "How come you listened to your mother?"

For the longest time, she doesn't answer. Finally, she shrugs. "Same reason you listen to Nonna, I guess. We ignore what our heart tells us when we think it could make someone love us."

I don't reply. Lucy wouldn't want my sympathy. I think of bossy Aunt Carol and of Nonna, and how I bow to her every need, squelching my own desires to please her, just as Matt said. Is it possible Lucy's right? Have she and I both sold our souls, hoping against hope that we might one day win the affection of someone whose love we can never fully trust?

It's six thirty when we return to the hotel, and the sun has edged west, gilding the city in liquid gold. True to her word, Aunt Poppy is raring to go after her afternoon siesta. She's freshly showered, dressed in a silky orange dress with purple pumps and a half dozen colorful strands of beads around her neck. She blots her coral lips with a piece of tissue and adjusts her wig. "Losing my hair was the worst part of this whole ordeal," she says, peering into the mirror. "Rico loved my hair."

Lucy shoots me a look as she rounds the corner to the bathroom, her arms loaded with shampoo bottles and cosmetics.

"You're welcome to use my bathroom, Emilia," Poppy says. "You'll want to get all dolled up for our first evening in Venice."

"Dolled up? Aunt Poppy, I'm exhausted."

She places a hand on mine. "Tired people

tire people," she says. "Now shoo! Go get ready. And put a bit of effort into it, won't you?"

Twenty minutes later, I emerge from Poppy's steamy bathroom, admittedly revived. My wet hair is pulled into a sleek ponytail, my glasses are smudge free, my scar is covered, and I'm good to go.

"Luce?" I call, catching sight of Aunt Poppy on the balcony as I return to our suite.

The bathroom door swings open, and a cloud of steam rises. "In here."

Lucy stands in front of a foggy bathroom mirror wearing the hotel robe, her head wrapped in a towel. A myriad of Avon cosmetics stretches along the vanity. I groan.

"You're not ready."

She gives me a once-over. "Unless you're waiting tables at the Olive Garden, neither are you."

I look down at my black slacks and red blouse and laugh. "What can I say? I'm a laid-back kind of girl."

"Just so you know," Lucy says, "laid-back girls rarely get laid back." She grabs a pot of lip gloss and hands it to me. "Do yourself a favor."

I step back, my finger moving instinctively to my scar. "No, thanks."

Lucy shakes her head. I turn when Poppy appears at my side, a bright floral scarf in her hand.

"May I?"

I hesitate for a split second before I bend down. My aunt's citrus perfume fills my nostrils as she wraps the soft fabric around my neck and knots it. I close my eyes, imagining it's my mother helping me get ready. She stands back with her head cocked, assessing me. "Better," she says, and she gives the scarf one last fluff.

"Not bad, Pops," Lucy says. She turns to me. "You know you've hit a low point, Em, when your fashion guru is eighty years old."

With Poppy in her orange dress, me with my bright scarf, and Lucy in a slinky silver bandage dress, we set out for dinner. Shadows fall and streetlights glow. I lock arms with Poppy as we get into the elevator. When she steps out, Lucy clasps her hand and walks her through the lobby. Together, we help her navigate the cobblestone calle. A block from the hotel, she throws her hands up. "Would you please stop treating me like a dying old woman? If I wanted pampering, I'd have gone to a spa."

Without waiting for an answer, she pivots and trots down the lane and over a bridge.

Lucy and I work to keep up with her. We turn down a wide calle. A woman waves to us as she leans out her window to gather her laundry. We pass houses, lit from within. The aroma of roasted herbs wafts into the street, and I imagine a family sitting down for their *cena*. I capture the sights and smells in my memory, hoping one day I can re-create the scene in a novel.

Poppy turns down a narrow alley, stopping just long enough to pluck a coin from the cobblestone walk and drop it into a ziplock bag. It's cooler here, and nearly dark. I suspect we're lost, but then she lets out a whoop. The sign appears for a restaurant called Carlucci, a tiny place tucked at the end of Calle Pezzana. She throws open the door and strides in as if she's the guest of honor.

A dozen candlelit tables fill the dusky room. My stomach growls from the aroma of fresh bread and garlic. From behind the bar, a short elderly gentleman with a winding mustache looks up. He catches sight of Poppy and his face erupts. He claps his hands and rushes to her.

"Paolina! Benvenuta, amore mio!" He captures Poppy into a bear hug and lifts her off her feet. She laughs like a schoolgirl as he spins her in circles.

"Luigi!" she says. She steps back, her gaze traveling from his unnaturally black hair to his wingtip shoes. "Arrest this man!" she cries. "He is stealing my breath."

Luigi blushes. "I have missed you, my flower." He holds her at arm's length. "You never age. What is your secret?"

"White teeth and dark hair." She leans in and cups her hand around her mouth. "Most people our age have the opposite." Luigi throws his head back and laughs. They stand gazing at each other until finally, Luigi remembers his role.

"Your favorite table awaits."

He leads us to a spot by the window, settling us into our chairs and fanning napkins onto our laps. Poppy introduces Lucy first. He bows and shakes her hand. *"Benvenuta.* Welcome."

"And this is Emilia."

I smile. "Hello, Luigi."

He looks into my eyes. *"Bellissima."* He takes my hand and kisses it. *"Come tua nonna."*

Beautiful. Like your grandmother. I smile at the compliment, and don't bother correcting him.

For two hours, Luigi showers us with attention. Each course is accompanied by a special wine, selected by Luigi himself. I'm

187

stuffed and a wee bit drunk when he brings a dessert of zabaglione — a light custard made with egg and sweet wine, served with fresh raspberries. It's more tart than mine, and better. Next time I make it, I'll use less sugar.

Luigi arrives with a tray of liqueurs and a trio of tiny glasses. "Fernet? Frangelico? Limoncello?"

I'm not the least bit thirsty, but according to Lucy, that's beside the point.

Lucy lifts her dainty glass of Frangelico and settles back in her chair. "Are you scared to die, Aunt Poppy?"

I choke on my Fernet. "Lucy!"

"I am, a bit," Poppy says, seemingly unfazed. "Yet I can't wait to solve the mystery of what lies beyond."

It feels odd having this conversation with my dying aunt, who, admittedly, seems quite comfortable with the subject. "Do you believe in God?" I ask softly.

"Oh, heavens yes! Though not in the conventional way I was taught. To me, spirituality is less about Sunday mass than it is about love. It's that simple. When you treat others with love, consistently and fully, you honor your god or goddess. Some of the holiest people I know have never stepped foot in a church. And I've met many church-going, self-righteous born-again Christians that God himself probably wishes had never been born the first time."

Lucy bursts out laughing. "Amen to that."

Poppy sips her Limoncello. "I'm most excited to see the film. Ah, what a joy that was to produce."

My aunt was a movie producer? "What film?" I ask.

"The one we're told will flash before us when we die. I must say, I get goose bumps when I think about it. You see, my film will be part drama, part mystery, a bit of a thriller, with romantic comedy scenes tossed in for good measure." Her dark eyes dance. "You, my dears, are still in the production stage of your movie. Make it riveting! Make every scene sizzle! When it comes time to watch the movie of your life, may tears run down your face, may you scream with laughter and cringe with embarrassment. But for Goddess's sake, do not let your life story be one that's so dull you fall asleep during the viewing."

Lucy grins. "I think she's talking to you, Em."

Poppy stares down at her glass. "But with every life, there's tragedy, too."

Luigi arrives at our table, interrupting

189

Poppy. "What else can I get you, *amore mio*?"

It sounds odd to hear Poppy's flirty friend call her his love. I imagine she reserves that endearing term for Rico. But Poppy hasn't seen her German love in decades. She's had other companions, like Thomas, and perhaps even this man.

She reaches into her purse and retrieves her bag of coins. "Nothing more, grazie. The meal was *fantastico*. And seeing you has made me so very happy."

"The pleasure is always mine." Luigi smiles, and his eyes never leave hers.

She takes his hand and presses a coin into his palm. "For luck."

"I will add it to my collection." He winks. "When will I see you again, Paolina?"

She rises from the chair and kisses his cheek. "Sooner than either of us can imagine," she says, a bittersweet gleam in her eyes.

But there will be no next time. She knows this. How agonizing and overwhelming and oddly fortunate it must feel, bidding a final farewell to those you love.

The velvet sky is peppered with stars, and we three walk back to the hotel. Poppy drapes an arm around each of us.

"Now, where did I leave off? Ah, yes, Rico

had just started playing his violin."

"No," Lucy says. "I'm sorry, Pops, but he was playing *you*. He had a fiancée, remember? Rehashing your tragic love story isn't going to make it easier. I know guys like him. He's going to be a no-show at the cathedral. You haven't talked to him in over fifty years. He's probably dead by now."

I gasp. "Lucy, please!"

Poppy stops. She takes Lucy's cheeks in her hands and stares into her eyes. "Tell me, Luciana, do you want me to break the curse or not?"

CHAPTER 20

POPPY

1960
Trespiano

Rico and I continued to meet in the square every Monday through Saturday. I refused to let the idea of a fiancée bother me. After all, I had a supposed fiancé, too, waiting for me in America. Rico loved me, I was certain. We would talk and walk and share a gelato or a pastry, hold hands, and sneak kisses. But I was growing frustrated. I wanted more of him.

It was a rainy Monday, the eighth day of February, a day I shall always remember. I hurried from the museum when my shift ended. Rico was waiting in the square, as always. He stood beneath an umbrella, a stem of orange freesia in his hand.

"I could not find papaveri this time of year." He kissed my cheek. "Would you like a coffee?"

My hands trembled when I took the freesia from him. I looked into his eyes, mustering all my courage. "I would rather go to your flat," I said, swallowing hard. "If you will have me."

I'd never felt more vulnerable. My heart thundered so fiercely I was certain he could see it pulsing beneath my blouse. After what seemed like ages, he cupped my cheek and smiled down at me. "Is this really what you want, *amore mio*?"

I nodded, unable to speak. He tapped my forehead with a kiss and led me down the street.

He rented a small room above a tailor's shop, four plaster walls that held a wooden bureau and a single bed, everything in the world we needed. The room was tidy and warm, a palace to me.

He kissed my neck, my lips, my cheeks as he slowly unbuttoned my blouse. I stood before him naked, the soft gray light seeping through the window. His eyes shone with tenderness. "Exquisite," he whispered. It was the first time I ever felt completely safe.

The rain tapped against the windowpane, and he laid me on the bed. Soon, the rhythm of the rain matched our bodies, followed by a crash of thunder that shook me to the core. Moments later, I lay in his arms, both of us moved to tears.

Neither of us spoke. There are no words when one has witnessed magic.

Il mio unico amore, he called me from that day on. I never asked about Karin, his fiancée. He called me his only love. That was all the assurance I needed.

For two months we shared a secret bliss, a life of two, unencumbered by friends or families, or even a future. Nobody knew of our afternoon trysts, where we'd walk and talk and make sweet love. It was a time suspended between past and future. We had no claim on tomorrow, so we cherished today, drinking in every bit of joy and laughter from each moment together, oblivious to the threat that loomed just beyond the horizon.

It was an extraordinary, ordinary Monday in April, and Rico and I were strolling through the piazza hand in hand. The papaveri were in bloom, and Rico stopped to buy me a bouquet. We continued on, pausing in front of the Palazzo Vecchio, where Rico told me about the first time he held his rail pass in his hands, allowing him to travel to Western Europe. "I will never forget the feeling," he said, his eyes bright. "Standing in another man's country, feeling so light, so completely untethered. It was overwhelming, this feeling of freedom, after what my people had been through."

I was dabbing tears from my cheek when, from out of nowhere, Rosa appeared.

"Paolina?" Her eyes shifted from me to Rico and back again. "What are you doing?"

I couldn't speak. My sister had caught me. For weeks I'd been tempted to tell her of Rico, how I'd fallen hopelessly in love, but I wasn't ready to divulge my secret. Not even to my most trusted confidant.

"Rosa," I said. "Meet my friend, Rico — Erich. More than a friend, actually." I giggled nervously and stuffed my hands into my pockets. "I love him, Rosa."

Rosa offered him a hand. "Pleasure to meet you, Rico. It must be difficult, knowing Paolina is engaged to marry a man in America, a handsome shop owner."

I gasped. Rico turned to me, his eyes shrouded in bewilderment and pain.

"No," I said. "I — I have changed my mind."

"We will be gone within a year," Rosa continued, as if I hadn't spoken. "You know this, sì?"

My heart shattered. I closed my eyes, unable to look at either of them. Then I felt his hand in mine.

"I am sorry, Rosa," he said calmly but firmly, "but that will not happen. You see, your sister and I are in love."

Rosa looked him up and down, taking in the patched sleeve on his pressed cotton shirt, the worn toes of his polished boots. "You are a good man, Rico, I am certain. And my sister is very fond of you, that is obvious. But you do not understand. You are jeopardizing Paolina's entire future. You see, my sister is the second daughter, and doomed to be alone forever. Ignacio is her only hope of breaking the curse. Please," she said, clutching her hands as she gazed up at him. "I am begging you, do not ruin her one chance."

My sister, my biggest protector, thought she was doing me a favor. Though she was crazy for Alberto, I don't believe she had ever experienced true passion. How could I expect her to understand our love?

"She will have a good life in America," Rosa continued, as if my fate were already decided. "What can you give her? Tell me. Do you have a plan? A business? A skill?"

"He can play the violin," I said.

The sympathy seemed to drain from my sister's eyes. "He plays the fiddle?" She turned to Rico, a mocking smile on her lips. "Can you tap-dance, too?"

Her desperation had unleashed a cruelty I had never seen in her. "Rosa, stop. Rico is smart and strong and talented. And I love him with my entire heart. I cannot go to America."

She stared at me for the longest time, until finally, her shoulders slumped in defeat. She shook her head. *"La mia sorella testarda.* How can I go without you?"

My heart burst with love. "You will be fine. I will visit, Rosa. Rico and I, we will come see you in America."

She studied Rico and bit her lip. "Rico, if you make my sister happy, you have my blessing."

Rico hugged her. *"Danke schön* — er, *grazie mille."* They shared a laugh. "I hope all of Pop — er, *Paolina's* family will be as welcoming as you, Rosa."

"Of course they will be," I said, without thinking. "You must come to our house in Trespiano. It is time you met my parents and brothers."

Rosa took a step back. "So soon, Paolina?" She was signaling me with her eyes, trying not to be rude to Rico.

I turned to Rico, ignoring her covert warning. "Please. Come to our house for dinner on Sunday. My family will adore you."

But I saw the fear in Rosa's eyes. My parents would never accept Rico, a penniless foreigner who threatened to upend their daughter's future in America. And Rosa knew it.

CHAPTER 21

EMILIA

Day Two
Venice

We're in full tourist mode Tuesday. We visit the market in Campo San Giacometto, an ancient square hosting the oldest church in Venice. Poppy gushes at a display of perfectly proportioned sfogliatelle — flaky pastries shaped like lobsters — and buys one for each of us. I tear the edge from the crust and nod toward the church's tower. "Check out that old clock," I say.

"Don't set your watch to it," Poppy says, dabbing her lips with her napkin. She turns to Lucy. "Like many things in life, it's attractive and flashy, but notoriously unreliable."

Lucy lobs her napkin into a trash bin, seemingly unaware of our aunt's not-so-subtle advice.

199

"I take it you and Rico broke up," I say gently, wrapping my scarf around my shoulders as we stroll. Since sharing her story last night, Poppy hasn't mentioned Rico. I don't want to push, but I'm dying to hear what happened next.

She looks at me quizzically.

"You know," I say, "when you realized he'd never be accepted by your family."

Poppy stops at a bridge and leans against its iron rail. Below, a gondolier steers his boat, seemingly oblivious to the young lovers snuggled on the bench behind him. "Rico and I never broke up. We're still together, in our hearts."

Lucy looks at me and rolls her eyes. "Mm-hmm. Of course you are. Now, about the curse." She slings an arm around our aunt. "When do we get to that part?"

"Perhaps in the next chapter."

We continue on to the Galleria dell'Accademia, then to Teatro La Fenice. "In the history of Italian theater, this is the most famous landmark," Poppy tells us.

"Bo-ring," Lucy says, playing some sort of game on my phone.

Poppy tsks. "Bored people bore people."

It's late afternoon, and we're sitting outside Caffè Florian, the world's oldest coffeehouse, enjoying *aperitivo* — the Italian version of happy hour on steroids. Pigeons fly overhead and I'm dreaming up stories set in this bustling old piazza. We sip our Aperol spritzes — Aperol, Prosecco, and a splash of soda, garnished with an orange wedge. A chubby man with an accordion winds his way through the tables playing the "Tarantella Napoletana." Poppy taps her foot to the music.

"La vita bella," she says and lifts her drink. "The beautiful life."

I raise my glass. "Best part of the day." I break off a piece of taleggio cheese from a plate heaped with Italian olives, pancetta-wrapped figs, and mini sandwiches filled with sun-dried tomatoes and marinated goat cheese.

"This café is where Casanova is rumored to have stopped for coffee when he escaped from prison," Poppy tells us.

"How cool," I say, taking in the array of arched stone windows adorned with white balloon curtains; the cream-colored awnings; the handsome waiters in their white jackets and black bow ties, balancing trays on their broad shoulders.

"Yes," Poppy says. "Caffè Florian was the only coffee shop in eighteenth-century Venezia that allowed women patrons. I suspect that influenced Casanova's decision."

"Typical guy," Lucy says, "hoping to hit it and quit it."

A young Italian couple sit at the table beside us, so close that it's impossible not to hear their entire conversation. The man — a good-looking thirty-something wearing too much cologne — talks nonstop about his job, the money he's raking in, the Mercedes he plans to buy. His date finally excuses herself to the ladies' room.

Poppy waits until the woman is out of earshot, then turns to the man. "Your first date?" she asks in her native language.

He nods. "That obvious?"

"Does she prefer a sunrise or sunset?" He scowls, but she continues. "If given the option, would she choose an extra month's vacation or an extra month's salary? What is her earliest memory of joy? If she could possess only one book, what would it be?"

He gives a mocking laugh. "Easy, lady. I told you, it's a first date."

"And if you'd like another," she says, "I'd suggest more this" — she points to her ear — "and less this" — she mimics a moving mouth with her hand.

I look on, horrified and embarrassed and undeniably awed. The man's smile fades. He rises and stalks off.

Lucy cracks up. "Way to shut down that

pompous gasbag!" She lifts her hand and slaps Poppy a high five. "So how about doling out some of that wisdom for me — us. I know you're sick and everything, so I'm not making demands. But . . ."

Poppy tilts her head. "But what, dear?"

Lucy takes a deep breath, and I can tell she's trying to keep her temper in check. "You promised you'd break the curse. Was that complete bullshit?"

Poppy leans in and pats Lucy's cheek. "We second daughters have nothing to fear. I promise you."

Lucy's nostrils flare. Poppy may have good intentions, but her statement is as helpful as telling a man in a wheelchair that his legs are perfectly fine. I grab Lucy's hand.

"Poppy's trying to tell you that you don't have to worry about the curse. It was unfair of Aunt Carol to put so much pressure on you."

She frowns. "Was it? Because you know what? My mom taught me to believe that I can break this damn curse. And I will."

"Forget what your mom says," I say, keeping my voice low. "It doesn't matter. If you never break the curse, if you're single forever, you'll be just fine, Luce, I promise. No, you'll be better than fine. You'll be great."

She plucks the orange garnish from her Aperol spritz and sucks it. "I'm going to be married one day."

"Okay. Sure. Maybe you will be. But, Luce, you're giving marriage way too much power. It's one part of a person's life — or not. You can still have a full and happy life without a ring on your finger, believe me."

"Believe *you*? If you want to know the truth, you're my incentive, Em. You inspire me."

I smile and push up my glasses. "I do?"

"Yup. You're the person I think of each time I put myself out there." She tosses the orange peel onto her napkin. "Because I refuse to end up with a sorry-ass life like yours."

The breath is knocked from me. I turn to Poppy for help, but she pins me with her gaze, waiting for my reply.

"What do you mean?" I ask.

"Your life sucks, Em."

I try to laugh, but it strikes the wrong note. "My life is great. I have a cute apartment, a sweet cat, no debts." I absently rub my scar. "I get to cook whatever I want, whenever I want, or not at all. At night, the TV's all mine." I'm on a roll now, and the talking points come effortlessly. "I can binge on Netflix for ten hours straight, in my pajamas. I come and go as I please. I don't have to worry about impressing anyone."

"And you've never had your heart broken, have you?"

For the briefest moment, Liam's sweet face appears, swollen beyond recognition. I block it out, as I've done for the past decade, and square my shoulders. "No."

"You've never been disappointed by some dickwad who promised to call but never did."

"See, there you go! No dickwad disappointment for me."

Poppy chimes in. "You've never watched the world turn to Technicolor when you've spotted your love in the crowd."

I laugh. "Aunt Poppy, that's a little dramatic, even for you."

She leans in. "You've never felt like you were going to die if you didn't get to hold him one more time."

"No. Of course not." My eyes shift from Poppy to Lucy. *Lovely.* I'm being tagteamed. "Okay, I get your point. Yes, I may have missed some moments. But those are fleeting. You know, studies show sixty percent of marriages are unhappy."

"So . . . what?" Lucy says. "You quit the game because you have only a four-in-ten chance of winning?"

"I didn't quit. I chose not to play. Honestly, curse or no curse, I want no part of the dating world."

"You're completely checked out." She turns to Poppy and talks as if I'm not here. "There's this guy, Matt, who's been in love with her since as long as I can remember."

"That's not true."

"He's actually kind of cute, if you're not a teeth person. But Em just shuts him down."

"Matt's my best friend. I feel nothing, *nothing* for him except friendship." Guilt rushes me. It feels treasonous, expressing this out loud. "Forget about me, Luce. Look at Aunt Poppy. She's a successful, happy woman with a full life, who travels the world. And she's never married."

"And then there's you," Lucy says. "A single female whose entire life could fit into a thimble. A woman whose obituary will read: A lonely girl who spent her life trying to please her nonna. A woman who lived up to everyone's expectations."

I throw up my hands. "Whatever, Luce. I'm happy. I'm safe." I bite my lip until I can no longer contain my silence. "Unlike you. I mean, my god, you may as well have a tattoo across your chest that reads *Next, please.*"

Lucy leans in, the vein in her forehead

bulging. "I'd rather go down fighting than forfeit the game, like you have."

"But I haven't . . ."

"That's right, Em. You haven't. You haven't done a damn thing to break this curse. Do you realize the pressure you've put on me? You've given up, and now it's all on me."

"I never asked you to break the curse, Lucy."

"Of course not!" Lucy explodes. "The truth is, you like the curse. Admit it. It gives you a perfect excuse to be a frumpy old lady, with those butt-ugly bendable glasses and that lame-ass ponytail. It's your pass from ever having to put yourself out there. So just spare me the bullshit."

"Ah," Poppy says, nodding her head. "You resent Emilia for being cowardly."

I hitch up my admittedly dated but perfectly functional glasses. "Cowardly?"

"Yeah," Lucy says. "That's right, Poppy. Em is a coward. And never once did she stop to think of me."

"Since when is it my responsibility to solve your problem?"

"Have you even once thought about Mimi? Or all the other future Fontana second daughters coming down the pike?"

I lift my shoulders. "Mimi will be just fine."

"Well, I'm not!" Lucy's face is red, and for the first time, I see pain along with the anger. "I'm on my own out here. And I'm drowning. It's like you're on this private island, comfortable and dry and boring as hell, watching as I flail and gasp and slip beneath the current."

My cousin, who never cries, bats tears from her eyes. My throat tightens. Though I claim to deny the curse, might I have fallen prey to it, too? I actually like being single, and I'm perfectly content if that's my status forever. But Lucy's not. She's overwrought with pressures and expectations and unfulfilled dreams. All her life she's been made to believe that without a man, she's worthless, incomplete.

In twenty-nine years, I've done nothing to try to break the curse. Until today, it never occurred to me that maybe I should.

On the way back to the hotel, we stop to look at necklaces behind a glass display. Lucy can't decide between the gold chain or the silver, and eventually marches away with neither. She refuses to look at me. Her words — and Aunt Poppy's, too — tag along like someone's unwanted kid sister.

Maybe I'm still jet-lagged, or homesick, or in mourning over Poppy's illness, because despite being in this magical place called Venice, nothing feels right. Instead, the accusation echoes in my head. *Em is a coward.*

That night, after I've picked at my baccalà mantecato — a creamy mousse made of dried cod, served with polenta — we return to the hotel. It's eleven o'clock and I'm ready to climb into bed and write a couple of pages. But Lucy, who drank nearly the entire carafe of wine with dinner, has come to life.

"Let's go out," she says, finally looking at me when she speaks. She throws up her arms and does a little dance.

I bust my own move by pulling my nightshirt over my head. "Seriously? Don't you sleep?"

"C'mon. Just one drink. We'll go downstairs to the hotel bar."

"Maybe tomorrow," I say, praying she'll forget the promise twenty-four hours from now.

Lucy opens her mouth, as if she's about to say something. But she doesn't.

I'm in the bathroom when I hear the hotel door open, then close. I step into the room, lathering my face.

Lucy has disappeared.

■ ■ ■ ■

It's two a.m. and I'm sitting on our balcony overlooking the Grand Canal. The water glistens in the moonlight, softly lapping against the docks. I gaze up at the blue-black sky dusted with stars. Here I am, in Italy, four thousand miles from home, against my family's wishes. How could I possibly be cowardly?

I turn when the French door opens. Poppy steps out, wearing a polka-dot robe and pink kitten-heel slippers embroidered with gold fleur-de-lis. Who knew they made slippers with heels?

"I had a hunch I'd find you awake," she says. "You've been upset all evening."

"Yeah, well, I'm not used to being called cowardly."

She braces her hands on the balcony and gazes out at the canal. "Luciana is threatening your beliefs. It's not comfortable for you. She's making you question whether perhaps, all these years, you've hidden behind the curse."

I absently rub my scar. "Yeah, well, I guess there's a bit of truth in that. For both of us. I mean, neither you nor I have tried to break the curse."

Poppy turns to face me. "Dear, you and I are nothing alike in that respect. You see, I've embraced my sexuality. There was Rico, of course, and later Thomas. I celebrate my femininity. I wouldn't dream of suppressing it. But Emilia, my child, I fear you have."

I stare at her. "Because I don't date? Because I'm not hell-bent on getting married?"

She flicks her wrist. "I don't give a whit whether you marry. That's entirely your choice. What I care about is you, being whole and authentic and fully feeling. And right now, you're behaving like a lily-livered lion."

"I'm just being myself."

"That sounds like a cop-out. Why not strive to be better than yourself?" Before I can reply, she continues. "You neutralize yourself, Emilia. You dress and act in a way that's deliberately unattractive. It's as if you've stuffed your femininity into a cardigan sweater and buttoned it up to your chin. You are undeniably female, my girl, yet you refuse to own it. I suspect your sweet Matt would vouch for that."

I cross my arms. "So I'm not a flirt. I'm not stylish. I don't look glamorous. This is me. It's who I am."

She studies me with her head cocked.

"Yes. This is who you've become. But Emilia, my dear, you don't have to die as that woman."

The bedside clock flips to 3:27. Where is Lucy? The hotel lounge closed at two. Is she okay? Why didn't I join her?

I stare up at the ceiling, remembering Liam and what happens when second-born daughters dare to love. But still, the little voice screams, *You're a coward!*

If only I could talk to Matt. He'd assure me that Lucy's off base, that I'm perfectly fine, exactly how I am.

Or would he? Matt clearly wants more from me than friendship. Have I been a coward, keeping him at arm's length? Could I have been the one in my family to break the curse and spare Lucy and Mimi? I love MC. Does it matter that I'm not "in love" with him?

I roll onto my side. Rather than easing my mind, Poppy only added to its clutter. What's so wrong with who I am? I don't want to be like Lucy — a woman who relies solely on her sexuality.

But Emilia, my dear, you don't have to die as that woman.

Have I been hiding? Have I allowed the curse to brand me, to define who I am? Has

212

the Fontana myth become my scapegoat?

Our hotel door jiggles. I grab my glasses to check the time: 4:07. The door opens and Lucy slips inside. Thank God! I click on the bedside lamp and she startles.

"Jesus! Way to give me a heart attack."

Her hair is mussed and her clothes are rumpled. I've got a gazillion questions . . . and I don't want the answers to any.

"Sorry," I say. "I was getting worried about you."

"I'm a big girl." She tosses her clutch onto a chair and kicks off her heels.

"Right. Sorry."

She drops onto the side of the bed and rubs her feet. She looks tired and lonely and defeated. I swallow hard and take a deep breath.

"I don't want to be a coward, Lucy."

She looks at me. She's waiting for me to elaborate, to give her something more than an empty statement. Something that might actually help her.

"And I'm willing to change."

CHAPTER 22

EMILIA

Day Three
Venice

It's eight thirty Wednesday morning, our final day in Venice before we head to Tuscany. Which means it's our final night, too. In the wee hours of the morning, I promised to change. But can I? Will I?

The elegant hotel courtyard is set with cloth-covered tables topped with vases of sunflowers. Poppy and I sit alone eating a *colazione* of fruit, homemade yogurt, and exquisite pastries. I catch a glimpse of azure sky as I stir cream into my coffee.

"Looks like a great day for walking."

Poppy fans her napkin onto her lap. "I suggest we take a vaporetto today."

I turn to her, taking in the slight tinge of gray in her skin, the sharp cheekbones jutting from her thin face. Because she's so

214

agreeable, it's easy to forget that Paolina Fontana is ill.

"Good idea," I say. "My feet could use a break."

Across the courtyard, a bedraggled Lucy plods past the buffet station. I wave and she works her way to our table.

"Is there a reason we start our days at the butt-crack of dawn?" she asks.

Poppy claps her hands. "We're going to the Doge's Palace today, one of the most famous landmarks in Venice. It has caught fire more than once, requiring restoration, but parts of the structure date back to the Middle Ages."

"And I'm pretty sure it'd still be there this afternoon, if we'd chosen to wake at a humane hour."

Poppy's eyes crinkle with amusement. "How was your night?"

Lucy scans the small courtyard, as if she's looking for someone. "It was okay."

My heart wrenches. Where was she last night? What must it be like, to be on a relentless search for love?

Poppy spreads apricot preserves on her croissant. "Some people have a certain relish for heartbreak. I hope you're not one of them, Luciana."

Lucy cuts her a look that could boil an

215

egg. "Trust me, I'm not."

"I'm glad to hear it. Because that type of person chooses a partner the way they'd choose a designer purse. It looks good on the arm and garners much admiration. But quickly, they realize they've paid too dear a price. They have a fancy purse, when what they really wanted was a backpack." She sets down her knife and smiles. "Just my two cents' worth."

Lucy looks just as puzzled as I am. What is Poppy trying to say?

I could refer to Piazza San Marco, Venice's most popular gathering place, as Saint Mark's Square, like most Americans do. Or *La Piazza,* like the Venetians. But the writer in me prefers Napoléon's romantic description: the drawing room of Europe.

I step onto a field of gray rectangular stones inlaid with white parallel geometric designs, reminiscent of a dazzling oriental carpet. Facing the entire length of the piazza sits the famous Basilica di San Marco, or Saint Mark's Basilica, all arches and marble and Romanesque carvings. It seems impossible not to feel small and young and insignificant in its domineering shadow.

"The four horses," Poppy says, pointing to a magnificent quartet of bronze beasts.

"A symbol of Venice's pride and power, brought to Venice by the Crusaders in 1204. Napoléon looted the piazza in 1797 and had the sculptures shipped to Paris. They were returned eighteen years later. Sadly, air pollution was killing them. The original horses are now safely inside the basilica."

Lucy moans and rubs her temples. "Just my luck. First time in Europe and I'm traveling with an art history teacher."

We walk the Bridge of Sighs, which connects the palace's interrogation room with the prison. "Imagine yourself a prisoner hundreds of years ago," Poppy says, stepping to the side of the limestone bridge. "This may have been the last glimpse of the outside world you would ever see. Lord Byron gave this bridge its name, surmising that the prisoners would sigh as they viewed their beautiful Venice for the last time."

I stop in front of a small block window and gaze out at the piazza below. People of all nationalities bustle across the square, darting into shops and restaurants and museums. No doubt they're speaking languages from all over the world, each carrying secrets and scars, unspeakable tragedies and moments of bliss. I, Emilia Josephina Fontana Lucchesi Antonelli, am part of this crazy maze of humanity. Tears sting my eyes.

I think of the prisoners, being pried away from these very windows, never to see this mad whirlwind of a world again. At once I feel like the luckiest woman alive. I'm not a prisoner — or at least I don't have to be. I can roam freely, travel broadly, make mistakes, welcome adventures.

I startle when Lucy's hand grips my arm. "You gonna spend all day looking out the window?"

"Nope," I say, smiling as I continue across the bridge. "Most definitely not."

It's almost six o'clock when we head back to the hotel to get "gussied up," as Aunt Poppy calls it. We're two blocks from the hotel when Poppy suddenly stops. She backs up a few steps and peers into a store window, where a sign reads *Occhiali da Vista.* "Emilia," she calls to me.

Thirty minutes later, I'm standing in front of a mirror, a dozen pairs of eyeglasses splayed on the counter in front of me. Once more, Poppy returns to the tortoiseshell frames and plants them on my face. They're large and bold and chic — a completely different look from my small indestructible wire-frames.

"Perfect!" She turns to Lucy. "Don't you agree?"

"Uh, ye-ah. About a hundred times better

than those lame-ass glasses you've had since you were, like, six."

I rise, rubbing a finger along my scar. "This is ridiculous. If you're trying to make me beautiful, it's not going to happen."

Poppy scoffs. "Beauty is overrated. I'd choose interesting over beautiful any day." She turns to the stylish optician who looks like she should be on a fashion runway. "How soon can we have these glasses made?"

"You can pick them up in the morning," she says, her voice cool and aloof. "But without a prescription, we will need the original lenses."

"Done." Poppy hands her the new frames along with my old glasses.

"No," I say, reaching for them. "I can't be without my glasses. And besides, they're just fine."

"With all due respect," the gorgeous optician says, "they are hideous."

Lucy bursts out laughing. I lift my shoulders. "But I can see perfectly. Seriously. What difference does it make?"

Poppy pats my hand. "How about we find out?"

The sun fades and I stand beside Lucy at the bathroom vanity, tying back my hair while she applies her makeup. Everything is slightly blurry. Thankfully, she hasn't mentioned going out tonight. Still, my aunt's words echo in my mind. *Emilia, my dear, you don't have to die as that woman.*

I take a breath and work a bit of enthusiasm into my voice. "So where should we go tonight?"

Her eyes find mine in the mirror. "Seriously? You really want to go clubbing?"

My stomach tightens into a knot. "Uh, sure."

She crosses her arms and surveys me. I'm dressed in black slacks again, this time with a gray sweater. "Well, for sure you can't wear that." She sets down her compact and disappears. A moment later, she's back, clutching a black skirt that looks like it would fit my niece Mimi.

"Try this."

I stare at the tiny band of spandex. The last time I wore a short skirt was on New Year's Eve with Liam, eleven years ago. And that ended in disaster. But Lucy's face is so hopeful I can't bear to disappoint her. I slip off my slacks and pull the skirt over my hips. The stretchy fabric hugs my every curve so tightly I can barely breathe. "It's too small," I say, ready to yank it down.

"It's perfect," Lucy counters. She drags

me from the bathroom, over to her closet, and pulls a see-through blouse from its hanger. "Put this on."

"Lucy, I can't possibly —"

"Try it."

Luckily, I'm wearing my white sports bra, because even without glasses, I can see straight through this flimsy fabric. I cross my arms. "It's way too revealing."

She scoffs. "That sports bra defeats the whole purpose. Don't you have something lacy? No," she answers for me. "Dumb question." She shrugs. "I guess it'll have to do."

She pulls me into the bathroom and yanks the scrunchie from my ponytail. My hair erupts like Medusa's and I cover my head. "What are you doing?"

She grabs a bottle from the vanity and squeezes a dollop of goop onto her palms. "I've always loved messing with hair. My first client was Lindsey — Carmella's American Girl doll." She rubs the product into my hair. "Carmella went ape-shit crazy, but the faux-hawk actually looked cute on Lindsey."

Rather than taming the waves, like I've tried to do my entire life, Lucy scrunches my locks, forming loose curls.

"It won't last," I say. "It'll turn to frizz the

minute I step outside."

"Hold still." She grabs her compact. Before I can object, she's stroking a brush across my cheeks. My nose itches and I go to rub it with my shoulder. "Close your eyes." She shadows my lids with various powders, stopping long enough to pluck a few hairs.

"Ouch!"

"*Addio,* unibrow." Next, she sweeps an eyeliner pencil into a bold cat eye, followed by several coats of mascara on my lashes. "Voilà!"

She pivots me toward the mirror. I blink until the reflection comes into focus. I take in the sultry woman with the see-through blouse and smoky eyes and I gasp.

"I can't go out like this!"

"Why not? You look hot!"

Poppy appears at the open door and literally jumps when she sees me. "Emilia?" She starts to laugh. "You *are* trying to change!" She grabs a pot of Lucy's gloss and starts to dab my lips.

"No," I say, stepping back and lifting a finger to my scar. "Absolutely not."

"She hates her lips," Lucy explains.

Poppy studies me, curious. "This tiny scar wields such power over you. From what I gather, it is your only source of vanity. Now, would someone please tell me its history?"

We move to the balcony, where the last rays of sun turn the lagoon cotton-candy pink. Lucy combs her wet hair and begins to tell the story she's heard a dozen times.

"You were, what — ten when it happened?"

"Eleven."

"Her dad and Uncle Bruno were out fishing on Coney Island. She and Daria tagged along."

I nod. "We begged them to let us come. The amusement park was our favorite place. But by noon, Daria and I had used up our tickets for the rides. We walked back to the pier where my dad and Uncle Bruno fished."

Lucy interjects. "Of course they got bored and started goofing around."

I smile. "That's right. We were rifling through their tackle boxes, exploring the lures and bobbers, probably making a mess of things. To distract us, my dad offered to teach us how to cast the fishing pole."

"Daria had to go first, of course," Lucy says.

"Uh-huh. I stood behind her, waiting my turn, listening to my dad explain how to point the rod at the target." I touch my finger to my scar, the image coming back to me with striking sharpness. "Daria lifted her arm and swung the pole back. But not in the gentle way my father instructed. It was more of a jerky whip."

Lucy winces. "I hate this part of the story. The hook got caught in Em's bottom lip!"

Poppy gasps. "Oh, heavens! That must have hurt like a . . . motherducker." She winks at Lucy.

I laugh. "It did! Like a wasp bite — ten wasp bites. I grabbed for my mouth, and felt something strange. Looking down my nose, I could see the fish hook, hanging from my lip. I started to scream.

"My dad rushed over to me. I'll never forget his face, a mix of horror and sorrow and fear. 'No!' he kept saying, over and over. 'No!' "

"He was scared shitless," Lucy says. "That's when Uncle Bruno took over. He grabbed a set of pliers from his tackle box."

"Pliers?" Poppy asks, her eyes wide.

"Tiny fishing pliers," I say. "He ordered me to hold still. I tried not to whimper, but I'd never felt such pain. I squeezed my eyes and gripped Daria's hand. Uncle Bruno clamped the pliers on the hook. Hot white fire seared my lip. That's the last thing I remember before I passed out."

"Uncle Bruno drove like an effing maniac

all the way home," Lucy says. "When they got back, Em's bottom lip had swollen to the size of a peach. Nonna was furious. But it was too late. Uncle Bruno had made a mess of her lip." Lucy's voice is wistful now, and she stares at my bottom lip. "It's a lot better now, but the scar is still there, if you look closely."

In the Grand Canal below, waves lap the concrete dock, methodical and rhythmic. The part of the story I've never told comes to me, as clearly as the twinkling lights across the Laguna Veneta.

"My dad's balled-up T-shirt was pressed to my lip," I say. "It stank of fish and sweat and salt water. He lifted it, so Nonna could see the injury. She leaned in and put a hand to her throat.

" *'Dio mio,'* she said, crossing herself. 'There is no hope now. She will never find a husband with a face like this.' "

Lucy clutches my arm. "No, she didn't!"

"My dad thought we should go to the ER. I remember so clearly. Nonna lifted her palms upward as she walked back to her apartment. *'Perché preoccuparsi?'* she said."

Why bother?

CHAPTER 23

POPPY

1960
Trespiano

The day of Rico's visit arrived with a torrent of rain. Sheets fell from the sky, turning the fields into a patchwork of ponds. But weather never kept Mamma from Sunday mass. The Cathedral of Saint Romulus of Fiesole was cold and drafty. I knelt with my icy hands clenched in prayer, begging for a miracle. *Please help Rico find the right words. Help us convince Papà of our love. Please, God, do not take away the one good thing in my life, the only person I have ever wanted.*

We left the church and traveled home, all seven of us squeezed into Papà's old Fiat. Rain ricocheted from the streets. Rico had planned to ride his bike — the buses didn't run on Sundays. Surely he wouldn't cycle

226

thirteen kilometers in a downpour. We had no phone at our farmhouse, so he had no way to contact me. He would have to wait another day before approaching my father, a thought that left me simultaneously crushed and relieved.

I went about my Sunday chores, plucking eggs from the henhouse, sweeping the barn. At two o'clock, I set the table for dinner. Rosa was making artichoke salad again, something she had heard increased fertility. "Alberto and I are ready to start our family," she reminded my mother, who stood at the stove, adding oregano to her marinara sauce.

I jumped when I heard a knock at the door. My stomach pitched. I will never forget the look that passed between my sister and me. She knew. She knew that Rico had arrived. And she was terrified. For him, and for me.

"It will be fine," I said, pretending to be calm.

I smoothed my hair and untied my apron on the way to the door. There he stood, his brown britches and white shirt drenched. He was wearing a necktie, and I stifled a giggle. I'd never seen him in such dapper clothing. His face bloomed when he saw me.

"Not for you this time," he said, looking down at his bouquet of soaking-wet daisies. "For your mother."

My heart overflowed. How could my parents resist his charm?

Before I had time to let him in, Rosa rushed over, pushing me aside. "Papà will kill you — both of you. Go. Now. Before you cause Paolina trouble."

"But Rosa, Rico has come all this way."

"That will make no difference to Papà. He and Mamma have put all their hopes in Ignacio. They will be furious at anyone who comes between you — especially someone who is not Italian." She looked at Rico. "Go, please. We must keep this our secret, for now."

"Just one moment with your papà," Rico said firmly, brushing past Rosa. "That is all I ask."

He entered the house. My heart was beating erratically, like a metronome gone haywire. I wanted to have faith in Rico, but Rosa's words rang true. Might Papà actually kill him?

In the kitchen, hiding my trembling hands behind my back, I introduced my mamma.

"Buongiorno, Signora Fontana," Rico said, extending the flowers.

She yanked them from his grip, craning

228

her neck toward the archway leading to our living room, where my papà rested.

"Grosso errore," she whispered. Big mistake.

But it was too late. There, in the archway, stood my father, his hands planted on his hips, his wide stance swallowing the room.

Time stood still as I watched Rico cross the floor. Though he was a tall man, he seemed to shrink before the mountain of my father. If he had prepared a speech, it was forgotten.

"I love your daughter," he blurted out.

"Fuori!" my father said. "Leave! Out of my house, now!"

"Papà!" I rushed to Rico's side and linked arms with him. "Please, listen to him."

My father turned to me. *"Stai zitta!"* he shouted. He flicked his hand. "Be quiet. Get this barbarian out of here. Now."

Tears sprang to my eyes. How dare he be so cruel? I wanted to scream at him. I wanted to storm off and prove my love to Rico. But if I did, I would lose my family. If I chose my family, I would lose Rico.

Rico made the choice for me. He looked up at my father, his voice calm and certain. "I will leave, but you have misjudged me, signore. Nobody will ever love your daughter the way I do."

My father huffed. "You know nothing. Paolina is engaged to marry a shop owner in America. She will have everything she wants, riches beyond belief, in this new land of opportunity. And most important, she will be with her family, something a German would not understand."

"Papà!" I cried, my heart breaking for Rico. "Do not say that."

He waved a dismissive hand in Rico's direction. "I read of men in East Germany, leaving their fathers and mothers, siblings and wives, all for so-called freedom." My father sneered. "It is not like that with us. The threads of the Italian family do not unravel."

Rico's jaw twitched, as if an electric current were passing through. But he kept his voice even. "You do not know of what you speak." He turned to me and kissed my cheek. *"Addio, mio unico amore."*

I started after him. How could I part with a man I loved, a man who called me his one love? But halfway to the door, Papà grabbed my arm, his thick fingers biting into my flesh. "Please, Papà. I love —"

My father's hand swept across my cheek, so swiftly I heard the crack before I felt the sting.

Rosa ran to me. "Papà! No!"

He shot her a look, silencing her, before turning his attention back to me. "You are risking everything, *everything,* we have worked for, everything we have dreamed of!"

I swallowed hard, unable to speak.

"Ignacio is a solid man. He is willing to take you for his wife, and you, a second daughter no less. How dare you squander this opportunity, you selfish fool. You must stop this nonsense now. That is an order! You will go to America. *Capisci?*"

My knees nearly buckled. I grabbed hold of Rosa's hand to keep steady. As my mind scrambled for a reply, Rosa answered for me.

"Sì, Papà. She understands."

CHAPTER 24

EMILIA

The wine bottle, empty now, sits beside a single candle in the middle of a cloth-covered table. Dusk has drifted into darkness, and streetlights reflect off the freshly washed sidewalk.

"That's enough for tonight," Poppy says, pulling her gaze from the window. "If I continue, you'll miss your night on the town."

"It's okay," I say, scooting to the edge of my chair. "What happened next?"

"Yeah," Lucy says, draining the last drops from her glass. "Was our great-grandpa simply a bastard, or did he really think you'd be happier with that Ignacio dude?"

Poppy smiles, but her eyes are heavy. "My papà loved me. He and Mamma wanted the best for me."

I choke on my wine. "You can't be ser —"

She lifts a hand, silencing me. "I've found

life much sweeter when I choose to believe the best of others, rather than the worst."

The waiter appears with a tray of liqueurs.

"No Frangelico for me," Poppy says. "I'll take the check, please."

Sweat breaks out on the back of my neck. "You still want to go out, Luce?" *Please say no. Please say no. Please say no.*

She scowls. "Ye-es." She breaks the word into two syllables, as if to emphasize the silliness of my question.

Poppy claps her hands. "You shouldn't miss Al Volto, the oldest wine bar in Venice."

"Never heard of it," Lucy says. "TripAdvisor says the place to go is Il Campo. Music and craft cocktails and lots of *ragazzi caldi.*" She does a jaunty little shoulder shimmy when she says the Italian phrase for "hot guys."

Poppy tsks as she signs the receipt. "Suit yourselves." She reaches into her purse as she rises. "For luck," she says, and places two coins on the table.

"Thanks, Pops!" Lucy says, snatching one of them. She looks at me and wiggles her eyebrows. "Here's hoping we get lucky."

A pit forms in my stomach. Poppy pushes in her chair and waves her fingers. "Ta-ta until morning."

"Wait," I say, panic setting in. "We'll walk

233

you back to the hotel."

"Nonsense. It's three blocks away. I'll be fine."

Yes, I imagine she will be. But what about me?

Lucy navigates using an app she's loaded onto my phone. "Where the hell is this place?" We round another corner, cross another bridge.

"Sorry. I'm no help without my glasses."

"This damn island is like a house of mirrors."

"Maybe we should go back to the hotel, Luce. We can go out tomorrow, when we're in Florence."

She cranes her neck to find a street name on the corner of a building. "Okay, this way."

She leads me into Campo Santa Margherita, and we navigate the perimeter. "Aha!" she says, pointing to a nondescript door with a tiny sign that reads *Il Campo.* "Here we are." She gives me a quick once-over, then fishes a lip pencil from her purse. She uncaps it and aims it at me.

"Stand still."

"Oh, no, you don't," I say, and step back.

"You heard what Pops said. You've got yourself a kick-ass battle scar if there ever was one."

My heart beats erratically as she outlines my lips. Next, she dabs them with thick wet gloss. I fight the urge to swipe my mouth with the back of my hand. She stands back and smiles.

"Nice."

It's funny how words can affect a person, how, with the slightest shift in perception, along with one person's faith, a lifelong belief can rise up like a flock of sparrows and fly away. I'm still a bit self-conscious. Others will notice my mouth now, and with it, my scar. The jagged blue line below my glossy bottom lip is as obvious as the sports bra beneath my blouse.

Tonight, I'm choosing to reveal, rather than conceal.

I follow Lucy through the door. Immediately, we're assaulted by techno music and a cloud of cigarette smoke. Lucy sidles up to the bar. Without my glasses, everything's a bit blurry. I blink and, for a moment, things come into focus. Throngs of kids — college aged, mostly — stand shoulder to shoulder. The entire place, it seems, is orange. Orange walls, orange chairs, orange sofa, orange rugs. I feel a headache coming on.

Lucy hands me a drink. My glossy lips

stick to the rim of the glass, and I sip something that tastes like lime . . . but has a spicy hotness.

"Green chile and citrus vodka," she shouts over the music.

"Oh. It's . . . thanks," I say, and choke down another sip.

She pays the bartender, seeming not to notice the dark-skinned guy with bloodshot eyes whose nose is practically pinched in her cleavage. His friend, a redhead who looks like a five-foot, three-inch version of England's Prince Harry, smiles at me. I spin away and walk alongside Lucy toward a shaggy orange sofa that looks super comfy. Thank God I'll get to rest these aching feet. How does my cousin prance around in these heels twelve hours a day?

We near a small round table, where a guy and a cute brunette stand, drinking martinis. As we pass, the guy looks me up and down without the slightest pretense.

"Asshole," Lucy snaps. She turns to me. "I can't stand a guy who checks me out when he's with another woman."

We arrive at the empty orange sofa and I plop down. "My feet," I groan, and kick off my — *Lucy's* — heels.

"Drink," she orders.

"Oh, Luce. I've already had wine with dinner."

"Drink," she repeats.

Cautiously, I take another swallow of my chile citrus vodka and shudder.

"Good girl," she says, smiling. "You really are trying to change, aren't you?"

I take a long swill of the awful drink, hoping for courage. *We ignore what our heart — and stomach — tells us when we think it could make someone love us.*

Thirty minutes and two citrus whatever-they're-calleds later, Lucy and I have befriended a quartet of tall blond women from the Netherlands. They speak perfect English — better than mine at the moment.

"You guys are great!" I say, but it sounds more like, "Who died in the lake?"

"To new friends," Lucy says, and we clink glasses. I throw back my delicious drink. Beside me, Lucy scans the place from wall to wall, as if measuring for carpet. She slams her glass on the table and rises.

"C'mon! Let's dance!"

The blondes jump to their feet and make their way to the dance floor. I try wedging my feet into my shoes, my heart battering in my rib cage. Lucy grabs my hand and yanks me from the chair.

"Wait," I say, as I stumble forward. "I

haven't danced in . . . forever."

The room sways. She pulls me onto the wood floor, crammed with sweating, writhing bodies. I shift awkwardly and tug at the hem of my skirt. A guy with a scarf around his neck scoots up behind me, thrusting his crotch dangerously close to my rear. I yelp and spin around. My tongue feels thick and I shout in Lucy's ear.

"Did you see that?"

She shimmies her shoulders and laughs. "Be nice!"

I look around at this blurry crowd of happy millennials, laughing, bobbing, hopping up and down with their arms raised to the ceiling. I'm probably the oldest person here. Besides Lucy, I don't know a soul in this entire place, or the entire city. A refreshing surge of freedom washes over me. Here, I can be whomever I choose to be.

I find my rhythm. People look at me, smile at me. Thanks to the alcohol, I'm almost able to ignore my aching feet — and the couple to my right who are basically dry-humping. It's actually fun, dancing with this laughing group of girls.

But one by one, my new friends scatter. The blondes find a flock of guys to dance with. Lucy moseys over to the tall, dark-skinned guy who'd been checking her out at the bar. She's on the other side of the dance floor now, her arms flung over her head as she prances around in front of him, arching and dipping to provide an unobstructed view of the Fontana mountain range.

I'm smiling when, without forewarning, my stomach rumbles. A queasy feeling comes over me.

I snake my way through the dance floor, trying to steady myself, when the short redhead — Prince Harry wannabe — appears. Uninvited, he grabs hold of my hands. What makes him think I want to hold his sweaty hands? He winks as he yanks me back onto the dance floor. Am I the only one who thinks winks are creepy?

I do my best to lose myself in the song — some techno tune with lots of bass. I'm at a bar in Venice, drinking and dancing — with a guy. Tonight, I'm actually putting myself out there, just like I promised Lucy I'd do. My stomach churns.

Speaking of Lucy, where is she, anyway? I gaze past the top of Harry's head, trying to keep a little rhythm in my step. The music slows. My neck snaps when he yanks me to his chest. Our bodies press together, sandwiched like a PB&J, except one slice of bread — my slice — is about twice the size of the other. Lovely. I'm dancing with a twelve-year-old. And what's that poking at my thigh? Oh, shit! Make that a *horny* twelve-year-old!

I struggle to create some distance between us and search the dance floor for Lucy. There she . . . hey, where's she going? She's walking off with the swarthy guy in black. I wave my hand until finally, she sees me. She points at the guy, wags her tongue, and gives me a thumbs-up. I manage a weak smile, one I hope conveys *Don't you dare leave me!*

"Relax, beautiful," Harry whispers.

But how am I supposed to relax, in the clutches of Shorty and his hard-on? I take a deep breath. This isn't about me. I'm here for Lucy. And tonight, she's happy.

The song ends and Harry grabs my hand. "Come," he says, pulling me across the floor.

My heart thuds. "Wait," I say, searching for Lucy. "My cousin —"

But Harry has a tight grip and he's dragging me along like a kid at a carnival. He's hurting my hand. My head is filled with cotton. I can't think straight. I stagger past the bar, trying to keep up with him, all the while craning my neck, hoping to spot Lucy. Everything's out of focus. Where is she?

The door pushes open and a cool puff of

wind hits me. Behind us, the door slams shut.

It's mercifully quiet in the piazza. I suck in deep breaths while Harry leads me around a corner. I realize he's on a mission and pull back. "Stop," I say, tugging my hand from his grip. "I have to find my cousin."

"She left with Ethan." Sure enough, he has a British accent.

"Who?"

"My mate." He tips his head to the right. "Let's go."

"Go? Where would we go at this hour? I don't even know you."

His eyes twinkle, as if I might be joking.

"I'm not leaving without Lucy. My aunt is waiting —"

Without warning, his thin, chapped lips clamp down on mine, stealing my words. I'm frozen with revulsion and shock. A wet tongue darts into my mouth. "Stop," I manage to say, but he hitches me closer. He tastes of garlic and stale beer and I fight the urge to gag. I try pulling away, but Harry's grip is too tight. He's groping my ass!

"Let me go!" I say, and manage to shove him away. But he's right back on me like a chimpanzee, his arm a vise around the back of my neck.

My stomach gurgles. The chile vodka whatever-it-was rises from my stomach. It's making its way up my esophagus, and I'm powerless to stop it. I put my hands to Harry's chest and push away with all my might. He staggers backward.

"The fuck!" he says.

I double over, vomiting down his pant legs, onto his Stan Smiths.

"Oh, bloody hell!"

I swipe my mouth with the back of my hand. "Now," I say. "Do I make myself clear? Leave me the hell alone!"

He stares at me with wide eyes, then lifts his hands. "You are one sick bitch."

I watch as he walks away. "Yes," I say proudly. "I am." Then I vomit once more, this time into a trash bin.

CHAPTER 25

EMILIA

I can't believe I barfed on the Brit. Serves him right. Men are pigs — all men except Matt and Liam, that is. Is this what Lucy has to contend with, night after night? No, thank you!

I return to the bar and search the place, but Lucy's nowhere to be found. Where could she be? Finally, I settle for my last resort. I stand outside Il Campo and wait for her to leave — or return.

Forty minutes later, I'm more or less sober, and panic is setting in. The bar is emptying. We need to get back to the hotel — which is where, exactly? Damn Lucy!

The last patrons tumble out at two a.m., the quartet of beautiful Dutch girls.

"Hey," I say, "have you seen Lucy?"

"Yes," one of them says. "About two hours ago. She left with that guy in black."

I hear the squeak of a door and turn to

see a man in a white shirt padlocking the entrance.

"Wait," I say to him. "My cousin's still in there."

He shakes his head. "No, signorina. It is empty."

My mind reels. What am I supposed to do now? What's the protocol for girls' night out? What happens when a friend hooks up with someone? Will she come back here for me? Do I wait? Or are we on our own now? Why didn't I ask her earlier? And why the hell didn't we borrow Poppy's phone?

I wait another twenty minutes. Campo Santa Margherita is nearly empty now, and I don't have a clue which direction we came from. Even after three days, Venice is nothing but a labyrinth of canals to me. Where are my maps when I need them? I pull up the app on my phone, but without my glasses, it's useless.

I clutch my head and spin in a circle. Slowly, I move in the direction I think we came from. I enter a narrow brick-walled lane. The light from the campo fades. A chill comes over me. Nothing looks familiar. Is this the way we came?

Raised voices spill from darkened apartments. My skin prickles with fear. I need to think, but my head is still foggy. I trot to the end of the calle, never mind that my feet are screaming in agony. I come to an intersection, where the lane branches off in three directions. "Damn it!"

It's dark, and I can't make out the street names on the corner walls. My heart races. I start down one corridor but reconsider. I spin around and scurry in the opposite direction. I'm struggling to breathe and my head feels light. I need Matt. He would talk me off the ledge, help me think clearly. But that's not fair. I can't use him to clean up my messes, like a handy stain-stick, and then toss him aside when my life is tidy.

A young couple approaches. I rush toward them.

"Excuse me," I say, my voice shaking. *"Mi scusate."*

The man raises his hand and they continue on, as if I'm a beggar trying to hustle them.

I travel down another narrow calle, over a bridge. Does this look familiar? I don't know! Damn it!

A memory finds me. I'm in kindergarten. School got let out early because of a winter blizzard. Daria and I are walking home, each rubber-boot step sinking into the drifting snow. Even though she's right beside me, I can barely see my sister through the blinding storm. Fear grips me. We'll never find our way home. "Don't lose me," I call to her, the wind stinging my face.

My big sister takes my mittened hand in hers. She tells me she'll never leave me. Suddenly, I'm safe.

I slip my fingers into the pocket of my purse, pausing to touch the Saint Christopher medallion before lifting my phone. It's evening back home. I squint until the star icon comes into focus. I blindly tap the first contact saved under *Favorites.* She answers on the second ring.

"Emmie?"

My throat squeezes shut. "Dar," I finally manage to croak.

"Are you home? Please say yes. Nonna is an absolute wreck."

I close my eyes. At this moment, alone in this alley, I would give anything to be back in my safe little Emville. "I'm lost."

"What's going on? Where are you?" Her voice carries the same urgency it did when I called her on New Year's Eve eleven years ago.

"I'm in Venice. Lucy and I got separated."

She lets out a sigh. "You're okay. You've got the hotel address, right? Call an Uber. Don't try to find Lucy. Just get back to the hotel."

"Okay," I say. I don't remind my sister there are no vehicles in Venice. She'd feel silly. "Thank you, Dar."

"Is that it?"

I peer down the lonely narrow alley. "No. There's one more thing." I lean against a stucco building, as if to fortify myself. "What happened to us, Dar?"

Silence fills the air. I rub my aching throat. "Did I do something to hurt you? Something that caused you to hate me?"

"What are you talking about?"

She knows. I know she does.

I swallow hard and force the words from my lips. "I love you, Dar."

It's awkward, expressing the sentiment we haven't spoken for years.

She waits a beat. "Yeah, well, you need to get home, like, presto. I've never seen Nonna so worked up."

Drunken sadness grips me. In the distance, I hear footsteps. I steal a glance behind me. The silhouette of a man takes shape, forty feet away.

"Oh, God. I have to go."

I slip my phone into my pocket. My heart speeds and I scurry onward. What was I thinking, stopping in this deserted alley?

The steps grow louder on the cobblestones. I quicken my pace. The footsteps quicken, too.

Ahead, another bridge appears. Where the hell am I?

My heels clomp against the concrete bridge. Fear claws the back of my neck and I break into a trot. And still, the footsteps grow nearer. My feet are on fire. I'm going to be kidnapped, or murdered, or sold into sex slavery. Is this my punishment for betraying Nonna?

The footsteps finally overtake mine. A half moan, half cry pushes past my throat, and I fear I'm going to pass out. A tall man looms at my side.

"Posso aiutarLa?" he asks.

I can't breathe. My legs are shaking. I'm about to collapse.

"Can I help you?" he repeats, this time in English. His features are clouded in the dim streetlight.

I fight to keep from hyperventilating. "Leave me . . . alone. Please."

"It is okay," he says. "I am not going to hurt you."

Finally, I turn to him. His dark eyes shine down on me like candles in a cave. "You are lost?"

I push back the threatening storm in my chest. "I — I'm trying to find the Ca' Sagredo Hotel, on Campo Santa Sofia."

He rubs his chin. "Sì. I know this hotel. Come with me."

"No. Just tell me."

"It is very complicated on foot. It is much easier to show you."

"Never mind," I say, and turn to leave.

"Wait." He lifts his hands. "I can see that you do not trust me. You are wise to be cautious." He points in the opposite direction. "Go that way. When you reach the end, turn right, then left, and another left. You will cross a bridge —"

"Stop," I say, interrupting. "Okay, just . . . please, show me."

The stranger leads me down a dark calle. But something — instinct, perhaps — tells me I'm safe. He takes my elbow, and we turn down a narrow alley and cross a bridge. Five minutes later, the calle merges into yet another bridge. Like stepping into a lit room, it's brighter here, almost cheery. A half dozen gondolas idle beneath the bridge, as if waiting for me.

He signals to a gondolier and helps me on board. I'm surprised when, instead of vanishing, he climbs aboard the gondola and takes a seat beside me.

"I am Giovanni," he tells me. "Giovanni Ghelli."

"I'm Em — Emilia Antonelli." I cross my

arms over my chest, keenly aware of my see-through blouse.

The gondolier pushes off, and the small boat drifts down the winding canal. We follow a moonlit path across the blue-black water, and the night's cool breath chills my arms. I shiver. Giovanni takes off his leather jacket and wraps it around my shoulders.

"Better?"

I smile. "Grazie."

Giovanni chats as we drift along, and I begin to relax. He tells me of his job, waiting tables at his uncle's restaurant.

"It is a pleasant job, but I prefer to hear about you. Where is it that you live?"

"New York," I say, letting him assume it's Manhattan, not Bensonhurst. He lifts his brows and nods.

"My dream is to visit California one day." He clutches my arm. "No offense. I hear wonderful things about New York as well."

I laugh, savoring the feel of his hand on my arm, the warmth of his thigh pressed against mine, the musky smell rising from his leather jacket. If Lucy could see me now! And Aunt Poppy, too. I'm trying, just like I'd promised. Perhaps it's a sad statement about the pathetic little world Lucy claims I've created, but in twenty-nine years, this is, without a doubt, the most romantic moment in my life.

Twenty minutes later, the gondola coasts to a stop. I look up. The Ca' Sagredo Hotel stares at me. My heart sinks. I want to stay right here, on this little wooden craft with this handsome Italian man who makes me feel safe.

"Here you are," he says, his voice soft. "Just as I promised."

"Grazie. You were a lifesaver."

"It was my pleasure, Emilia. Truly." He takes my hand and helps me off the gondola. "Enjoy the rest of your evening."

He smiles down at me, his eyes tender. My heart thumps in my chest. Should I invite him for a drink? What would my character do in this situation? What would Lucy do? I swallow hard. "Good night," I say.

He lifts a hand. *Buonanotte.*

I walk toward the hotel, regret churning in me. Lucy will never forgive me for squandering this opportunity. I'm almost to the entrance when he calls to me.

"Emilia!"

I turn. "Yes?"

His head is tipped, and he's wearing the slightest smile on his beautiful face. He crooks his finger.

My heart leaps. I make my way toward

the boat, forcing myself to walk, not run. With each step, my confidence grows. *This is who you've become. But you don't have to die as that woman.* Poppy's right. I can be whomever I choose to be. And tonight, I choose to be bold.

I take one last step. I'm close enough to touch him. Before I have time to chicken out, I lift myself onto my tiptoes. I close my eyes and press my lips to Giovanni's.

His body snaps back, as if he's been Tasered. He swipes his mouth with the back of his hand.

"La mia giacca," he says, pointing to the jacket draped around my shoulders.

"Oh, God," I say, the chafe of his whiskers burning my lips. "I thought you —" Humiliation sears my cheeks. "I'm so sorry." I yank off his coat and thrust it at him. "Thanks again," I say with a curt wave.

I scurry toward the hotel as gracefully as I can, silently cursing myself. I am such an idiot!

"Emilia," he calls.

I close my eyes and suck in a breath. When I turn around, his eyes twinkle in the moonlight.

"My wife," he says. "She would not like it if she knew I gave away my jacket to a beautiful woman I shared my dreams with on a magical moonlit night."

A slow smile makes its way to my face. Giovanni's eyes lock on mine as the gondolier plants his oar on the dock and pushes off. I stand, watching my hero — my *married* hero — disappear into the darkness.

CHAPTER 26

EMILIA

Day Four
Venice

I lie in bed, my notebook beside me, staring up at the ceiling, thinking of Giovanni and Daria and my cousin who's still not home. In the wee hours of the morning, as dawn spins the room from charcoal to lilac, the door finally creaks open.

"Hey, Luce." I prop myself onto my elbows.

"Shhh," she says. Without bothering to change into her pajamas, she burrows beneath the covers and closes her eyes.

Where has she been all night? Is she okay? How did she get home?

I study her pale face in the feathered light of dawn. Her cheeks are puffy from too much alcohol and her hair is a tangled mess. But in sleep, with her lips slightly parted, I see a softness, a tender vulnerability she keeps hidden by day.

Did Lucy spend the night with the guy from Il Campo? I shudder, thinking of his friend Harry, groping me outside the bar. Is this the way it works, being single? Are we expected to hook up with strangers, without the slightest hint of affection? With no promise of tomorrow, no guise of love?

"Em?" Her sleepy voice cracks the silence.

"Yeah, Luce?"

"Do you think there's any chance, any chance at all, that Poppy could actually break the curse?"

I look down at her. In the first blush of daybreak, her face glows with hope.

"I — I don't know. I don't really see how she could."

She nods and drifts off to sleep.

I brush a lock of hair from Lucy's face, a warrior in the treacherous minefield of Dating Land. Unlike me, this brave woman puts herself on the battlefield time and time again. Tears sting my eyes. Poor, poor Lucy. And cowardly me.

If there really is a curse, at this moment I swear I would do anything, *anything,* to break it.

An hour later I give up on sleep. I tiptoe

across the wooden floor and quietly open the French doors. The sun mops the sky with pinks and purples. I step onto the balcony. The canal is quiet now, save for the gentle stroking of water against the concrete dock.

"Buongiorno."

I startle. Aunt Poppy sits on a chaise, sipping coffee in her robe and bare feet. She smiles and beckons me with her open arms.

"Good morning," I say, leaning down to give her a hug. "You're up early."

"I've never been one to waste a sunrise." She pats the chaise and I ease in beside her. "Tell me about your evening," she says, wrapping her arms around me. "Did you and Luciana have a good time?"

I gaze out at the pink horizon. "It was pretty much a disaster, with a few lighter moments of disgust and humiliation. Oh, and a bit of terror thrown in for good measure."

"It's always tricky when you pretend to be someone you're not," Poppy says.

"What do you mean?"

"Last night you were disguised as Lucy."

I turn to face her. "But you encouraged me."

She wipes a smudge of mascara from beneath my eye. "Sometimes we must try

256

on several personas before we find one that fits. You see, until you decide who you are not, you will never know who you are." Her eyes twinkle. "Now go on. Continue with the evening."

I groan. "The bar was so crowded I couldn't find Lucy. I got lost. I had no idea how to get back to the hotel. Every street, every bridge, every square looked the same." The panic from last night rekindles, and my breath quickens. I sit up straight. "It was dark, and I was . . ." I try to ignore the sly smile on Poppy's lips. "I was hoping someone would help. But people passed me by. They just kept walking and . . ." I scowl at her upturned lips. "Why are you smiling? I could have been killed."

She lifts her shoulders. "Yes, and I trust you won't find yourself alone on the streets after a night of drinking ever again. It could have ended in disaster. But luckily, you kept your wits about you. You are a smart, capable woman who had an adventure."

"An adventure? I was terrified."

"You've learned a valuable lesson, one that will serve you well when you finally decide to be true to yourself." She whispers now, as if she's imparting some very wise and weighty advice. "Being lost is where the beauty lies. Lost in a book. Lost in someone's eyes. Lost in a symphony so sweet it brings you to tears." She smiles. "Lost in a beautiful floating city on a starry night. This is magical, yes? It's being found that's the disappointment."

I was alone in Venice, justifiably petrified and panic-stricken. But could Aunt Poppy be right, too? I danced with some cool women. I stood up to a lecherous man. I made my way home safely. And aside from the fact that Giovanni was married, it *was* a magical night, sitting beside him on the gondola. I have a memory now, a story to tell, perhaps a scene to re-create in a novel one day.

I gaze out at the rippling Laguna Veneta, dappled in rose and coral, and a sense of pride comes over me. For a moment, I allow myself to believe I really am capable, that when I'm back in Bensonhurst, in my safe little neighborhood surrounded by family and friends, I might seek to get lost once in a while. Because now I know that's where the beauty lies.

"Next time I decide to get lost," I say, "I'm doing it stone-cold sober. With my glasses!"

"Didn't I just say you were smart?" Poppy's laughter fades. "About your cousin," she says. "Luciana is a different kind of lost. We must help her find herself. If we don't, she just might disappear completely."

L'ottico is busy Thursday morning. I sit in front of a mirror as the optician-slash-supermodel positions my new glasses on my face. She leans back and smiles.

"Bellissima!"

I catch sight of a man in a leather coat, watching us. "You will get used to the attention," she whispers.

At ten o'clock, wearing my stylish new specs, we board the train at Venezia Santa Lucia station. I follow Poppy down the aisle. Her face looks almost ghostly this morning, in direct contrast to her flashy clothing. She's sporting wide-legged yellow slacks and a white blouse imprinted with little bananas. A raspberry ascot is tucked into her collar. And despite this, people stare at *me.* How did I get talked into such conspicuous glasses? I want my comfy old wire-frames back, where nobody noticed me. I settle into my seat and reach into my purse for my beat-up glasses case.

Lucy's hand seizes mine. "Don't even think about it."

I drop the case back into my purse. I have to admit, my vision's great through these big lenses.

The train eases out of the station at 10:25 sharp. Aunt Poppy sits across from Lucy and me, her nose pressed to the window, waving good-bye to nobody in particular.

Soon, the islands of Venice draw out like a shadow behind us. I bid a silent farewell to the magical floating city with its endless canals and gilded sunsets, its maze of cobblestone streets and ancient bridges.

I plug my phone into the charger, but it doesn't seem to be working. I turn to Lucy in the seat beside me. She's massaging her forehead, looking stale as day-old bread. "How was your night?" I ask for at least the third time this morning.

She stretches and a slow smile makes its way to her face. "You saw him. He was hot, right?"

"Yes," I say, trying to picture the guy. "And he was really into you, Luce."

Her smile vanishes. "Of course now we're leaving, and I'll never see him again."

"You can keep in touch. Did you get his email?"

She rolls her eyes. "Right, Em. The guy's dying for a pen pal."

Poppy turns to her. "Imagine the possibilities of actually getting to know someone."

Lucy pulls a tube of lip gloss from her

purse. "What's that supposed to mean?" She offers me the tube. I hesitate briefly, then dab some onto my fingertip.

"True intimacy is a connection of the mind as well as the body," Poppy says. "When you settle for only one of these two, the result is either emotionless sex or platonic friendship. Nothing more. Nothing less."

Lucy huffs. "Gee, thanks, Dr. Phil."

Lucy may not like the advice, but the words ring true to me. Could Matt and I have more than friendship if I tried harder?

"She's only trying to help," I whisper to Lucy, once Aunt Poppy's attention returns to the window. "Seriously, I don't understand, either. You're putting yourself in danger, leaving with these guys. I mean, sure, you like sex. I get that. But —"

"What makes you think I like sex?"

She looks directly at me. The pain in her eyes renders me speechless. My cousin, who's been AWOL two out of the last three nights, who gives herself so recklessly to any guy who shows interest, doesn't even enjoy sex.

We ignore what our heart tells us when we think it could make someone love us.

The train glides past yellow fields and green hills, an occasional stone farmhouse, a pasture of sheep. Soon, I'm lost in my story, imagining my characters spending a clandestine weekend in this quaint setting. While I mentally sketch the scene, Lucy fiddles with my hair. I smile as she separates strands, mumbling to herself about which type of braid would be best for my oval face. Careful not to disturb her, I open my notebook. With my back to her, I lose myself in my writing.

Ten minutes later, I put my pen down. I pat my head, feeling a braid cascading down one side. I turn to find Lucy leaning over my shoulder . . . reading my story!

I flip the notebook shut.

"Hey!" she says. "I wasn't finished."

"How long have you been snooping?"

"Long enough to know you're writing a book." She grabs the notebook.

"Give me that."

She holds it above her head and reads aloud, *"He stroked her soft cheek, his touch sending shivers up her spine."*

"Stop!"

"She turned to him, her eyes filled with need."

I finally yank the book from her.

"Don't leave me hanging!" she says. "What happens next?"

I stuff the book into my bag and shake my

head, choked with humiliation. "Just stop, Lucy. You're not funny."

She shrugs. "I wasn't trying to be. I mean, isn't that the point of writing, to have people read it? By the way, that braid looks awesome. Hey, Pops, check out the new do!"

Poppy's ashen face brightens a shade. "Now there's my girl! Well done, Luciana. Rico loved it when I wore a braid."

Lucy positions the braid so that it spills over my shoulder. "Did you ever see Rico again? You know, after your dad basically cut off his balls?"

Poppy shakes her head. "It was the longest night of my life, that April day when Papà sent Rico away. I did not dream. I did not sleep. I could no longer breathe. Instead, I prayed.

"By the next morning, my head had cleared. I made a promise to myself. I would never again allow someone else to make decisions for me." She turns to the train window. "If only I had kept that promise."

CHAPTER 27

POPPY

1960
From Florence to Amalfi Coast, Italy

I was the first one off the bus at Piazza della Signoria. I ran all the way to Rico's flat. I couldn't wait to see him, to tell him my news. I had chosen him. I was breathless when I quietly let myself in.

"Rico?" I whispered, my eyes adjusting to the dim lighting. I blinked once. Twice. The room was empty. Every piece of him — his razor, his hair comb, his violin case — was gone. My heart sank. The only man I ever loved had vanished.

The door behind me creaked open. I spun around, expecting to find Rico. Instead, a woman barged into the room carrying a bucket and a mop. I rushed to her.

"I'm Poppy, Rico's — *Erich's* — friend. Do you know where he is?"

She reached into the pocket of her smock and removed an envelope. *Poppy* was written across the front. I tore it open.

Mio unico amore,

By the time you read this, I will be on the train to Naples, a broken man whose heart is bleeding. I must move on, and so must you. There is a place called Amalfi, wedged into the cliffs, cascading down the hillside to the Gulf of Salerno. I hear the crowds there are large, even bigger than in Firenze, filled with wealthy tourists waiting to be entertained. I will start fresh, a new life in Amalfi, just me and a beautiful coast where I can live in sunshine and freedom. This is what I came for. But now that I have tasted you, I realize I will always be missing the most important thing in life. Love.

Please honor your father's wishes, and know that I understand and respect this. No person should have to choose between blood and water. Do not look back in sadness, but only in love, a reminder of a sweet time when two souls collided in song.

I wish you the best in your journey to America. Your life will be prosperous and easy, and for that I am grateful. I will pray for you every night of my life, asking for your safety and happiness. I have faith someone will hear my prayers. Of one thing I am certain: I will continue to love you until my dying breath — something I both cherish and fear. I am the luckiest unlucky man in the world.

I will love you a million times over, my beautiful papavero.

Rico

I didn't hesitate. Not even for an instant. I dashed from Rico's flat and made my way to the train station. I left Firenze two hours later. When the train stopped, I boarded a bus. It was dusk when the bus finally arrived in the seaside town of Amalfi. I asked the first person I saw for directions to the main square.

And there he was, new to Amalfi but already surrounded by a small crowd in the Piazza del Duomo. They cheered and cried for the German violinist. He had been practicing our favorite song, an international hit by Doris Day called "Que Será, Será." Now he was performing it in public for the first time. I whispered the words as he played. *"Que será, será. Whatever will be, will be. The future's not ours to see."*

His bow slid up and down the strings, at once tenacious and tender. I stood clutching my hands, my heart soaring. And then he saw me. His bow fell to his side. He ran to me.

"Mio unico amore!"

He lifted me into his arms. I couldn't see through my tears. The crowd cheered, and I knew, right then and there, I was home.

We rented a room above a bakery, in a small town called Ravello, three kilometers up the cliff from Amalfi. I was soon hired in the little bakery downstairs. Rico played his violin every afternoon and evening. Just as he was told, the crowds on the Amalfi Coast were larger, wealthier. Even so, we did not have much money. But we felt rich as royalty. Our palace was the tiny room where, from the rooftop each evening, we would sip wine, catching a sliver of sun as it set over the Tyrrhenian Sea.

Summer merged into fall. October arrived and the nights grew cooler. We had no heat, and we'd huddle beneath the covers in the mornings, our breath steaming the air. Soon, I would turn twenty-one. Every day, Rico would ask me what I wanted for my birthday. I think he feared I was lonely, that I missed my family and regretted my decision to follow him. Each time, my answer was the same. "You."

That year, October twenty-second landed on a glorious Saturday. The bakery owner had given me the day off work. Rico and I spent the entire day together, drifting in and out of stores, stopping for a cappuccino, later a glass of wine. As the sun set, I sat in the piazza watching him perform, thanking the goddesses for my beautiful, talented music man. It was the best birthday I'd ever had.

I returned to our flat at half past eight to prepare dinner. An hour later, Rico waltzed up the stairs, clutching a mysterious box with a bright purple ribbon. He lifted me off my feet, kissing me with all of his passion.

I vowed I would always remember that moment — the smell of garlic sautéing on the stove, the comfort of his strong arms around my waist, the golden flecks in his blue eyes.

When he finally set me down, he brushed past me and clicked off the stove. Then he handed me the box. "For you," he said, his eyes mischievous.

I removed the bow. Inside was the prettiest dress I'd ever seen, a gauzy white linen I knew we couldn't afford.

He lay on the bed with his hands behind

his head, smiling as he watched me change. The fabric was so soft, so fine. I felt like a princess. I couldn't believe it. In all my life, I'd only worn hand-me-downs from Rosa, or an occasional dress stitched by my mother or me.

"I love it," I said. "But it is too expensive."

"Nothing is too grand for you, my beautiful Poppy." He bounded from the bed and took me by the hand. "Come with me."

"Where are we going?" I asked, laughing as Rico pulled me down the stairway and out the door.

The evening air was crisp, and Rico wrapped his arm around my bare shoulders. Above, a slice of the moon played peekaboo with the clouds, creating shadows on the streets. While the city prepared for sleep, he led me up the steps of the Ravello Cathedral.

"We're a little early for church," I joked. Rico silenced me with a kiss. When our lips finally parted, he bent down on one knee.

"Paolina Maria Fontana, will you marry me?"

CHAPTER 28

EMILIA

Day Four
Firenze — Florence

The train glides to a stop at the Firenze Santa Maria Novella station. Poppy sits up and looks around, as if she's forgotten where she is.

"So what happened?" Lucy asks, clutching Poppy's arm. "Did you marry him? And break the curse?"

"Rico was not an Italian citizen," Poppy says. "And I had no birth certificate. I'd left everything behind when I walked out of my papà's house."

Lucy groans. "So what does that mean? Did you break the curse or not?"

Poppy gives her a wistful look. "I shall continue the story later."

Lucy drops her head on the tray in front of her and gently bangs it.

The station is swarming with tourists, and everywhere I see posters taped to the walls, encouraging fair wages for the train workers and announcing an upcoming *sciopero,* whatever that means. Poppy searches the platform for the driver she's arranged to take us to Trespiano. Her face lights up and she waves her hand.

"Gabriele!" she cries, moving stiffly down the platform in her suede flats. She's not running today, or even trotting. I watch as a tall Italian man wearing jeans and a white shirt lifts Poppy into the air. She plants kisses on his cheeks. I can't help but smile. How has she managed to collect so many friends in this country, four thousand miles from home?

"Come," she says, waving Lucy and me over. "Meet Gabriele, our driver. He is all ours for the next three days."

Lucy does her usual dip and flip. First, she bends at the waist, so Gabriele can check beneath her hood. Then she flips her hair so that it covers one eye, something I'm sure is meant to convey sexiness but only makes me want to search my purse for a hair clip.

"Hey," she says, her voice breathy. "I'm Lucy."

To his credit, Gabriele looks directly into

her eyes . . . or eye. "Pleasure to meet you, Lucy." His deep voice is perfectly gilded with a sexy Italian accent. He turns to me, and for some reason, I startle. He laughs. "I do not mean to frighten you."

I shake my head and lift a hand. "No. You don't." But my racing heart tells me a different story. He does scare me. Those dark eyes are too penetrating, that wry smile too seductive.

"I am Gabriele Vernasco," he says, his warm hand pressing mine. "Please, call me Gabe."

He leads us out of the station, our bags slung onto his back like a pack mule. Lucy trots alongside him, chatting. Poppy and I trail behind, both of us, I suspect, admiring his broad shoulders, his unruly dark waves, his tight round —

Poppy elbows me in the ribs, interrupting my thoughts. "He's scrumptious, isn't he?" She winks. My face heats and she laughs. "Perhaps you are coming to life, learning to be Emilia."

When Poppy announced Gabriele was ours for the next three days, I assumed his duties were limited to travel. But apparently, he's not only our driver — he's also our tour guide and innkeeper.

272

He loads the bags into a black SUV and closes the trunk. "I thought we would have lunch in the city before going to the inn."

Poppy claps her hands. "Marvelous!"

Together, we walk the streets of Firenze — Florence — the very town where Poppy gave tours and met Rico. This gorgeous medieval city, divided into two sections by the River Arno, has a different vibe from Venice, sacred yet cosmopolitan, hip while holding fast to its old-world charm. I catch whiffs of roasting meat and fresh bread, and my stomach growls.

"Ah, my favorite *trippaio*," Gabriele says, coming to a stop at a street-side kiosk, where the awning reads *Lampredotto*. "Would you like to try our version of the American hot dog?" he asks me.

"Sure," Lucy answers, elbowing her way to his side.

"It is a soft bread filled with meat."

"I'm all about meat," she says.

"Lampredotto is made from a cow's fourth stomach," Poppy says. "It's named after the lamprey, which it resembles."

Lucy gags. "How do you say *W.T.F.* in Italian?"

Gabriele smiles. "I take it that is a no?"

"It's a hell no," Lucy says.

He laughs. "How about pizza?"

We enter the heart of Florence, the lively Piazza della Signoria. Young men sell selfie sticks and trinkets. Tourists mill about with their cell phones poised, snapping photos of the replica statue of David and the Palazzo Vecchio — once the old palace, now the town hall. I turn in a circle, slowly panning the L-shaped square, barely able to believe I'm here, in the cradle of the Renaissance, surrounded by historical relics I've only read about and masterpieces by geniuses from Michelangelo to Michelozzo.

"Look," I say, pointing to a sign with an arrow. "The Uffizi must be that way. That's where you worked, right, Aunt Poppy?"

"Yes," she says. But she's staring in the opposite direction. I follow her gaze to the Fountain of Neptune, the place where her Rico performed. The octagonal fountain hosts a marble statue of Neptune, surrounded by laughing satyrs and bronze river gods and marble sea horses rising from the water. How strange it must feel, coming back to a city that seems impervious to change, a place that looked the same back in the sixteenth century as when she strolled the piazza, hand in hand with her Rico. Every statue, every fountain, in this town must remind her of her love.

Gabriele points us to a small café and we

settle into a table beneath a giant red umbrella. As we drink wine and devour an amazing pizza topped with fresh mozzarella and basil, he tells us about his first job, selling high-end automobiles at a private dealership off Via Valfonda.

"There is no sexier vehicle than the Lamborghini Diablo. But soon I tired of the job. I was making good money, selling luxury items to wealthy people. But it was corrupting my soul."

I nod, appreciating his honesty, admiring his integrity and, I admit, his muscular forearms. I think of my own job. I'm not getting rich selling pastries, and my clientele certainly isn't wealthy. So why is it that today, it feels as if the little kitchen at Lucchesi's Bakery and Deli is corrupting *my* soul?

"Did anyone famous ever come into the store?" Lucy asks, completely missing the point.

Gabe laughs good-naturedly, as if he's humoring a young child. "Several. I once sold a Ferrari to Sting." He returns his focus to me. "I found my true calling when I stumbled upon the inn. Of course it wasn't an inn at the time. It was a dilapidated farmhouse that had been vacant for two years. But still, I saw the potential."

His eyes twinkle as they penetrate mine, and it feels like he's sending me a cryptic message, telling me he sees the potential in me. I should probably warn him, I tried to find my potential last night and ended up puking on a guy.

"I knew that with the right love and care, the crumbling old house could become a jewel."

He smiles and Poppy's words return to me: *You don't have to die as that woman.* For the first time ever, I realize how much I want to find that woman I just might be.

It's four in the afternoon when we return to the SUV. Gabe opens the back door and Poppy steps forward.

"No, Aunt Poppy," I say. "You sit up front."

"Nonsense." She climbs into the backseat. "I've seen this land before."

Gabe helps buckle her seat belt, then opens the front passenger door.

"Shotgun!" Lucy calls.

Gabriele's eyes grow wide, as if he's expecting to find an actual shotgun on one of us American tourists.

"It's a figure of speech," Lucy says. "It means I'm going to sit —"

"Emilia?" he says, interrupting her. He

276

makes a sweeping gesture with his arm.

"Me? Up front?"

"Please."

I avoid Lucy's eyes as I climb into the passenger seat. I'm sure she's annoyed, but what am I supposed to do? I fasten my seat belt and turn to the backseat, offering her an apologetic smile. She rolls her eyes.

Soon, the city falls quiet. Traffic slows and the congested street morphs into a country road. Gabe slows the SUV each time we come to a hairpin turn.

"I say this road has more curves than Aphrodite."

I smile. "I was thinking Beyoncé."

He laughs and I puff with pride.

I gush at the landscape, a bucolic scene that makes me long to run through the fields. We pass hills and terraced vineyards, fields dotted with spools of hay, and, every now and then, a pasture with grazing cows or sheep. Tiny stone farmhouses spew smoke from their chimneys, and I conjure up a fictitious family, enjoying a meal at a long wooden table.

We come upon a quartet of cyclists. I roll down my window and wave, breathing in the fresh scent of straw and lavender. Gabe grins and lowers his window, too.

"I love the smell of this land, the feel of

the breeze on my face."

I spy a band of horses, lazily grazing on clover. I turn to the backseat to tell Poppy, but her eyes are closed. She looks so vulnerable with her chin against her chest and her wig slightly askew.

"You are a — ?" Gabriele's voice startles me, and once again I jump. He chuckles and reaches out a hand to me. "Please, Emilia, I am not dangerous."

I laugh. "I know! I'm sorry. What were you asking?"

"I wonder if you are a country girl."

"No." I grin. "But I am today."

"You must come back in the spring, when the fields are ablaze with red papaveri. It is spectacular to see them in the early morning, sprinkled with dew. And this field," he says, pointing to our left. "In the summer it is a blur of smiling sunflowers. It is impossible to be moody when you see their happy faces gazing up at the sun."

I smile, impressed with this masculine man's poetic descriptions.

We ride in silence, making our way up and down and around the voluptuous hillside. "What are those mountains called?" I ask, pointing to the horizon.

Gabe's eyes crinkle at the edges. "We call them hills."

I groan and shake my head. "Right. Hills. I'm from Brooklyn. Every hill looks like a mountain to me."

He nods. "I understand. Some people see the grandeur in ordinary things. I sense you are one of those people."

I mull it over, wondering if I am, and whether that's a good thing or a bad thing.

He reaches over a hand and pats my arm. "It is a wonderful trait," he answers for me.

Soon, the vehicle veers down a long dirt driveway. A shaggy black dog greets us midway, barking and wagging its tail as it races alongside the car.

"Ciao, Moxie," Gabe calls out the window.

We come to a stop in front of a charming two-story home built of irregular stones and occasional terra-cotta bricks.

"Here we are," Gabe says.

"It's beautiful," I say, and twist in my seat. Poppy sleeps with her mouth agape, looking childlike and frail. Lucy gently pats her cheek.

"Poppy, we're here."

She doesn't stir, and a surge of alarm goes through me. I watch, relieved when I see the soft rise and fall of her chest. "Maybe we should let her nap."

Lucy nods, and together we stare at Poppy. I suspect we're thinking the same thing. The traveling is too much for her. Our vibrant Poppy is fading.

Leaving the windows open, we quietly step from the car.

Terra-cotta roof tiles add a splash of color, and everywhere, bright flowers spill from clay pots. We wander down a path of cobblestones bordered with fragrant red roses. Above an old wooden door, a painted plaque announces *Casa Fontana.* I point to it.

"Fontana. That's my family name."

Gabe nods and opens the door. "Sì. This is Poppy's childhood home."

I stop short. "It is?"

"I did a complete renovation when I purchased it from her eight years ago."

"Wait . . . Poppy owned this place?"

"She bought it almost forty years ago, when the landlord was raising the rent yet again, and her papà could no longer afford it."

I rear back. "She bought it for her father?"

"That is right. She risked a great deal, taking a bank loan that size. If it had not been for Poppy, he and Signora Fontana would have had to live with relatives. She allowed them to stay in their home until they died."

I blink. "So she made peace with him."

Gabe nods. "She even paid for a nurse to

live here during Signor Fontana's final months."

Do Rosa and Dolphie know that Poppy saved their parents from homelessness? I gaze out at the cascading fields, more thoughtfully this time. I imagine young Rosa bringing water to Alberto and Bruno as they tilled the soil. I take in the creeping red rosebushes, the same flowers my great-nonna Fontana may have tended decades ago. But this house harbors ugly memories, too, memories that would be impossible to forgive. This is the farmhouse where Poppy's father forbade her from seeing Rico. Why would Poppy choose to return here now?

We enter through the kitchen, just as Rico did that fateful Sunday. The floors, probably the original stone, are polished to a glossy sheen. Cheery yellow and red tiles cover the walls, but double gas stoves, a Sub-Zero fridge, and chic new light fixtures give the room a modern, upscale feel. Even so, I can't help but picture my great-grandmother at her old stove, warning Poppy and Rico they're making a big mistake. A shudder goes through me.

"This way," Gabe says.

We pass through an arched doorway into the living room. The high ceiling, supported

281

with rough-sawn beams, gives the spacious room a rustic feel. A stone fireplace hunkers in the corner. Modern oil paintings cover one wall, and a floor-to-ceiling bookshelf another. Gabe's weathered leather furniture and overlapping rugs create a coziness I'm guessing was absent in the 1950s. My eyes land on a chair near the fireplace, and I picture Poppy's father rising from it, the Sunday when Rico came to call.

I turn when I hear footsteps, and gasp when Poppy creeps into the room. She looks like a caricature of the vibrant woman who appeared unannounced on my telephone two months ago. Her shoulders sag and blue-black circles hover beneath her eyes.

"Spettacolare!" She casts her gaze upon the room, taking in the modern art pieces alongside beautiful antiques. "The old place is looking *meraviglioso,* Gabriele." She pats down her wig. "Which is more than I can say for myself at the moment."

She laughs, but I can't manage a smile. How can she be so cheerful, standing in the home that once betrayed her, clinging to a body that's doing the same?

Poppy insists on climbing the stairs to her old attic bedroom, where Lucy and I will sleep the next three nights. The door squeaks when Gabe opens it, and all four of us manage to squeeze into the small space beneath the eaves. A tiny bathroom sits to the left, probably an addition. The polished wooden floors boast years of wear, but the colorful rugs brighten the place. Between a set of twin beds, an old casement window allows for much-needed sunlight and air. I imagine Poppy and Rosa staring out this very window, wishing on stars and sharing secrets.

Poppy studies the place but says nothing. Finally, she turns and makes her way back down the stairs. We drop our bags and follow.

Gabe holds Poppy's hand, leading her down the first-floor hallway to a bright orange bedroom he calls "the Poppy Suite." Fresh wildflowers adorn the bedside table. The tile floor is covered with a sisal rug, and a white down comforter hosts a flock of colorful pillows. A perfect room for my colorful aunt.

Poppy takes Gabe's face in her hands and kisses his cheeks. "Grazie," she says, then lowers herself onto the side of the bed. She lets out an exhausted sigh.

"Dinner will be at eight," Gabe says. "Is there anything I can get you? A cup of tea?"

She looks at Lucy, at Gabriele, at me. "I've got all I need."

I wait until Lucy's and Gabe's voices disappear down the hallway. "Aunt Poppy," I say, helping her off with her shoes. "I don't understand. You bought this home for your father? The same man who tried to ruin your life?"

She removes her wig and takes a bottle of water from the bedside table. "That's what families do — we take care of one another." She points to her purse. "My pills. They're in the side pocket."

I remove an orange vial, catching sight of the warning label. *Do not drive or operate machinery while taking this medication.* I shudder and shake a red capsule onto my palm, then hand it to Poppy.

"Did your papà ever apologize? Did your mother?"

"It wasn't necessary. I had forgiven them years ago." She swallows down the pill, and I help her settle against the pillow. "Love. Forgive. Love again. Forgive again. That, my dear girl, is the circle of love."

I'm stunned at her grace. "Did they ever try to come to America?"

"That was their plan. But you see, my father's sister, your great-great-aunt Blanca, died unexpectedly from a burst appendix."

I lift a blanket from the foot of the bed and cover her. "Still, their children were in

284

America. Why did his sister's death change their plans?"

"Papà's mother — my nonna Fontana — was still alive. Aunt Blanca was expected to care for her."

"But Blanca died suddenly," I say. "So your papà had to care for his mother?"

"Sì. And their dream of America vanished. It never once occurred to them that Blanca wouldn't be around. She had a budding relationship with a widowed farmer, but nobody thought much of it. She was healthy and six years younger than my father. They assumed she had nothing else to do besides care for her mother. After all, she was the single second daughter."

CHAPTER 29

EMILIA

Fading sunlight dapples our tiny room, and Lucy softly snores on the bed beside mine. Smells from the kitchen drift up the old staircase. I lower my notebook, grab my phone from the charger, and rise.

I find Gabe at the kitchen island, his shirtsleeves rolled up as he chops tomatoes. It's probably my imagination, but his face seems to brighten when he sees me.

"There you are." His full lips part, and I'd bet my life he was voted "best smile" in his senior class. He lifts a glass filled with a pretty red liquid. "Can I interest you in an aperitif?"

A cocktail now? Didn't we just have wine with lunch? "I'd love one!" I say.

"I shall make you our famous Negroni, created right here in Tuscany by Count Camillo Negroni, one hundred years ago."

"Perfect." I perch on a barstool and try

not to stare at his tanned forearms, with just the perfect smattering of dark hair, as he mixes gin and Campari.

"Did you enjoy a little siesta?" he asks, adding a jigger of sweet vermouth.

"I'm not much of a napper."

"Nor am I. It used to frustrate my nanny."

"You had a nanny?"

He lowers his gaze while he slices an orange, and an errant lock of dark hair spills onto his forehead. "My father was a successful jeweler. He and my mother traveled a great deal. My sister and I were left at home with any number of nannies. I describe my childhood as calm, cool, and neglected." He gives a sardonic laugh. "I often wondered why they even had children."

Despite his effort to sound lighthearted, there's an aching undercurrent in his tone. At once, I feel a certain kinship with this man who grew up without his mother, like me.

"I'm sorry. You must have been lonely."

He carries the drinks to my side of the counter and takes the stool beside mine. "You should not feel sorry for me. Look around. I am living in paradise. I could not have bought this inn without my inheritance." He raises his glass. *Salute.*

I sip my drink and mentally bombard him with questions. *Are you married? Do you have children? How do your lips taste?* "Delicious," I say — and quickly point to my Negroni.

"How about you, Emilia? You had a happy childhood, sì?"

"Yes," I say, reflexively. But today, I take a moment to examine it. "My mother died when I was two. I have a recurring memory of her." I look out the kitchen window, where the setting sun ignites the fields in orange and gold. "She was at the stove, stirring something. I remember her eyes, gazing down on me with pure kindness. She set down the spoon and scooped me into her arms and hugged me so tightly I could feel her heart beating against mine, as if we were one person, not two." I look up and shake my head. "Of course it's probably not a real memory at all."

"But it is real, Emilia." He's turned to me now, his face so close that I can see a tiny scar on his jaw. "That feeling is primal, as if instinctually, we are born knowing of this mother's love. And when it is absent, it leaves us with a thirst that can never be quenched."

He lowers his eyes and shakes his head. "I

am sorry. I did not mean to get philosophical."

"No," I say, touching his arm. "It's fine. It's good. You've articulated so beautifully what I've felt my entire life."

His gaze falls on mine, refusing to budge. His dark eyes are shadowed, and I have to resist the urge to run my hand over the dark stubble on his beautiful cheek.

"Need any help?"

I leap from my stool, my heart thundering. Lucy stands at the kitchen entrance, dressed in black jeans and red heels, wearing the most curious look on her face, as if she's stumbled onto a mystifying experiment and she's hypothesizing about the smoking electrical current she's witnessing.

A jazz ballad floats on the warm evening air. Lucy and I prepare a table in the courtyard beneath a pergola of twisted wisteria vines. We set out the first course, antipasto. Cured meats and fresh cheeses, artichoke hearts and Leccino olives dress the table. Poppy comes out just as Gabe opens a bottle of Chianti.

"Lovely," she says, but her voice is strained. And she's moving so slowly, even after her nap.

My phone chimes. It's Daria again. I'd

missed an earlier call, too, when my phone was dead.

Lucy holds out her glass. "Cheers to you, Gabriele," she says, in her most seductive voice.

I send Dar a quick text before turning off my phone. Call u tomorrow. xo

"Salute," Gabe says. When he clinks his glass to mine, my hand trembles. He winks. "No need to be nervous, Emilia."

I turn away, clutching my glass with both hands.

"Where is Sofia?" Poppy asks, looking around. "She is here tonight, yes? And the boys?"

My heart skids to a halt. Sofia? Kids?

"Sì," Gabe says. "You will see her tomorrow. She insists we dine in peace tonight."

My face flames, and I'm grateful for evening's cover. I was flirting with him. How could I not have known?

"Nonsense!" Poppy says. "Go get them. Remind her that age trumps beauty."

Gabe shakes his head and laughs. "You are as stubborn as ever, Poppy." He rises and travels down a flagstone path to a tiny cottage.

A moment later he returns, his arm draped around a twenty-something woman with a short, funky haircut, wearing high-waisted jeans and a sleeveless blouse. Two curly-haired boys let go of her hand, and the oldest runs to Poppy.

Poppy grabs the boy in a hug.

"Franco! Look how you've grown."

"I am four and a half," Franco says.

"A boy who is almost five deserves a lucky coin." A shiny penny seems to appear from out of nowhere. Poppy tucks it into Franco's pocket.

"Dante is only two," he says. "He has to wait for his coin, right, Mamma?"

"Sì, Franco," his mother says, rubbing the little one's head.

Poppy opens her arms. "My beautiful Sofia!" She kisses both the woman's cheeks, then looks down at the younger boy, who's clutching his mother's leg, his thumb in his mouth.

"Hello, my friend." She goes to lift him, but can't get him off the ground. She's too weak. My heart breaks. I look away, hoping to spare Poppy her dignity.

"Meet Sofia," Gabe says.

Lucy reaches out a hand. "Nice to meet you, Sofie, I mean *Sofia.*"

Sofia laughs. "I like this name, Sofie. You may use it, if you like."

"Cool." Lucy leans in to examine Sofia's bare upper arm, where a wreath of roses forms the feminist symbol of Venus. "Nice tat."

"Grazie," Sofia says and lightly touches the symbol. "A reminder that females are strong and capable, something women in America accept naturally."

"Not all of us, I'm afraid." Lucy's introspection surprises me. Then she jabs me in the ribs. "Meet my cousin Emmie, a perfect example of a timid American woman."

"Thanks, Luce," I say, and roll my eyes. I take Sofia's hand in mine, my head still trying to come to terms with my silly heart. Of course Gabriele is married. Of course his wife's a natural beauty, with big dark eyes and a pretty smile. And she's young. And nice. Damn her. "It's lovely to meet you. Your inn is beautiful."

She smiles. "My brother's inn. But thank you."

"Brother?" The word charges from my mouth before I have time to censor it. Over Sofia's shoulder, I see Gabe's eyes twinkle with humor. I turn to Sofia. "So you — you're Gabe's sister?"

She nods.

"Shall we eat?" Gabe says and winks at me again.

My heart grows three sizes. Whatever made me think winks were creepy?

Gabe lights a fire in the stone pit and the night becomes golden. The seven of us gather at the long wooden table for our antipasto. Lucy sits between Franco and Dante, teasing them by stealing their noses. They squeal each time she displays their nose — her thumb caught between her fingers.

"Do it again!" Franco insists.

Sofia pats his head. "Enough, little man. Let Lucy eat in peace."

Gabe clears the dishes and returns with steaming bowls of homemade ribollita, a delicious Tuscan soup made with beans and bread and fresh vegetables. More wine is poured. Voices overlap. Stars collect in the sky. The breeze carries the scent of grapes and lavender and smoke from the fire. I soak in the sweet scene, knowing this day . . . this moment . . . is one I shall re-create many times, both in memory and on paper.

A star slips from the sky. "Make a wish!" Poppy cries. "Ask for it, whatever it is your heart desires."

Tonight, my cousin doesn't argue. She lifts her face to the sky and closes her eyes.

I make my wish for Poppy and Rico. And then, for the first time, I make a wish for myself, too.

Later, when we're sipping sweet iced wine,

I whisper to Lucy in the moonlight, "What did you wish for, on the falling star?"

She pretends not to hear.

CHAPTER 30

EMILIA

Day Five
Trespiano

I wake Friday morning, surprised to see Lucy pulling a shirt over her head. She looks especially pretty this morning, with her hair gathered in one of my clips. Her face, barren of makeup, shines.

"You're up early," I say.

"Why waste the day?"

She disappears into the tiny bathroom and I burrow beneath the covers, expecting she'll spend the next thirty minutes applying makeup. I'm stunned when she slips from the room two minutes later with only a touch of gloss on her lips, smelling of toothpaste.

"See you downstairs," she says. Just before the door closes, she pokes her head into the room. "And don't touch that braid. It looks even better with all those loose hairs around your face."

After a long and luxurious bath, I wrap myself in a towel and scan the blouses hanging in the tiny closet. My clothes look dated and dull, like Nonna's faded wallpaper. When I get home, I'll buy something new. It won't be a short skirt or a see-through blouse, but something fun and stylish, something that reflects who I want to be. This morning I opt for a pair of black leggings and a white blouse that hits just below my hips, my only decent option.

I dry my toothbrush and place it in a cup. From the vanity, Lucy's makeup bag taunts me. I hesitate, then reach inside. Carefully, I open a compact. I take a deep breath and fish a long-handled makeup brush from the bag. Using the slightest touch, I dip the brush into the powder. I lean into the mirror and stroke crystals of copper across my cheeks and nose. Instantly, I look sun-kissed and healthy.

My gaze zeros in on the scar below my lip. I reach for my cover stick but stop myself. The jagged blue line isn't telling me I'm ugly and unworthy anymore. It's telling me I'm brave. I dab my lips with gloss, place my new glasses on my face, and step back.

"Warmer," I whisper to my reflection.

"You're getting warmer."

I rush downstairs and throw open the French doors. Thick white clouds muddle the sky, and I breathe in the fresh Tuscan air. Poppy sits on the patio looking like a little girl at the grown-ups' table. A bowl of fresh fruit sits untouched as she works a crossword puzzle.

"Good morning." I kiss her soft cheek, surprised by the heat of her skin. "How do you feel today?"

"Peachy," she says and gives me a once-over. "Aren't you fetching!"

I smile. At the last minute, I swapped my bra for a black tank, and left my blouse unbuttoned an extra two inches. "Really? I look okay?"

"A-OK." She pulls a bright pink scarf from her neck. "Bend down, dear."

"No. I can't take your scarf."

"Please. It's making me claustrophobic today."

I lean in and she snakes the scarf into a casual coil. "There you go."

I touch her forehead, once more alarmed by how warm she feels. "We should visit a doctor today."

She cocks her head. "You're feeling ill?" I give her a look and she bats her hand. "A doctor would only confirm what I already know. Who needs that?" She returns to her puzzle, end of discussion.

I should insist we go to a doctor, but she'll never allow it. I squeeze her shoulder as I step away.

A flagstone path leads me to the terrace, where Lucy and Sofia sit on chaise lounges. Sofia wears a long flowing skirt and a denim blouse tied at the waist. Her short hair is pulled away from her face with a headband, revealing a trio of earrings in each lobe. She smiles when she sees me.

"Emilia! Join us."

I perch on the side of Lucy's chaise and sip my coffee, listening as they resume their conversation.

"We —" Sofia looks at me and quickly fills me in. "My ex and I — split two months after Dante was born. My brother invited us to live here, with him, so he could be part of his nephews' lives."

"Do you work?" Lucy asks.

She shakes her head. "Our father made sure my brother and I were well provided for in our adulthood, perhaps to atone for his absenteeism in our youth." She shrugs. "That is a story for another day. But for now, I enjoy the freedom of raising my boys. And during the busy season, I help Gabriele with the cooking." She tips her head.

"How about you?"

Lucy tells Sofia about waiting tables at Rulli's. "It's a job," she says. "Not exactly a career. Someday I'd like a place of my own, a business I can pass on, you know, to my kids or whatever." Her cheeks turn pink, as if she's embarrassed to have shared her dream, and I've never loved my cousin more. Is that what she wished for on the falling star?

At the far side of the lawn, the door to the guest cottage pushes open. Little Dante appears in his pajamas, followed by Franco. They look in both directions until they spot Sofia.

"Mamma!" they cry, charging toward her.

Sofia leaps from the chaise and meets them in the soft grass. She squats down and they fall into her open arms.

"My little men!" she says, kissing them both.

Lucy and I watch as the two boys climb atop their mother like she's their jungle gym. She topples over and the three of them scream with laughter.

"That," Lucy whispers to me, keeping her eyes on the trio. "That's what I wished for."

My throat seizes.

"That's a lovely wish, Luciana." I turn to see Aunt Poppy coming up behind us. "I wonder what it is that's keeping you from it."

Lucy's eyes meet Poppy's, and I'm guessing she's got a dozen blazing replies at the ready. *I haven't found a boyfriend, never mind a husband. Thanks to Em, I'm still in the dating trenches. Perhaps if you'd break the damn curse, I'd have a chance!*

But Lucy seems to be pondering the question in earnest. "I'm a single waitress. Not exactly mom material."

"What you do isn't important," Poppy says. "It's what you're *going* to do that matters." She takes Lucy by the shoulders and gently pivots her toward Sofia's little family. "Believe in your dream, my dear. It's possible."

After a lunch of Caprese sandwiches — crusty bread topped with fresh mozzarella, juicy tomatoes, and basil — I gently suggest that Poppy take a nap. She huffs, as if the notion of a siesta were ludicrous. "Why lie in a bedroom when you can sit in the park?" I can't help but notice how raspy her voice sounds. "Nature is the best healer, don't you agree?"

Gabriele grins. "Okay, stubborn one." He grabs his car keys from the counter. "We will go to my favorite park — the Bardini

Garden. You will love it." He glances over at me. "I believe you will, too, Emilia."

My heart does a little jig.

"Sounds like a plan," Lucy says, coming up beside me.

"I must get sunscreen for the boys," Sofia says.

Twenty minutes later, all seven of us pile into Gabe's SUV and head to Florence. This time, Lucy sits up front with Gabriele. I have to tamp down a flicker of jealousy.

We enter the bustling city, where buses and taxis and cars jockey with scooters and bicycles. "The statues in the park are magnificent," Gabe says. "And you will notice all kinds of birds — rock pigeons, wood pigeons, blackbirds."

"Any rides?" Lucy asks. "Ferris wheels? Roller coasters?"

He laughs, as if she were joking. "No, Lucy. It is not Disneyland."

We cross the Arno River, where a single rower sweeps the sleepy water with his oar. The city quiets. Gabe parks along a wide boulevard. Poppy leans against me as we walk toward the park entrance. Despite the day's warm temperature, she's wearing her bulkiest sweater, and still her hand is like ice in mine. Fear prickles my skin. Earlier, she felt too warm.

Sofia and Lucy stroll ahead of us, trying to keep up with Franco and Dante. "Slow down, little men," Sofia calls. They don't listen. Franco runs full force, his shoelace trailing behind him. Seconds later, he's planted facedown on the pavement, wailing.

"You are okay," Sofia says, examining his bloody knee. But Franco isn't convinced. His cries grow louder, and soon Dante joins in.

"Ah, not you, too, Dante," Gabe says, bending down. "What have I told you? Vernasco men do not cry."

Lucy huffs and elbows her way to Dante. "Don't worry," she says, squatting down beside the boy. "Your brother is okay." She turns to Sofia. "You go ahead. I'll hang with these two."

Sofia looks at Lucy as if she'd just offered to donate a kidney. "You would do that?"

"I'm not a huge fan of statues and birds." She tousles Dante's hair. "And I'm dying for some gelato. How about you?"

Dante squeals. Franco jumps to his feet, his knee miraculously healed. "Me, too?"

Lucy slaps him a high five. "Absolutely!"

Sofia crosses her arms. For the longest time, she simply smiles at Lucy and the boys. Finally, she turns to Gabe. "Shall we meet back here at four?"

"You are not coming inside? You love the Bardini."

My cousin shoos her away. "Go. Have fun. I've got this."

Sofia shakes her head. "Today, I prefer gelato."

I watch, curious, as my cousin and her new friend Sofia disappear down the street alongside the boys. She's passing up a day with Gabriele?

"Your cousin is very sweet," Gabe says, his eyes lingering on the happy quartet.

Cute, yes. Funny, definitely. But sweet is not an adjective I'd typically use to describe Luciana Fontana. An uncharitable thought strikes me before I can extinguish it. *Might my cousin be trying to win over the boys, in hopes that she'll also win over their uncle?*

Gabe and I escort Poppy up a cobblestone walk, where young couples stroll hand in hand and children race across the perfectly manicured lawns. I smile at a group of elderly gentlemen playing bocce ball. Poppy clutches my arm, and every now and then I hear her wheeze.

"Shall we rest for a bit?" Gabriele asks her.

"Why? Are you tired?"

He catches my eye and we smile.

We arrive at a lush green garden adorned with flowers and fountains and gorgeous sculptures.

"Belvedere Terrace," Gabriele says. "My favorite spot."

Ancient oaks and cypress trees dapple the sunlight. Overhead, blackbirds and robins and pigeons chatter. Poppy clasps her hands. "The majesty of Mamma Nature!" She lifts her face and inhales deeply. "However did I miss this place?"

"It is a hidden gem, sì?" We settle Poppy onto a concrete bench overlooking her beloved city. Below, the Arno River swirls like a serpent. Red clay rooftops pepper the landscape. I spy the massive cupola of the Florence Cathedral, or Duomo, alongside Giotto's famous bell tower. With Poppy snuggled between us, Gabe begins to tell of the garden's history. "This place was once a private estate. These gardens only opened to the public in 2005."

Before he finishes the sentence, Poppy's head drops onto her chest. He steals a glance at me. "I must learn to be more engaging."

I smile, certain that would be impossible. "She should be in bed," I whisper.

"She refuses to miss a moment. I suspect we could all learn from her *joie de vivre,* as the French say. Her joy of life."

Together we admire the city. Gone is the traffic and other noise — save for the birds, chirping in the distance. I rise and shield my eyes from the afternoon sun, admiring a breathtaking view of the Florentine cityscape. Gabe comes up beside me and places a hand on my back. A shiver runs through me.

"This place is magical," I say.

"I was hoping you would like it. I find the gardens here very romantic. Much quieter than the more popular parks." His eyes find mine. "But that is just me. I prefer understated."

My face heats, and I can think of no reply. He meanders onto the lawn and lowers himself onto the soft grass. "Come," he says, patting a spot beside him. "Sit with me."

My heart pounds in my ears. As I sink onto the grass, I lose my balance and nearly crush his thigh on my landing. "Sorry," I say, horrified. I scoot over. "I'm not the most graceful."

He spreads his long legs out in front of him and leans back on his elbows, his eyes twinkling with humor. "You, Emilia, are what I call easeful."

"Easeful? Like peaceful?"

"Much the same, sì. On the other hand,

there is Lucy." He chuckles. "I sense she can be very . . . turbulent."

I pluck a blade of grass and gaze out at the city. "It's not her fault. She's the second daughter, like me." Without intending to, I divulge the Fontana Second-Daughter Curse.

"So you see, our ridiculous family myth is making her crazy. All she really wants is a husband and a family, and she's terrified it'll never happen."

"And you?" he asks. "Do you believe you are cursed?"

"Cursed?" I give him a smart-aleck grin. "You think I'm that naïve?"

He doesn't laugh. His dark eyes bore into mine, seeking the truth. My breath catches. This is where I say, *No, of course I don't believe. Never did.* I wrap my arms around my knees and stare off into the distance.

"I didn't believe at first. Not for a long time."

"And then?" His gentle voice acts as truth serum.

"And then something happened with this guy I was seeing in college, the first real boyfriend I'd ever had."

He gives me a knowing smile. "Your first heartbreak. That will make anyone feel cursed."

"We'd both gone home at winter break. Liam invited me to Delaware for New Year's Eve. His best friend was throwing a big party. My nonna forbade me to go, but I snuck out while she was at work. New Castle was a two-hour drive from Bensonhurst, a straight shot down I-95. Daria loaned me her car — a cool red Jeep she called Rita.

"I was excited — and super nervous — to meet his parents and his little sister. But they were really great. Anyway, that night, as Liam and I set out for the party, the rain was changing to ice. His mom freaked out about us driving in the weather, but Liam was determined to go. We decided I'd drive — Daria's Jeep had better tires than Liam's car."

I raise my head to the sky. A puffy white cloud skates past.

"I never saw it coming. One moment we were laughing and singing along with Rihanna, the next minute the car was spinning, swerving wildly. I couldn't control the steering wheel. We were skidding into the other lane. And then nothing."

My heart is hammering now. Gabriele's hand closes over mine.

"I woke when the paramedics were loading Liam onto the ambulance. I tried to call his name, but my voice was this pathetic little croak. I turned to the medic who was examining my leg. He shook his head, as if reading my thoughts. 'Say your prayers,' he said."

Gabe runs a hand over his face. "Oh, *cara mia.* I am so sorry."

I take a deep breath, images I've tried to forget coming back to me now. The blood on the Jeep's dashboard. The sight of Liam's lifeless hand, dangling from the gurney.

"He suffered massive internal injuries. His family arrived at the hospital. I swear his mom had aged ten years. While Liam was in surgery, I called Daria. I was crying so hard, I could barely speak. When she finally figured out what had happened, she let out a wail. I'll never forget it. She sounded like a wild animal. 'That fucking curse!'

"My sister's no saint, but it was the only time I've heard her use the f-word. At first, I didn't understand. But then it hit me. Daria, my biggest cheerleader, the one person who had always promised me there was no curse, actually believed in it."

I close my eyes, a chill coming over me, just as it did eleven years ago, when the cause and effect of my cursed state settled in. "Until Daria said that, it never occurred to me that Liam's near-death condition had anything to do with my curse. He and I had gotten too close, and the curse was determined to stop us. Just as it had done for centuries."

Gabe's arms encircle me. "*Carissima,* surely you were not responsible for his accident."

"Over the next four days, Liam grew weaker. He was unresponsive. His organs were shutting down. On the fifth day, I went to the hospital chapel. I got down on my knees and begged God to let Liam live. I swore that if he spared Liam's life, I'd break off the relationship. I promised I'd never see him again."

"But Emilia, this makes no sense."

"The very next day, Liam opened his eyes. By the weekend, he was answering questions by squeezing our hands. Ten days later, he was breathing on his own.

"As soon as he was well enough, I broke up with him in the gentlest of ways."

Gabriele shakes his head. "Even though you loved this young man."

I watch a robin circle an oak tree. "Which is why I couldn't continue the relationship. The risk was too great. He was a beautiful person. I could've killed him."

"But you broke his heart."

"He was very civil about the whole thing.

We would have fizzled out sooner or later anyway. My uncle Bruno got sick, and I ended up transferring to Brooklyn College so I could help at the store."

"And of course your friend lived?"

I nod. "He made a full recovery. We talked and sent text messages for a while. But I kept my promise. I never saw him again."

Gabe takes my head in his hands and gently smooths my hair. "It is simply *coincidenza*. This accident — his recovery — these had nothing to do with that preposterous curse."

I lower my gaze, but Gabriele lifts my chin with his finger. "Please tell me you believe this."

I look into his eyes. "I believe this," I say.

And I realize how very good I've become at making believe I don't believe.

CHAPTER 31

EMILIA

Day Six
Trespiano

Saturday morning, we gather around the old wooden table, feasting on a breakfast of hard rolls and cheeses, fresh prosciutto and melon. Gabriele claps his hands. "Today we will tour the countryside. Everybody in?"

"Sure," I say.

"I've got the kids," Sofia says. She looks at Lucy. "But you have fun."

"I'll stay back with you guys," Lucy says.

She's choosing not to go with Gabe? Again? She's definitely up to something.

"How about you, Poppy?" Gabriele asks.

She coughs and shakes her head. "I have much to do here, preparing for Ravello."

A ripple of fear passes through me. The woman who never says no is begging off today. She's ill — seriously ill. I should insist

311

she go to the doctor, but for what? My aunt has a terminal illness. There is no pill that will cure it.

I bend down and kiss her cheek. "I'll stay with you."

"You most certainly will not!"

"Then promise you'll rest today. And eat some fruit. Don't forget to wear your sweater."

She waves me off. "Don't worry about me. I'm saving my energy for Ravello."

It dawns on me as I follow Gabe around the front of the house, he and I will be alone. All day.

"We can cancel the tour," I say, offering him an escape clause and praying he won't take it.

"And break my heart?" He holds out his hand. "Come." He leads me into an old stone garage. "With just the two of us, we can take the Vespas. It is best to see the countryside on two wheels."

I freeze.

"Go on," he says, gesturing to a pretty aqua Vespa. "Sit."

My temples throb. I creep toward the motorbike as if it's a caged beast. *I will not ruin this day.* I place my shoe on the footrest. Immediately, my body tenses.

"You do not like this one?"

"No. It's beautiful." I back away from the bike and take a deep breath. "But I don't drive. Not anymore."

He tips his head and studies me. I turn away, feeling silly and cowardly and utterly petrified. Finally, he holds out his hand and leads me over to a shiny black Ducati. "Then you will be my passenger." He pats the seat. "Hop aboard."

He smiles as he fastens my helmet, then settles himself in front of me. My thighs press against his; my arms clutch his waist. He turns his head.

"You have ridden on the back of a motorcycle in the US, yes?"

A surge of terror and excitement shimmies up my spine. "No. Never."

He tips his head and laughs. God, even his nostrils are sexy. "*Buonissimo!* I am honored to give you your first ride. I promise, it will be thrilling. You will be hooked for life."

Thrilling doesn't adequately describe my day with Gabe. I try to sketch each moment into my memory, so that one day I can call upon this myriad of emotions when I'm writing a beautiful scene about a pair of young lovers.

He handles the motorcycle with great

skill, but still it unnerves me every time we come to a hairpin curve, or when he overtakes a rumbling motor coach a mile long. Every now and then he leans back and calls to me. "Everything okay back there?" Or, "How is my girl holding up?"

I can't keep the smile from my face. We pass groves of olive trees, fields of lavender. The wind grazes my skin, and I've never felt so alive, so free.

We stop for lunch at a hilltop vineyard. Gabe parks the bike beneath a tree and helps me off. From the stone building beyond the house, a giant man appears. His long black hair is snarled and he walks with a limp.

"Gabriele!" he calls.

"Giuseppe Natoli!" Gabe rushes to greet him and pulls the big guy into a hug. "Meet my beautiful friend Emilia. She is here from New York."

Giuseppe takes my hand and kisses it. "*Benvenuta a casa mia.* Welcome to my home."

Giuseppe leads us to an intimate patio overlooking terraced hills of twisted grapevines. Soft music plays in the background. A single table sits in the middle of the stone patio, topped with a red linen cloth and a vase of sunflowers. It is set for two. Gabe pulls the chair out for me.

"Just as you had hoped?" Giuseppe asks.

"Perfetto," Gabe tells him.

I freeze. Gabe arranged this . . . for me?

He squeezes my shoulder as he moves to his chair, and my entire body tingles.

He's right, I think to myself. This is perfection.

"Wine is a family tradition here in Tuscany," he tells me over lunch. "This vineyard has been in the Natoli family for four generations. We are drinking their Chianti Classico."

"It's delicious," I say, embarrassed by my unsophisticated descriptor.

With his thumb, he swipes a drop of wine from my lip, then places it in his mouth. *"Sì. Delizioso."*

Another flutter lets loose in me.

After lunch, we continue our trek through the countryside, stopping every now and then to explore a neighboring village or visit another of his friends' vineyards. Always, Gabe is welcomed like family.

The sky is tinged with violet when the motorcycle makes its way toward home. I knew the day would end, but still, my spirits dip. Eventually the country fields become dotted with houses, and the horizon reveals the outline of buildings; I'm puzzled when

Gabe slows the bike on the outskirts of Florence and finds a parking spot on the street. He pulls off his helmet.

"No reason to stop when we are having such fun, do you agree?"

"One hundred percent!"

He takes my hand, and together we stroll through streets narrow as bike paths, lined with boutique shops and shoe stores, gelato counters and restaurants. Smells of roast lamb and garlic spill onto the streets, softly lit by streetlights. We stop at a leather shop and I splurge on a pair of gloves for Daria. The beautiful woman behind the counter eyes Gabe as she rings up my purchase. A surge of pride wells in me. Is this really me, Emilia Josephina Fontana Lucchesi Antonelli? Yes, I think it is.

It's dark when we finish our dinner, a feast prepared by Gabe's friend Claudio, in a tiny restaurant hidden in the basement of an old art gallery. The evening air is cooler when we step outside, and Gabe drapes an arm around my shoulders. We wander through Piazza della Signoria, just as my beautiful aunt and her yellow-haired love once did. A throng of teenagers laugh and chatter as they dart past us. Perfectly coiffed old women, dressed in dark coats and flat shoes, promenade arm in arm, the evening ritual of lifelong friends, I suspect.

We stop in front of the statue of David. I study the naked shepherd boy as he must have appeared when sizing up his opponent, the giant Goliath. His face is stamped with determination, his body exquisite. The genius is staggering. I choke up unexpectedly, awed by the talent of Michelangelo, my fellow human.

"This is a replica," Gabe tells me, taking hold of my hand. "For protection, the real statue was moved to the Accademia Gallery in 1873. I will take you tomorrow if you'd like to see it."

I shake my head. "We're leaving in the morning."

"Ah. Yes. We will save it for your next visit." He squeezes my hand. A bubble of joy rises, so immense it threatens to lift me off my feet.

We move on. Young people hustle past, speaking languages I don't know. Their gazes seem to linger on us, as if we — Gabe and I — project some sort of energy.

A voice in the distance catches my attention. A note here. A chord there. Gabe hears it, too. Without a word, we quicken our pace, the melancholy drawl of a violin luring us nearer. Ahead, people have gathered in front of the Loggia dei Lanzi, a covered open-air space on the piazza filled with statues and marble inscriptions. Gabe pulls me through the crowd. Beneath one of three wide arches, a young man in a T-shirt and jeans glides his bow across his violin strings.

"Rico," I whisper and put a hand to my lips.

Beside him, a pretty redhead waits with her eyes closed, swaying to the music. Finally, she opens her mouth, and an angel's voice rings out, gilding every note from Schubert's opus.

Ave Maria.

Chills blanket me. The entire square seems to still. People draw near, silently making their way to the sound of magic. The woman's voice reverberates on the tile flooring. A bird passes overhead, making its way into the night, its wings beating in time with the music. In the background, even the statues seem to listen, statues created hundreds of years ago by then little-known sculptors.

"Ave Maria," she sings. *"Gratia plena."*

My eyes well. Gabe pulls me to his chest, where I fit perfectly. He wraps his arms around me and rests his chin on my head.

"Ave, Ave, Dominus."

Her voice is heartbreaking and haunting.

The song reaches a crescendo. Tears spill down my cheeks. She hits her last note. The music fades. For a moment, the entire square falls silent. Then, it erupts in applause.

"Brava!" I cry through a haze of tears. "Brava!"

I turn to Gabe. He's cheering, too, his face wet with tears. He wraps me in his arms, but neither of us speak. We don't need to. As my wise aunt once said, there are no words when one has witnessed magic.

It's midnight. The bike's engine quiets, giving rise to the din of night — a dog howling in the distance, the chirping of cicadas. Gabe leads me up the walk, his hand in mine. The house creaks its welcome when we step inside. An amber light shadows the kitchen. Without a word, we make our way toward the staircase.

My chest fills with a dozen clamoring hummingbirds. Together, we climb the stairs. Do I assume I'm going to his room? We're almost to the landing. Or should I continue up the stairs to my room in the attic?

We reach the landing and Gabe stops. He turns to me. I can't breathe. In the darkness, his eyes seem to question mine. He finds a stray lock of my hair and spirals a curl around his finger. My heart thunders. His hand slips behind my neck. He pulls me toward him, his breath grazing my cheek. His mouth inches toward mine. I'm in agony until, finally, our lips meet.

My head swims and my mouth fills with the sweet taste of port wine. A ripple goes through me. I step back.

"I'm a little out of practice," I say, and give a little chortle.

"It is okay, Emilia." He pulls me against him, but I put a hand on his chest.

"Seriously. It's been, like, eleven years."

"That is fine."

"I've only been with one —"

He silences me with his finger. "We can discuss this later, sì?"

Finally I know what the fuss is about. All my life, I thought sex was overrated. My brief dalliance with Liam was nice — really nice. But being with Gabriele is magical. I pray one day Lucy finds this.

I lie in the crook of Gabe's arm, the pad of his thumb absently grazing my arm. He kisses the top of my head. My throat squeezes shut. I never knew . . . I never let myself realize . . . how deeply I was missing the sound of a heartbeat next to mine.

"You are a woman of great passion, Emilia. I only wonder how you could survive eleven years without love in your life. Your heart is so full it is spilling over."

I swallow hard. Later this morning, I will leave this beautiful Tuscan innkeeper. Poppy, Lucy, and I will be on the Amalfi Coast by nightfall. Gabe and I live on different continents. It's likely I'll never see him again. I knew this when I opened my heart. But already I am homesick for him.

"I'm going to miss you," I whisper, smoothing the hair on his belly.

"I will miss you, too, my flame." He pulls me closer. "You see, most people create a spark. Sparks are fine. But you, my love, are a flame." He raises himself onto an elbow, so that he's looking down at me. "You lit a fire in me, Emilia. And I shall never, ever forget you."

I smile in the darkness. Aunt Poppy promised she'd break the curse. I never should have doubted her.

We make love again, this time more slowly, more thoughtfully. I allow myself to explore his body and welcome his touch, which rocks my entire soul. When we finish, Gabriele collapses against the pillow and closes his eyes. His breathing slows.

I wait. What am I supposed to do now?

I've just had the best sex of my life and I'm wound tighter than a Timex. I feel like I'm at a sleepover, and I'm the only one who wants to party.

"Gabriele," I whisper in the dark.

"Hmm."

"Did you enjoy that?"

His hand falls limply on my arm. "Sì. Very much."

A smile takes hold of my face and won't let go. "Should I go back to my room now?" I whisper, half out of courtesy, half to hear him beg me to stay.

"Sì," he says. "I will see you in the morning, *carissima.*"

"Oh. Okay."

Seconds later, deep, contented inhalations come from his slack mouth, ebbing and flowing like ocean tides. Soon, the sun will appear. I pad barefoot across the wooden floor. Gabe is right. There are children here, after all.

His bedroom door creaks when I open it. Just before stepping out, I peer back into the dusky room that still smells of us.

"Grazie, Gabriele," I whisper. I turn, leaving his bedroom door ajar on the off chance he'll call me back to his arms.

Lucy stirs when I cross the floor. Very

slowly, I slide into my bed, trying not to wake her. My head reaches the pillow. From the opposite bed, Lucy's hand rises. She gropes the bedside table until she finds the clock.

"It's two in the morning. Shouldn't you have a tongue in your ear about now?"

I can't help but laugh. "Oh, Luce. I will never forget this day. Gabe is incredible."

She groans and rolls over. "Then why the hell didn't you dock the boat?"

"Dock what boat?"

"You should have finished the job, Em. Gabe's a guy. Guys expect that."

I could confess that I've just had the best sex of my life . . . twice in one night. She'd probably be impressed. But I don't. That's my secret, and Gabe's.

"Good night, Luce."

It's still dark when I wake again. I glance at the bedside clock: 4:13. Thoughts of last night send a rush of heat through my body. I close my eyes and grin. I did it. I fell in love. Or as close to love as I've ever come. Pride and excitement and the purest of joys rise in me.

When will Gabe and I see each other again? Christmas is just two months away. I'll invite him to New York. My chest flutters with anticipation. I feel like an Italian Jennifer Aniston. I'll decorate Emville and make all my favorite holiday treats. I'll get a real Christmas tree this year. We'll pick it out together. Dad will love Gabe. Nonna . . . she'll tolerate him. But Daria will be thrilled. Lucy and Mimi will be free!

I shake my head. I'm getting ahead of myself. I need to put on the brakes. But Poppy's right — it's possible. The curse — the one I actually, *foolishly* embraced — is lifting, just as she promised.

I roll onto my side. Do I dare wake Lucy? I want to tell her everything. She was right. I was checked out. I never gave love a fair shot.

In the darkness, I try to make out her figure.

"Luce?"

Her bed looks flat. And the room is strangely quiet. She's not snoring tonight. I prop myself onto an elbow, my eyes slowly adjusting to the silvery moonlight.

"Lucy?" I say, louder this time.

I pull back the covers and grab my glasses. My heart speeds. I rise and flip on the bedside lamp.

Lucy's bed is empty.

My gut turns inside out. No. No. She would never do that. I rub my temples and spin in a circle. She must be in the bathroom. Or maybe she's downstairs already.

But the bathroom light is off. My cousin does not rise at four in the morning.

My stomach churns. I'm going to be sick.

I let myself out of the room. Quietly, I tiptoe down the steps. Never have I more desperately wanted to believe my instincts are wrong. *Please be open!* I reach the end of the hall.

The door to Gabe's bedroom, the one I purposely left open, is closed.

Chapter 32

Emilia

Day Seven
Trespiano

I yank my suitcase from the closet and pitch it onto the bed. I will not cry. I throw open the dresser drawer and heave my clothes into the suitcase. I need to get out of here. I cannot bear to see Gabe. How will I ever forgive Lucy? We've got forty-eight more hours of this damn trip. The forty-eight most crucial hours.

My hand hits something hard buried beneath my leggings. I lift my notebook from the drawer. I haven't written in two days. I hold it to my chest like my neglected best friend. Then I reach for my pen.

I shove the suitcase aside, making space for myself on the bed. Propped against the headboard, I write fast and furiously. Words flow with greater clarity, deeper emotion, more honesty than I've ever dared put on paper. I fill one page. Then another. By the time Lucy steps through the doorway two hours later, I've written three chapters of a new book. This time, it's not a happily-ever-after romance.

Lucy's hair is a tangled mess — sexy bed-head, to be exact. She's wearing her pajamas — cotton shorts that come up to her ass and a tank top that's so tight it may as well be stamped on.

"Em?" she says and takes a step back. She smiles, but not before a flash of guilt strikes. "You're up early." The girl who barely speaks before noon is cheerful today. "And you've already started packing." She gestures to the suitcase. "Could you be any more organized?" She plops down on her bed and looks around. "I don't want to leave this place."

I slap shut my notebook. "I'm sure you don't!"

She looks at me and scowls, then her face falls and she looks away. "Oh, shit. You followed me?"

I clench my jaw, not trusting myself to speak.

She hangs her head. "Don't be mad at me, Em. Please."

My anger erupts. "Right. You expect me

to give you my blessing? God, you're disgusting."

Her face flushes. "Nothing happened, I swear. You've got to believe me, Em. It's freaking me out. And I was hoping maybe, just maybe, you'd be cool with it."

"Cool with it?" The fury in my voice simultaneously scares and delights me. "You just assume ol' Em the doormat will take the hit, like she always does, don't you?" I open my arms. "Go ahead, Luce, take another stab at my heart. Go on, walk right over me, just like Dar and Nonna. Stomp your muddy feet on me. I'll even point out a few places you haven't crushed, so you don't miss a single fiber."

Lucy rears back. "What are you talking about?"

"Shut the hell up! The old Em is gone." I jump to my feet and lean over her bed, so that I'm inches from her face. "I am nobody's doormat. Do you hear me? You will not sleep with the one person I finally . . ." My voice cracks and I steel myself from tears. ". . . finally opened my heart to, and expect me to say it's okay, all is forgiven. No! I am sick of being nice. I have a right to happiness, too!"

My hands tremble and I turn away. I hear her bed creak. Then her warm arms enfold me. I bite my cheek, hoping to keep the tears at bay as she gently rocks me.

"I wasn't with Gabe," she whispers. She draws back and pivots me, so that we're standing face-to-face. Her lashes are spiked with tears, and when she smiles, her chin trembles.

"I was with Sofie."

The smell of baking bread wafts up the stairs, into our tiny room beneath the eaves. Lucy and I race downstairs like a couple of kids on Christmas morning. I stop when I see him, and my heart overflows. He's pouring cream into a pitcher, smiling as he yaks into his cell phone.

"Va bene. Sì." He raises his head and smiles when he sees me. *"Ciao, amico mio."* He plants the phone in his pocket. *"Buongiorno!"* He wipes his hands on his jeans as he crosses the room to come kiss my cheek. "Did you sleep well, *carissima*?"

"Sì." I rise on my toes and kiss him again, and then boldly whisper, "Next time, I want to wake up beside you."

He tips his head. "You are here another day?"

I laugh. "No. I mean next time I see you. Whenever that might be."

"Ah, yes. That would be a treat for me."

He squeezes my hand and turns to a fancy coffee machine. "Cappuccino?"

Sofia enters the kitchen and lights up when she sees me. "Emilia! We missed you yesterday. I hope my brother showed you a good time?"

"The best," I say. "How about you?"

"We had great fun. Lucy taught Franco how to play soccer. You should have seen them."

I'm smiling when Lucy bounces in with Dante on her hip and Franco riding on her back.

"Morning," she says to Gabe and lowers Franco to the floor.

"No!" Franco cries. "I want to play Horsey."

"Later," Sofia says and gives him a stern look. "Uncle Gabe has breakfast waiting."

Lucy bends down and cups Franco's rosy face in her hands. "After we eat, little man, we'll show Emmie how you can score a goal."

"Yay!" he cries. Lucy laughs and kisses his nose.

I can't keep the smile from my face. My cousin looks positively effervescent.

"Where's Poppy?" I ask.

"She was down earlier for coffee," Gabe

says. "She's skipping breakfast this morning."

Alarm shoots through me, followed by a wave of guilt. I barely saw her yesterday. While Lucy and I were exploring and laughing and falling in love, Poppy was withering.

"I'll go check on her."

"Let her sleep awhile longer," Gabe says, his eyes infused with worry and warning.

After breakfast, Sofia, Gabe, and I stand in the damp grass, watching Franco clumsily kick the ball Lucy tries to steal. "Stay focused," Lucy tells him. "That's it."

"Your cousin is a very patient coach," Sofia says, shielding her eyes from the morning sun. "Franco adores her."

"I see that."

She turns to me. "What is New York weather like in November?"

"Gray, cloudy, wet." I cock my head. "Why?"

She stuffs her hands into the pockets of her billowy pants and shrugs. "I was wondering if Franco would be able to play soccer when we visit."

"You're visiting? Next month?"

She squeezes shut her eyes and nods, her entire face scrunched with excitement. "Sì!

331

This is the plan."

I throw my arms around her. "That's awesome." I turn to Gabe. "Did you hear that? Sofia's coming to visit. Come with her! It's beautiful in November."

He smiles, his eyes on his nephew. "Beautiful? You just said it was gray."

"But it *would* be beautiful if you were there."

He claps when Franco scores a goal. "I am afraid that is not possible. I have a business to run."

"Close the inn," I say, unable to contain myself. "It's the off-season. Come to New York."

I'm moving too quickly. I'm being clingy. I hate the neediness in my voice. But I can't stop myself. Sofia must see it, too, the desperate woman inside me who's lost all subtlety. She moves away, giving us our privacy.

"Please, Gabriele, say you'll come. If not in November, then for Christmas. I'll show you the city. The storefronts will be decorated and —"

He silences me with a finger. "Ah, Emilia. I knew when I met you, you are one who sees the grandeur in the ordinary. I am but a hill. I am afraid you have mistaken me for a mountain."

■ ■ ■ ■

I stand in the tiny attic space, biting my knuckle to keep from crying out. How could he sleep with me, whisper sexy thoughts into my ear, then act today as if I'm nothing more than another guest at the inn? Because I'm cursed, that's why.

I check the time. In ten minutes, Gabe will be taking us to the train station. How will I endure the thirty-minute ride? Without warning, a sob charges from my chest. My knees buckle and I slide to the floor, clutching my ribs. I wanted love. I pretended not to, but I did. I wanted it so badly.

If only I could talk to Matt. He'd call Gabe a stupid piece of shit. He'd make me feel lovable again. But of course I can't call Matt.

I manage to pull myself upright. I blow my nose and dry my eyes. I have to be strong. For Poppy.

I drag my bag down the stairs and poke my head into Aunt Poppy's room. I work my face into a smile. We're about to embark on the most anticipated part of this journey, and I will not spoil it for her.

"Hey, soon-to-be birthday girl. Can I get your bag?"

She sits on the edge of her bed, clutching a box of tissues. Lucy helped her bathe and dress this morning. She's wearing black slacks and a bulky red sweater. The turquoise beads around her neck look heavy enough to topple her. Even her wig looks too big. As if to keep it from slipping off her head, she's created a headband with a turquoise scarf. My self-pity momentarily vanishes. I lower myself beside her and adjust the scarf on her forehead.

"Are you feeling well enough to travel?"

"Of course," she says, always the warrior. But her voice is even more gravelly than yesterday, and absent all enthusiasm.

Today's travel will be especially tiring, a three-and-a-half-hour train ride to Naples, followed by a two-hour bus ride to Ravello.

"Aunt Poppy, you need to see a doctor."

She pulls a tissue from the box and rises. "Rico is waiting. We must go."

I shake my head, and lead her to the SUV. Though I dreaded the thought of sitting beside Gabe on the way to the train station, I feel cheated when I see Sofia holding the keys.

"Set your bag right there," she tells me. "I will get it."

"You . . . you're taking us to the station?"

"Sì." She gives me a doleful smile. "I am

sorry, Emilia. My brother is a generous hello man. He is stingy when it comes to good-byes."

I stare out the backseat window, half listening as Sofia and Lucy chatter in the front seat.

"I live my life, day after day, not worried about what others think of me," Sofia tells Lucy. "Do you not do the same?"

"No," Lucy says. "Not since I was eight. But starting now, I do."

I'm so proud of my cousin, and I'd tell her, if I trusted my voice. I turn to the window. Trespiano, and my dream of Gabriele, disappear along with the countryside. My eyes sting and I blink back tears. Today, my heart breaks. Tomorrow, it will be my aunt's. What is it with love, anyway? Lucy was right: I never wanted to be in the game. I was fine, living my life as a single woman. I finally step onto the field, and — *bam!* — I'm knocked unconscious by a curveball. Never have I felt so rejected, so humiliated and lonely and empty. Who needs this kind of pain?

As my mind rationalizes a life without love, my heart remembers how magical it was, lying in Gabe's arms, how alive, how fully connected I felt, like the world around me — the one I'd never felt quite comfortable in — had welcomed me at last.

Traffic picks up when we reach the outskirts of Florence — the place where, just last night, I stood in Gabe's arms, as happy as I'd ever felt. Was none of that real? I think of Lucy. I was completely unsympathetic about her love life. I felt so superior, convinced she should have been able to see these guys for what they were — players. But the truth is, they were no different from Gabe. And I'm no different from Lucy.

Sometimes it's our mind we ignore when we think we could make someone love us.

I turn when Poppy's chilly fingers intertwine with mine.

"You will find, Emilia, life is not always a circle. More often, it's a tangled knot of detours and dead ends, false starts and broken hearts. An exasperating, dizzying maze, impossible to navigate and useless to map." She squeezes my hand. "But not a single corner nor curve should ever, ever be missed."

Her eyes are soft and she hands me a tissue. Somehow she knows. She pats the space beside her and I slide over. It should be me, comforting her. I know this. But still, I can't resist. I lay my head on her shoulder and she strokes my hair.

"I am proud of you, Emilia."

"Proud? I was made a fool."

"Nonsense. You left the fool behind."

I study her face, wondering who she's talking about: Gabriele or the old me.

"You have finally experienced love." She leans in and whispers, "Even if it was with a no-good, dirty dog."

"What? You knew Gabriele was a dog?" I glance at Sofia. Luckily, she and Lucy are busy talking. "Why didn't you warn me?" I whisper. "You let me go off with him yesterday! Do you realize that we . . . ?" My voice trails off.

"Of course I do. It was high time you experienced some passion. And a dirty dog like Gabriele knows a lot of tricks." She winks at me.

I massage my forehead. One day, maybe I'll look back on this conversation and find the humor.

Maybe.

La Stazione di Santa Maria Novella is a jungle of cars and taxis and frenzied passengers. Sofia insists on walking us to our train. My phone dings when we enter the bustling station. A text from Daria.

Where RU?

Damn. She's ticked, and I don't blame

337

her. I'd promised to call her . . . three days ago. But I was so consumed with Gabe I completely forgot.

I type as I walk. Train station. Florence. Will call in 5 minutes. Promise!

I mean where, exactly??

I practically ram into Lucy before I realize she and Sofia and Poppy have stopped. I look up, struck by the chaos. People storm past us, angry and agitated. Voices are loud, frustrated. To my left, a huge line snakes beyond the ticket counter. A man hands us a pamphlet. I make out two words: *Salario Equo.* Fair Pay.

"Oh, hell," Sofia says, shepherding us over to the side of the platform. "The train workers have gone on strike."

Poppy clutches her chest. "I should have been paying attention. They announce these things in advance."

"They announce their strikes?" I notice a poster on the wall, the same one I spotted when we arrived Thursday, telling of an upcoming *sciopero.*

"We better hightail it to another station," Lucy says.

"It's *nazionale,*" Sofia says, reading the pamphlet. "The whole country is affected for the next twenty-four hours."

"So what do we do now?" Lucy asks. "Can

338

we fly to Ravello?"

"No. But you can catch a flight to Naples, and take a bus from there."

An American man beside us pipes up. "All domestic flights are booked solid." He holds his iPhone out to us. "I've checked all the carriers. The soonest anyone can get out of here is tomorrow afternoon."

My heart sinks. I can't even look at Poppy.

"You can rent a car," Sofia says. "Or, you can come back to the inn." She smiles at Lucy. "My brother and I will welcome another day of your company."

My head spins. Could this rail-worker strike be fate, forcing our return to Casa Fontana? Might Gabe have had an epiphany in the past hour? Might he run to me with open arms, having realized he almost lost me?

Lucy shakes her head. "We have to get to the cathedral."

I close my eyes, shamed by my selfishness. "Absolutely."

"Is that the line for rentals?" Lucy asks, lifting her head above the crowd. "Shit. We'll be here all day."

I spot the car rental booth just as the agent pulls down the gate. He tapes a sign to the wall. *Esaurito.* The crowd erupts with curses and boos.

"They have sold out," Sofia says.

Poppy whimpers, a sound so faint it breaks my heart. I grab her hands.

"Don't worry. We'll get there. I promise." But inside, I'm not the least bit convinced.

"You will take Gabriele's car," Sofia says.

"No," I say. "We can't do that."

"You can. I promise. He would want this."

Uh-huh. To ease his guilty conscience?

"He can arrange for someone to return it. Until then, he and I will use the Vespas."

Lucy claps her hands. "Sounds like a plan. Let's hit it."

We move against the crowd, inching our way to the exit. I lock eyes with a brunette about fifty feet away, coming toward us. She's wearing a denim jacket with a backpack slung over her shoulder. She looks like Daria. So much like Daria. Exactly . . . like . . .

"Daria?" I say. I call again, louder this time, and wave my arms. "Daria!"

Lucy shoots me a look. Before I can utter a word, she sees her, too.

"What the hell? Daria's here? In Italy?"

CHAPTER 33

EMILIA

I edge my way through the crowded platform, overcome with love and confusion
and joy and disbelief. "You're here!" I grab
Daria in my arms and squeeze her with all
my might. "You came all this way. I can't
believe it."

"Easy, sister," she says and gives an awkward chuckle before untangling herself. "I
barely recognized you. You got new glasses."

I start to thank her, before I realize she
didn't actually compliment me. "How did
you find us?"

"I followed the itinerary you left with
Dad."

"I can't believe you're here! Oh, my god,
thank you."

"What was I supposed to do? You call me
from Venice in the middle of the night, lost
and terrified. Then we're cut off and I hear
nothing. I finally get one measly text telling

me you'd call. And do you? No."

My sister was worried. She came here to rescue me. I can't stop smiling. "Sorry about that," I say. "I made it home safely, as you can see."

She turns to Lucy. "And you. Do you never answer your phone?"

"I broke up with that ugly-ass Samsung the minute I got here," Lucy says, without skipping a beat. "I miss it about as much as my old headgear." She slings an arm around Sofia. "By the way, this is Sofie."

Sofia extends her hand and offers a shy smile. "Nice to meet you."

Daria's gaze shifts from Sofia to Lucy, and back again, before she finally takes Sofia's hand.

Lucy aims a thumb at our aunt. "And of course you know Aunt Poppy."

Poppy steps forward, cupping Daria's cheeks in her hands. "My dear girl. It's so lovely to see you."

My sister literally recoils. I want to grab her by the arm and tell her to behave. "Thanks," she says coolly, adjusting her backpack.

"You've arrived just in time for Ravello," Poppy continues, seemingly unfazed.

"Yes!" I say. "Perfect timing. Ravello is the capstone of our trip. Wait until you hear

Poppy's story. We'll fill you in on the way."

"We'll be there by sunset," Poppy adds. "Depending on how fast Luciana drives."

Lucy rears back. "I'm not driving. I don't even have a license. Em will drive."

My heart begins to pound. I feel Daria's eyes on me. She's got a sly grin on her face.

"So you're driving, Emmie?"

My sister knows I don't drive, and she knows why. I clasp my shaking hands. "No," I whisper.

Sofia studies us, as if trying to understand the dynamics between these strange American sisters. "I would drive you myself, but I need to get back to the boys. Besides, I am terrified of the cliffs."

Poppy bats a hand. "Not to worry. I will drive."

If it weren't so sad, it would be laughable. Poppy can barely walk. And the label on her pill vial prohibits her from driving.

There's only one obvious solution.

"What about you, Dar?"

Her head snaps to attention.

"Will you drive us?"

"Me?"

"Yes, you!" I clasp my hands in prayer. "Please, Dar, I'm begging you. Say you'll drive us to Ravello?"

She checks her watch, then turns to Lucy

343

and Sofia and, finally, Poppy. She heaves a sigh.

"Which way to the car?"

The parking lot is a frenzy of panicked travelers, clamoring for taxis, shouting who came first and who needs to go to the back of the line. Sofia shudders and hands Daria the keys. "I am sorry to leave you," she tells us, "but I must get back to my little men."

"We'll drive you back to the inn," Lucy says.

"No. Gabriele will pick me up down the block, where it is not so busy. You must get on the road. It's a six-hour drive to Ravello."

She hugs me first, and then bids Poppy a tearful good-bye. It seems to take all of Poppy's strength to reach into her purse and fish out her bag of pennies. She places one in Sofia's hand.

"For luck," she says. "Now, go spread your sunshine in this world."

Sofia kisses each of Poppy's cheeks. "I will."

Her eyes are misty when she turns to Lucy. "See you in November." She tucks a stray hair behind Lucy's ear. "Be safe."

Lucy nods. "Grazie," she says, her voice thick. "Grazie."

Sofia walks away, then turns around. "Ciao! Be careful. The bends in the roads can be treacherous."

While Daria punches an address into Gabe's GPS, Lucy and I settle Aunt Poppy into the backseat. She winces and rubs her temples. We buckle her seat belt and wrap our coats around her. Despite the balmy weather, she's shivering. My aunt should be tucked in a warm bed, maybe even a hospital bed. But no. We've come all this way for one reason. We cannot give up now.

"Try to rest," I tell her. She leans her head on the window and closes her eyes.

Daria maneuvers through the city streets of Florence with confidence, obeying the directions displayed on the GPS. I sit up front with her, following along on my finally useful map. She exits SS67 at Viale Francesco Redi and heads north. According to my map, she should have stayed on SS67. I open my mouth to tell her, but close it. Daria doesn't like to be second-guessed. She's come all this way. She's here, in Italy. We're going to spend the next two days together.

"Thanks again," I say. "I can't tell you how much this means to me. It's unreal. For starters, you must have spent a fortune to get here."

"Nonna paid."

"Nonna?" I laugh. "I would have thought Nonna would consider this trip a *colossale* waste of money."

"Nope."

"But you took time off work, just for this. And time away from the girls, and Donnie."

"Forget it."

"No. Seriously, I really, really appreciate it." I pivot, so that I'm facing her profile. "I know we're not as close as we once were, Dar. But deep inside, I've always known you've had my back. This just proves —"

"Stop, Em. Just . . . stop, please."

"Okay. Sorry." I sit back, stung. We ride in silence for another mile before I realize I've got my finger on my scar. I clasp my hands and gaze out the window, watching a plane take off. Then another. Ahead, I see the sign for the Aeroporto di Firenze — Peretola. I check my map.

"Dar, I think we might be going the wrong way."

She ignores me. I'm confused when she takes a right into the airport entrance. From the backseat, Lucy pipes up.

"It's a waste of time, Daria. A guy at the station told us all domestic flights are sold out."

Daria doesn't reply. She follows the signs to the international departure deck. Suddenly, I feel sick.

"What's going on, Dar? We need to get to Ravello. Tomorrow's Poppy's birthday."

The terminal comes into view. Daria zips into a spot at the curb and shuts off the ignition. She grabs her phone and scrolls, then holds the screen out to me.

"This is my plane ticket home." She swipes to the next page. "And this one is yours."

I stare, openmouthed, at the e-ticket for Emilia Antonelli, with today's departure date. "I — I can't go home."

"Lucy will take Poppy from here. Nonna needs you."

I clutch my head, thoughts rushing me. Why, exactly, is Daria here? Because she was worried about me? Because she cares about me? A wave of nausea rolls over me.

"You . . . you came all this way, just to bring me home?"

She stares at the Alfa Romeo in front of us, attempting to parallel park. "Nonna insists."

"Is she crazy? This is the most important part of the trip. Tomorrow is Poppy's birthday. It's the only reason we're here."

She turns to me. "Think about it, Emmie.

The trains aren't working. The flights are full. None of you can drive." She tips her head toward Poppy, asleep in the back. "This one's running out of juice. You think the universe might be trying to tell you something? Nothing good is going to come of this trip. Nothing."

A shiver runs up my spine. From the backseat, Lucy's voice rises, strong and firm. "Cut the crap, Daria." She leans in between the two front seats, her eyes narrowed. "This trip has changed everything. We're no longer cursed. You should've seen Em, with Sofie's brother. She was flirty and fun. You wouldn't have recognized her, I swear."

"Really?" Daria turns to me. "And how did that turn out for you?"

I picture Gabe's beautiful eyes, brimming with counterfeit love and false promises. I drop my head in my hand. What more does the curse have in store for me?

"We have to get Poppy to Ravello," I mumble.

Daria lifts her shoulders. "Good luck, without a driver."

I clench my jaw. I want to scream out, *I will drive!* But the words won't come. I rub the back of my neck, my hair sticky with sweat.

"Let's go," Daria says, unbuckling her seat belt. "Our flight leaves in ninety minutes." She opens her door and steps out of the SUV.

My heart thunders. I glance back at Lucy. "Maybe we should go home, Luce — all of us. We'll change the tickets. The sooner Poppy gets back, the sooner she can get to the doctor."

"I am not leaving." Lucy's face is branded with determination.

"Hurry up," Daria says.

I chew my lip. Daria's waiting for me. She needs me. Finally, I let out a sigh. I unbuckle my seat belt and turn to Lucy. "Okay. Um, you and Poppy will go back to the inn? Poppy has Gabe's number."

Lucy glares at me. "I cannot believe you're letting your sister manipulate you."

"She's not manipulating me. I can't drive, Luce! It wouldn't matter if I stayed. We can't get to Ravello. So why wouldn't I return early and make Nonna happy?"

"Don't you dare try to justify this, Em." Her nostrils flare. "I thought you'd changed."

A dagger enters my heart. I peek at Poppy. Thankfully she's still asleep. What would she say if she knew I was bailing on her now?

Daria leans into the car, her backpack

slung over her shoulder. "C'mon, Emmie."

I rub my scar, paralyzed with indecision.

"You'll be back in time for work tomorrow," she continues. "Nonna will be so relieved. And trust me, Emmie, she'll be forever grateful. Nonna values loyalty above all else." My sister lowers her voice. "It absolutely broke her heart to think you chose her sister over her. I mean, my god, Em, the woman's been like a mother to us."

My breath catches. "No. She was a mother to you. Not to me."

"Whatever," Daria says. "Let's go."

Blood races past my temples. "And you haven't been a sister to me, Dar. Not in years."

"Right. I came all the way here, and that's my thanks?"

I dig my nails into my palms. "You came here to ruin my trip." I speak through clenched teeth, years of anger bubbling to the surface. "You couldn't bear to see me, the inferior second-born daughter, doing something fun for myself. You've been brainwashed by Nonna, just like Dad. Just like I was."

"You're delusional."

I let out a maniacal little laugh. "I was, yes. But not anymore. I see things clearly now. The curse works for you. Because you're the superior one, the anointed first-born daughter. You're Nonna's protégé, her pride and joy. And you're so afraid of losing your status that you've sacrificed me, my life, our entire relationship, just to please her. I'm nothing but your personal hand-maid."

"Go to hell, Em."

My hand shakes when I open the car door. My heart beats a wild and erratic rhythm. I step out and round the car until I reach Daria. I look into the eyes of the person I love more than anyone else in the world.

"No." My mouth twitches and my chin trembles, but my words are steady and strong. "I am not going to hell. I'm going to Ravello."

Daria's eyes bore into mine. Perhaps she's hoping I'll burst out laughing and tell her it's all a joke. And I almost wish I could. Almost.

I muscle past her and slide in behind the wheel.

"Don't do this, Emmie," she says as I close the door.

I start the engine. My stomach drops. I slide the gearshift into drive.

"Stop. You're making a huge mistake."

Ever so gently, I press my foot on the accelerator. The car inches forward. I watch,

feeling sick and petrified and oddly de-
tached, as my sister disappears from my
rearview mirror.

I get as far as the next terminal before I
pull over. I drop my head onto the steering
wheel. My knees quake. What the hell have
I done? From the backseat, I hear clapping.
I look over my shoulder.

"Brava! Brava, my pollia berry." Poppy
reaches out and clasps my shoulder. "You
are shining right now. You are positively
shining."

I blink back tears, unable to speak.

Lucy chuckles. "Looks like ol' Emmie has
grown a pair of balls." She raises her palm
to me. "Way to show that bitch who's in
control."

I give her a halfhearted high five, though
it feels treasonous to celebrate. Daria is my
sister. I love her. Unconditionally. But for
the life of me, I cannot defend her today.

Lucy climbs over the seat back and lands
in a heap beside me. She straightens her
shirt and turns to me.

"So, you were joking about not being able
to drive, right?"

CHAPTER 34

EMILIA

I'm telling Lucy about the bargain I struck after Liam's accident, when an airport security guard knocks on the car window. *"Partite!"* he says. "Go!"

"Shit." My breath catches and I give him a little wave.

"So everything you told Daria was bullshit?" Lucy's propped against the passenger door, facing me. "Tell me, Em, do you believe in the curse or not?"

"I honestly don't know, Luce." I rub my temples, realizing how screwed up I must sound. "And I don't want to push our luck."

"I don't get it. I mean, sure, you freaked out after that accident and promised never to see Liam. But what the hell does driving have to do with the curse?"

"You just met Sofie. You're happy, right?"

"Um, like, for the first time in forever."

"And that's exactly when it happens. Now,

just to prove its power, the curse will strike. That's when we get in an accident, and you're hurt or disfigured or . . ."

"Dead? Is that what you're afraid of? That you'll kill me?"

"Yes . . . no . . . I'm afraid my *curse* will kill you. Just like it almost killed Liam." I take a deep breath. "I would never forgive myself if I were the cause of —"

Lucy throws up her hands. "Oh, get over yourself, Em. I'm telling you in advance, before I'm brain-dead or missing a nose or nothing but an urn of ashes, I forgive you."

We lock eyes for a moment, two once-cursed daughters, testing our fate.

"Let go, Emilia." We turn to the backseat. Has Poppy been listening the whole time?

"Let go," she repeats, the two words packed with hope and possibility and danger. Let go of fear. Let go of guilt. Let go of false beliefs.

Outside, the airport guard marches up to our car. He blows his whistle and jabs his finger. *"Partite!"*

My stomach pitches and I lift a finger. "Okay," I mouth to him. I look away. "Damn!"

I take a deep breath. Very slowly, and with the greatest trepidation, I press down on the accelerator. And let go.

An hour and a half later, I finally loosen my grip on the steering wheel. From the back-seat, Poppy softly snores. I rock my neck, trying to work out the kink, and catch sight of the GPS. "Wait . . . we've only traveled eighty-three kilometers?"

"Uh, yeah, about that," Lucy says. "According to my calculations, we should make it to Ravello in plenty of time for Poppy's birthday. Her *ninety-seventh* birthday."

"We need to get there safely." I stare at the road. "Will you text Dar for me? My phone's in my purse. Tell her I'm —" The word "sorry" sticks in my throat. What was that favor Poppy once asked of me? *Stop apologizing when you're not sorry.* "Tell her safe travels. And that I'll see her in three days."

"Here's hoping," Lucy mumbles as she types the text. "I'll tell her you finally had an orgasm." She looks up at me. "If you die now, at least you've got that, right?"

I try to smile, but it's still too raw. Was it just yesterday that I was falling in love? For a brief moment, I was an "us." I blink quickly. I can't be sad, not now, not when Lucy's ecstatic and Poppy's filled with hope.

With all my will, I block out the sound of Gabriele's voice, forget the feel of his skin against mine. And then, I tuck the memories away in some secret corner of my heart, to be opened later.

"Luce, do you know that I'm thrilled for you? I mean, really, truly thrilled. Sofia is one cool woman. And so are you."

"Thanks. I'm a little freaked if you want to know the truth. Carol and Vinnie will have three strokes apiece when they find out."

"They'll come around. Your parents will see what I see. You're Lucy again, the real Lucy."

She breaks into a smile. "Yeah?"

"Yeah. I'm proud of you. All love takes courage. Your kind of love takes a special kind of valiancy."

"Valiancy? That's good, right?"

"Really good."

She turns to the window. "You know, for years now I've tried to ignore what felt natural. And it's not that I suddenly decided to become a dick dodger. I didn't set out to fall for a chick. It's more like I just stopped resisting."

We travel in silence another mile before Lucy speaks again, her voice soft. "I suppose I should welcome you to the Laid and

Played Club."

Is she poking fun at me? My fingers tighten around the steering wheel.

"It's not exactly a club you'd want to join," she continues. "But I'm guessing at one time or another, most people are initiated."

I wait until a truck passes before I peek at her. Her eyes hold a tenderness I've never seen. I let out a sigh. "I was so stupid."

"You were inexperienced. You didn't know the rules. You'll learn. And if it makes you feel better, I've been laid and played, too."

"That Jack guy," I say — a statement, not a question.

She nods. "And about a million and twenty-seven other douche bags."

My laugh gets captured in a groan. "Oh, Luce, what am I going to do? Where am I supposed to put all these feelings?" I shake my head. "I know what you're thinking: I'm being dramatic. I only knew him for three days."

"Doesn't matter," she says. "It's all about connection. When you have it, and then it's ripped away, you feel like your lungs cannot fill, like you're emptied of every atom of joy. You can't breathe, let alone eat or sleep. And you're certain, absolutely sure-as-shit certain, that you will never be the same again."

I sneak a glance at her. "But eventually you are, right?"

She shakes her head. "No, Em. You are never the same."

I groan. Dread fills me, and I imagine a lifetime of misery.

She pats my knee. "You become better. A hell of a lot better."

Five hours later, just when I'm finally starting to relax behind the wheel, we reach the province of Salerno. To the west, I glimpse the silhouette of Naples. Only fifty-nine kilometers until we reach Ravello. Almost instantly, the landscape changes. Gone is the long stretch of Highway A1, replaced by narrow passages with harrowing switchback curves carved along the cliff's edge.

The vehicle groans as we climb the jagged mountain. Lucy sits up straight, her face taut.

"You've got this," she tells me. But she's clutching the dash in front of her as if clinging to the rocky ledge. My hands sweat. I gasp when I catch sight of the foamy Gulf of Salerno beyond the jagged cliff.

"Damn!" I cry, fighting a wave of dizziness.

"Don't look down," she says.

My heart thunders in my chest. "I hate this!"

"On the bright side," Lucy says, "if we crash, we'll take out Gabe's precious SUV."

My eyes strain to focus on the road in front of me. I hold my breath as we navigate around another hairpin curve. I let up on the gas when we come upon a tour bus. It's following an RV, and we slow to a crawl. Behind me, a line of cars begins to build. I glance in the rearview mirror. The driver behind me is right on my tail. He's ducking in and out of the lane, obviously anxious to pass me . . . and the bus . . . and the RV.

"Relax," Lucy says. "Ignore all those cars you're holding up."

"What am I supposed to do? I can't pass."

The car behind me honks. Lucy whips around and holds up her middle finger.

"Stop. You'll encourage road rage."

The driver lays on his horn again. It's too dangerous for him to pass me, along with the bus and RV. He wants me to lead the way. "Damn it!"

We round a curve, and straight pavement stretches before us.

"Go!" Lucy says. "Pass these snails! Now!"

"What? No!"

From the long line of cars behind us, a

chorus of horns begins — plural. My chest squeezes. It's up to me to move the traffic. My entire body trembles. I put on my blinker and, with utmost caution and trepidation, enter the passing lane.

"Move it!" Lucy shouts.

I step on the accelerator and the car lunges. I'm almost past the bus when a curve appears in the distance.

"Oh, God!" I cry. The engine groans, downshifting on the mountain's incline. I start to wedge between the bus and the RV, but there's not enough space.

"Let me in," I shout, at the same time Lucy cries, "Go for it!"

I press my foot on the gas. I have no choice but to try to overtake the RV as well. Sweat breaks out under my arms.

"Wahoo! You've got this, Em."

From a hundred yards ahead, a car rounds the curve. It's heading straight at us.

"Holy fuck! We're gonna die!" Lucy covers her head, screaming as she slides down the seat.

My heart's in full-blown tachycardia. I grip the steering wheel. Please, God! Help me! I punch the gas. The approaching car grows nearer. The RV stretches beside me, an endless box of aluminum. "Let me in, asshole!"

With seconds to spare, I crank the wheel and dart back into the lane. The car whizzes past.

I let out a half cry, half groan. "Oh, my god!"

I turn to Lucy. She's crouched on the floor of the car, clutching her head.

"You can sit up," I tell her.

She eases her way back onto her seat. "Jesus, Em, you almost killed us!"

I give a nervous chortle. "I warned you."

She grins. "I'd prepared myself for the missing nose, not the urn of ashes."

In that dark place inside of me where fear has festered, a door opens. Light spills in. I let out a laugh, softly at first. Lucy joins in. Soon, it's full-on hysteria, an intoxicating release of fear and shock and frayed nerves. Lucy pounds the dashboard, tears running down her cheeks. "The look on your face when that car appeared out of fucking nowhere!"

A little chuckle rises behind us.

"Sorry, Aunt Poppy," I say, glancing in my rearview mirror. "We'll be quiet. Go back to sleep."

"And miss all the fun? Never!"

CHAPTER 35

POPPY

1960
Ravello, Amalfi Coast

The massive cathedral door groaned, that evening of my twenty-first birthday. We dipped our fingers into a basin of holy water and crossed ourselves. The shadowed church was empty and smelled of incense and musty carpets. Tiered candles glowed in the prayer booth, white-capped flames in a sea of silence.

Rico led me down the center aisle until we reached the altar. He turned to me then, his eyes bright, and took my hands in his.

"I, Erich Joseph Krause, do take thee, Paolina Maria Fontana, to be my wedded wife. I promise to love you and cherish you all the days of my life, until death do us part."

I put a hand to my quivering chin and said

362

my vows, my throat so tight I could hardly get the words out. ". . . Until death do us part."

"May I kiss the bride?"

He took my face in his hands. Just as his lips touched mine, footsteps startled us. Out of the darkness, a priest emerged, not Father Pietro but a youthful man with dark hair and a long, thin nose.

He climbed the three steps to where we stood on the altar. "Bow your heads," he said, and he placed his hands upon us.

"May God bless and protect you. May he smooth the path that lies before you, and give you the grace and humility to accept both fortune and sorrow. May you be strong as the redwood when troubles arise, and bend like the willow when forgiveness beckons. Above all, may you love joyfully, gratefully, faithfully, in Christ's name. Amen."

"Amen," we repeated, stunned by this unexpected prayer, awed by this mysterious holy man who appeared out of nowhere. We thanked the young priest and left the church, a married couple if ever there was one.

We barely made it outside the cathedral before Rico drew me into his arms. With his lips at my ear, he whispered, "My wife. My life."

"How do you say 'my husband' in German?"

"Mein Ehemann," Rico replied and stroked my cheek. "And one day, when your parents come to accept me, we will come back here for a real ceremony, and I will truly be your husband."

"Real ceremony? Real husband?" I shook my head. *"Mein Ehemann,* we are married. It could not be more real."

"I feel it, too." He squeezed my hand.

Something shiny caught my eye. I bent down and plucked it from the concrete step. "A lucky coin," I said, showing it to Rico.

Together, we gazed at the coin, as if it held some magic power. Rico put his hand over mine. "May we be here, in this very spot, on your next birthday, as in love as we are today."

A chill came over me. Despite the day's joy, I believe we both sensed, in some secret place in our hearts, that darkness lay ahead.

"Next year?" I said, trying to lighten the sudden weight of our futures. "That is too easy."

"Okay," he said, rubbing his chin. "We will be back here on your thirtieth birthday."

"Nine years from now? Still too easy." I

clutched the coin and searched the sky for my favorite star, wondering how we might guarantee our future. "We will be here, together on the steps of the Ravello Cathedral, on my eightieth birthday. Promise me this, *mein Ehemann.*"

He smiled, but his eyes glistened. "Yes. On your eightieth birthday," he said. "It is a promise."

CHAPTER 36

EMILIA

Day Seven
Ravello, Amalfi Coast

I've heard of people who enter a place — a big city or small town, an old castle or a lakeside cabin — and feel as if they'd returned home, following a long and lonely journey. Poppy called it *hiraeth,* a yearning for a place, a home, one you might never have realized you were missing. I steer the car into the hilltop village of Ravello, and I think I understand.

The sun dips behind the Tyrrhenian Sea, bathing the pristine town in watercolor pastels. Hedges of magenta bougainvilleas create lush pops of color, and everywhere I see urns of red geraniums and baskets of purple hollyhock and yellow snapdragons.

"Home!" Poppy cries. She rolls down her window, letting in a fragrant breeze of roses and sea salt. "At last!"

Beyond the cliff's edge, the Mediterranean hums a soothing lullaby. The day's stress seems to vanish in this quiet village of fewer than three thousand residents, but there's an energy, too. Hikers with walking sticks climb the winding sidewalks; cyclists wave as they zip past.

I slow to a stop in front of an elegant boutique hotel in the heart of Ravello's Piazza del Duomo, taking in the gorgeous fountain through the open courtyard. My hand aches when I pull the key from the ignition. I let out a sigh. "Thank you, God."

Lucy smiles. "You did it, Em. You drove. You were friggin' awesome."

Poppy squeals and goes to lift her door handle, but Lucy turns to her in the backseat.

"Not so fast, Pops. All this time you've been married? Why didn't you tell us?"

I twist around, anxious to hear Poppy's response. She gazes out the window.

"We had no witnesses, no papers. We'd been living in sin. Looking back, we should have tried harder. It never occurred to us to marry outside the Catholic faith. The truth is, we didn't know then that time was running out."

Lucy looks from Poppy to me, then back

to Poppy. "Still. That means the curse is broken, right? All this time, there never was a curse!"

"Rico and I believed that God, our God, had blessed our marriage. We bought silver bands at the jewelry store, cheap as bottles of milk. We returned to the cathedral, time and again, asking to see the young priest who'd appeared that night. But Father Pietro, whose hair was white as ash, insisted he was the only priest in the parish. We waited after Sunday mass and asked the church members. Nobody knew of the dark-haired priest with the long, thin nose."

"So what does that mean?" Lucy says. "Are you legally married or not?"

Poppy lifts her hands. "Was it legal? Was it moral? Will others believe me? Criticize me? Abandon me?" She clamps a hand on Lucy's shoulder, and I know she's talking about Sofie now, not Rico. "Perhaps they will. But when you come from a place of love, of truth, you will be confident in your answers. And more often than not, the answer is, 'So what if they do?' "

Our room at the Michelangelo is even grander than the one in Venice, with Wedgwood blue walls topped with ornate moldings, splashy oil paintings, a sitting room, and two king-size beds. Lucy and I unpack, but Poppy stands aside, staring out the second-floor window. I tuck my suitcase in the closet and go to her.

Across the cobblestone piazza, a pretty white church faces us, its pyramidal spire topped with a simple cross. Twin arched windows, like a pair of eyebrows, hover over a set of green double doors.

"There," she says, pointing her finger, "is where I will meet Rico tomorrow."

Her voice is heartbreakingly hopeful. I open my mouth to caution her. But then I close it again. What's the harm in letting this ferociously positive old woman believe it's possible for one more day?

The church bells chime seven times, and well-dressed couples set out for dinner. The mild evening calls for sandals and skirts, but Poppy opts for a pink faux-fur vest. She suggests we stop at Villa Rufolo on our way to the restaurant. "A wealthy merchant built the ancient villa in the thirteenth century. Rico and I adored its gardens."

Most of the tourists are gone now, and it's quiet when we enter what looks like an ancient watchtower. Stepping through an arched opening, we continue down a path lined with lime and cypress trees.

Poppy stops. "Close your eyes."

When I open them again, my jaw drops. It's as if we've been transported into a fairy-tale Italian courtyard. A circular fountain sits in the center, surrounded by geometric borders hosting lush tropical plants and roses of every variety and color. I'm drawn to the edge of the terrace. As if perfectly staged, an umbrella tree rises from the flora. Three hundred feet below, the Gulf of Salerno sparkles against a sky bruised with purples and golds.

"They call this the Garden of the Soul," Poppy says, coming up beside me. "Rico played his violin in this garden from time to time." She turns and slowly pans the perimeter. It takes a moment before I realize: she's looking for him.

"Anyone hungry?" Lucy says, forcing us back to the present.

We make our way to L'Antica Cartiera, an intimate seafood restaurant perched on the rocks, overlooking the coast. Poppy orders a bottle of Greco de Tufo, a crisp white wine from Campania that puckers my tongue. Waves crash against the cliffs, and we feast on fresh tuna tartare, chunks of lobster the color of coral, and seafood soufflé with wild fennel and fresh tomatoes. Every few minutes, Poppy pats her wig, making sure it's in place. Each time someone steps onto the terrace, her head pops up. And each time, my heart sinks.

The waiter refills our wineglasses. "To my beautiful girls," Poppy says and lifts her glass. "Luciana, you finally realized you didn't need that fancy purse."

Light dawns on Lucy's face. "Yeah . . . I get it now. I was choosing fancy purses, when all along I've been a backpack kind of girl."

"You're becoming the woman you were meant to be."

"You really are," I say to Lucy as I clink her glass.

"Me? Look at you. You stood your ground with Daria. And you drove across the flipping country."

A surge of pride comes over me. For a decade, I've lived within a walking-distance little bubble. I allowed myself to be manipulated by fear, and that really was a curse.

"And what's more," Poppy says, tapping her glass against ours, "Emilia survived her first real heartbreak."

I groan. "Thanks for reminding me."

"Finally, you can write your romance novel."

"I was already writing my novel."

"An artist's most important tool is right

here." She points to my heart. "And you've finally uncovered yours. Until now, you were writing from your head. At last, my dear, you will write from the heart."

I want to be angry. I want to play victim a bit longer. But as always, she's right. I'm an insider now, rather than one with her nose pressed against the window, watching and wondering what it is to feel love.

Our waiter slides a huge Neapolitan pastiera onto the table. Poppy is the first to plunge her fork into the creamy molded cake. She closes her eyes.

"Deliziosa!" She pats her lips with the napkin. "Legend has it, a woman once left a basket on the seashore, filled with eggs and ricotta, candied fruits and orange blossoms. It was her sacrifice to the gods, to ensure that her husband, a fisherman, would return safely from the sea. When she came back to the shore the next morning, she discovered that the waves had mixed the ingredients. Her husband arrived home safely, and she had a beautiful pastiera for him to eat."

"Sweet," Lucy says, licking her fork. "But we'd rather hear your story. You left us with a cliff-hanger." She elbows Poppy. "Your wedding night."

Poppy giggles and waves her off. "Suffice it to say, it was stupendous." Her smile fades. "But as they often do, things changed."

CHAPTER 37

POPPY

1960–61
Ravello, Amalfi Coast

It was a cloudy Friday in November, just four weeks after our wedding. Rico and I strolled the market, buying melons and fresh tomatoes, when someone called out.

"Erich? Erich Krause? *Sind Sie das?*" The accent was unmistakably German. My heart began to race. I could sense Rico's alarm, too. Though people were escaping East Germany in large numbers, in all of his months in Italy, he'd never once seen a familiar face. Now I could see the toll it took on him, being an escapee. He looked stricken, as if the border guards had finally caught up with him.

His grip on my hand tightened, and slowly he turned around. Before us stood a round-faced young man with rosy cheeks and an infectious grin. Rico let out a sigh, the tension easing from his shoulders.

"Fritz Kuhlman!" he cried. The two clasped hands and slapped each other's backs. "How long have you been in Italy?" He spoke in German, but I was able to understand most of what he was saying.

"I escaped last month. I arrived here just one week ago."

"Darf ich vorstellen?" Rico said, drawing me near. *"Meine Frau."*

A flush of pride warmed me. He was introducing me as his wife. Whatever else might happen, we were united, until death do us part.

Fritz looked at me, then back to Rico. *"Frau?"* he asked, his brow creased. He began speaking so rapidly that I couldn't keep up. But I recognized one word. *Karin.* He used her name several times, along with *Verlobte.* Fiancée.

Rico flinched each time her name was spoken. *"Nein. Nein,"* he said, shaking his head. "I do not love her. She knows this." He turned to me, no doubt trying to change the subject. "Fritz is from my city of Radebeul," he said. "He was in school with my sister, Johanna."

I listened as Fritz told of the food shortage back home, the tightening at the border, the way the Communist government was taking over private businesses. My hands trembled and a knot formed in my stomach. Fritz had invaded our little bubble, and I was certain he hid a needle in his pocket.

"My family," Rico said, stepping forward and letting go of my hand. "Is my father's business still safe? How is my mother? Is Johanna well?"

"You do not know?"

"Know what?" Rico asked. "What news do you have?"

Fritz looked down and rubbed the back of his neck. "Your father . . . he suffered a stroke. He's . . . he's . . ."

"My god!" He grabbed Fritz by the arms. "Is he alive? Spit it out!"

"Yes, last I knew, he was alive. But he is a changed man. It is only a matter of time before the VEB takes over your father's repair shop. If they haven't already."

We sprinted to the post office. It had been weeks since Rico had called home. His family knew nothing of me, or his new life in Ravello. We'd been so caught up with our love and our life together that everyone else seemed superfluous. Now we recognized how selfish we'd been.

He spent three hours trying to place a call

to his family's shop. I stood beside him, rubbing the knots from his shoulders, bringing water in paper cups, listening as he chastised himself. Finally, at four p.m., the call was connected. We held our breath as the phone rang once. Twice.

"Krause Autoreparatur." I huddled beside him, close enough to hear the woman's voice through the receiver.

"Johanna," Rico said, his voice so thick he could barely speak.

They spoke in German, Rico and his sister, a rapid-fire volley of questions and answers. Again, words and phrases jumped at me.

"Komm nach Hause."

"Du musst."

"Wir brauchen dich."

Come home now.

You must.

We need you.

We left the post office, my beautiful world suddenly out of focus. Rico sat me on the edge of Villa Rufolo's concrete fountain. Clutching my hands, he told me of his father's condition.

"His right side is useless. He cannot lift a fork, let alone a wrench. He has lost his speech and sits all day in a wheelchair. My

377

mother feeds him, bathes him, like a small child. It has made her very weary, Johanna tells me."

He looked away. I rubbed his back until he could speak again.

"Johanna is trying to keep the business going, but how? She knows nothing of auto repair. Her husband tries to help, but they are losing business. The authorities have come twice. They are pressuring Johanna, and my mother, too. They demand to know where I am, why I have not returned. My maximum travel permit expired long ago. The authorities threaten Johanna. They tell her if I do not return, my father's shop will be turned over to the VEB — the Volkseigener Betrieb."

A shiver ran through me. If Rico didn't return, his family business — the one his father built and loved — would be owned and operated by the government.

"We must go," I said softly. "At once."

He shook his head. "No. My home is with you. Here, in Italy."

But I could see the future. His soft heart would never recover if he didn't try to help.

"Family is first. You told me this much. We will go. You will work in the shop until your father is healthy."

He took a deep breath and then let it out,

his shoulders sagging with the weight of his decision. "You are right. I must go." He looked me straight in the eyes. "Alone."

I rose like a shot. "I am your wife. I will go with *mein Ehemann.*"

"East Germany is not a place for a holiday!" He had never spoken so firmly, and I blinked quickly to keep back tears. He softened his voice. "You will return to your papà's house in Trespiano." He stroked my cheek. "I love you, Poppy. I will always love you. But I must go home. And so must you. Once my father is well, I will return, this time as your husband, not your suitor. Your papà will not stop us."

Though he tried to sound positive, his eyes were shrouded with grief. I wanted to help ease his pain. But I was too selfish.

"No. I cannot live without you."

"You will never be without me," he whispered, and he kissed my forehead. "When I return, I will build you a grand house. We will have children. They will have your eyes. They will live in freedom." He cupped my face. "And on your eightieth birthday, we will walk the steps of the Ravello Cathedral, I promise you."

That evening, I found his old leather satchel. From our closet shelf, I removed the jars of coins we'd been saving, surprised at how heavy they'd become. In a few years, we might be able to purchase that small home we'd dreamed of. But that wish seemed so far off now.

I was placing the jars in his satchel when Rico entered the room. "No," he said. He opened the first jar, pocketing just enough to get him through his journey, and handed it back to me. "You will need the money for your train ticket to Firenze."

Terror gripped me. How would I be greeted when I returned home? Rosa would be my ally of course. But my father hated me. My mother would make my life miserable. Even so, going home would be easy compared to what my Rico would be facing.

When he left the room, I removed enough money from the jars to pay for my train ticket and some essentials from the market. The rest I dropped into an envelope, along with a note.

Come back safely, my love. Until then, please know that I love you, that I pray for you, that I long for you, every second of every hour of every day.

I swiped the tears from my cheeks. For as certain as I tried to sound, I was terrified for him. I taped my luckiest coin to the note, the one I'd found on the steps of the Ravello Cathedral. *I'll see you very soon. And remember, we will be together at the cathedral on my eightieth birthday.*

We shared our last sunset on the rooftop, sipping wine until the saffron sky faded to black. The next morning, I helped him finish packing. Already I felt empty, vacant. My eyes pooled as I wrapped bread and ham in waxed paper for his long journey ahead. Would he be imprisoned when he eventually arrived home? Would he be beaten by the guards?

His plan was to travel by train to the border of Italy. From there, he would rely on his bicycle, or the generosity of passersby to give him a lift. When he arrived in West Berlin, he would use his return train ticket, the one he had purchased almost two years before and never intended to use, to take him back into East Germany, the prison that was once his home.

The guards would interrogate him at the border, harass him, and demand to know where he'd been. Of course in the end they would allow him to return to the insular world of East Germany. "Their mission is to keep people inside," he explained, "not turn them away."

Because who in their right mind would choose to return to the East?

"I will contact you once I am safely back in Radebeul."

"You will have letters waiting when you arrive," I promised.

"Wait until you receive my first letter." He kissed the tip of my nose. "Then you can write to me every day of the week."

"But why must I wait?"

"The authorities open and censor the mail — sometimes they destroy it altogether. If they intercept a letter from you, they will know I have tried to escape. They will make me pay for this when I try to reenter."

I shuddered, trying not to think of my husband being beaten by East German guards.

He took a small knife from his pocket and stood on a chair. Above our bedroom door, he carved a simple sentence.

We chose love.
PF & EK

We stood back and read the words. I fell into his arms, wishing I could die there.

I could have begged him to stay. He would have, I know this with my entire heart. But as he once told me, no person should have to choose between blood and water.

For the first time in my life, I was alone. My train left at four, giving me time to pack up the tiny apartment. But I couldn't muster the energy. I wandered aimlessly around the simple flat, as if I'd been hollowed out, as if the very soul had been shucked from my chest.

I'd promised Rico I would return to Trespiano, but the thought of the cold stone farmhouse, my papà's temper, made me weary. It's possible I would be forgiven in time. But my parents' forgiveness would come with a price. I would be expected to leave, to go to America with Rosa and marry Ignacio. And that was unthinkable. I was already married, bound for life, to a man I loved with my entire soul.

The hours passed. I didn't pack — I couldn't. I decided to wait one more day before returning home. I felt a little less alone in our sweet apartment, where Rico's shirt still hung in the closet, where his toothbrush stood next to mine in a cup beside the sink, where I could sleep beneath the same tattered quilt we had shared.

Another day passed. Then a third. The trip back home loomed before me like a smoke-filled forest, one I'd soon have to enter.

Dread set in. Then strength. By the end of the week, I'd made a decision. I would not return to the farm. I would not, could not, leave this little place above the bakery, the only place that had ever truly felt like home.

But Rico thought I was returning to Trespiano. And I'd agreed to wait until he was safely home before writing to him. He would be sending letters to Papà's address. I wrote to Rosa and asked her to forward the letters from Rico that would surely come.

Within a week, I'd taken on a second job. In the mornings I made bread in the bakery downstairs, and now, in the evenings, I worked in the kitchen of a pizzeria a short walk away. Two paychecks, however meager, would provide enough money to scrape by.

Each day, I prayed for Rico's safety, begged God to keep him healthy, to give him strength and courage. A month passed. Every morning, after my shift at the bakery, I hurried to the post office, my silly heart thrumming with hope that I might find a letter, forwarded from home. Instead, I found letters from Rosa, page after page, pouring out her heart to me, telling of the chasm she sensed between her and Alberto. She was convinced she didn't deserve him, that he would one day leave her. She would wake at night crying, terrified Alberto would abandon her. And when she turned to him for comfort, he did not know how to give it. He called her silly, which only made her feel worse. She shared her fears with Mamma, who assured her that things would be fine as soon as she was with child. And then, at the end of each heartbreaking letter, she would add, *Still nothing from Rico.*

I sensed a change in my sister, a bitter obsession brewing. She had turned inward, consumed by her inability to make Alberto love her.

In my darkest hours, I wondered if love even existed. Was it possible we were both doomed to an agony of the heart, a longing to recapture something that was never ours to begin with?

In the dreary month of February, despair set in. I felt no sunshine. Laughter was a foreign sound. I spent my few hours of free time writing letters, begging Rico to return. Letters I knew I could not send. I filled pages, pouring out all my misery, admitting to him that I wasn't as brave as I'd pretended to be. Nor as selfless. I needed him. It didn't matter that his family did, too. I needed him more.

Each day was a monotonous grind,

twenty-four hours of nothingness. I washed dishes at the pizzeria until midnight, and rose at four to bake bread downstairs at Piacenti's Bakery. Exhaustion set in. From two in the afternoon until six, I lay on the bed in our tiny room, staring at the words Rico had carved above the door, desperate for sleep. But the bright sunshine stalked me. The four walls that once held laughter and passion became an oven, stealing my slumber. Sounds from the street paraded through the open windows — girls gossiping in front of the bakery, a woman's pealing laughter. Sounds of a person I once was.

My lips were cracked. My mouth tasted like cardboard. I couldn't keep anything down, not even water. One day, after hearing me vomit in the bathroom, my boss at the pizzeria sent me home early. It was nine o'clock, the streets already dark. In my mind, bad men were stalking me. Shadows that I was certain were wolves lurked in doorways. Faster. I had to move faster. But my feet were weighted in concrete. I could barely move. I made it to our building before collapsing in the stairwell.

I lay on the hard wooden stairs, my breathing ragged, trying to garner the strength to climb six more steps.

That's when I heard it — the creak at the

top of the stairs. A door opened. Not any door, *our* door! I lifted my head. I blinked several times, trying to make sense of the face I saw before me. For the first time in two months, my heart rose. And then everything turned black.

CHAPTER 38

EMILIA

Day Eight — Poppy's Birthday
Ravello

Sounds of running water wake me. The hotel room is still cloaked in darkness, but beneath the bathroom door, light seeps. Poppy is already up. Her day has arrived.

Last night Lucy and I bombarded her with questions. Who was on the staircase? Was it Rico? Did he come back for her? But she'd gone silent, as if the lonely memory had left her spent.

I grab my glasses and my phone. At least I know his last name now. I type *Krause Auto-reparatur, Radebeul* into my phone's search bar. Damn. Not one entry. Next I try *Erich Krause.* Over three hundred thousand links appear.

"What are you doing?" Lucy asks, her voice groggy. She flips on the bedside lamp and curls onto her side.

"Trying to find Rico." I hold out my phone. "Check out all these entries. Most of them are written in German. I'll start with the marriage licenses and death certificates, so we can rule those out."

"That'll take forever." She gently peels the phone from my hand and sets it on the table. "How about we let fate take over from here, and give Poppy her day?"

I'm taken aback by my cousin's sensitivity. Just a week ago, she was ready to bolt, to run back to the States and forget about Poppy's dream. But she's different now, more generous, no longer bitter. Whether or not she believes the curse is lifted, I can't say. But I do know she has hope. And that makes all the difference.

"May fate be kind to Poppy," I say.

"I have a good feeling," Lucy says, with a sparkle in her eye.

I turn away. When did my cousin start believing in miracles?

And when did I stop?

The morning air is cool, and puffy clouds at the horizon shed a lavender haze over the town. People mill about in the piazza, some clutching newspapers and coffee cups, others with maps and umbrellas. Poppy leads the way to the cathedral. Her gait is still slow, but she's peppier than I've seen her in days. I linger behind, carrying our raincoats, and marvel at her. She's dressed in a white frock. It's yellowed and wrinkled, and two sizes too big for her, but she's belted it with a strip of red leather. Around her neck she's donned a bright purple scarf and her turquoise beads. As always, an array of bangles garnishes her arm.

"It's a pretty morning for your birthday," I say, trying to ignore the menacing clouds gathering over the sea.

She looks back at me. "I knew it would be. I've waited fifty-nine years to celebrate eighty. I even wore my wedding dress."

"That's your wedding dress?" I trot up beside her and study the aged white linen more closely. "The one Rico bought you?"

"No. The one from George Clooney." Laugh lines crease her cheeks, then quickly fade. She's stopped now, and gazing at a pink stucco building with a faded sign beneath an awning that reads *Piacenti's Bakery.*

"That's where you worked," Lucy says.

But Poppy's not looking at the first-floor bakery. Her head is raised, focused on the light in the second-floor window.

"Your old apartment," I say, peering up at it.

"Rico's, too." She stares up at the building as if it's her lost love himself. Finally, she crosses herself and continues toward her destination.

Morning mass has just let out, and a half dozen people amble down the Ravello Cathedral's concrete stairs. Poppy studies each face, her hand at her throat. When the last person descends, she plants a foot on the first step. She peers up at the dozen remaining steps in front of her. It may as well be Mount Everest.

Lucy and I scamper to her side, but she waves us off. She straightens her shoulders and grabs hold of the concrete parapet. It takes her six minutes to reach the top, but she does it, with grace. She's holding her chest when I come up beside her.

"Brava," I say, and kiss her cheek.

"Rico may be watching. I wouldn't want him to think I couldn't climb a single flight of stairs."

I gaze out at the piazza below. But of course Rico isn't watching.

The first hour is hope filled. I open the door to the cathedral and Poppy steps inside. She does a quick perusal of the church's interior, in case Rico forgot that they were to meet on the steps. When she doesn't find him inside, she laughs.

"It's only eight o'clock. The man always loved his sleep."

Above us, the church bells clang nine times. All traces of the sun have vanished, and mist falls from the sky like holy water. Poppy stands beneath the eaves at the cathedral's entrance, surveying the piazza like a queen overlooking her kingdom. But this queen is searching for one person, and one person only. And he's nowhere to be found.

She remains undeterred throughout the damp morning. She loiters on the stair steps in her yellow slicker, ducking inside the cathedral only once, to "powder her nose." I take off my sweater and create a cushion for her on the top step, insisting she sit. Why hadn't I thought to bring a chair, or even a pillow? She's reluctant, but finally she agrees. It takes both Lucy and me to lower her onto the step, and I briefly worry that we won't get her back up. Though she doesn't complain, I see her grimace. I hear the rattling in her chest. She's not well.

Behind us, the cathedral door opens. A white-haired man with a long, thin nose steps out of the church, wearing a clerical collar. He stops when he sees Lucy and Poppy and me, perched on the top step like a trio of pigeons.

"Father," Lucy says. "Would you please take our picture?"

"I'd be happy to."

I hand my phone to the priest, who tells us his name is Father Benedetto, while Lucy helps Poppy to her feet.

"Bei sorrisi!" Father Benedetto says. "Beautiful smiles!"

He hands me the phone. While I check out the picture, I notice Poppy inching closer to the priest. She studies his face, peering closely at his nose. Her hand flies to her throat.

"You," she says. "You married my husband and me. Fifty-nine years ago, right here at Ravello Cathedral. My husband was German. Surely you remember."

His lips tighten and he shakes his head. "No, signora. I have been the priest in Ravello only forty years."

"But . . ." Poppy's voice drifts off.

He turns and makes his way down the wet steps.

"It must have been a different priest," I say, rubbing her back.

By the time the bells chime twelve times, the clouds are spitting rain and my stomach is growling. "How about we break for lunch?" I suggest.

"There is no room for food. My stomach is packed with butterflies. I'm about to see Rico."

"C'mon. Let's stretch your legs."

Poppy won't hear of it. "You girls go ahead. I wouldn't want to miss Rico."

"He'll wait for you," Lucy says.

"Yes, but why make him? He's waited much too long already."

CHAPTER 39

POPPY

1961
Ravello, Amalfi Coast

The room was out of focus, and a wet washcloth bathed my forehead. Where was I? I had a vague memory of lying in the stairwell. I tried to sit up, but a firm hand was holding me down.

"Lie still," a voice from far away called to me.

I was too weak to fight. I closed my eyes and drifted off again. In my dream, Rosa was calling to me. "Open your mouth."

Suddenly, something hot seared my lip. I flinched and opened my eyes.

Rosa sat beside me on the edge of the sofa, a steaming bowl in her hand. She lifted a spoon to my lips. "Eat," she demanded.

The weak broth tasted of salt and burned my throat as it made its way to my stomach.

"Another," she said.

I ate, obedient, until the bowl was empty. Then she held a cup to my lips and made me drink water. When I'd swallowed twice, I found my voice.

"What are you doing here?" My words were hoarse.

She set the cup down on the table. "A letter arrived last week." She removed an envelope from her pocket. "From Germany."

I let out a cry of relief. "Thank God. You came all this way. Grazie, Rosa." I reached for the letter, but she held it from my grasp. "Lie still. I will read it."

My dearest Poppy,

I pray that you are reading this letter, and that you are well and safe in your parents' home. Perhaps you've read other letters I've sent. Perhaps not. As I warned, mail from East Germany is likely to be intercepted or even confiscated altogether.

I am home now, though it feels nothing like it should, or once did. My heart is in Ravello, in our tiny flat above the bakery. My home is wherever you are.

I had hoped that upon my return, I would find my father much improved. I hoped I could say good-bye, once again, and make my way back to you, my love.

Sadly, this is not the case. My mother, who was always fragile, has aged two decades. She cannot finish a sentence without breaking into tears. She is so thin I fear her bones will snap.

She refuses to venture beyond the house. She will not leave my father's side.

Johanna is the only strength in our family, but she alone cannot keep our family business intact. Her husband is useless. Johanna must go to town each day, where food is scarce and lines are so long it can take hours to receive a loaf of bread. Yesterday, she was able to get a tiny can of mango juice. It came all the way from Cuba, one of our Communist trading partners. A sip of that sweet nectar was a bit of heaven in this place I call hell.

I have rolled up my sleeves, and already a dozen cars are waiting to be repaired. I lie beneath them, changing oil, exchanging fan belts. With my head inside the hood, I daydream of you, my beautiful wife. The image of your face is what gets me through these endless days of darkness.

I have thought of nothing else since I left, and I have come to the conclusion, you must go to America.

I gasped, and Rosa stroked my cheek. "Listen to him," she said. "Rico is right. He wants what is best for you. We all do."

"No," I said. "I will never leave Italy. Not until *mein Ehemann* returns."

A flicker of alarm lit Rosa's face. "Please, Paolina, do not be foolish. I know it hurts, but he is not coming back, *la mia sorella testarda.*"

I looked away. Finally, she returned to the letter.

The place where I grew up, the beautiful town of Radebeul, has grown dark and cold. Armed guards keep watch at the borders between East and West twenty-four hours a day, making it increasingly dangerous to escape. But the truth is, amore mio, I cannot leave. Each day, it feels as if the door to freedom is closing for me. I am my family's only hope for maintaining ownership of our father's business, of eking out a meager existence that is just a notch above starvation. And worse, I believe it would kill my mother now if I were to disappear again.

Once, you spoke of coming here, so we would be together. I forbade it then, and I forbid it even more today. I live in a prison. I would never allow you to enter such madness.

So go, please, mio unico amore. Go to America, land of the free, and blossom. I want you to marry again. Yes, take the man's hand — your brother-in-law's uncle — if he pleases you. It will bring me peace, knowing that you are safe and happy and cared for, that I have not ruined your life with my silly dream. But know, please, always, that I love you, and I will continue to love you until my last breath.

One day, we will meet again. I get through each day, dreaming of your eightieth birthday, our fifty-ninth anniversary, and the joy of holding you again at the Ravello Cathedral. Until then, I will guard you — your memory, our love.

Eternally yours,
Rico

I took the letter from Rosa and reread every word three times. "He is gone," I murmured. Panic rose, stealing my breath. I tried to sit up. "My husband is not coming for me."

Rosa held my hand. "Husband? Wife? Why are you using these words?"

I explained the private ceremony at the Ravello Cathedral, the mysterious young priest who blessed our marriage. "We are married," I said. "And I miss him so much."

Rosa's face clouded with tears. "I had to bid good-bye to my Alberto four weeks ago. On the twelfth of January, he and Bruno finally left for America."

I took her hand, shamed by my selfishness. My poor sister was without her love, too, and all I could think about was myself. "Oh, Rosa, I am so sorry. You are in pain as well."

She nodded and dabbed a handkerchief at her nose.

"I understand how you are feeling," I told her. "I realize the power of love now, how it is all-consuming, how you swear you will die if you cannot hold Alberto in your arms. Just like me, without your husband, you feel like a leaf, fluttering in the wind with no direction."

"Sì. That is right." She looked down at her hands. "I only wish my Alberto felt this same way."

"Of course he does. What do you hear

from him? Are he and Bruno happy in their new home? Alberto must be so anxious for you to arrive. He sends you letters, yes?"

Tears filled her eyes. "One. One single letter from my husband, while Bruno has sent a half dozen to Mamma. He tells Mamma of the pub next to the store, the modern American women he meets. Surely Alberto is meeting these same women."

"Rosa, stop. He loves you very much."

But as I spoke the words, I knew in my heart this was not true. Now that I knew love, I recognized its absence. Never had I witnessed Alberto gazing at my sister with tender eyes. I'd never once seen him brush a stray hair from her face, or knead the back of her neck, or stroke her cheek with his thumb. And at night in the attic, on the other side of the partition, I never once heard the sounds of love that Rico and I found impossible to silence.

"He still wants me to come to America as quickly as possible. He still wants to start a family. I must get there before he changes his mind."

"He will not change his mind," I said. "You have much to look forward to."

She smiled, but her face was etched with anxiety. I quickly calculated how long she and Alberto had been married. Seventeen months. And still, no baby.

"Papà says in six more months we will have saved enough to purchase our tickets."

As she spoke, smells from the bakery drifted up through the vent, as they often did. Sweat broke through my skin. I swallowed back a wave of nausea. "But, Rosa, I told you, I will never marry Ignacio. You must understand. I will not leave without Rico."

My eyes landed on the letter. "I must write to him. I must tell him I will wait for him. Surely his father will get better."

"Lie back," she said, and she kissed my forehead. "Tomorrow you will write to Rico. Tonight, you must sleep."

I woke the next morning, alone on the sofa, a tattered blanket covering me. I struggled to rise, my limbs stiff and cramped. The pink of dawn painted the room, like the inside of a seashell. What time was it? The bakery. The bakery! I had to get downstairs to the bakery.

I managed to crawl from beneath the blanket. I stood still, one hand on the sofa, waiting until my legs felt trustworthy. I crossed the room, barefoot, grabbing hold of the walls as I made my way to the bathroom. As I passed our bedroom, I saw my sleeping sister. My heart cried out and I put a hand over my mouth. The small bed where Rico and I slept, the coral-colored quilt beneath which we alone mingled, the one that still smelled of him, no longer felt sacred.

I turned to the bathroom and filled the tub, the rush of the water drowning my tears. I cursed my selfishness. Rosa traveled all the way here to bring news from Rico. Surely she deserved to sleep in the bed. I only wished I'd had one last moment to press my face into the frayed patchwork, to breathe in the scent of my husband's skin, before saying good-bye.

I was standing in the tub, drying myself, when Rosa entered. She took one look at me and let out a strangled cry. She backed up a step, as if I were a hideous creature she was frightened of.

My sister and I had shared a bedroom for all of my life. We didn't knock before entering a room. We didn't hide our bodies from each other. But so much had changed in the past year. I was no longer a girl. I clutched the flimsy towel, trying to cover my nakedness.

She took one tentative step closer to me, then another. With one swift pull, she yanked the towel from my clutches.

"No!" she cried.

I cringed with embarrassment, lowering my eyes. Surely I looked too thin — "skeletal," my full-figured sister might say.

"Incinta," she said, her mouth agape.

The hairs on my arms rose.

She took me by the shoulders and pointed me toward the mirror. "My god, Paolina, you are pregnant."

CHAPTER 40

EMILIA

Lucy and I wrap our arms around Aunt Poppy, trying to shield her from the painful memories. The pregnancy didn't end well. Uncle Dolphie told me.

"I worried Rosa might resent my pregnancy," Poppy says. "But she never appeared to. Not once."

"She was pregnant, too, right?" Lucy says. "That took the sting out of it."

"She was not yet aware. But yes. Once she knew she was going to be a mother, my sister seemed . . . reborn."

"And more sure of Nonno's love?" I ask.

"Yes. Parenthood bonded them."

Two pregnant sisters, but only one with her parents' support, and a husband, and, eventually, a healthy child. I gaze past the square, beyond the pretty little town of Ravello. The terraced hillsides host pergolas of chestnut poles draped with grapevines. An

405

idyllic scene that looks — and feels — forlorn on this misty day. What was it like, living in this magical village while your heart was being torn from your chest? Did she find comfort, listening to the purr of the gulf, gazing out at the frothy Tyrrhenian Sea beyond? Or did the infinite horizon fill her with despair? How long did she stay? Did she continue working at Piacenti's Bakery, living in the upstairs flat? The flat . . .

I rise. "I'll be back."

I dart across the piazza, my idea gaining momentum. What if Poppy could step inside her old apartment, revisit the place she and Rico once shared? Might it comfort her?

The rich aroma of bread and fresh coffee intensifies as I near the old bakery. Up close, I can see that the pretty stucco building is in need of a coat of paint. The door opens, and a tall Italian man steps out, casually dressed in a black Henley shirt and a relaxed knit beanie. With a novel in one hand and a to-go cup in the other, he holds the door with his elbow. An elderly woman shuffles in.

"Grazie, Nico," she says. "You will be taking your grandfather to mass Sunday?"

He grins. "We would not miss it, Signora Cappello."

"You are a good boy." She pats his cheek

as she passes.

His eyes are still smiling when he spots me. "Please," he says, his elbow remaining on the door.

"Grazie," I say. "But I'm not going in."

He steps out and the door swings shut behind him. "Okay, but do not wait too long. Signor Piacenti makes the best espresso in all of Ravello, and he just informed me he is closing his bakery at the end of the year." He gazes into the cloudy shop window. "If I had nine lives, I would take over this lease."

"You're a baker?" I ask.

"I can open a tin of biscotti."

I laugh. "That's a start."

"No," he continues, "I have a different plan for this place."

"It looks like you've got your opportunity."

He gives me a wan smile. "It must remain a dream. You see, I am *un avvocato.*"

I scowl. "You are an avocado?"

He tips his head back and laughs, a rich, full-throated melody that warms me. I bat my head, immediately recognizing my mistake.

"You're a lawyer," I say. "Sorry. That's not a word I use often in Brooklyn."

"Yes, my adorable American friend, I am an attorney. Just like my father, and his father. But if you prefer to think of me as a Mexican fruit, you may."

I laugh. "Okay. Avocado it is."

We stand, facing each other, smiling. Moments pass before I realize I'm staring at this perfect stranger — emphasis on *perfect* — while I'm supposed to be on a mission. "Oh, well, I better go."

"Please, join me for a pastry."

"I'm sorry, but I can't." I hold out my hand. "Good luck to you, Avocado."

He grips my hand and gives me the most genuine smile, one that reaches all the way to his dark eyes. "And to you, American girl. Until we meet again, ciao."

I look back only once as I make my way toward the back courtyard. He's still watching me, with that beautiful smile on his face. I lift a hand and grin, then turn away, another step closer to the woman I want to be.

I round the corner and arrive at a shaded courtyard crowded with potted plants and wandering vines and a perfectly proportioned lemon tree. A shiver runs through me as I climb the staircase to the second floor, imagining my aunt, collapsed on these very same stairs, fifty-nine years ago.

I reach the apartment door, take a deep breath, and knock. Immediately, doubts surface. Am I being rude, asking this favor? Does my aunt even want to see this place again?

Before I have time to turn away, the door opens and a pretty twenty-something woman appears. She's wearing a pair of jeans and a T-shirt.

"Posso aiutarLa?" she asks, leaning to look behind me. Can I help you?

"Sì," I say. "I'm sorry to be so bold, but my aunt lived in this apartment years ago. We're leaving Italy tomorrow. I wondered if perhaps you'd allow her to take a quick tour. It would mean a lot to her."

The woman fidgets with her necklace, and I count at least four rings on her long fingers. "Uh, now is not a good time."

"I understand. I just had to ask. You see, this is her last trip to Italy."

"I am sorry. It is my boyfriend's place, not mine. He is not here, and it is not up to me to allow it."

"Of course."

I return to the steps of the cathedral. I don't tell Poppy about my attempt to arrange a tour of the apartment. The last thing she needs is another disappointment.

It's midafternoon, but the gunmetal sky makes it feel later, colder, lonelier. I sit beside my aunt, holding her chilled hand. She coughs, a deep, chest-rattling cough. She should be in bed. This isn't good for her.

Below, Lucy sits on a bench in the square, using my phone to talk to Sofie. The wind stirs and I tuck the purple scarf around Poppy's neck.

"How about you take a break? I'll walk you back to the hotel, then come right back to watch for Ri—"

"Absolutely not," she says, her face set in granite.

"Let's step into the cathedral," I say. "Just for a minute."

This time, she acquiesces.

I hold open the massive wooden door, assailed by the smell of damp concrete and candle wax. It's not much warmer in the drafty interior of the church than it was outside. Poppy crosses herself with holy water and pauses a moment to catch her breath.

She grips my arm and leads me toward the far side of the cream-colored cathedral, stopping when we reach a statue mounted on the wall. The Blessed Virgin smiles down at us. Poppy clings to the wooden kneeler and slowly drops to her knees. While she prays, I light a candle.

Moments later, she crosses herself and I help her to her feet. She turns toward the nave, looking from one side of the aisle to the other. The cavernous cathedral is empty except for one woman near the front, kneeling in a side pew.

I turn to leave, but Poppy freezes. I follow her gaze. Beside the kneeling woman, almost hidden in the shadows, sits a wheelchair, its back to us. I make out the black collar of an overcoat and the back of someone's head, covered with a spattering of gray fuzz.

"Rico?" Poppy whispers, at once a question and a call and a plea. The hairs on my arms rise.

She charges forward at a snail's pace, grabbing hold of each pew as she moves down the aisle, closer to the man, closer to her dream.

"Rico?" she calls again, her voice a mist of air.

My heart quickens. *Please, God,* I pray.

She moves with urgency, as quickly as her diseased body will carry her. Finally, she's only feet from his chair.

"Rico?" she croaks. The man doesn't move. "Is . . . is it you, Rico?"

The woman pivots in the pew. She smiles

kindly. *"Mio padre,"* she whispers. "Salvatore."

But Poppy doesn't trust her. She grips the metal handle and makes her way around to the other side of the wheelchair. She peers down at the man. Her face falls and her hand goes to her mouth. *"Mi dispiace,"* she says, her voice hoarse. "So sorry."

I don't look at Poppy as we walk back down the aisle. It's a journey for her, one she's waited nearly six decades for. And it's coming to a bitter end.

It's six o'clock and the piazza lights flicker on. Our raincoats are soaked, and Poppy's voice is raspy.

"You are thinking there was no Rico."

"That's not true," I say.

"We know Rico was real," Lucy says. "But for whatever reason, he can't be here today."

Poppy looks from Lucy to me, and back again. "You think he never loved me? That he forgot about me?"

I do believe there was a Rico. And it's entirely possible he loved my aunt fifty-nine years ago. But he may not even be alive anymore. Or maybe his love wasn't as powerful, as lifelong and unwavering as hers. But I don't voice my doubts. Instead, I wrap my arm around her shoulders, hoping to cushion the blow.

"For nearly sixty years," Poppy continues, her raspy voice surprisingly forceful now, "I have held fast to the belief that I was loved. This is what got me through the darkness." She turns her head and gazes up at the cathedral, as if it were an angel. "And now, when the curtains of my life are closing, I don't have to stop believing, not if I don't want to."

It's nine o'clock and darkness has fallen over the Piazza del Duomo. In the distance, thunder cracks. Lucy and I stand under our umbrellas at the foot of the stairs, looking up at Aunt Poppy. She's huddled in the same spot on the steps, a hotel blanket on her lap. We've covered her in a cape of plastic to keep her dry. To anyone passing by, she'd be thought a homeless woman.

"Please take her back to the hotel," I say. "I'll wait here for Rico."

"Forget it, Em. She won't budge. We have to let her wait it out."

"He's not coming," I say. "She's getting sicker by the hour."

"I know," Lucy says, biting her lip. "But how do you make someone give up on something they've been waiting for their entire life?"

413

Her eyes are filled with sympathy, and something else . . . wisdom. It occurs to me that Lucy understands my aunt's determination far better than I do. My cousin knows what it's like, waiting a lifetime for a dream that others desperately want you to abandon.

The twelfth bell chimes. We three make our way across the empty piazza. We reach the hotel. Poppy stops. She turns to face the cathedral one more time, as if still expecting to find Rico, as if somehow she had missed him.

CHAPTER 41

EMILIA

The next morning, we drop our bags in the hotel lobby and settle Poppy onto an over-sized sofa. We've got ten minutes before our driver arrives to take us to the airport.

"Anyone want coffee?" I ask.

Lucy lifts a finger. "Double espresso, grazie."

"How about you, Aunt Poppy?" I squat in front of her. "Can I get you an espresso?"

She looks lost among the sofa pillows, a different woman from the one I watched just weeks ago, bustling around her house with a martini shaker. She's ditched her wig for the first time, and turbaned a silk scarf around her bald head. Her skin is colorless today, her eyes sunken. Still, her beauty is unmistakable.

She shakes her head and raises a hand. A knot of sadness cramps my throat. Earlier this morning, Lucy and I discovered our

415

aunt had not booked a return flight. She'd expected to remain in Ravello, with her love, for the rest of her life. We purchased her a ticket online. She hasn't spoken a word since.

Unlike yesterday, I need sunglasses today, and from the east, a warm breeze laps my skin. I take a deep breath, hoping to shake the ashes from my heart, and trot across the cobblestone piazza toward Piacenti's Bakery. Flowering trees and rosebushes scent the air. Below, the mountain dips to the sea, where foamy white waves lick the shore, a view so spectacular it stops me in my tracks. If only Rico had been at the cathedral yesterday. Instead, Poppy will live the rest of her short life absent a dream, knowing she'll never see the man she spent her entire adult life yearning for.

"American girl!"

I spin around. A man in a white Panama hat rises from a table at an outdoor café. It takes a moment before I recognize him. He's wearing dark sunglasses today . . . and a grin that could melt the polar ice caps.

"Avocado!" I say. *"Buongiorno."*

He waves me over. "Come join us, won't you? Meet my grandfather, Benito."

An old man sits across from him, one side of his face droopy. His hand trembles as he tries to extend it.

"Piacere di conoscerLa," I say, taking his limp hand.

He mumbles something incoherent.

"My grandfather is the smartest man I know," the younger man says, gazing down at his nonno. "He taught me everything I know about law . . . and life."

Benito lifts his misshapen face, his misty eyes brimming with love. He can't speak, but he understood his grandson perfectly. Avocado squeezes his shoulder and calls to the waiter.

"Giorgio! Un altro caffè, per favore." He begins folding his newspaper to make room for me.

"Thanks," I say. "I'd love to join you, but I'm about to leave. I'm making a quick stop for coffee, and then I'm off."

"Tomorrow, then?" His face is so hopeful that I almost believe he'll be crushed.

"I'm flying home today, back to America."

He seems to deflate. "No. Extend your stay. You must. I will show you the beautiful town of Amalfi, where I live and work. It is not far."

I laugh and wave as I walk away. "Enjoy your day, Avocado."

I arrive at Piacenti's and place my order, all the while recalling Avocado's beautiful

417

smile, the compassion he showed to his grandfather, his disappointment when I couldn't stay. After yesterday's bitter defeat, the fleeting encounter feels like a sliver of hope. Maybe I'll actually find love one day, a love like Poppy and Rico's. And maybe, just maybe, the old memories that have surfaced during our trip, however bittersweet, will allow my dear aunt some closure.

Five minutes later, I turn to leave. I fumble with my sunglasses, trying to balance my latte and Lucy's espresso, and practically collide with a woman entering the store.

"*Mi dispiace,*" we say in unison. We laugh and she points at me.

"You are the woman who came to the apartment yesterday."

"Yes," I say, recognizing the rings on her fingers. "And again, I'm sorry for being so bold."

"I spoke to my boyfriend. He said I should have allowed your friend to see the apartment."

"My aunt," I correct her. "Please thank him for me."

"He is there now, if you would like to see it."

I shake my head. "Thanks, but we're leaving this morning. The driver's probably waiting now. But thank you. You're very kind."

How nice to be recognized, twice in one morning, almost like I'm part of this small Ravello community, like I belong. I breeze into the hotel lobby and stop when I spot Lucy in a chair, engrossed in . . . No. No way. Not my notebook!

I march over, plop the coffees on the table, and snatch it from her hands. "What are you doing? I told you, that's private."

She shrugs. "Why? I mean, it's not going to win any prizes or anything, but I'd read it."

I blink several times, bracing myself for a cutting remark. But her eyes hold no malice. And she's grabbing her coffee now. My jaw unclenches ever so slowly.

"You would read it? Seriously?"

She blows on her espresso. "Hell, I'd even buy it. This new story's a hundred times better than the one you were working on in Venice. This one has soul."

Joy breaks free and I laugh out loud. "Thank you!" I hug her neck and she pretends to choke.

"Jesus, kill me, why don't you? Hey, let's grab breakfast."

"Breakfast? We don't have time."

"The driver called. Our flight's delayed. He's picking us up at noon."

My heart quickens and my thoughts scurry. "Forget breakfast. I have a better idea." I turn to Poppy and quickly explain that we've been invited to tour the apartment. "The owner is there now. Shall we go?"

Poppy's ambivalence surprises me. I expected her to be excited. Instead, she drags her feet as we walk.

"You really think this is a good idea?" Lucy whispers to me. "I mean, it could totally bum her out."

"She's already bummed out," I say.

We enter the shady courtyard. Poppy pans the space, then moves to an iron bench beneath the lemon tree.

"Need a minute before we go up?" I ask.

She doesn't answer. Is she afraid of the memories hidden in this place where she last loved? Or worse, is she doubting Rico's love, wondering if the man she devoted her heart to for the past fifty-nine years was a fraud?

CHAPTER 42

POPPY

1961
Ravello, Amalfi Coast

My body was thin to the point of gauntness. But even so, there was no denying the fullness of my breasts, the widening of my hips. No longer could I ignore the tenderness in my nipples, the nausea. Or the two cycles without one drop of blood.

The startling news, the effort of the bath, exhausted me. I had to lie down. Rosa helped me into a dress. Once I was on the sofa, she ran downstairs to beg the baker for three more days off work.

When she returned, I was sitting up. I had two lines written. *My dear Rico, Our love has multiplied. You are going to be a father.* The thought that terrified me only an hour before now thrilled me. I was carrying Rico's child! We were going to be parents.

"What are you doing?" Rosa asked, coming up beside me.

I leaned my throbbing head against the sofa. "This changes everything. Rico will want to be with me and our baby. I will go to him. We will live in Germany with his parents and his sister. Even if it is a poor existence, we will be together."

"In a place he calls prison? You think this is what he wants for his child? No, Paolina. You heard what he said in the letter. He wants you to go to America."

"Maybe his father is not so ill," I said, ignoring her, along with my every rational thought. "Maybe he will choose to escape, and he will come back to us."

She planted her fists on her hips. "And get killed trying to cross the border? How could you live with yourself?"

A shudder rolled over me and my eyes grew heavy. "I know him. He will want to be with his child."

Rosa perched at my side. Very gently, she took the pen from my hand.

"*La mia sorella testarda.* If you are certain this is what he would want, I will help." She touched the pen to the paper. "You talk, I will write."

It felt awkward, revealing my deepest thoughts to Rosa. I longed for a private conversation with Rico, an intimate penning of my joy, sharing the news of our child. But my sister was right. I hadn't the strength to write.

By the time I finished dictating, I was spent. When Rosa held the pen in my fist and helped me sign my name, it was everything I could do to keep my eyes open.

When I woke, Rosa was coming through the door. "Rest easy," she said, perching beside me and stroking my forehead. "The letter is in the mail."

I closed my eyes, grateful for my sister's help, and drifted off to sleep again. My news was on its way to Rico. Soon, we would be reunited.

Rosa was a godsend. I am certain I would have died had she not arrived. She stayed another week, nursing me back to health. While I slept, she negotiated a reduced rent with my landlord and begged my employers to keep me on. She helped me write three more letters to Rico. She shopped at the market each morning and filled my cupboards with fresh fruits and cheeses, hard rolls and meats. When I was able to keep food down, she cooked my favorite dishes.

"You must eat. The baby needs nutrition."

I put a hand to my stomach, loving the

feel of the tiny bulge in my belly, the beautiful oval shape of our child.

I cried when we had to say good-bye. "You saved my life," I told my sister at the train station. "You saved my child's life. I shall never, ever forget it."

She hugged me tightly. "I am happy I could help. And now you will do me a favor." She patted my belly. "Promise to take care of my niece . . . or nephew."

My sister, who was hoping for a child of her own, could not have been more gracious.

"I will make an excuse to come back in six months, before you deliver." She cupped my cheek. "I would come more often, but you know we do not have the extra money."

"It is okay," I assured her. "Rico will be back before the baby comes."

Her eyes clouded, and she nodded. "In case he is not, I will be here."

A wave of anxiety rolled over me. The idea of being alone during labor made me shudder. I clutched Rosa's hands, struck with homesickness I'd not expected. "Will you tell Mamma?"

She shook her head. "I think it would kill her."

I reared back. "But I am married."

"Not according to Mamma's rules, and

God's. Your marriage is not legal, Paolina.
You have nothing from the church that says
you are man and wife. I think it is better to
keep this our secret, sì?"

The following week I woke without nausea.
It was as if a switch had been flipped, and I
was healthy again. No, not healthy . . . radiant! I had a newfound energy, more ambi-
tion than ever before. I found a small bas-
sinet at a junk shop and spent a day painting
it white. The following afternoon, I added
red and blue and green polka dots. That
weekend, I splurged on a ball of yarn and
knitting needles. When I wasn't working, I
was preparing for our child. I chose names
— Erich if it was a boy, and Johanna for a
girl, after Rico's mother and sister. The
future would be kind to our little family of
three, I was certain.

CHAPTER 43

EMILIA

A leaf falls from the lemon tree, landing on Poppy's lap. She looks up, her eyes bright. I wrap her in a hug. "You don't need to tell the rest. I know what happens. And I am so very sorry."

She pulls back and looks at me quizzically.

"Uncle Dolphie told me you lost the baby. I'm so sorry. I know how hard that was for you."

"I went full term." Her voice is shaky and she looks down at her hands. "I delivered Johanna. I held her. She even suckled my breast." She puts a hand to her mouth. "I loved her instantly. It was a magical time. I never dreamed it could end so abruptly."

I'm rubbing Poppy's back, the three of us in tears, when the woman with the rings on her fingers rounds the corner.

"Buongiorno!" she says, her voice bright. Her gaze travels from my weepy aunt to

426

Lucy's red nose. She freezes.

I stand up and swipe my cheeks. "Sorry. We're . . . reminiscing."

"You have time to take the tour?"

I turn to Poppy. "Shall we do this?"

She covers her chin and nods.

We introduce ourselves while climbing the steep staircase. "I'm Elene," the woman says. She holds the apartment door open with her hip and waits until Lucy and I finally reach the landing, Poppy wedged between us.

The space is bright and cheerful, with large windows and whitewashed wooden floors. Though it's small, the high ceilings create an airy feel. Poppy lifts her chin, taking in the place. The walls are painted a soft shade of gray and covered with bold colorful paintings.

Poppy gasps. I follow her gaze to a large painting hanging above the sofa — a giant bouquet of orange poppies. "Papaveri," she says. My body erupts in gooseflesh. What are the odds?

Footsteps fall, and a handsome young man with a striking face enters the living area. His hair is thick and blond.

Poppy gasps. *"Mein Ehemann,"* she whispers. Ever so slowly, she steps forward and extends her arms. *"Mein Ehemann!"*

The man — a twenty-something who obviously is not Rico — looks at her, his brow knit. I can barely stand to watch. He crosses the hardwood floor and gives her an awkward hug. "Hello. I am Jan."

His accent is unmistakably German. I rub the chill from my arms.

"This is my aunt Poppy — Paolina Fontana," I say. "She once lived here . . . with a man named Rico."

He gives Poppy a sympathetic smile. "I am sorry. There is no Rico here."

Poppy shakes her head. "But you look . . ."

"This place belonged to my grandfather Erich."

"Erich?" She clutches her chest, her eyes imploring. "Erich Krause?"

We sit on a modern cream-colored sofa across from Jan, while Elene retreats to the kitchen to make coffee. Jan explains how his grandfather purchased this pied-à-terre the year his wife died.

"Last March, he gave up his home in Germany and came here permanently, to this tiny place, to live out the last of his life."

I swallow hard. They missed each other by only a few months. "Oh, Aunt Poppy," I whisper. "He wanted to be here."

She nods, her chin quivering. If there was

ever a doubt, it's gone now. She was loved.

"He kept the place exactly the same — the tiny kitchenette, the scarred wooden floors."

"Really?" Lucy says. "Because I'm thinking it looks awesome."

"You should have seen it two months ago," Elene says, entering the room with a tray of coffee. She places it on a teak coffee table. "We're selling the building now, so we've updated."

"Come," Jan says. "I will give you a tour."

By tour, he means moving from the combined living room/kitchenette, poking our heads into a sleek marble bathroom, and stepping into the small bedroom overlooking the piazza. Immediately, Poppy turns to the door and lifts her head.

"Do you see it?" I ask, standing beside her, helping search the freshly painted wall for Rico's inscription.

"No," she says, her voice thick. "But it's there. It will always be there."

She steps into the hallway. Without asking permission, she opens a door. A staircase beckons us, presumably to the rooftop deck. She peers up at it before gently closing it again, either too weak or disappointed to climb the dozen steps.

We return to the living room sofa. Jan

leans forward and plants his arms on his knees. "So tell me, Poppy, how do you know my granddad?"

I try to read Jan's face as Poppy reveals the tale of their love. Is he upset? Angry? Embarrassed? It can't be easy, hearing that your grandfather had a wife in another life, a woman he loved so deeply that he purchased the place where they once lived, just to feel her nearness.

"So that's why we're here," I say. "Your grandfather and my aunt promised they'd meet on the steps of the Ravello Cathedral on their fifty-ninth anniversary."

"Incredible," he says. "This explains a lot." He rubs the stubble on his face. "My grandfather's health was failing quickly. We knew he had to get back home to Germany. But he insisted he had to be here on his wedding night, to meet his wife. We thought he was losing his mind. You see, Grandmother Karin had already passed."

"He married Karin," Poppy says, mostly to herself. She stares off into the distance, as if trying to digest this information.

"They were married forty-seven years. My father was the eldest of four children. His name is . . ." He looks up, as if surprised. ". . . Paul."

My throat swells. Had Rico named his son after his love, Paolina?

Poppy reaches into her purse and pulls out a stack of letters, at least a dozen of them, bound with a ribbon. They are addressed to Krause Autoreparatur, Radebeul, Germany.

"These were returned to me," she said. "Eventually, I stopped writing."

She hands them to Jan, and I catch sight of a handwritten note on the top envelope. *Do not write no more. Please.*

Jan turns them over in his hand and examines the note. "My grandmother's handwriting." He shakes his head. "Aunt Joh received all the mail at the shop. I suspect she gave these to her future sister-in-law, rather than to her brother. You see, both women were desperate to keep my grandfather in Radebeul." He stares down at the letters. "Please understand, she was not a bad woman, my grandmother Karin. She was a fine mother and wife. She and my grandfather seemed . . . compatible. Before the wall came down, people did not expect joy."

"When did he pass?" Poppy whispers.

Jan looks at her quizzically.

"She wonders when your grandfather died," I say.

431

"He is still alive, as far as I know. My father arrived last week to take him home to Germany, but Grandfather wasn't strong enough to travel. He was admitted to L'Ospedale Leonardo — the hospital in Salerno. The doctors diagnosed him with a blood infection."

"He's alive?" Poppy says, her voice wavering.

"He's alive!" I repeat, rising. "We need to see him."

"I am afraid it would be a disappointment. My grandfather is completely . . . what is the word . . . unresponsive. Father says he no longer eats. He hasn't uttered a word since he left Ravello."

"I must see him," Poppy says.

"But you are leaving today, sì?" Jan shakes his head. "Salerno is an hour to the east; Naples International is three hours northwest."

From her place on the sofa, she rises. "I will not leave *mein Ehemann.* Not this time." Her voice is strong and fierce. She's never looked prouder or more certain.

Before Italy, I would have hidden behind a thousand excuses, for fear of Nonna's wrath. *Poppy's too sick. Rico won't even know she's there. Nonna expects me back at work.* But today, I don't hesitate. I lace my fingers with hers. "I'm staying, too."

She squeezes my hand and turns to Lucy. "I know you must get back to that new job of yours."

"And miss all the fun?" Lucy cracks a smile. "Nice try, Pops, but this chick's going nowhere."

Ninety minutes later, we five — Jan and Elene, Aunt Poppy and Lucy and I — race down the sterile corridor of L'Ospedale Leonardo. My heart thumps wildly as I push Poppy in a borrowed wheelchair. She's applying lipstick as we move. *Please let Rico live long enough to share a final good-bye.*

I'm out of breath when we reach room 301. A nurse flags us down, handing us each a paper mask. Jan offers Poppy a hand, but my proud aunt rises from her wheelchair independently. Once on her feet, she pats her head, as if to smooth her hair. But today, of all days, she opted not to wear her wig. Her hand goes still upon her bare scalp, partially covered with the scarf. She sucks in a breath, and I can almost hear what she's thinking. Her beloved will see her bald head.

"You're gorgeous," I say through my mask and point her toward the door.

CHAPTER 44

EMILIA

Salerno, Italy

The blinds are closed, and the dusky room smells of disinfectant and decay. Machines blink and hiss. Elene, Lucy, and I stand aside as Poppy steps up to the hospital bed. She clutches her throat.

"Rico."

He wears a veneer of silent agony on his lifeless gray face, a patchwork of age spots and yesterday's whiskers. An IV needle punctures his arm, and an oxygen tube fills his nostrils. Poppy leans in over the bed rail and cups his face. Tears well in her eyes. "Rico, it's me, Poppy."

The old man in the bed — Rico — doesn't move. A shiver runs over me. Is he even breathing? Poppy smooths his hair, still thick but gray and coarse looking now. Wiry hair sprouts from his nostrils and ears. But

I can still detect the strong jawline Poppy described, and somewhere in my mind's eye, I see the handsome man who played the violin in Piazza della Signoria.

"Rico," Poppy says again, her voice strained. "Wake up. It's me, *mein Ehemann.*" Desperation clings to every syllable.

Rico lies motionless. From the other side of the bed, Jan calls to him, each word loud and deliberate. "Opa, you have company."

"Poppy," she says, her voice quivering. She lowers the metal bed rail. With shaking hands, she removes her paper mask. Slowly, she bends down to kiss his sunken cheek. "It's me, Poppy."

She adjusts Rico's hospital gown, smoothing the green fabric. A ghastly scar appears on Rico's shoulder. She runs a finger over the thickened skin.

"What happened to you, my love?"

"Bullet wound," Jan says. "My grandfather tried to escape from East Germany in 1961, and again in 1963."

Poppy drops her bald head onto the old man's chest, and I can almost see the pride, the vindication, the regret pouring from her. "I knew it. I knew you would try to come back for me. I should have waited for you. I am sorry. I am so sorry."

She finally straightens, and Jan presses a

wet washcloth to the old man's cheek. "Poppy is here. Wake up, Opa."

"Please, Rico, I have so much to tell you."

The room goes silent. From the hallway, muted Italian voices call from the PA. We wait, wishing, hoping, praying, he will respond. Poppy strokes Rico's hand, his cheeks, her eyes pinned to his hollow, vacant face, whispering her love over and again. Despite the ache in my heart, it was worth the four-thousand-mile journey just for this — Poppy's one last glimpse, one last touch, of her beloved Erich.

A tiny movement startles me. I inch closer.

Ever so slightly, Rico's eyebrow twitches.

"Rico!" Poppy cries. "It's me. Poppy. Wake up, *mein Ehemann.*"

Rico's forehead creases. Shivers blanket me. My heart batters in my chest. *Please, open your eyes!* In all of my life, I've never wanted anything more. I will every ounce of my strength to this man.

Softly, Poppy begins to sing. *"Que será, será. Whatever will be, will be."* Her voice is craggy and she sings off-key. I've never heard a more beautiful rendition.

Rico's lids flutter. I can almost feel the strain of each muscle as he battles to lift his eyelids. Poppy moans and leans in, stroking his cheek.

"It's me, Rico," she says, her voice breaking. "I came here. To Ravello. To see you. On our anniversary. All day, I waited."

His right eye cracks open for an instant, then slams shut again.

"Yes!" Poppy's laughter gets tangled in a sob. "It is me, my love, your Poppy!"

Slowly, almost imperceptibly, as if using every bit of strength he can muster, his eyes strain to open.

"Opa!" Jan cries. Quickly, he fumbles to place a pair of glasses on his grandfather's face. Rico stares blankly through the lenses. From over Poppy's shoulder, I gaze into rheumy eyes the color of aquamarine.

Poppy sobs. "Mister Blue Eyes. I love you, my sweet man. I love you." She bends over and presses her wet cheek to his face. She whispers her love, her undying love, all of the tender words she's longed to share with him for the past fifty-nine years.

His eyes fall closed again.

"I never gave up on you, Rico. I never stopped loving you."

I wonder if he hears her, or if he's drifted back to sleep. But very slowly, his eyes lift again. A leathery hand rises, the one that once so deftly held a violin bow. He touches his fingers to my aunt's face.

"Poppy," he mouths. When his crusted lips

move, they carry no sound. But the words are unmistakable. *"Mio unico amore."*

For the rest of the day, Rico's eyes remain closed, as if he'd spent his last drop of energy to profess his love and the effort left him drained. Maybe it's my imagination, but the earlier agony etched upon his sleeping face seems to be replaced now by a contentedness, a serenity. I like to think the glimpse of his love, after all these years, was the missing peace he'd been searching for.

Visiting hours are almost over, and Jan and Elene have gone to retrieve the car. Lucy and I step from the room, allowing Poppy a private good night with her sleeping prince, one that very well could be their last.

While Lucy meanders up and down the hallway, talking to Sofia on Poppy's phone, I tap open my text messages. It's mid-afternoon in New York, and Matt's probably out on a job. How can I possibly put the week's events into words?

So much to tell you, MC. My aunt met the love of her life today. We're staying in Ravello until he . . . I swallow hard and say a silent prayer . . . recovers.

I press send, then punch in Carmella's number. As I predicted, my sweet cousin is thrilled to continue staying at Emville, taking care of Claws.

"Stay as long as you want, Emmie," she tells me. "Now, sit back while I catch you up on my life. Do you have a minute or thirty?"

"We're getting ready to leave and I need to call my dad."

"No worries," she says. "Just know that I'm loving life in Emville. Claws is cranky as ever. We'll talk when you get home."

Finally, I make the call I've been avoiding all afternoon. My dad answers on the first ring.

"Thank God you're home." I imagine him behind the meat counter, shouldering his flip phone while he replenishes sausages for the after-work customers. "Your nonna can finally rest. Are you coming in today, or will I see you at home?"

My heart thumps. "I'm still in Italy, Dad. Lucy and I are staying here with Poppy."

Through the phone, a heavy sigh escapes him, one he's likely been holding for the past ten days. "No. Emilia, be reasonable. You must get back now. Let Lucy take over from here."

"Aunt Poppy needs me."

"Your nonna needs you, too. She is expecting you at work. You must be respectful of her."

I gaze past the open door of room 301, where my aunt cups Rico's sleeping face in her hands.

"One who demands respect will never command it." Out of nowhere, the statement comes to me, a "Poppy-ism" if ever there was one. My chest puffs with pride.

"What are you saying?" my father asks.

"I don't know when I'll be back," I say. "I'm staying here as long as Poppy needs me."

The October moon is full tonight, illuminating the road as we wind our way back to Ravello. Poppy sits between Lucy and me in the backseat, her head pressed against my shoulder. A soft ballad plays on the radio, and I say a silent prayer of thanks. Poppy and Rico shared a moment, however fleeting. What a trip this has been. We, all three of us Fontana second daughters, found love. The still-cynical part of me wonders whose, if any, will last.

Lucy turns to Poppy in the moonlight. "Can I ask you something, Pops? Those letters you brought, the ones Karin returned to you, they were mailed from Italy. What about the letters you wrote from the US?

You think he ever got those?"

"I never sent a letter from America. I was too ashamed." She lets out a sigh. "You see, a mother has one job: to protect her child. I couldn't tell Rico that I had failed that singular task, not in a letter." She turns to the darkened window. "It would have to wait until I saw him in person."

CHAPTER 45

POPPY

1961
Ravello, Amalfi Coast

Rosa stepped from the bus the second day of August, a shawl draped over her shapeless gray dress. She looked different — older yet softer — than the last time I'd seen her, six months earlier. Her face was full and her eyes somehow wiser. And her figure had become lush, with ripe hips and large breasts. She caught me gawking and her face turned pink.

"I have been eating too much pasta," she said.

"You do not fool me. You are pregnant!"

Her eyes flooded with tears and she crossed herself. I pulled her into a hug. "We are both having babies, like we'd always dreamed!"

"Stop. Please. Can we not talk about this

442

yet? It is your time now."

I understood. After trying for so long to get pregnant, she was afraid she might jinx it. "You look gorgeous," I told her. "Alberto will be mad for you."

This time she did not turn anxious at the mention of his name. "Alberto is writing to me every week. He is very excited for me to come to America."

I smiled at my sister. "Of course he is." I patted my round belly. "I appreciate you being here for the baby's arrival." And I was. But my gratitude was tempered by disappointment. In my heart, I believed Rico would be here when I gave birth. My faith was wavering. Was he alive? "Have I received any mail from Rico?"

Even though he should have known to write to me here in Ravello, I held my breath, hoping against hope she'd say yes.

"A letter arrived last month."

My heart nearly leapt from my chest. "He still thinks I am in Trespiano? Where is it? Let me see!"

She shook her head. "Papà found the letter before I could hide it. He was livid. I risked my life by snatching the envelope while he was talking to Mamma."

I smiled at my sister's unusual burst of courage. "Grazie, Rosa. Now please, I must read it."

"I do not have it. I threw it into the fireplace before Papà could see it."

I gasped. "You destroyed it?"

"I had no choice. He would have killed us both. I am sorry. But I did manage to read it first."

"You read it? What did he say? When is he coming?"

"He cannot leave." She shook her head. "He wants you to go to America. He wants you to marry Ignacio."

The air became scarce. I put my hands to my head. "No! Rico is my husband! How dare he ask me to commit adultery?"

Sympathy welled in her eyes. "Listen to him, Paolina. He loves you. He wants what is best. He refuses to raise the child in his homeland. It is a prison there. The people are desperate to escape. Have you not read the paper? East Germany is no place for a baby. He wants you to have a good life, and more important, he is trusting you to provide the same for his child."

Tears blinded me.

"Think of the baby, Paolina. Not yourself. You can no longer be selfish."

We walked arm in arm back home, each of us lugging a suitcase. I listened as she told me about her travel journey. She had concocted a story, telling our parents that I'd had a change of heart, that I no longer loved Rico. She was coming to get me. We would travel together to America. She had already said her final good-bye to Mamma and Papà.

"I have our papers, your passport, everything we need, in these suitcases. Our ship leaves from Napoli next month."

"But Rosa, I am not going to America. I must wait for —"

She held up a hand, silencing me. "Mamma and Papà were so relieved, Paolina. Their daughter has come to her senses. They were worried I would have to make the journey to America alone."

But I knew better. It was Rosa who was worried. She knew she must travel to Brooklyn, especially now that she was carrying Alberto's child. And she still hadn't given up on the idea that I'd join her. I forced myself to hold my tongue. When Rosa had her mind made up, there was no reasoning with her. Soon enough, she would find that I could be just as stubborn as she.

"I convinced Papà to purchase two tickets," she continued. "Our ship leaves in six weeks. Which means . . ." She turned and looked me up and down. "You must deliver this child soon, so we can leave and start our new lives with Alberto and Ignacio, in America, land of the free."

Five days later, on the seventh of August 1961, with the help of Signora Tuminelli, a grouchy midwife my sister found in the next village, Johanna Rosa Krause was born. She had thick, dark hair and blue-black eyes, and Rico's dimple in her left cheek.

They say that motherhood changes a woman. That when she holds her child for the first time, something shifts. Priorities change.

I lay upon the fresh sheets, baby Joh asleep on my chest. I gazed down at her in awe, the miracle of life created by Rico and me. I studied her downy skin, the long lashes splayed against cheeks pink as a sunrise, the ten little matchstick fingers, each capped with a miniature pearl.

"Welcome home," I whispered to her. "May the essence of kindness fill you. May you be blessed with goodness, and carry with you the best parts of me and the best parts of your father." Tears blurred my vision. "Your papà may not be here, but he loves you. He — we — want only good things for you. You are going to have a wonderful life, full of opportunity and riches and joy. I promise you. And I promise him."

Eight days later, Rosa blew into the apartment waving a newspaper. "They've built a wall!" she cried. "Two days ago, the free passage between East and West Berlin was sealed off with barbed wire. Today, they are building a wall out of concrete, five meters high." She held one hand to her belly as she read from the article. "It will be topped with barbed wire, guarded with watchtowers and machine guns and mines." She tossed the paper onto the table and took my hands. "Access to the West is closed, Paolina. Permanently. Rico will never return."

CHAPTER 46

EMILIA

I dab Poppy's wet cheeks with a tissue, worried that the painful memories are too much for her fragile spirit. She leans back and closes her eyes.

"How could I celebrate the birth of my child while grieving the loss of Rico? The cruelty of the Berlin Wall was too much. I allowed my Joh to slip away. In my sadness, in the darkness of my despair, I didn't realize how quickly she was fading."

So that's it. The Berlin Wall was erected. Rico was trapped. Poppy suffered from severe depression, so all-encompassing she didn't even realize her baby was dying. I shudder, wondering what, exactly, happened to baby Johanna. Rosa was wise to bring Poppy to America. But she left all hope of Rico behind. Two hearts separated by war and wounds and a godforsaken wall. I kiss Poppy's hand.

"I am so sorry."

"Ditto," Lucy says, her voice thick.

"Rosa's waiting was finally over. We were both taken by surprise. When my sister arrived in Ravello, she wasn't expecting motherhood to come so soon. She chose the name Josephina, after our mother's mother."

A shiver goes through me. One sister gives birth, the other buries her child. And the names — Johanna and Josephina — so very similar. Could the gods be any crueler? It's no wonder Poppy transferred her love to Josephina.

From the car stereo, a sonorous ballad plays. The melancholy notes make my nose sting. Lucy shapes her sweater into a pillow, and soon she's propped against the door, softly snoring. Poppy sighs when I reach for her, almost a purr. She's a small child in my arms, in need of comfort tonight. Her breathing slows. Her body falls limp against mine. My arm goes numb and begins to tingle. I don't move. I breathe in the sweet scent of my aunt, feel the faint rise and fall of her breath, hoping that years from now, I can close my eyes and retrieve this very moment.

"I should have tried harder to connect

with you," she whispers. "Please forgive me."

I stroke her downy head. "There is nothing to forgive. You tried. But I allowed Nonna . . ." My words trail off. I'm an adult now. It's not fair to blame Nonna.

"Next time you speak to Rosa, please tell her I'm sorry. That I love her."

Uncle Dolphie was right. Reconciliation would give Poppy peace — and probably my nonna, too. "Why not tell her yourself? We can call her tomorrow."

She shakes her head. "I phoned Dolphie just before leaving the States. We had a lovely conversation. But Rosa . . . she will not speak to me."

I clench my jaw, anger burning in me. "She's stubborn," I say, "like my sister."

"Yes. I've tried many times to reach out to Daria."

I look down at her. "Really? She never told me."

"You and I are together. That's enough."

"Thank God," I whisper, and I kiss her head. "And thank you."

"I love you, Emilia."

"I love you, too, Nonna."

I catch my mistake, but for some reason, I don't correct myself. Neither does my aunt.

Jan drops us off at Rico's old apartment above the bakery. "It is yours for as long as you need it," he says, handing Poppy an old-fashioned brass key. "I will stay down the hill at Elene's."

Lucy helps Poppy into her nightgown before retreating to the living room sofa. I dampen a cloth and wash Poppy's soft cheeks.

"I always dreamed I'd sleep in this room again," Poppy says, staring up at the wall above the door. "He carved our initials. They are still there, somewhere."

"I know," I say. "He loved you very much."

"He still does," she reminds me, and I'm ashamed that I referred to him in the past tense.

The sheets are crisp when I pull them down, and Poppy burrows into them like a little kitten. I climb in beside her and turn off the lamp. Amber light from the piazza stripes the room.

"Did you get in touch with Brody?" Poppy asks.

"I did." I say a silent thanks to Brody, Poppy's helper back home. "He's happy to continue watching over the farm until we return. He wants you to know he's riding Higgins every day, keeping him exercised."

Poppy nods. "Brody refuses to accept a raise, though God knows he could use the money. Did I tell you he lost his leg in Vietnam? Never utters a complaint. The man is a peach, just like his father was."

It seems strange now, to think that Poppy had a whole other life without Rico, that she had a relationship with Brody's father, her "man companion." As my beautiful aunt's life comes to a close, I can't help but wonder, does she have regrets?

"Did you ever want to get married again? Have children?"

"No," she says without hesitation. "Though I did love Thomas."

"Brody's dad? He wasn't just a . . . consolation prize?"

She turns to me. "You'll find the older you get, the less stingy you become with the word 'love.' Thomas taught me to laugh again. And I believe I was a comfort to him, after his wife died. We were wonderful comrades, Thomas and I." She smiles, as if recalling a sweet memory.

A breeze rustles the sheer curtain. "Does it bother you that Rico married Karin?"

"I'd be sad if he hadn't. You see, Emilia, not every love requires passion, nor does all

452

passion require love."

The air seems to still. A vision of Matt's sweet smile comes to me. I prop myself onto my elbow and search her shadowed face. "Do you honestly believe that, Aunt Poppy? Do you really think it's possible to be with someone — maybe even marry someone — if you don't feel passion?"

"I believe it happens all the time."

A shiver blankets me. I feel as if I'm speaking to a wise sage who holds the answer to the question I've pondered for years. And everything hinges on her reply.

"But is that fair? Is that enough? Or should I — should everyone — hold out for the kind of love that sets your skin aflame?"

She smiles. "That, my dear, is a question we can answer only for ourselves. All I can tell you is that, after eighty years, I realize that love plays many roles. Paramour. Comforter. Protector. Mate. Though Rico is my heart's only true passion, there's much to be said for a love that provides deep friendship, or simply companionship, in a world that can sometimes feel like a fisted glove."

Her eyes glisten in the night's glow. "In the end, life is a simple equation. Each time you love — be it a man or a child, a cat or a horse — you add color to this world. When

453

you fail to love, you erase color." She smiles. "Love, in any of its forms, is what takes this journey from a bleak black-and-white pencil sketch to a magnificent oil painting."

She touches my cheek. "It's the sweet fruit that paints the field and wakes our senses. I'm not saying you must be on a constant quest for it, but please, if love comes to you, if you find it within your grasp, promise me you'll pluck it from the vine and give it a good looking-over, won't you?"

Her words wash over me as I try to reconcile the idea of Matt-my-pal becoming Matt-my-potential-love. Is it possible I haven't given him a good enough "looking-over"?

As I begin to drift off, she grabs my hand, her grip stronger than I'd have expected.

"Your mother loved you very much."

I freeze. I was only two when she died. Much of that time, she was ill. I've always wondered, was I the one who caused her illness? Did she resent me? Was I a bother to her?

"How do — ?" I force the words over the knot in my throat. "How do you know for sure?"

"You were her angel. That's what she called you."

Tears slide past my temples. All my life,

I've longed to hear these words. "But she never knew me, the person I am. I was just a baby."

Poppy's grip tightens. "A mother's love isn't measured in time, Emilia. It's instantaneous and everlasting. And this, my dear, I know for certain."

CHAPTER 47

POPPY

1961
Aboard the SS *Cristoforo Colombo* En
  Route to America

Rosa got her way in the end, as she was accustomed to. But to be fair, I went willingly. It seemed my only option. The eight-day voyage from Napoli to New York was mercifully calm. The days brought warm breezes and only the occasional thunderstorm. But newly born Josephina had her days and nights confused. Each evening, after we'd tucked ourselves into our stuffy cabin, Josephina's eyes grew wide and curious. The duties of motherhood exhausted Rosa, and I did everything I could to keep the baby quiet while she slept. Often, I'd bundle her up and sneak out onto the deck, where we'd stand facing eastward, looking back toward the land where my Rico lived. Together, we'd watch the following black sea rise and fall. I'd point out the constellations, and we'd talk about her future.

Though Rosa understood I was grieving, she was prickly when I was alone with Josie. She'd caught me, more than once, pretending to be a new mother en route to see her loving husband. The roles of wife and mother, she gently reminded me, belonged to her.

But Josephina and I shared a connection Rosa could not deny. She was a listener, my little vessel of joy. She'd study my face, wrinkle her little brow when I spoke of my Rico, the greatest man on earth. And when my eyes grew misty, she'd latch onto my finger, as if to reassure me that she understood my pain.

I called her my tiny miracle, and told her she was the reason I breathed. Because she was.

CHAPTER 48

EMILIA

A long and lonely voyage, taking her farther and farther from her love and the infant she lost . . . nights spent with a new baby, with a name so similar to her own child's. No wonder Poppy displaced her maternal longing and became overly attached to Josie.

"It all makes sense now," I say, facing her. "You grew to love Josephina as your own. You were grieving. You meant no harm."

She's gripped with a wracking cough. I pat her back, a sense of foreboding coming over me. Poppy is dying. Earlier, she asked for forgiveness. I treated the request dismissively. But I realize now, she needs to hear it. Even if it's not from her sister.

"I don't blame you," I say, my voice soft, "for what you did to my mother, for taking her."

"Kidnapping," she whispers. "That's what they called it."

458

"You weren't yourself. Nonna should have understood."

"I believe she did, deep in her heart. It was Alberto who insisted I leave. And of course Rosa agreed with her husband. I put her in a horrible position, having to choose. It is my biggest regret. Not a day has passed when I didn't question my decision, or curse myself for acting so recklessly."

"Shh," I say. "That's all behind you. You've created a beautiful life for yourself, filled with people who love you. You should feel proud."

She turns to me, her eyes imploring. "When you see Rosa again, tell her I'm sorry. That I love her. That I've never stopped missing her."

My heart shatters. And then a thought strikes. I study Poppy in the moonlight, my mind reeling. What if I were able to bring Nonna to Italy for a final sister reunion?

They say time heals all wounds. But in witnessing the simultaneous recoveries of my aunt and her beloved Rico, I can profess it's not time but love that heals.

I insist on taking Poppy to the doctor first thing Wednesday morning. All along, Lucy and I assumed the advancing brain tumor was causing her decline. We're surprised when the young physician treats her for a respiratory infection, giving her an intravenous cocktail of antibiotics and steroids and fluids. By Thursday afternoon, she's champing at the bit, ready to get back to Rico's side.

I rent a car — a sporty white convertible Poppy insisted we splurge on — and for the next week and a half, we rise at dawn and drive to Salerno. Even on cool mornings, she makes me put the top down. "That's what heated seats are for," she tells me. "Now, give it some gas. My goddess, Emilia, it's a Maserati, not a minivan."

While Poppy sits at Rico's bedside, combing his hair, shaving his face, whispering her love, he slowly comes back to life. Every day, we see progress. He opens his eyes again. He smiles. He utters words, then speaks in short sentences. The doctor calls it a miracle. Poppy calls it fate. I call it beautiful.

By the second week, Rico's eating on his own again, and most days he's sitting in his wheelchair when we arrive, plucking his violin strings or fiddling with his old Leica camera. The color has returned to his face, and it's easy to see the dashing German violinist who charmed the crowds — and my aunt. His jawline may not be as chiseled, his body might not be as taut, but I can clearly see the piercing blue eyes, the head of hair still thick and wavy, the brilliant smile that Poppy adored.

As if we'd struck some tacit agreement, Lucy and I talk in future tense, both of us intent on staying in Italy until our aunt's dying breath. We take up a comfy spot in the hospital visitors' lounge, giving Poppy and Rico their privacy.

Lucy sits at the hospital's complimentary computer for hours at a time, researching something, though she won't tell me what. Lucky for us, I still write the old-fashioned way — in my notebook. But now, the words stream from my pen, as if all around me the air is charged with love and light and a resurgence of life. When, hours later, we return to Rico's room, we often catch them snuggled together in the hospital bed, Rico stroking Poppy's bald head. Other times, they're laughing at an old memory. Still other times we find them in tears, and I suspect they're talking about the child — and the time — they lost.

"I want to marry you at the cathedral," Rico tells her one rainy Monday, his voice deep and raspy. "I have all my paperwork completed for the government."

She bats a hand at him. "We're already

461

married!"

My independent aunt, a second daughter who, after all these years, feels no need to prove their love, kisses her husband's cheek. "You have been *mein Ehemann* for nearly six decades. You always will be."

He smiles. "And you shall always be my wife."

Poppy claps her mouth, as if catching herself, and spins around to where Lucy and I stand. "Oh, dear," she says. "How thoughtless we are. Might it be important for you two that we marry?"

She's letting us know, in case we're concerned, that she will put an end to the Fontana Second-Daughter Curse with a legal marriage certificate, in a way nobody can dispute. I have zero need for this sort of closure. But perhaps Lucy does. I let her answer for us.

"If you marry," Lucy says, her voice slow and deliberate, "just to disprove some effed-up, whack-a-doodle curse that never was, I, for one, will not be attending the wedding."

It's November third, a warm, overcast Saturday, and we're sitting at a table in the hospital courtyard playing Shoot the Moon, a card game Poppy taught us.

"You had a club in your hand, but you

played a spade," I say to Rico. "No wonder you always win."

Rico tsks and shakes his head, laugh lines shooting from the corners of his eyes. "You are a poor loser, *mein Mädchen.*"

My girl. Just like my aunt calls me. He places the cards into a box and reaches beneath the table for his old Leica camera.

"Enough with the pics," Lucy says, sticking out her tongue as he snaps a picture of her. She yanks the camera from him. "You three," she says and motions for us to gather.

Poppy comes up on one side of me, Rico on the other, their hands intertwined. Poppy kisses my cheek. I turn to Rico, his blue eyes bright with joy and love.

"Say *formaggio*!" Lucy says, making me laugh just as she snaps the photo. She sets down the camera and scoots to the edge of her chair.

"Guess what?" she says. "I've finally decided what to do with my life. Ready for this?" She mimics a drumroll. "Duh-duh-duh-dah! I want to cut hair. That's right, I'm not exactly sure when or where, but at some point I'm enrolling in barber school!"

"Marvelous!" Poppy says, clapping her hands.

"So that's what you've been researching on the hospital computer." I hold out my

463

hand for a fist bump. "That's awesome, Luce."

"I emailed all the info to Carol and Vinnie. My mom thinks I should go to cosmetology school instead, but I like cutting men's hair. I'm not into waxing and facials and all that stuff."

I cannot believe this is the same girl who once chose her eyeliner over her toothbrush.

"I talked to Grandpa Dolphie about it," she continues. "He says I can do an apprenticeship in his shop."

I picture Uncle Dolphie's forlorn shop, with the opera music and empty chairs. He has no idea what he's in for. His granddaughter will flip his sleepy shop on its axis, providing a much-needed shot of adrenaline. Uncle Dolphie will complain every step of the way. But deep inside, he'll love it. Finally, he'll have a purpose again. His shop — the business he worked so hard to build — will continue on to the next generation. He will not be forgotten. Isn't that what we all want?

"You're becoming the character your playwright intended," Poppy says. "Next year, after you've finished barber school and Emilia has completed her novel, we will all celebrate together."

"Sure thing," Lucy says without hesitation. But I remain silent. Will our aunt even be alive a year from now? Will Rico?

Poppy's eyes hold mine until finally, I agree.

"But the novel," I say. "You're thinking I'll have it finished in a year? I'm not sure it's poss—"

"It's possible," she says and winks.

Lucy's explaining the difference between a cosmetologist and a barber when Rico's doctor approaches. "There you are!" She's wearing her white lab coat, an iPad tucked beneath her arm. "I have good news, Mr. Krause. Your lab results remain stable. I am signing your discharge papers. Tomorrow morning, you are free to go home."

Rico chokes up, and I can only imagine what these words mean to a man who's spent much of his life behind a wall.

Tomorrow he will return home, to the tiny apartment he shared with Poppy. He's healthy now, and so is she. My mission here is accomplished. But might there be a greater mission? A mission Uncle Dolphie proposed last fall?

I motion to Lucy, and she follows me over to a little flower garden, where patients' names are memorialized in carved stepping-stones.

"I know what you're going to say," Lucy

says. "The lovebirds need some space. Those apartment walls are pretty thin." She wiggles her eyebrows.

"Uncle Vinnie really should have invested in charm school." I shake my head. "I'm going home, Luce."

She rears back. "No. Not yet. We'll rent our own place, here in Ravello."

"I've got to go. Just for a few days." I fill her in on the rest of Poppy's story, the heartbreak of baby Johanna's death, how crossing the Atlantic with a newborn baby was too much for Poppy, resulting in a displaced affection that eventually ended in Poppy's biggest regret.

"I will convince Nonna to come back here with me and patch things up with Poppy before . . ." I stop short of saying, *Before it's too late.*

CHAPTER 49

EMILIA

Two days later, as Monday's dawn flirts with the horizon, Lucy and I stack our suitcases at the door. Rico focuses his old Leica camera on Lucy, Poppy, and me. "Are you sure you must leave?" he asks for at least the fifth time.

"We're coming back, you know," Lucy says, making a face at the camera. "As soon as I break my parents' hearts and Em finds someone to rent Emville."

We haven't revealed the plan to bring Nonna back here for a final sister reunion. The odds are too slim to get anyone's hopes up.

"Safe travels," Poppy says, tucking a penny into each of our purses. "Remember to spread your sunshine. Never underestimate the importance of your light to someone living in a bank of clouds."

"Aw, c'mon!" Lucy says. "We'll be back in

a flash." She looks at Aunt Poppy and winks. "So, you might want to take advantage of your alone time. Just saying."

Poppy laughs and grabs her in a hug. "Luciana, you slay me!" She looks at me, her face growing serious. "You'll talk to Rosa? Tell her I'm sorry?"

I kiss her cheek. "Absolutely."

Rico opens his arms to me. Though he's certainly stronger than he was, he's still too thin.

"Auf Wiedersehen, meine schöne Enkelin," he says to me in his native language. He pulls back, his eyes misty, and strokes my cheek with his hand. In his gravelly voice, he whispers, *"Ich liebe dich."*

I don't need to translate the German words. His eyes tell me everything I need to know. "I love you, too," I say.

Lucy and I walk to the end of the street, where a lone taxi idles. The driver leans against the hood, smoking a cigarette. He flicks it onto the pavement when he sees us and pops the trunk. While Lucy helps load our bags, I turn back to the little pink bakery. Poppy and Rico stand at the courtyard gate, the first hint of dawn drenching them in lilac. I wave a final good-bye.

"I love you," I call, hoping they hear me.

Rico's arm is draped around Poppy's

shoulders, and she's dabbing her eyes. He leans in and, ever so gently, kisses her cheek. He says something, and even from here, I can hear her laughter.

Love, in any of its forms, takes the world from a bleak pencil sketch to a magnificent oil painting.

The flight to New York is full. I stuff my purse beneath the seat in front of me, still reeling with thoughts of my aunt and Rico. What a privilege it has been, witnessing their love. Will I ever have that kind of connection?

I rub my throat, and one man appears in my mind. One man who loves me, who'd wait for me while I finish my duties in Italy, no matter how long it might take. One man who makes me laugh, who cheers me on, who makes me a better person. One man who I know, without a doubt, would gladly be a character in my final chapter, when I'm old and ill and fading to gray.

I reach for my phone. On my way home, MC. I take a deep breath. Let's talk.

My future with Matt comes alive in my mind. Once Poppy is gone, I'll return to the States. Bensonhurst will be my world. Forever. Despite myself, a wave of loneliness rolls over me. My little life, working at

469

the bakery, watching Netflix with Matt, seems stifling now. But that's natural after being on an adventure, I assure myself. I'll adjust again. Before long, it'll be like I never left.

I toss my phone into my purse. In the aisle beside Lucy, a handsome flight attendant pours drinks. My cousin lowers her tray table. "I ordered you a club soda while you were texting."

"Danke schön," I say, choosing German for some reason.

She tears open a bag of pretzels. "You really speak German? Like, did you understand a word of what Rico said to you this morning?"

I snag a pretzel from her bag. "I could make out most of it. I have a pretty good ear, and I took two years of German in college."

She rolls her eyes. "My cousin, the brainiac."

"He said, Good-bye, my beautiful something-or-other." I smile. "It sounded like, 'my beautiful ankle.' "

Lucy laughs. "Who knew ol' Rico was a leg man?"

The flight attendant places a Diet Coke on Lucy's tray and looks over at me. "Granddaughter."

"Excuse me?"

"*Enkelin.* It's the German word for granddaughter."

Time slows. The hairs on the back of my neck stand erect.

Lucy lets out a laugh. "Wrong!" she says. "Guess your ear's not as good as you thought it was."

CHAPTER 50

EMILIA

Brooklyn

It's almost four o'clock when Lucy and I arrive at Kings Highway subway station in Bensonhurst. Sounds and smells I once ignored now accost me. Blaring horns. The rumble of a garbage truck. The pounding of a distant jackhammer. I miss the briny scent of the sea, the chiming of church bells, the feel of my aunt's warm hand in mine.

The November sky has turned to slate when we reach the corner of Seventy-Second Street. I catch sight of the redbrick house and my stomach drops. It's as if the past month has vanished and I've slid backward into my old life. But the difference is, now I know there's a whole other world out there.

Lucy hoists her bag higher on her shoulder. "Good luck talking to Rosa."

472

"Thanks," I say. "Good luck telling your parents about Sofie."

She nods and sucks in a breath. "Ol' Carol's gonna shit bricks when she finds out."

My poor cousin. Above all, she still wants her parents' approval. Don't we all?

"I can be there with you, Luce, for moral support. I mean, if you wanted."

A slow smile forms on her lips. "Whatever made me think you weren't cool?" She tips her head and studies me. "Oh, wait . . . it must've been those pleated khakis. Or maybe the bendable glasses."

I swat her arm. "Very funny."

"Thanks, anyway," she says. "I've got this."

"I know you do." I gaze up at a plane passing overhead. "You know, your mom can hardly be upset. I mean, you were only following her advice."

"How do you figure?"

"At age eight, when your mom explained how you'd break the curse." I try to keep my face straight, but laughter is bubbling. "You took that first rule straight to heart."

She looks at me, puzzled. It takes a second, but then she bursts out laughing. So do I. At the same time, we cry, "No balls!"

I trudge up the familiar staircase and let

myself into Emville. The usual aroma of coffee beans and lemon oil fills my nostrils. On the coatrack, a ball cap embroidered with *Cusumano Electric* hangs from a rung. I shake my head. Like a dog who marks its territory, Matt came to retrieve his hoodie but left his ball cap in its place.

"Claws?" I call. I plop a canvas bag onto the table and find a note from Carmella.

Welcome home, Em. Thanks for loaning me Emville while you were gone. I LOVED having my own space. Claws missed you, and so did I. I have so much to tell you, but I'll wait until you're settled. See you at work tomorrow. xoxo

I smile and step into my living room. From his spot on the window seat, Claws stretches and leaps to the floor, lazily sauntering over to me as if determined to prove I wasn't missed.

"Well, hello, handsome," I say, scooping him into my arms. "I'm home." But it doesn't feel like home. I'm slammed by a question Poppy posed to me just as we were leaving for Italy. *What if, after nearly thirty years of life, you discover you've been planted in the wrong place?*

But no. For as much as I love it, Italy is

only temporary. Bensonhurst is my world. Matt's here. His business is starting to take off. It'll be a great place to raise a family.

My fingers tremble when I tap my phone. I'm home, MC. Want to grab a beer?

A full five minutes pass before he replies. At Homestretch but leaving soon. Tomorrow night work for you?

I'm ashamed when I let out a sigh of relief. Even better.

I need to get out of here. For the first time since that day at the Florence airport, I call Daria.

"You're back." Is that relief I hear in her voice?

"Yes," I say, not daring to tell her I'll be leaving again soon. "How've you been? How are the girls?"

"Oh, you know, fine." She's returned, once again, to the flat voice reserved just for me.

"Look," I say, rubbing my temples. "About what happened . . ."

"Yeah, about that."

She's waiting for my apology. Instead, I say, "Can we put it behind us?"

"I can't believe you did that, Emmie."

I tamp down a smile. "Me, neither."

"Where are you?" she asks.

"I'm here, at my apartment. I'll walk

475

down, if you're home." I pull two porcelain dolls from my bag, and the beautiful gloves I splurged on for Dar. "I have some souvenirs for the girls." I run a hand over the expensive black leather. "And I bought something special for you."

"Okay, well, Donnie's sister and the kids will be here any minute. They're coming for pizza. Can you bring the stuff to work in the morning? You will be at work, right?"

Smells of stale beer and popcorn greet me when I step into the Homestretch. The pub has a decent crowd for a Monday evening. A pair of blondes stand at the jukebox, laughing as they feed money into the slot. Four men gather at the pool table, three leaning on their cue sticks while one prepares to shoot. My stomach rumbles as I scan the bar. I spot a navy work shirt and my heart thumps. He's still here.

Slowly, I step forward. He's got his back to me, one hand scrolling his phone, the other clutching a beer mug. For some odd reason, I choke up. This is it. This is the man I'll spend the rest of my life with, right here in Bensonhurst. He's solid. Dependable. Funny. Adorable. And he loves me. So why am I on the verge of tears?

I creep toward the bar, stopping when I

reach his stool. He doesn't know I'm behind him. As I bend down to kiss his neck, I catch a whiff of the same Avon cologne my uncle Vinnie wears. I turn away, hit with a wave of nausea. I suck in one breath. And another. It's okay. It's only cologne. I'll get used to it. Better yet, I'll find him a new brand.

Take two. I wet my lips. I bend down, this time trying not to inhale. My lips meet his neck.

He jerks his head and lets out a laugh. "Hey," he says, spinning around in his stool. He rears back when he sees me. "Ems?"

I smile. "Same girl, different glasses."

"Whoa," he says, looking everywhere except at me. "I didn't expect to see you tonight."

I slide onto the stool beside him and set a gift bag on the bar. "For you."

His phone chimes. He quickly checks it before planting it facedown on the bar.

"Go on," I say, pushing the bag closer to him. "Open it."

He hesitates before reaching into the bag. His hands shake when he lifts the scarf, something I've never noticed from my steady electrician. "Nice," he says. "Thanks, Em."

"You okay?" I force myself to take his

477

trembling hands in mine. The intimate gesture feels just as awkward as I remember. I'm thankful when he pulls them away and grips his mug.

"Yeah. Fine." He takes a long swill of beer, then shakes his head, as if clearing it. "How was Italy?"

"Great."

"And Poppy?"

"She's amazing." My mouth is so dry I can barely speak. "She made me realize some things." I inhale deeply. "I'm ready to make some adult decisions."

His phone chimes again. He lifts it, just inches off the bar. As if in slow motion, he rotates his wrist as he goes to peek at it. In that split second, I catch the name on the caller ID.

Carmella.

I order another pitcher of beer. *"Salute!"* I say. Matt grins and clinks his mug against mine.

"It's good to have you home, Ems." He turns pink and shakes his head. "You sure you're cool with this?"

I slug his arm. "Cool with it? I'm thrilled. Seriously, MC. How could I not see this coming? You both love to bowl, you're into craft beers, she's a sweetheart, and, well, you're not so bad yourself. I should have set you up with Carmella years ago."

"She always seemed like a kid. But now that we're in our twenties, five years is nothing."

"Nothing," I agree. "You look really, really happy."

He studies me for a moment. "Yeah, well, I couldn't wait for you forever."

I look away.

"Seriously," he says, and he touches my arm. "I'm not the one for you, Ems. I wanted to be, but I wasn't."

"I wanted you to be, too," I say, my voice choked. "Carmella's a lucky woman."

"I'm the lucky one." He smiles into his beer. "She gets me, Em. I feel . . . I don't know . . . at home when I'm with her. You know what I mean?"

Emotions I wasn't expecting rise in me. Love. Joy. Relief. And a bit of sadness, too, if I'm being honest. "Yes, I know what you mean," I say, hoping someday I will.

CHAPTER 51

EMILIA

It's still dark when I dash out the door Tuesday morning, my new scarf knotted around my neck and a bag of souvenirs in my hand. A light in Uncle Dolphie's barber shop catches my attention. Since when does he open at six a.m.?

I trot up to the glass door and knock. "Hello," I call. The bells jingle when I enter. "Uncle Dolphie?"

The shop is in complete disarray. Four cardboard boxes line the floor, partially filled with old hair dryers and half-empty shampoo bottles. For a moment, I think he's been robbed. But then it strikes me: he's cleaning the shop, already preparing for his granddaughter Lucy.

From the back room, a note rings out, clear and powerful. Then another. I stand still. Soon, the shop erupts in an aria that's at once fierce and tender and heartbreaking. I don't recognize this one. I put a hand to my chest and close my eyes, swaying as the melody slowly rolls over me.

I'm disappointed when the gorgeous piece finally ends, and I open my eyes. Uncle Dolphie stands watching me from the other side of the room. His hands are folded, his face a mixture of curiosity and apprehension.

"You like?" he asks softly.

I put a hand to my quivering chin. "It's your aria," I say, a statement, not a question.

"I rented a studio," he says sheepishly. "We recorded it in 1979."

"And the voice?" I ask, already knowing the answer.

He nods. *"La mia."*

I rush over and wrap my arms around him.

"It's so beautiful," I say, my voice cracking. "Find a producer, Uncle Dolphie. Sell it. It's not too late."

He holds me at arm's length. "This" — he swipes my wet cheek with his thumb — "is enough. I have touched someone's emotions. It is all I ever wanted."

I open my mouth to protest, to argue all the reasons why he must market this gorgeous piece of music. But he's already turned away, tossing old brushes into a box.

"Soon, Lucy will be joining me here," he

481

says. "I will leave my business to the next generation." He shakes a comb at me. "Never underestimate the blueprint for a dream, Emilia."

Nonna and I bustle around the kitchen, me rolling dough and cooking cherry filling, she boiling pasta and roasting peppers. She never mentions my trip. Never welcomes me back. Never asks about Poppy. I look over at her again, wondering how, exactly, to broach the subject of a reunion. Her face is pinched, and the ever-present scowl between her brows is more pronounced than ever. I try to imagine her as the loving sister she once was, the young woman who nursed Poppy back to health and traveled across Italy to help deliver baby Johanna. But I can't.

At ten o'clock, my sweet cousin Carmella — Matt's new girlfriend — flies into the back kitchen, wearing torn jeans and Converse sneakers.

"Emmie!" she cries, planting a kiss on my cheek. "God, you look amazing. Love the new glasses!"

I grab Carmella into my arms and spin her in a circle, trying to ignore Nonna's glowering stare. "I am so, so happy for you!"

She raises her head to the ceiling and

482

sucks in a huge breath. "I can't believe it, Emmie! Matt's a doll. How did I not know this? I owe you, big-time. If you hadn't let me stay at your place, if Matt hadn't come over to get his hoodie, we never would have —"

I shake my head, interrupting her. "Yes, you would have. It was just a matter of time."

She dons a hairnet and snags an apron from the bin. "Enough about me. I want a blow-by-blow of your trip. How was Italy? Were the men gorgeous? Was the food awesome? How weird was Poppy?"

"The trip was . . . life changing," I say. "Poppy is the most amazing —"

"Silenzio!" Nonna snaps from the other side of the counter, her chest wheezing. "I do not wish to hear about that woman."

"Nonna, stop," I say. "She's the same sister you once adored — loving and kind and wise and fun. You should reach out to her, before it's too late. Please. Despite everything the two of you have been through, she loves you."

Nonna's eyes narrow. "What have we been through? What did she tell you?"

"Everything. She told us all about Trespiano, and how she ran away with Rico. How you nursed her back to life after find-

483

ing her on the apartment steps. How you brought her to America. Even her deepest regret," I add. "Taking Josephina."

She lifts her head and studies me, as if trying to decide if I'm being truthful.

"Come back with me to Ravello," I say, my voice soft now, pleading. Every word matters. Somehow, someway, I must convince her of the urgency. "Your sister has brain cancer. And she's sorry for what she did. She wants to make peace with you. Go see her, Nonna. Please. Before it's too late."

Her nostrils flare when she draws in a breath. "That woman is dead to me. Get back to work." She turns away and slides the peppers into a stainless steel pan. "You are not on holiday."

I clench my fists. "You stubborn —"

She whirls around. "You have something to say to me?"

My heart bangs against my rib cage. I force myself to look her straight in the eyes, and speak the same words she once said to my father, when he wanted to have my lip examined. *"Perché preoccuparsi?"* Why bother?

She glares at me for a full ten seconds. Finally, she marches from the kitchen, the double doors snapping behind her.

Carmella looks on, her hand over her

mouth. Without a word, I pivot toward the counter and crack an egg against a bowl, cursing as I pluck broken shells from the goo. My hands are still shaking when the store bell chimes. I look out the back-kitchen window. Mrs. Fortino waltzes in for her Tuesday morning visit. She checks herself in the mirror. My father sucks in his gut. Nonna hisses. A fog settles in my chest.

"My life has become *Groundhog Day,*" I say to myself.

Carmella lets out a laugh, more from relief, I suspect, than humor.

The bell chimes again. I rise up and see the Cannoli Man. "Carmella," I say. "Check out this guy. He came in last August, raving about the cannoli."

She peeks through the window. "Yup. He was in last week. Aunt Rosa dragged me out to meet him."

"Really? Nonna wouldn't waste his time on me."

"She told him I was Bensonhurst's *bella pasticciera.*" She laughs. "As if the guy gives a shit whether his baker is beautiful."

I watch him cross to the bakery counter. I turn to Carmella. "Is he here to see you?"

"Oh, heck no. I only met him that one time."

Before I have time to talk myself out of it,

485

I yank off my hairnet and untie my apron. Then I step through the double doors, my shoulders squared.

"Emmie?" Carmella calls after me.

From behind the bakery counter, Rosa scowls. "Get to work," she hisses.

The truth hits me: she doesn't want me to find love. But why? So she can continue to control me? So she will always have one person in this world to take care of her when she needs help?

Ignoring her narrowed eyes, I stroll down the aisle. The Cannoli Man stands at the register now, handing Daria his credit card. He's wearing an expensive-looking suit, and his hair is perfectly cut. He glances over when I approach. My heart beats double time. I come up beside him and extend my hand.

"I'm Emilia Antonelli. I hear you're a fan of my cannoli."

His hand is warm in mine, his nails trimmed and buffed. "You're the baker?" He spins around, as if expecting to see Carmella. "I thought . . ."

"Nope. It's me. I'm kind of the family secret."

His blue eyes sparkle. "The best-kept family secret, I suspect. It's nice to meet you, Emilia Antonelli." His gaze drops, giving me an agonizingly slow once-over. "I'm Drake," he finally says, pulling a business card from his Hermès wallet. "Call me. I'll trade you lunch at Luke's Lobster for a dozen cannoli."

He squeezes my hand and strides away. The door closes and I glance at the card. *Drake Van Buren III.* I smile and slip it into my pocket.

"What the hell?" Daria says.

I hear the swish of nylon stockings and turn to see Nonna marching toward me. Her face is pinched and pink, and she's wheezing louder than ever. She shakes a finger at me. "You make me to be a liar! How could you do that? Now we have lost this man's trust!"

"You're right. I shouldn't have done that." I step closer to her. "I should have walked out of that kitchen last August, when he first asked to speak to the baker. But I was fully indoctrinated back then."

Rosa bats a hand at me, dismissively. My blood pressure soars. Behind her shoulder, Mrs. Fortino and my father stand watching us. But right now, I'm too angry to care.

"For all of my life, I've let myself believe I wasn't worthy of love. You — and generations of Fontanas — have created a myth, and I bought into it. The truth is, there is

487

no curse. There never was."

My hand moves to hide my lip, but I catch myself. I lower it and look Nonna straight in the face, my scar — and my courage — beautifully visible. "For years, this little line made me feel ugly and ashamed. But it's a powerful reminder now. My spirit was never broken by you, Nonna, no matter how hard you tried."

She gasps.

"Emilia!" my father says.

I lift a hand to silence him. "I will not be manipulated any longer. I'm finished here. I'm going back to Italy. I was hoping you'd join me, Nonna. Your sister loves you. She needs your forgiveness. She's longing for one last reunion."

Nonna sneers. "That woman is evil."

Blood surges past my temples. "No. Your sister is kind and loving and forgiving." I jab a finger at her. "Everything you're not."

As I march toward the back kitchen, I catch a glimpse of my father. His mouth is agape, like a cartoon character who has just been clobbered with a bowling pin.

"And you," I say to him. "Are you going to spend the rest of your life kowtowing to your mother-in-law? Jesus, Dad, get a backbone!" Beside him, Mrs. Fortino stifles a smile. I drape an arm around her shoulders. Together, we face my dad. "You've got a chance at love," I tell him. "Here's a woman who's sweet and generous. And she likes you. Take a chance, for God's sake! Be the man that my mother fell in love with."

His eyes mist. I draw him into a hug, trying to ignore Rosa's frosty glare from down the aisle. "I love you, Dad," I say, the long-unspoken words awkward on my tongue. And I realize how much I do.

"Love . . . you," he whispers, barely loud enough to hear.

But I do hear. And I smile.

My chest heaves and I throw open the kitchen double doors. Carmella grabs me into a hug and spins me around. "Oh. My. God!" she bellows. "That was, like, a five-star Netflix performance! I never knew you were such a badass!"

I let out a breath. "Can you take over?"

"Yes. Absolutely. Take a break. You deserve one."

"No. I'm leaving, Carmella." I grab my phone from beneath the counter. "I'm not coming back."

A slow smile blooms on her face. "It's about time."

"Know anyone who'd want to sublet Emville? Someone who'd be willing to cover the utility bills?"

Her eyes go wide and she nods. "Is Claws included in the deal?"

"Only until I figure out how to get him to Italy." I pull Drake Van Buren the Third's business card from my pocket and toss it in the trash.

"Wait!" Carmella cries. "What are you doing?" She rushes over and plucks the card from the trash bin. "Call him, Em. He wants to have lunch. You never know what might —"

"Not my type." I take the card and tear it in two. "But it felt good, all the same."

I trot down the back hallway. As I pass the cement-block break room, I catch sight of the souvenirs I bought for Daria and the kids, on the table where I placed them this morning. Daria's box is open, the gloves splayed on the table.

I step into the room and lift the gloves, breathing in their rich leathery scent. My sister didn't tell me she'd opened her gift. Or that she liked it. Or even say thank you. I slide my hands into the gloves. They feel heavenly. I turn from the room and nearly collide with Rosa.

"Such a disrespectful girl," she says, her arms akimbo. "You go away, and return thinking you are better than us?"

I study her, my mind whirling. This angry

woman who has belittled me since I was a child, this bitter, broken caricature of a grandmother . . . and a sister.

"You break my heart, Emilia," she continues. She lifts her apron to dab her dry eyes, the same dramatic stunt she's used my entire life. "A disappointment, that is what you are."

What kind of a grandmother would say such things? What kind of a grandmother would treat her granddaughter . . . ? Rico's words call to me. *Meine schöne Enkelin.* My beautiful granddaughter. Goose bumps rise on my arms. Am I off base? Might my hunch be wrong?

I step forward. My heart thunders. Without warning, I yank the apron from her face. "Enough, Rosa."

Her head snaps to attention. Her scowl deepens.

"That's right. *Rosa.*" I look her straight in the eyes, my chest heaving. "You are not my nonna. You never were."

Her mouth goes slack. The color drains from her face. My premonition is confirmed, as clearly as if she'd confessed the words aloud. Her eyes narrow and fill with venom. I force myself to hold their gaze, knowing, without a doubt, I've uncovered the truth.

It was Rosa who stole my mother from Poppy, not the other way around.

CHAPTER 52

EMILIA

I told my family there was no curse. But that's not entirely true. The Fontana second-daughter myth was very much alive. But it was never about being single. Like all stereotypes, the real curse was the sense of hopelessness the myth created, the erosion of self-confidence, the failure to believe in one's dreams . . . and oneself.

I race up the cement stoop and pound on the screen door. "Lucy! Open up. It's me. I'm going back to Italy."

The door swings open and I take a step back. My perky aunt Carol slumps against the doorframe. Her face is barren of makeup, her eyes red rimmed. My heart sinks. Lucy has told her family. And I wasn't there for moral support.

"Aunt Carol," I say, inching closer. "Are you okay?"

"No," she says, pinching her nose. "I am

not okay."

I place a hand on her arm. "Please, Aunt Carol, try to —"

"For twenty-one years I have prayed," she says, interrupting me. "But the curse is too strong. Luciana will never find love." She gives me a sad little smile. "Nor will you."

"Oh, hell," I mumble aloud. "Why quit when I'm on a roll?" I plant my fists on my hips. "Lucy is not cursed. I swear. She's found herself at last. I know, because I witnessed it firsthand. This might not be the relationship you envisioned. It might take a bit of getting used to. But your daughter is happy. She's met someone special, someone she cares for. It's beautiful, and it's real, and it's pure. And nobody — not you or Uncle Vinnie or that damn curse — can deny her of that."

She begins to weep. I soften my voice. "The way I see it, you have two choices. You can be a super-cool mom and accept your wonderful daughter as is. Or —"

She finishes the sentence for me. "Or be a narrow-minded, miserable homophobe, as Lucy says, and lose her forever."

I give a weak smile. "Yeah. That's pretty much it."

She drops her face into her hands. "She's asking too much. I'm afraid it's im—"

"Possible," I say, interrupting. I sling an arm around her shoulders. "You'll find life is much more interesting when you learn to say 'It's possible.' "

From behind my aunt, Lucy appears, a new phone in her hand. Aunt Carol scurries away, as if she cannot bear to be near her daughter. Lucy rolls her eyes and waves me inside. "Hey, Pops," she says into the phone. "Guess who's here?" She points the phone at me.

I smile into a bright yellow screen, imagining my nonna and nonno on their rooftop deck, not realizing that their phone is aimed at the afternoon sun. "Hello, Aunt Poppy."

My stomach flutters with joy. I'm desperate to call her "Nonna," to blurt out the truth and claim her as my grandmother. But I'll wait for her to tell me, once we're together again in Ravello.

"Hello, my sunshine!" Poppy's face finally appears on the screen. She's not on the rooftop. She's sitting inside, on the sofa next to a lamp. Rather than her wig, her head is covered in a pink knitted cap with kitten ears. Did she really bring that hat to Italy? My smile fades. Something is wrong. She's wearing her robe, and her lips aren't painted.

"Are you okay?"

"Dandy," she says, for my benefit, I'm certain. She tips her head. "Aren't you supposed to be at work?"

I huddle beside Lucy so she can see both of us. "Lucy and I are coming back to Ravello." I glance at Lucy. "Right?"

Lucy cranes her neck toward the kitchen, as if hoping her mom hears. "Damn right!"

Poppy claps her hands. "You've already found someone to take over your lease, Emilia?"

I lower myself onto the arm of the sofa. "Yes, and I'm ready to be out of here."

She gives me a sympathetic smile. "Oh, dear. I had a hunch things might go awry once you found your voice."

From behind her, Rico — my opa — steps into the room, balancing a cup of tea on a saucer. Where's her wine? Or even coffee? Italians drink tea when they're ill.

He bends down. "*Guten Tag,* Emilia." His face is too close to the screen, and I can't help but laugh.

"*Guten Morgen* — it's still morning here, Rico. How are you?"

"I am fine," he says in his gravelly German accent. "It is this one I am worried about. She woke with a migraine."

I jump to my feet. "Lucy and I will be on the next flight."

496

Poppy's face returns to the screen. "My sister." She looks me in the eyes, her voice urgent now. "Have you talked to her?"

My heart breaks. Poppy is still hoping for absolution from the one person who refuses to give it. Her clouded eyes plead with me, waiting, hoping to hear of her sister's love.

I want nothing more than to tell her the truth. That she doesn't need her sister's love, that her sister is evil and manipulative and will never, ever make peace with her. Instead, I force a smile.

"Yes," I say. "She wants me to tell you . . ." I try to steady my quivering voice. "She regrets what happened with the two of you."

"She forgives me?"

I nod, barely able to produce the words that she longs to hear. "All is forgiven," I whisper.

She squeezes shut her eyes, and a soft moan escapes her.

"Your sister loves you," I say.

She lowers her head and a tear spills from the tip of her nose. Rico comes up beside her. "What did I tell you?" he says, dabbing her cheek. "You are loved. You are forgiven." He looks at me through the screen. "Thank you, Emilia. Finally, she can rest."

Maybe I shouldn't have lied, but I like to think that somewhere inside Rosa's rusty heart, she would want her dying sister to hear the words she's too terrified to voice.

My open suitcase hunkers on my bedroom floor. I add one more sweater before snapping it shut. I'm pulling cat treats from the cabinet when I hear a knock at my door.

"It's no use, Dad," I call, dropping fish-shaped kibbles onto the window seat. "I don't care what you say. I'm finished at the store. I'm going back to Italy, where I belong."

"Emmie, it's me. Open the door."

Daria? I turn. What's she doing here? I throw open the door and step back, my arms crossed over my chest. "You're here for your gloves, I presume?"

My sister, who never cries, puts a hand over her mouth. I step forward.

"Dar? Are you okay?"

She closes her eyes and shakes her head.

All my anger vanishes. I take her by the arms. "Come in," I say, leading her to my kitchen table. "Sit down. Can I get you something? Water? Coffee?"

"No. Stop. Just . . . listen to me." Her voice is choked. "I am a bitch, Emmie. That's . . . what I came to tell you."

The old me would have protested. I would have spent thirty minutes reassuring my sister that she is a doll, an angel, a ray of sunlight.

"Yes," the new me says. "You have been a bitch. For about ten years, if you want to quantify it."

"More like eleven."

She's right. "You changed when I went off to college. You resented me. And you lied to me all those years. You actually believed in the curse."

"No, Emmie."

"My entire childhood, you claimed you didn't believe, but you really did."

"That's not true."

"You were feeding me a line of bullshit. You've been lying to me since —"

"I wasn't lying! I didn't believe the curse!" Her voice bellows, and the little vein in her forehead bulges. She takes a deep breath. "Not back then. Not when we were girls."

"So what changed?"

"Nothing." Her eyes dart to the wall.

I pound my fist on the table, startling us both. "What?"

"It changed when you met Liam!" She props her elbows on the table and massages her temples.

I wait, hoping she'll fit the missing piece into the puzzle that's been lying unfinished for years.

"Nonna was furious when she found out you had a boyfriend at Barnard. She told me the curse would never allow you to love."

I'm tempted to blurt out the truth, to expose Nonna as the impostor she is. But Rosa is the only mother figure my sister has known. If, or when, I choose to tell Daria, the conversation needs to be handled with sensitivity, and right now, I don't have it in me. "She's crazy," I say.

"That's what I told her. But she insisted the relationship would end badly. And then winter break rolled around and I let you borrow my Jeep. Nonna was livid that you'd gone to Liam's for New Year's Eve, and royally pissed at me for being your accomplice. She paced the floor in the back kitchen, clutching her rosary beads. She swore something bad would happen, the curse would never allow you to love."

I picture Liam's lifeless body. Goose bumps pepper my arms.

"We got into a huge fight. I told her the curse was bullshit." She looks up at the ceiling and takes a deep breath. "And then you called me from Delaware, hysterical, saying you'd been in an accident." She shakes her head and looks away.

I reach over and put a hand on hers. "And you thought she'd proven herself right."

She looks up at me, her lashes spiked with tears. "It totally freaked me out, Emmie. I was terrified for you. All my life I'd heard stories of the Fontana second daughters, like Great-Great-Aunt Blanca, still in her thirties, who died just after she met some widowed farmer. So, I did everything in my power to keep you from finding love. Because I knew — I *thought* — that if you did, it might just kill you."

My sister was trying to protect me. I turn to the window. Snow softly falls from a white sky. "So that's why you came to Italy, trying to drag me home."

"I was furious when you wouldn't get on that plane. I mean, three second-born Fontanas traveling together? I was sure something awful would happen."

"But it didn't."

"I know. There is no curse. I know this now, just like I knew it when we were kids." She lets out a half laugh, half cry. "I'm a grown woman. I can't believe I fell for it."

"I fell for it, too." I lean back in my chair, trying to digest the words, trying to understand my sister's actions. "I get it now. Sort of. But why did you treat me so badly? Did you do it to please Nonna?"

"I'm not trying to make excuses, Emmie, I swear. But being the, quote, anointed firstborn daughter wasn't easy, either."

"Oh, spare me."

"It's true!" She looks off into the distance. "You had the one thing I wanted: freedom."

I look up with a start. She lifts a hand. "Don't act so surprised. You knew I had doubts about Donnie before we married. Remember when I wanted to move to Colorado with Carleana Garagiola? It was you who nixed the idea."

I rear back. "I did not! Rosa put the kibosh on it."

"Yes. And you took her side."

The memory returns to me in bits and pieces. Daria squeezing my hand as she dragged me into the back kitchen. My heart heavy, like someone had filled it with wet sand. Rosa standing at the stainless steel sink, loading dishes into the bubbly water. Dar stumbling over her words, trying to spit out that her engagement was off, that she wasn't cut out to be somebody's wife. The relief pouring over me when Rosa shouted down the idea. *If you do not marry this man, your poor father will have no grandchildren.* My sister's face as she turned to me, hopeful, imploring me to take her side. Me, unable to speak.

I hang my head. "I'm so sorry, Dar."

She shrugs. "I should have known it was

too much to ask. You were petrified of crossing Nonna."

My heart pitches and I take a deep breath. "The truth is, I was petrified of losing you." I rub my temples. "You were all I had. And I put my happiness above yours. I'm so sorry." I place a tentative hand on her arm. "Will you please forgive me?"

She looks into my eyes and gives a wobbly smile. "It's all good. Donnie's a great dad. I adore the girls. You know that, right?"

"Of course. You've got a great family."

She takes a deep breath and nods. "Which is why I feel like a selfish bitch when sometimes I look at my life and think, 'Is this it?' I mean, why couldn't I have been the second-born daughter? You have so many possibilities, Em, but until Poppy came along, you'd squandered them. You took up residence in this boring little Emville like it was your retirement home. All that was missing was a rocking chair and a crocheted tissue box."

My quick burst of laughter fades to silence. "But you did nothing to encourage me. You did just the opposite."

"I know. I wanted it both ways. I was afraid to let you leave, but angry when you didn't. And then I got pregnant, and married Donnie. It became clear pretty quickly, it was useful to have you here." She gives a little laugh and looks down at her hands. "In fact, I don't have a clue what I'd have done without you all these years. I figured, if you felt needed, you wouldn't leave. And if you didn't leave, you'd be safe. But, Emmie, the fact is, you deserve so much more."

"I know," I say, and swallow the knot in my throat. "Poppy taught me this."

She sniffles. "I was proud of you today, the way you stood up to Nonna. Screw the store! You're going places, Em, mark my words."

My chin quivers. "But, Dar, you could have more, too."

She gives a wan smile. "Nah. I'm okay with the store. I get to set my own hours, come and go as I please. Who else is going to let me do that?"

I smile. She's right. Nonna spoils Daria, her fellow firstborn daughter.

She scoots her chair back and rises. "I better get back to work." She nods at the suitcase beside the door. "And you need to get to the train station."

My nose stings and I know, without a doubt, I would stay here forever if my sister asked. But luckily, she doesn't. Instead, she pulls me into a hug. It's not the tepid hug

I've grown used to. It's a Daria full-body squeeze. Tears blur my vision. I'd almost forgotten how beautiful it feels, a sister's love.

"I love you, Dar."

I feel her crying softly. "I love you more." She turns to leave. "Call me when you get to Ravello."

"Wait, Dar. I have something for you."

She lifts the gloves from the kitchen counter. "I opened them earlier. They're gorgeous, Emmie."

I reach into my pocket. "I meant this."

She stares down at the medal in my palm. Saint Christopher, the patron saint of travelers, her prize possession. She closes my palm around it.

"Mom would want you to have it. And so do I."

She kisses my cheek and closes the door behind her.

CHAPTER 53

EMILIA

Ravello

The evening sun spills over the Gulf of Salerno, mopping the rooftop in pinks and golds. It's hard to believe that just two days ago, I was at work in Bensonhurst, and now I'm here with Lucy and my grandparents, feasting alfresco on a rich seafood stew heaped with clams, sea bass, and herb pesto. A half dozen candles flicker in the breeze. My nonna Poppy is wearing a flowing, lemon-yellow caftan, with what looks to be a double strand of brightly painted Easter eggs around her neck. Her wig is freshly styled and she swears she's feeling grand.

As I watch Lucy steal a clam from Rico's plate, I wonder, could she and I have continued faking it, pretending we were people we weren't, in order to be accepted? Before Poppy introduced us to Italy, I wasn't even aware of my discontent. I might have spent the rest of my life in Benson-hurst, seemingly happy. But now I realize, living in Emville is like wearing a see-through blouse with three-inch heels. I could certainly do it if I had to. But all the while a part of me would feel conspicuous and uncomfortable and a million miles from my true self. I suspect my cousin would agree.

Rico opens another bottle of Taurasi Ri-serva, and we three listen as Lucy tells us how she broke the news to her parents.

"Carol freaked, as expected. But my dad took it like a champ. Who knew?"

Rico smiles. "One of life's loveliest mo-ments is witnessing another person's grace."

His statement is laced with German, and Lucy scowls. Poppy pats her hand. "He said that it's a wonderful surprise, discovering that your father's not the judgmental prick you thought he was."

We burst out laughing.

"Right?" Lucy says, high-fiving Rico. "And he's convinced ol' Carol will come around, once she picks herself up from the floor."

"Perhaps all along," I say, my gaze pinned on Poppy, "they were waiting for you to tell them the truth they already knew."

My heart ricochets against my chest. Since

we arrived last night, I've been dropping hints, hoping Poppy will tell me the truth, reveal that she's my grandmother, and Rico my grandfather. Our time together is measured now, and we've wasted so much already.

Poppy smiles and gazes out at the mango sunset, ignoring my not-so-subtle comment once again. "For fifty-nine years, I prayed for this," she says. "Another Ravello sunset." Her face glows in the waning sunlight. "I'd like one more Tuscan sunset, too." She locks eyes with Rico. "Please, take some of my ashes to Trespiano, when the time comes?"

He rubs her arm. "Whatever you wish, *mio unico amore.*"

Despite her glow of love, her newfound energy, she's still dying. I'd almost convinced myself otherwise. They deserve more time. *We* deserve more time. Does she not want me to know the truth? Does she not wish to call me her granddaughter?

Rico raises his glass, lightening the mood. "To sunsets . . . and, more importantly, sunrises."

"Salute," Lucy says.

My hands quake when we clink our glasses, and I try to tamp down my frustration.

"I'll say good night now," Poppy says, rising.

Wait! I want to scream. *Why have you kept the truth from me, from my mother, all these years?* She's nearly to the steps when I can stand it no longer.

"Can we talk?"

She pivots, and for a brief second, her eyes flash with fear. "Of course," she says breezily. "Another day." She waves her fingers at us. "Ta-ta for now."

I jump to my feet, my heart thundering. "I know what happened."

Time stills. Ever so slowly she turns to me. She blinks once. Twice. I take a deep breath, and when I speak again, my voice is soft. "But I'd love to know why. And how. Tell me. Please."

She puts a hand to her chest. From his place at the table, Rico whispers. "It is time, *mio amore.*"

Her troubled gaze travels from him to me. Finally, she pivots and disappears down the staircase.

Tears sting my eyes and I drop my head. I had such high hopes that she might want me. Rico's warm hand rubs circles on my back. "Our Poppy has strong principles," he tells me. "Too strong, I fear."

Footsteps sound on the stairs. I lift my

509

head. Poppy appears, a large manila envelope in her hand.

"I had planned to keep this secret for as long as Rosa was alive. It seemed the right thing to do." She looks at Rico. "For weeks, *mein Ehemann* has been trying to convince me otherwise. Perhaps he is right."

She pulls a document from the envelope and sets it on the table in front of me. "I wrote this from my suite in Venice, while you girls were exploring the city."

I swallow hard. "That's why you insisted on a private room."

"Huh," Lucy says. "And I thought you were hoping to get lucky."

She whacks Lucy's arm playfully and slips into the chair beside mine. "Before our trip, I made a promise to you, Emilia. In hearing my story, you will finally learn of your mother's."

I stare down at a stack of pages, stapled at the upper right corner, titled *Poppy's Final Chapter — 1961.*

CHAPTER 54

POPPY

1961
From Italy to America
With Rico trapped behind the Berlin Wall, Rosa was my bedrock. Without her grit, I may have crumbled. She was the one who insisted I get up every day. She was the one who walked me through the markets, helped me care for Johanna.

Even through my grief, Johanna was thriving, taking to my breast like a little champ. Mercifully, Rosa finally stopped badgering me about coming to America. She understood, even with the news of the wall, I could not leave Italy. Rico would come back for me, I was certain. And when that day came, I needed to be in Ravello.

On a Monday morning, four weeks after I'd delivered Johanna, my sister finally admitted defeat. "I am disappointed in you, *la mia sorella testarda,*" she said as she folded laundry. "But I cannot force you to come to America. Tomorrow, we will pack. By the end of the week, you must return to Trespiano."

"Trespiano? No. Ravello is my home."

She spun around, a clean diaper in her hand. "No, Paolina. I can no longer help with Johanna. I am leaving for America in ten days. You will live with Mamma and Papà."

Fear shot through me. I was a single mother, with no money, no options. How was I to support Johanna on my own? But the thought of returning to the farm drained my soul.

"Do you think Mamma will be angry?" I asked, hoping against hope my fears were unwarranted.

"Sì. She is. But not as angry as Papà."

I gasped. "You told them?"

"I am sorry, Paolina. It slipped."

I gazed down at the bundle suckling my breast. "They will grow to love her. She is their grandchild."

Rosa shook her head. "Love her? My sister, how can you expect love?" She peered into my eyes as if I were a small child in need of a lecture. "Mamma is a proud woman. You know this. Now, she is humiliated. First her daughter runs off with a German. A year later, she returns with his bastard child, for all the village to witness. This has broken her heart. You will always have my love, Paolina. But Mamma's? I am afraid not."

A headache kicked at my temples. No matter what rosy future I'd promised my baby girl, at that moment I could only imagine a scorned life, the poor illegitimate daughter of the Fontana whore, living on the farm, resented by her grandparents, ridiculed by the village. For the first time, I became furious at Rico. How could he leave us? How could he choose his father and mother over his wife and child?

"When is he coming for us?" I said aloud.

"Rico will not be returning." Rosa reached for me, but I pulled away.

"You don't know this."

"There is a wall, Paolina! What further proof do you need? You will never see your Rico again. Stop your foolishness!"

Tears sprang to my eyes. "He loves me. He will return, you will see."

"Yes," she said, her voice oozing sarcasm. "Your Rico will leave his ailing father's bedside. He will abandon his fragile mother and the sister who is counting on him for her very existence. Or maybe he will risk his

513

life and escape the guards at the border, poised with their machine guns, all for you."

I looked away, suddenly aware of my naïveté.

Rosa pulled me into her arms. "Shhh," she whispered, stroking my back. "You, of all people, should not be surprised at this unhappy ending. You are the second daughter. You've known all along you would never marry."

"But I am married!"

She ignored me and stepped back to straighten my collar. "Now, it is time you returned home. Mamma will raise baby Johanna, regardless of her disgust. You will help Papà in the fields. When Joh is old enough, she will work on the farm, too. That is, if they will allow it."

Fear gripped me. I would never accept such a life for my child. But what could I do? I had nothing to offer her. I swiped my cheeks, desperate to save my daughter. There must be a solution! My child's entire future weighed on my shoulders. Johanna was counting on me.

Slowly, one anemic spark at a time, a fire flickered to life. "No," I said firmly. "Johanna will not live her life as a disgraced child."

Rosa folded a towel, silent.

"My daughter will be proud . . . and free!"
Rosa shifted her gaze toward me.

"If . . ." I began, cautiously. "If I came with you to America, who says I must marry Ignacio?"

A sad little smile appeared. "Stop. You do not want to go to America. I know this."

"I — I must do what is best for Johanna. That is what Rico would want."

Rosa slid the laundry basket beneath the bed and shook her head. "I am afraid it is too late. The government will never allow an illegitimate child into the United States."

I reared back. "You tell me this now? You have been begging me to come with you, to raise my child in America. And all along you knew it was impossible?"

"I only found out last week, after doing some checking."

I closed my eyes, all of my options vanishing before me. What seemed like an act of treason just minutes before now appeared the obvious solution. I must get to America with Joh, and allow her to have the bright future that neither Italy nor Germany would allow.

Rosa paced the floor and shook her head. "If only you were a married woman, with a husband waiting for you in America. Then you and the baby would be welcome, no questions asked."

I spun in a circle, clutching my head. "Help me, Rosa. I need a plan. I am responsible for my child's life, her happiness. Her only chance is in America."

"I would love to help you. You know this. Alberto and I would gladly take you in and help you raise Johanna. He has money and a fine apartment. But first, you must get to America." She bit her thumbnail and paced the room. "Perhaps you could hide baby Joh, sneak her onto the ship."

"No. That is much too dangerous. God knows what the officials might do to her if we got caught." I chewed the inside of my cheek. "There must be a better way."

And then an idea struck me. It might actually work. I looked up.

"What if . . . ?" My voice trailed off.

"What?"

"Never mind."

"Tell me."

My head spun. I took a breath, my thoughts taking shape as I spoke. "What if . . . what if you pretended Joh was your child? Just until we arrived in America."

"Oh, no," Rosa said. "I do not look like her mother — anyone's mother. Not yet."

"But you do. We can disguise your pregnancy. See, it is easy to believe you've just given birth." I pulled her shapeless dress a bit tighter at the waist, surprised that her belly wasn't bigger. Alberto left for America seven months ago. She should be round by now.

"Rosa, when are you due?"

She batted my hands away and fluffed her dress. "The authorities will know that I am not Johanna's mother," she said, ignoring my question. "She is too attached to you."

"But I will be there, too." I took her by the arms, my urgency rising. "Nobody will suspect a thing. I will continue to feed her and care for her. Only when we are in public will you pretend to be her mother."

She frowned. "The birth certificate. They will want to see it."

"We'll get another. Surely that old battle-ax midwife will create a new one if we grease her palm. This one will list you as the mother and Alberto as the father."

"Oh, Paolina, if I get caught —"

"You won't. I promise. Please, tell me you'll do it."

She let out a heavy sigh. "Let me think about this, Paolina. You are asking so much from me."

One day passed. Then another. It was all I could do not to scream. I needed an answer.

517

But Rosa's face looked suddenly old, and I caught her more than once on her knees with her rosary beads. I had placed her in a horrible position, having to choose between the truth and Johanna's future. Finally, on the third day, just one week before the ship would sail, I could stand it no longer.

"Rosa, please! I beg of you. Say you'll pretend to be Johanna's mother. If you won't do it for me, do it for your niece."

She closed her eyes and then crossed herself. A slow smile came to her face. "You mean, for my daughter."

I laughed and grabbed her into a hug. I'd never felt so much love and gratitude for my sister. "Yes! For your daughter!"

I wept the first day I tried to wean Johanna off my breast. Neither of us liked the clunky bottle that invaded our intimacy. I missed the feel of her skin against my chest, the contented sighs when she suckled from me, as if I alone could nourish her. But Rosa was right. Weaning was necessary if we were to cross the Atlantic as niece and aunt.

As we'd guessed, with the help of a few coins, Signora Tuminelli was happy to create a bogus birth certificate. And for an additional coin, she would forge the signature of the county official.

The ink was still wet when the tight-faced midwife handed the single slip of paper to Rosa. "I know nothing of this," she said, slicing a finger through the air. "Nothing!"

My heart battered against its cage. I was a criminal. Together, Rosa and I inspected the new certificate. The line above "Mother's Name" read Rosa Lucchesi. The father: Alberto Lucchesi. I swallowed hard.

"It looks very official," I said. "Nobody will ever guess it is not valid."

But then I caught sight of the child's name: Josephina Fontana Lucchesi.

"Wait," I said. "Her name is Johanna."

Rosa placed the birth certificate between two pieces of cardboard and taped the edges shut. "Don't be foolish. Alberto and I would never choose a German name."

She'd thought of everything. Why give the officials anything to question? But still, the hairs on the back of my neck prickled.

Rosa looked every bit a mother that mid-September afternoon, boarding the SS *Cristoforo Colombo* with Johanna in her arms. The authorities gave little more than a cursory glance at the baby nestled in the pink blanket I'd crocheted, before stamping Rosa's papers. I approached the desk next, my heart thumping in my chest, playing the role of dutiful aunt, loaded with our suitcases and a small bag for Joh. Within minutes, I, too, was welcomed aboard the ship. I let out a sigh of relief. So far, our plan was working perfectly.

"Look!" Rosa exclaimed, pointing to the crowd that had gathered at the harbor, family members and friends who'd come to bid farewell to their loved ones.

I shielded my eyes from the sun and followed Rosa's finger. And there, standing side by side in their Sunday best, stood our mamma and papà. They'd traveled all the way to Napoli to say good-bye. I lifted my hand, tears blinding me.

"Mamma!" I shouted over the grunt of the ship's engine. "Papà! I love you!"

Papà lifted his hand. Mamma waved and threw a kiss.

"Your granddaughter!" I shouted.

Beside me, my beaming sister proudly lifted baby Joh. Mamma clutched her heart, and Papà dabbed his eyes. *"Bellissima!"* Papà cried. He raised the camera that hung from his neck and snapped a photo.

"They love Joh," I said to Rosa. "I knew they'd love her."

"Yes," she said. "They are very proud of their new grandbaby."

My chest puffed with pride. *"Grazie!"* I

yelled to Papà, my voice choked. *"Grazie mille!"* I stroked Johanna's downy hair, her rosy cheeks, and laughed through my tears.

That moment marked the last time I would ever feel such joy. I didn't yet know that during this passage to find a brighter future, somewhere over the blue-black waters of the sea, I would lose my baby girl.

I spent every evening with Johanna. And each morning, as the sun rose, my baby's eyes would grow heavy, just in time for Rosa to take over. As we three strolled the decks, female passengers would stop Rosa to coo at the sleeping angel in her arms. "Your first?" they might ask.

"Yes," Rosa would say. "She's seven weeks old, my little sweetheart. Her father is waiting for us in Brooklyn."

An odd mix of pride and resentment churned in me. I said nothing of course. It was crucial that nobody learn of our charade. But inside, I felt robbed.

Soon, Rosa met other mothers who were traveling with their children. The lot of them would sit beneath umbrellas discussing motherhood, their husbands, gushing at photos. I wanted so much to join their conversations. But Rosa reminded me to keep quiet. She insisted I go to the cabin and rest. Later, when the women wanted to play cards, or when the baby needed to be changed, or when she simply grew tired of Joh, Rosa would fetch me.

Mothers, it seemed, shared a bond. I felt excluded, isolated, alone. My heart ached for Rico. I never should have left Italy. When I voiced my frustration, Rosa correctly reminded me, "This was your idea, Paolina. Do not forget it."

And then she would tell of the wonderful life Johanna would have in America, something that would not have been possible had she not agreed to lie for me. All of this was true. Feeling left out was a small price to pay. Rosa had risked so much for me and Johanna.

We'd spent seven nights aboard the giant ship, each day drawing closer to America, to Joh's future. But I could almost hear the past calling to me, chastising me for abandoning it, beckoning me to return. I had nightmares where Rico had come back for me, pounding on the apartment door while I was locked in a closet, unable to answer. I would wake, exhausted and emptied, reality creeping in with the dawn. I had given up on Rico. And it was too late to go back.

On the eighth night, neither Johanna nor I

could sleep. I stood on the ship's deck jostling her. "Shhh," I whispered. "It's okay. It's okay." As the chill of the night crept over me, I wondered who I was reassuring — my child or myself.

The eastern sky gradually came to life, a watercolor of peaches and lavenders. I blinked once. Twice. For the first time in eight days, something shone in the distance.

Cheers rose from the captain's deck. A chill came over me. I positioned Joh at my chest, so that she could see what lay before her.

"Look," I said, my wet cheek pressed against her downy head. "See that distant land, my beautiful girl? This is our new home, the place where you will grow to be wise and free and become anyone you want to be."

The tears continued to flow. I couldn't stop them. If anyone had asked, I would have claimed they were tears of joy. But they were anything but. The full gravity of my decision struck me. I'd given up on my husband, my love. I was thousands of miles from my home. And there was no turning back.

A fierce grip on my arm startled me. I turned to find Rosa, her eyes wide with horror. "What are you doing?"

I could see how it looked: me, sobbing, leaning too far over the ship's rail; baby Joh wrapped in a blanket, wailing in my arms.

"I can't live without Rico. I must return home."

I heard the crack of her hand against my face. My hand flew to my cheek and I gasped for breath. As if she, too, felt the heat, Johanna began to scream.

"Stop this nonsense!" Rosa said, yanking Johanna from my arms. "You think you are the only one in pain? No. But do you see me wanting to throw myself overboard?"

Had my sister lost her baby? I wanted to set her straight. I would never take my own life. But now was not the time to defend myself.

"Oh, Rosa," I said, clutching my chest. "I am so sorry. What happened, my sweet sister?"

She put her hand to her lips, but I could see the downward tug of her mouth. "It happened quickly, back home, the fifth of June. She had stopped growing weeks earlier." She swallowed hard. "You are never to speak of this. Nobody is to know."

"But Mamma knows, sì? And Papà?"

She shook her head. "The disappointment would be too great. Papà was so proud of me. He expects many grandchildren from

524

his firstborn daughter."

For the first time, I realized the pressure the curse had placed on Rosa. "But surely you told Alberto."

"Especially not Alberto." Her eyes fixed on mine. "Not until I am in America. He would have told me not to come if he thought I could not bear children."

Shivers blanketed me. Had she miscarried before? I took her by the arms, all self-pity vanishing. "The doctors in America will help you. You will have many children. We Fontana women are strong. We are resourceful. When a door closes, we take an ax to it."

She smiled then, a troubled smile that never reached her eyes. How was I to know how fully Rosa would embrace my advice?

Alberto cried when he first laid eyes on Johanna. He stooped, pressing his lips to baby Joh's forehead. My throat squeezed. It should be Rico, giving his daughter her first kiss, not her uncle Alberto. Rosa placed the baby in his arms, a contrived portrayal of a loving mother and proud papà. Johanna latched on to Alberto's pinky. He stood gazing at her, as if she were a beautiful apparition he couldn't quite believe. Finally, he turned to Rosa. For the first time ever, I saw affection in his eyes.

"My love," he said, and he planted a kiss on her lips. "You have made me a happy man."

Had my sister not told him our plan? My heart thrummed. I waited for Rosa to explain. Instead, she gazed at her handsome husband with such devotion it nearly blinded me.

I tried to calm myself. Of course she couldn't explain at that moment. The news of the miscarriage would break his heart. And besides, we were still within sight of customs officials. Once we got to Brooklyn, she would stop pretending.

Rosa wore her prettiest dress — a navy frock, belted at the waist, meant to show off her curves. But the fabric across her bottom stretched, and the buttons at her chest threatened to burst. I fought a wave of sadness. My sister had the body of a new mother, with no child to show for it.

I smoothed the wrinkles from the old red and white polka-dot dress I'd made back in Trespiano. I refused to wear my best dress. That white garment was packed away, secured in a bag in remembrance of my wedding day.

We stood on the edge of the harbor, shivering. New York's autumn air felt like the refrigerated room in the bakery, and I rubbed the chill from my arms. I looked up and noticed for the first time an older man standing behind Alberto, eyeing me as if he were judging cattle at the market.

I crossed my arms over my chest and listened as he whispered to Alberto in broken English he foolishly assumed I didn't understand. "I thought you said her skin was like cream. And she is much too scrawny. No hips, that one."

I seethed. I'd lost weight on the voyage, it was true. And the sun had darkened my skin. But who did he think he was, this pink-headed man with a watermelon belly?

"I suppose she will do," he said and pulled a set of keys from his pocket. My stomach lurched. Did Ignacio think I was here to marry him? Had Rosa not made it clear?

He cast me a smile, one I'm sure was meant to charm. It did not.

We climbed into Ignacio's automobile, a snazzy turquoise car that said *Oldsmobile* on the back. Alberto hunkered in the back-seat beside Rosa, holding Johanna. I had no choice but to sit up front with Ignacio.

Ignacio flipped on the radio. Of all songs, "Que Será, Será" rang out. I bit my cheek to keep from crying out. Rosa let out a whoop and leaned over the seat. "Can you

527

believe it, Paolina? He has his own automobile!"

I turned and reached for Joh. "I can take her, Alberto."

He smiled down at the baby. "She is happy right here, aren't you, Josephina?"

The car sped off with a squeal. The belt of dread around my belly, the one I'd been trying my hardest to ignore, tightened another notch.

Alberto lived in a sparsely furnished one-bedroom apartment above a butcher shop. He held Joh tightly to his chest as his wife inspected the drafty place that smelled of blood and raw meat. A tiny wall of cupboards created a kitchen, along with a filthy range and dented refrigerator. I could almost hear my sister's thoughts. Where was the beautiful home he had promised? Where was the machine that washed clothes?

"You will sleep here," Alberto told me, tipping his head toward a ratty sofa in the main room. I glanced at him, sheepishly. Surely he'd rather have his wife all to himself. But to his credit, he gave me a welcoming smile. "This is your home, too, Paolina. Until you and Ignacio become husband and wife."

"But Alberto, I'm —"

528

"Hush," Rosa said, silencing me. "We will talk of wedding plans later."

Joh began to fuss. When I went to take her, Alberto swooped away. "It is okay. Mamma will change you." He planted the baby in Rosa's arms.

I stood, my mouth agape. Rosa giggled nervously, avoiding my eyes. Beside us, Alberto smiled, a dreamy look on his face. *"La mia famiglia è qui, finalmente."*

My family is here, at last.

For years I've thought of that moment, cursing myself for not making it clear, in that instant, Johanna was mine. In part, it was the sorrow I felt for my sister. In part, the loyalty. For what she thought would be a brief moment, she allowed her husband a glimpse of fatherhood. She hadn't considered how instantly he would fall in love. And once dispensed, she didn't have the heart to steal that joy from him. How could she explain, when he was holding a beautiful healthy baby in his arms, that his own child had died months earlier?

And so the nightmare began. The following week, while Alberto worked in the store, Rosa and I spent ten hours a day alone with Johanna. I demanded she tell the truth. And every day she promised she would. But each night, when Alberto entered the apartment, he would kick off his shoes, scrub his hands at the kitchen sink, and go straight to Johanna. He sang songs to her, rocked her, whispered as he smoothed her downy hair. And another day passed with a hole in the truth.

Had something broken in my sister's heart, when her body would not produce a healthy child? Was her fear of losing Alberto so overwhelming that she would do anything to keep him — even if it meant claiming her sister's child as her own? Or did she truly believe she was doing what was best?

By the end of the week, my sister stopped making promises. She only looked at me with sadness. "*La mia sorella testarda.* How can you be so selfish? Do you not see? I am doing what is best for Josephina. She will have a good life now. She will have a mamma and a papà and a loving aunt."

"She has a mother!"

"What can you give her, Paolina? You are so distraught you were willing to throw yourself off the boat!"

"That's not true. I could never do that."

"You are the second daughter. You were not meant to have a child; I was."

That evening, I finally took charge. I was holding Johanna when Alberto arrived home. When he reached for her, I kept her

530

firmly in my grip. "You need to hear the truth. This is my baby, Alberto. I am so sorry."

He reared back, his face a heartbreaking mosaic of shock and confusion. "Rosa?" he called into the kitchen. "What is she talking about?"

It seemed to take hours for my sister to turn around from her place at the stove. She looked at Alberto, not me, when she finally spoke.

"Poor Paolina is struggling with grief. I told you this already, Alberto. Do not agitate her."

"This has nothing to do with grief." My heart was pumping wildly, but I forced myself to remain calm. I explained to him, clearly and concisely, my idea to pretend Rosa was Johanna's mother. When I finished, he only looked at me sadly.

"No, Paolina. Rosa shared the good news many months ago. It was a letter I shall never forget. *Our love has multiplied. You are going to be a father.*"

I collapsed on the sofa, the gravity of the situation hitting me full force. The letter I'd dictated to Rico had been sent to Alberto — or at least, copied. Did Rico even know I was pregnant?

"Those were *my* words!" I screamed

531

through my tears. "That letter was meant for Rico, not you."

His voice boomed. "Enough, Paolina. I saw the name tag you wore at the Uffizi, pretending to be Rosa. But you are not her, do you understand? And Josephina is not your baby. This game is over, *capisci*?"

"Rosa miscarried," I said softly. "You lost your baby. I am sorry, Alberto."

"What proof do you have?" he said, his face bloated with rage. "If this child is yours, show me."

A sinking feeling came over me. I thought of the bogus birth certificate, the ticket stub with Josephina Lucchesi's name. Even my breasts had dried up. With the exception of slightly wider hips and a few faded stretch marks, my body had contracted as effortlessly as a rubber band. It was Rosa, with her flabby belly and pendulous breasts, who looked as if she'd just given birth.

I lifted my eyes to my sister, the only person who could corroborate the truth. "Tell him, Rosa," I begged. "Please. Now is the time."

"Yes," Alberto agreed. "Tell me."

My sister's face went white. Her hands trembled and she shoved them into her apron pockets. Despite my disgust, my feelings of vengeance, my heart went out to her.

She was frozen with fear. When she finally spoke, her voice was little more than a whisper.

"It was you who miscarried, my poor sister. The day I found you on the stair steps."

Did Alberto realize the truth? Sometimes, I suspected he did. But there were no DNA tests back then. I begged for all of us to test our blood types, but Alberto wouldn't hear of it. And because he and Rosa were believed to be the parents, I couldn't force it. Joh looked nothing like him or Rosa. Her skin was creamy, not nearly as dark as theirs. Her hair had a softer texture, and when the sun shone, gold highlights appeared. Her eyes eventually changed to brown, as Rosa claimed they would. But in the right light, they held fast to a hint of blue, as if my baby were insisting upon her true heritage.

But to everyone else, Johanna was Josephina, Rosa and Alberto's new baby, the only child they would ever have.

I begged my big brother, Bruno, to listen to me, sure he would be my ally. But he only looked at me with pity. He went to a drawer, removing letters Mamma had written in the months earlier. Each page chronicled Rosa's pregnancy, her growing belly, and the family's excitement.

"I know about your stillborn baby. I am very sorry." He pulled me to his chest. "It was not your fault."

I pushed him away with such force he staggered backward. "They are lying!"

He gave me a grave look, one my father might have delivered. Then he marched to his bureau and retrieved a photo. "You must stop, Paolina! You are scaring everyone with your behavior." He thrust the photo at me.

It was the picture Papà had taken at the harbor. A glowing new mother stood on a ship's deck, proudly displaying her infant. On the back, Mamma had written, *Rosa and Josephina, 17 September 1961.* I burst into tears.

Bruno took my head in his hands and brushed the tears from my face. "You love this baby. I see this very clearly. But she is only your niece."

"No! She is my daughter."

Bruno gathered me in his arms. "Shhh. It is okay. You will have another child, one who is healthy, and all yours. Ignacio is still willing to marry you. Imagine that! You, the second daughter, the first to find a husband."

I wanted to scream. Nobody would believe

me. I hated America. I hated Alberto. My sister was a stranger to me. We spoke only when necessary, exchanges that inevitably ended in fierce arguments. To keep from going crazy, I busied myself with cleaning and cooking, all the while weighing my options. Marrying Ignacio was out of the question. My dream of going to the university was lost now. I had no money, and I would never leave my baby.

If I stayed with Rosa and Alberto, I could be with Johanna, but I would never be her mother. As hard as it was to live that lie, at least we'd be together. I could help shape her, guide her. That's what Rico would have wanted.

Joh and I already shared a special bond, one that seemed to infuriate Alberto. He seethed when I called her Johanna, or when he caught her gazing into my eyes as I sang to her. He pretended not to see her smile when I blew kisses into her chubby neck. His face would turn crimson when she would cry and I was the only one who could soothe her. My heart swelled with love. She and I knew the truth.

Alberto grew weary of my presence. Within a month, he secured Rosa a job in the store, working ten hours a day. He insisted she bring the baby to work, an attempt, I knew, to keep Joh and me apart. When it became apparent I wouldn't marry Ignacio, Alberto began pestering me about finding an apartment of my own, suggesting places in other boroughs. It was clear, Alberto loved his family of three. I was not welcome.

Every day I grew more anxious, more desperate. I had to get my child away from Rosa and Alberto, before I lost her forever.

I made a horrid mistake, one I have forever regretted. I left with Johanna, without the knowledge or resources a single mother needs. Had I stayed, perhaps I could have remained in her life, rented a small apartment nearby, convinced Alberto that I wasn't a threat.

I escaped with Johanna one winter morning, on Rosa's day off. I waited until Alberto had left for work and Rosa was in the bath. With a bag of our belongings and Joh wrapped in a blanket, I snuck from the apartment. We traveled as far from Bensonhurst as the city bus would take us.

Suffice it to say, Harlem was a dreadful place back then. What's more, I had underestimated the cost of living on my own. One week later, I returned to Bensonhurst, penniless and defeated. I showed up at Bruno's apartment with my sick child, begging him to take us in.

While Bruno warmed a pot of milk, he informed me that Alberto had filed kidnapping charges.

That was the final blow, when my knees finally buckled. He had won. I would be of no use to my daughter if I were imprisoned.

Perhaps I should have been grateful to my brother. Bruno brokered the deal. He went to speak with Rosa and Alberto and returned three hours later with a proposition. The kidnapping charge against me would be dropped. I would not go to jail. Instead, I would leave Brooklyn. Forever. I would be allowed to visit at Christmas and Easter. I could send Josephina cards on holidays. But I must promise never to claim her as my child.

I tried to convince myself she'd be better off. She had the chance to grow up with two caring parents, free from ridicule and poverty. I had nothing to offer my daughter except love, and despite what I once believed, love was not enough.

My grief nearly leveled me. I taped a shiny penny to the backside of her crib, where nobody would see it. Then I walked three blocks to the bus station, hollowed out and empty. I spotted a travel poster at the depot for a place called "the Sweetest City on

Earth." I bought a one-way ticket to Hershey, Pennsylvania. If there was anything I craved at that time, it was sweetness.

But for nearly two years, life wasn't so sweet. Almost immediately, I regretted my decision. But there was no turning back. Any chance of convincing even one person of the truth was no longer an option. What kind of mother gives up her child? I was shackled by guilt and self-loathing. What would Rico think if he knew I'd given away our child? I grew intimate with the term "self-destruction." I acted recklessly. I wanted to die, it's as simple as that. But thanks to friends like Thomas and a hidden, deep-seated resiliency, I eventually found my bearings again. I had someone who needed me, and I would not let her down.

I spent the next twenty-seven years living for the holidays, the only time I was allowed to see my daughter, Johanna Rosa Krause.

CHAPTER 55

EMILIA

I place a hand over my trembling mouth. "I'm sorry," I say. "I am so, so sorry."

Her eyes are bright with tears and she opens her arms to me. "My girl."

I burrow into them, feeling the blessed comfort of a mother's love, the feeling I'd been yearning for, for as long as I can remember.

"My nonna," I say, the word finally finding its sweetness. "All my life, I've been hoping for you."

"And I you," she whispers.

I look over to where Rico sits, tears raining down his cheeks.

"Opa," I whisper, moving toward him through a hazy blur.

"Meine schöne Enkelin," he says, his wet cheek pressed to mine. He smells of cologne and peppermint candy, exactly how I'd imagined my grandfather would.

"I've never had a grandfather," I croak.

"I've never had a granddaughter," he replies. "You cannot imagine how happy I am that you're mine."

"That makes Jan my . . . half-step-cousin. I have a whole other family in Germany." Tears spill over my lids.

"So now you understand," Poppy says, taking my hands. "My Johanna did die, in a sense, when 'Josephina' was born. And Rosa did, indeed, become a mother, that very day I proposed she play the role."

"Did Aunt Josie ever know the truth?" Lucy asks.

Poppy nods. "I suspect she did. A soft heart is a keen observer of the truth."

My chest aches for Poppy . . . *my nonna.* She kept this enormous secret her entire adult life. She showed such grace, allowing herself to become ostracized and scorned, a woman considered a thief.

"You deserve to be vindicated," I say. "Not just by me and Lucy but by our entire family. It doesn't matter that Rosa is still alive."

Poppy shakes her head. "Rosa has paid her penance."

"No. She's —"

"I'd placed my vulnerable sister in a horrible position, and for that I am truly sorry."

"How can you be sorry? She stole your child."

She nods. "Unbeknownst to me, Rosa was in a state of grief when, all those years ago, I asked her to pretend to be Joh's mother. I provided an easy solution to her problem, and the temptation was too great. Once Rosa decided to lie, it became impossible for her to recant. She believed she would lose her husband, and possibly the love of our papà, if they discovered she could not bear children. How overwhelming that secret must have felt. To keep it, she had to be fierce, to rule with anger. Those who cannot win hearts with love often control people with fear."

"How can you be so sympathetic?" I say. "She ruined your life."

She reaches over and our hands intertwine. "Few of nature's creatures are born scared. It is desperation that begets fear. Fear creates cruelty. Rosa was a desperate person."

I gaze out at the twinkling lights of the piazza, finally understanding why Rosa believed so fiercely in the curse. She needed it to absolve herself. As long as the Fontana myth was alive, she could make believe Poppy's fate was the fault of the curse, not of her. Everyone knew the curse would not allow a second daughter to love.

"It gave me no pleasure when, years later, my sister suffered the ultimate consequence. Josephina was ill and Alberto was asked to donate blood." Poppy shakes her head. "Had he agreed to the blood test I'd suggested years earlier, he would have known that Rosa's A-positive blood type and his A-positive blood type could not have produced a child with type B blood. He died soon after Josephina passed, but not before apologizing to me. I believe he died of a broken heart."

"My god," I say. "He must have felt so betrayed."

"Yup," Lucy says. "Kind of like Poppy did when he refused to believe her. Karma sucks."

"You finally had the proof you needed," I say.

"Yes, but I no longer had the desire. Rosa was a broken woman. She'd lost her daughter and her husband. I could not turn the family against her." Her eyes meet mine. "I'm asking the same of you, Emilia."

I lower my gaze. "I've already confronted Rosa."

Poppy takes my hand. "Of course you did, my little pollia berry. But please, promise me you'll keep it from the rest of the family, at least until Rosa passes."

My beautiful, generous nonna, still protecting her sister.

She reaches into the manila envelope. As if handling an ancient relic, she gingerly places a photo on the table in front of me. "My favorite picture."

I stare down at the old, yellowed Polaroid snapshot. I recognize my dad's old brown sofa immediately. Wearing a hideous sweater with huge shoulder pads, a young brunette sits, her shadowed eyes gazing at the baby in her arms. She looks sweet . . . and fragile. I laugh through tears and trace her face with my finger. "Mom," I whisper.

"Jesus!" Lucy cries. "You and Em look exactly alike."

I turn my attention to the forty-something woman beside my mother. Slim, with dark eyes, she smiles into the camera, her arm around my mother and two-year-old Daria on her lap.

"I get it now," I say, unable to pull my gaze from my beautiful young nonna. "I finally know why Rosa never liked me." I look up, into the eyes of the courageous and selfless, wise and wonderful woman who gave life to my mother. "I was a constant reminder of you — and the truth."

CHAPTER 56

EMILIA

Eleven Months Later
Trespiano

I shield my eyes from the morning's haze. A warm breeze brushes my skin, carrying the faint scent of roses and sage. Beneath a pergola canopied with pink bougainvilleas and braided vines, I spy Lucy and Sofia. A rush of love comes over me. I soak in the scene, Sofia on a chaise with her nose in her iPad, and Lucy at a small iron table with her bare feet propped on the chair in front of her, gazing out at the vineyard.

I make my way down the flagstone path. Lucy smiles when she sees me, her skin tawny from the Tuscan sun, her dark hair cropped and unruly.

"Finally," she says, "someone who'll talk." She thrusts a thumb at Sofia. "I can't get this one to put down that damn novel."

544

"Don't interrupt," Sofia says, lifting a finger but not her eyes.

My future novel! I can hardly believe it. It's only a Word document now, and I still have months of revision ahead of me, but my editor predicts it'll hit the shelves next fall. It's the story of a beautiful Italian woman in 1960, who fell in love with an East German violinist. I close my eyes and say a silent prayer of thanks to Nonna Poppy. If not for her, there would be no book. Until Poppy, I didn't have the courage, or the heart, to share my words with the world. I imagine Poppy shaking a finger at me. "Of course you did. You just needed to find your voice. But your next novel, Emilia, must be *your* story."

Is she still hoping I'll find love? Some people think having a ring on your finger is the ultimate goal. Not Nonna Poppy. And not me. In Italy, Poppy broke the curse. She helped me find my freedom. Not freedom to marry, necessarily, but freedom to believe. I may choose to love — or not. But I know one thing for certain: it's possible.

"You and Sofie seem really happy."

My cousin smiles, the kind of smile that comes from deep down in her heart and carries all the way to her eyes. "Things are great, with the exception of having the friggin' ocean between us." She raises her shoulders. "*Que será, será.* Who knows what the future will bring? We're happy with what we have now, a week here and there. The boys love Bensonhurst. Did I tell you Franco wants to be a barber?" She laughs. "Grandpa Dolphie has a chair reserved for him. Oh, and they're all coming for your dad's wedding in April."

"Perfect." When my dad proposed to Mrs. Fortino last month, they insisted it would be a small wedding. But when two Italian families merge, "small wedding" is an oxymoron. Secretly, I think he's pleased.

Lucy studies a persimmon tree, its autumn fruit a mosaic of ocher and orange. "You know, all that time I was looking for someone to love me. But what I really wanted was to love."

"You found it, Luce."

She nods. "And look at you, Em. I can't believe my cousin is a famous author."

I wave her off. " 'Famous' and 'author' are mutually exclusive terms."

She rolls her eyes. "I don't know what the hell you just said. All I know is that I'm proud, and you should be, too."

My phone chimes and I peek at it. "Daria," I say. "I'll call her back."

Lucy tips her head. "You still haven't told

546

her, have you?"

"Not yet."

"But you're allowed to now," Lucy says. "Poppy said you could spill the beans once Rosa died."

"It's only been six months. Dar's still grieving. She and Rosa were tight. But one day, I will. The girls need to know how incredible their great-nonna was."

"And how evil Rosa was."

"No. Poppy was right. Rosa was trapped in a lie, and it poisoned her. When Poppy and I FaceTimed with Rosa, just hours before she died, she actually cried."

"No shit? Like real human tears?"

I can't help but smile. "Yup. I think even her nurse was shocked."

I startle when someone comes up behind me and kneads my neck. I lift my face and pat his hand. "Good morning, Gabe."

"Buongiorno, bellezza."

What a flirt. A year ago, I would have melted at Gabe's touch. I shake my head, thinking of that naïve girl who shrank back to her room, red-faced and mortified, heartbroken and humiliated. To this day, it was the most romantic date of my life.

Back then, I thought kisses held promises, and sex implied a future. I'm wiser now, and more realistic. But of all the men who could have delivered my first real heart-break, I'm oddly proud to say it was Gabriele Vernasco.

I sit up at the sound of a car engine. Dust kicks up in the driveway. "He's here!" My chair scrapes against the flagstone and I dash to the front yard.

Wearing khaki slacks and a straw Belfry hat, Rico shuffles his way to me. He's clutching his old violin case in one hand, a metal box in the other. He lowers them to his sides and opens his arms. *"Mein Mädchen."*

"Opa!" I press my face against his chest, my heart overflowing.

He finally steps away. "How are you holding up?"

"I miss her so much."

"She would be overjoyed to know we are all together for her birthday, as promised."

All except her, I imagine we're both thinking.

"You gave her the happiest ten months of her life."

His voice breaks. "We both did."

Arm in arm, we make our way toward Casa Fontana, the house where his beloved once lived. He stops before we reach the porch, and fishes into his pocket.

"Our pied-à-terre in Ravello," he says,

holding out an old-fashioned brass key. "Poppy and I want you to have it."

I step back. "No. I can't."

He gently places the key onto my palm. "Jan agrees. The apartment belongs to you, our granddaughter. You will need to see Poppy's attorney friend in Amalfi to sign the papers, and then it will be all yours. We have great hope that it will be the launching pad of many happy memories."

I stare at the key, and all the possibilities it holds. "Thank you, Opa. You and I will live there together. I'll buy a sleeper sofa for me —"

He pats my cheek. "I must return to Germany. But purchase that sofa — I will be visiting often." He smiles. "Luciana will enjoy the apartment, too. And Sofia, of course, and the boys. Perhaps one day even Daria and the girls will visit."

"Daria," I say, already imagining it.

We wait until dusk before setting out to the field where my great-grandparents and their children once toiled. It's a warm evening, silent except for the chirping of insects and the thrashing of the grasses as we climb the hill. I spread out a blanket and Rico sets down his violin case. He gazes down at the metal container in his hand and gently kisses it.

Lucy, Rico, and I reach into the tin, each taking a handful of our Poppy's ashes. Rico turns, facing west, where the horizon is dusted with peach and lavender. "As we promised, *mio unico amore.* One last Tuscan sunset."

He strikes up his violin. Bittersweet notes cry out, *Que será, será.* I throw my arm to the pastel sky and release my clenched fist. A breeze rushes over the hill, catching the ashes and setting them afloat. For the briefest moment, Poppy's remains become iridescent in the sun's golden halo. Then they're swept away, into the ethereal, infinite horizon.

An image of my nonna Poppy and her Johanna comes alive. Together, they're laughing, hugging, dancing in the heavens.

"It's possible," I whisper.

CHAPTER 57

EMILIA

Days Later
Amalfi Coast

Daylight softens. Along the beach, two men dressed in black work to fold umbrellas and stack lounge chairs. I check my map, then trot up a hill and wind my way through the seaside town of Amalfi.

I reach the pretty tree-lined Via Pomicara and check my phone again for the address of Poppy's attorney friend. I pass a white stucco building wreathed in vines and bougainvilleas and almost miss the small placard beside the door. *Studio Legale di De Luca e De Luca.*

The polished cherry door squeaks when I step inside. I take a deep breath. In a matter of minutes, I'll have my own home. A balloon of gratitude sets afloat in me.

I gaze about a stylish but deserted recep-

551

tion room. Has everyone left for the day? Somewhere down the hall, a radio plays. I step forward.

"Hello?" I call softly, taking another step.

The music grows louder. I reach an open door and freeze. A thirty-something man with a close-cropped beard sits with his feet propped on his desk and a novel splayed on his chest. His head is tipped back and he's snoring. I can't help but smile.

I clear my throat and he bolts upright, sending the novel hurling to the floor.

"Merda!" he says, the Italian word for "shit." He glances at me as he scrambles to retrieve the book — some sort of crime mystery. *"Scusi."*

"It's okay," I say. "I'm sorry I . . ." I start to say "woke you," but opt for the less embarrassing, "startled you."

He rakes a hand through his wavy hair and straightens his tie. "I apologize," he says, grabbing a pair of dark-framed glasses from the desk and planting them on his face. "I was not expecting —" He leans in to peer at me. "Do I know you?"

"No. But I spoke to someone on the phone earlier this week — maybe you? I said I'd be coming in today to sign some papers that my aunt — my *grandmother* — and my grandfather had drawn up."

He shuffles through several folders on his desk. "You must have spoken to my father. He has left for the day." He lands on a stack of papers and squints at the top page. "You are Emilia Antonelli?"

"That's me."

"Ahh, Poppy and Rico's granddaughter, at last." He places his warm hand in mine. "Hello, Emilia. I am Domenico De Luca." He cocks his head and stares directly into my eyes. "But you and I have met, I am certain."

"Nope. Not me."

"Maybe six . . . eight months ago? I would not forget a face so beautiful."

I stop short of rolling my eyes. "You must be mistaken."

"No. I do not think so." He stands, stroking his beard, gazing at me, until finally I point to the pages.

"Are those for me?"

"Ah, yes." He gestures to a rectangular table and pulls out a chair for me before taking the seat beside mine. He's tall, with broad shoulders and long legs. When he positions the first page in front of me, I catch sight of his long, tapered fingers, minus a ring — not that I'm looking. In a deep voice that, I must admit, does sound vaguely familiar, he explains the legal jargon

553

as I read along. He smells of soap and heat — the way a man should — making it hard to concentrate.

I look up when I realize he has stopped reading. He studies me with knit brows. "I remember your face, those eyes." He vaguely lifts his hand toward my face. "I have thought about it many times. I believe we met at Giardini Caffè? Am I right?"

I shake my head. "Never heard of it."

His eyes twinkle. "Perhaps you would allow me to take you to dinner sometime, so we can uncover this mystery?"

I get it. You're incredibly charming, and lines like this probably work on many an unsuspecting signorina. But let's cut the bullshit.

"Shall we sign the papers?" I say, pulling a pen from my purse.

I roll my suitcase up the cobblestone walk, greeting a couple as they pass. Ravello is cast in bronze now, and the thrashing sea croons in the distance. Poppy's old Welsh word *hiraeth* springs to mind. She predicted one day I'd understand its meaning, and she was right. It feels as if this seaside town, half the world away from the city where I was raised, is the home I've been yearning for my entire life.

I stop when I reach the pink stucco building. A dim light shines in the old bakery, and I imagine my young nonna inside, some sixty years ago, making bread before sunrise. A faded sign sits in a clouded window, marking the business *Affittasi* — For Lease.

I gaze through the large window, taking in the tin ceiling, the wall of ovens, the uneven plaster walls. Instead of a bakery I see the perfect bookstore, a cozy shop with shelves up and down the center, and a small reading area in the back.

My mind wanders as I move around back. Does Ravello need a bookstore?

The hum of the piazza quiets when I step into the wonderfully rebellious courtyard, overgrown with vines and tangled roses. A café table and a pair of chairs are housed beneath the sprawling lemon tree — the perfect spot for writing.

I catch sight of the staircase and my smile fades. Will I ever climb these steps without thinking of my pregnant nonna Poppy, collapsed and near death? What strength she had, what resilience and grace. Just like my scar of courage, these steps will remind me that I can endure anything, that nothing is impossible. After all, I am Poppy Fontana's granddaughter.

I fit the key into the lock. The old wooden door creaks when I open it. I step into Rico and Poppy's old apartment — my new home in Ravello, the place I'll launch memories and write my next novel. Yes, it's possible.

I flip on a light switch. The colorful poppy painting comes to life, along with a new piece of art, my favorite. I move into the living room, my eyes already misty. Hung in a thick, contemporary frame, it's the photo Lucy snapped almost a year ago in the hospital courtyard. Printed in a cool black-and-white, giving it an artsy vibe, the picture covers much of the wall. I'm sandwiched between my grandparents, laughing, as Poppy kisses my cheek and Rico gazes at me with a tenderness I only now understand.

I travel from room to room, giggling, saying prayers of thanks to my nonna and opa. The place is gorgeous. How did they know this is where I was meant to be planted?

I spot a note on the kitchen counter, written in Italian.

Welcome home, Emilia. Best wishes settling in. I trust you will love this place as much as your nonna and I did. Remember us at dusk, when you take a glass of wine to the rooftop and bid farewell to the sun, before it ducks beneath the sea.

Elene and Jan send their best wishes. They would love to see you, once you are settled. We will all have dinner when I visit next month. Until then . . .

All my love,

Opa

P.S. I hope the signing with the lawyer went well. Mr. De Luca has been a godsend to us during this transaction.

My eyes fix on the Italian word for "lawyer." The hairs on my arms stand erect.

At once, I remember.

I glance at my watch. It's almost seven. Is he still there, reading his novel perhaps?

A memory finds me. *It's time we found you someone . . . I'm thinking someone cerebral. A dreamer . . . a lover of books.* My arms erupt in gooseflesh, and I know for certain my nonna has led me here, to this moment.

I fumble through my paperwork. Finally, I find his number. I lift my phone. My heart batters in my chest. He answers on the second ring.

"Nico De Luca."

"I remember now." A smile overtakes my face. "I called you an avocado."

He is silent for a moment, and then deep,

rich laughter pours over me. "Yes! That is right! It wasn't Giardini Caffè. We were in front of Piacenti's Bakery."

I smile as I meander down the hall. "I think you were wearing sunglasses that day. And a hat, too, if I'm not mistaken."

"If you tell me I was without a beard, you are completely forgiven."

I laugh. "The beard! That's what threw me off!" I step into Poppy and Rico's — *my* — bedroom. In the distance, the bells of the Ravello Cathedral chime. I pull back the gauzy white curtain and gaze across the piazza at the beautiful church, aglow with the last rays of sunlight. "I can't believe you remembered me, after all that time."

"It was an unusual encounter. You were like an angel who appeared out of nowhere, reminding me of my dream."

"You had a plan for the bakery," I say, recalling our conversation.

"Sì. And now you own that building."

I freeze. "I do? I own this entire building? Including the bakery?"

"Sì. I explained this before you signed."

My chest floods with gratitude and excitement . . . and anxiety.

"So I need to find a tenant? I don't know the first thing about commercial real estate."

"Do not worry. My father can help you.

Or my uncle." He pauses, and when he speaks again, his voice is tinged with hope, and trepidation, and seduction. "Or perhaps you will choose me?"

My breath catches. I know, somewhere in my heart, that his simple question comes loaded with possibilities. But I am happy now. I own this beautiful pied-à-terre, in a place that feels like home. I have a wonderful opa, and my sister's love again, along with my cousins', Lucy and Carmella. Matt Cusumano is my future cousin-in-law — or would that be my second-cousin-in-law? Whatever the title, he's my best friend again. And I have a new family in Germany, too, one I'm excited to meet. And on top of everything, I'm a soon-to-be published author. Do I dare risk the happiness, the genuine joy I feel now, for the possibility of love . . . and heartbreak?

His offer stretches between us like a bridge, waiting to be crossed . . . or circumvented. I can almost see my nonna Poppy, feel her soft hand enfolded in mine. *If love comes to you, if you find it within your grasp, promise me you'll pluck it from the vine and give it a good looking-over, won't you?*

"I am sorry, Emilia," Nico says. "I did not mean to be so forward."

I let go of the curtain and turn back to

559

the room. The day's final shaft of sunlight follows me, landing on a scratch etched above the door. I step closer, squinting up at it. It's been painted over, but I make out one letter . . . and then another. Shivers blanket me. A word comes into focus, then an entire sentence.

We chose love.
PF & EK

"I won't need your father," I say. "Or your uncle." I close my eyes, gathering all my courage. "I choose you."

Dear Reader,

Several years ago, I received a six-page letter from a reader in Germany. Dieter "Dieto" Kretzschmar, an elderly man from Germany who grew up during World War II, had suffered unspeakable atrocities during the Nazi regime, and later behind the Iron Curtain under the German Democratic Republic. In 1965, Dieto and the love of his life, Johanna, made a harrowing escape from their home in Dresden. Dieto went on to become a world-famous juggler. He wanted me to write his memoir.

I replied to Dieto, explaining that, although his story was fascinating, I write fiction. In no time, we were corresponding regularly. We've become great pen pals, and even met in person when Dieto visited the United States.

Though Dieto's story was not mine to tell, I couldn't stop thinking about the heartbreaking life he had endured, his spirit and resiliency. What happened to a relationship when a couple was split, one living in freedom, the other trapped behind the Iron Curtain? Soon, a story formed, this one contemporary fiction with a female protagonist. Though vastly different from my German friend's story, with his permission (and delight) I was able to sprinkle the novel with bits of his journey — his father being part of a troupe of prisoners that entertained the Russian soldiers, his mother finding shelter for her children in a sawmill in the village of Clausnitz, the angst he felt when leaving his family behind, his escape route using the trains and his bicycle.

I hope you enjoy Poppy and Rico's story — and Emilia's and Lucy's, too — as much as I enjoyed writing it. As Dieto signed off to me in his very first letter:

With kindest regards, yours sincerely,
Lori

ACKNOWLEDGMENTS

One of the first rules of writing is to show, not tell. Though I've tried to show my heartfelt gratitude to those who've traveled with me on this novel's journey, I have no doubt I've fallen short. Therefore, I must resort to telling, using mere words in an attempt to convey my deepest appreciation.

First and foremost, I give humble and hearty thanks to my dear friend Dieter "Dieto" Kretzschmar, the inspiration for Erich. Dieto, thank you for reaching out to me, a novelist thousands of miles from your home in Germany, and trusting me with your bittersweet memories. Though your life story is merely touched upon in this novel, your strength and resilience in times of adversity, your golden heart, and your good humor shone through during the entire writing process.

Aunt Poppy must have given me a lucky penny, because I've had the tremendous good fortune of being represented by my dream agent, Jenny Bent, along with her fabulous team of international agents. To each of you, I offer my sincere gratitude.

I'm over the moon to be working with the fantastic team at Berkley, led by the esteemed Claire Zion and my brilliant editor, Sarah Blumenstock. Your attention to detail, your patience and expertise, have created a far richer story. Additionally, I give a world of thanks to my ambitious and dedicated sales and marketing teams championed by Jeanne-Marie Hudson, Craig Burke, Jessica Mangicaro, and Tara O'Connor.

Grazie mille to my dear friends Joe and Elaine Natoli, for regaling me with tales of their Bensonhurst neighborhood and helping capture the essence of a big Italian American family. A million thanks to my wonderful friend and walking partner Vickie Moerman, for snapping and sending photos from Italy. Your eloquent descriptions helped bring Italy back to life in my mind's eye.

I give a huge shout-out to my invaluable cast of supportive friends during the penning of this novel, especially Linda Zylstra, Kathy O'Neil, Julie Lawson Timmer, Kelly O'Connor McNees, Kathryn Sue Moore, David Strickland, and my sister Natalie

Kiefer. As always, I pay homage to my early reader and fellow writer, the brilliant, hilarious, and endlessly encouraging Amy Bailey Olle. And to the generous authors who graciously gave their time to read and share their thoughts about this novel, you have my everlasting gratitude.

To my lovely reader friends, book bloggers, and booksellers, I am grateful and honored to have been welcomed so warmly into your hearts and onto your bookshelves. Thank you for embracing my novels, for sharing them with others, for reaching out to me with your thoughts. There is no greater joy for me as a writer than knowing that my story has touched another person's emotions.

To my wonderful parents and family, to God and my angels — I am humbled by your love. And finally, I thank my dear husband Bill. Without you, there would be no story.

■ ■ ■ ■

Readers Guide:
The Star-Crossed
Sisters of Tuscany

LORI NELSON SPIELMAN

■ ■ ■ ■

QUESTIONS FOR DISCUSSION

1. When she first steps foot on Italian soil, Poppy cries, *"Hiraeth!"*: a Welsh word conveying a deep longing for home, a nostalgia — a yearning — for the place that calls to your soul. Do you understand this feeling? Have you ever been to a place that feels inexplicably familiar or eerily unsettling? How do you explain it?

2. In chapter two, Emilia calls Bensonhurst home. When she returns from Italy, her perspective has changed. Have you ever felt trapped by a place you once loved? In what ways does travel change us? Are you more closely aligned with Poppy, an adventurous spirit who's always in search of something, or the earlier version of Lucy, someone seemingly content in her small but predictable world?

3. Poppy claims that life is much more

interesting when you learn to say, "It's possible." How likely are you to embrace the "it's possible" philosophy? Can you think of a time when you assumed something was impossible or out of your reach? What might have happened had you said, "It's possible"? In your experience, do you have more regret for things you did, or for things you didn't do?

4. Throughout Lucy's life, her mother tried to mold Lucy into the woman who would eventually break the curse. Do you think her mom had Lucy's best interest in mind, or do you think she was acting selfishly? Could both be true? How did her mother's expectations affect Lucy?

5. Lucy's desperation for love is apparent early in the novel. Later, she falls in love with Sofia. Was Lucy aware of her homosexuality prior to meeting Sofia? Was her mother? How might her life have been different had she acknowledged her sexuality at an early age? Would she have felt the same desperation to fall in love?

6. Poppy claimed the curse was a self-fulfilling prophecy. In what ways was she correct? Have you ever fallen prey to expec-

tations, whether familial, peer, or societal? How did you rise above them?

7. In what ways did the New Year's Eve car accident change Emilia's life? Without this twist of fate, do you think she would have found love, perhaps with Liam, and broken the curse? How might the family dynamics have been different had Emilia broken the curse?

8. Even after a heinous betrayal, Poppy still loved her sister. Should love for a sibling be unconditional? Poppy believes she put her sister into a horrible position, having to choose between her husband and her sister. Do you agree? Could you be as forgiving as Poppy? In the end, who was most hurt by the lie, Poppy or Rosa?

9. Rosa was once a loving sister. She experienced many life changes between her childhood in Trespiano and her adult life in Brooklyn. Who or what do you believe is most responsible for her bitterness? Do you feel any empathy for Rosa?

10. Daria admits that she resented Emilia for squandering her freedom. She implies that marriage and motherhood steal this freedom from women. Do you agree? Why

or why not? If you had complete autonomy, what might your life be like today?

11. Emilia says, "Young girls often dream of a white dress and a diamond ring. I suppose I had that dream, too, when I was younger. But I'm over it now." What if, as a young girl, you were told with certainty that you would never find love? How might you be different today? Would you look physically different? What articles of clothing would you banish from your closet? Is it likely you'd have more confidence, or less? Would you have the same friends, or different ones? Might you have lived more authentically, or less authentically? In what ways might your life be happier? In what ways might it be less fulfilling?

12. In the end, Emilia's single life is rich and full. Even so, she decides to take a chance on romance. Was her openness to love a necessary part of her character arc? How important is romantic love in a woman's life? If you were to write an epilogue, would the future Emilia be single or in a relationship? Why?

13. Even after telling Emilia and Lucy the truth about Johanna, Poppy wanted to wait until after her sister's death before telling

the rest of the family. Why was this important to Poppy? Do you agree with her decision to protect her sister?

14. Poppy and Rico's love withstood decades of separation. Do you think this kind of love is possible? They recited their vows on the church's altar without papers to prove it. Do you believe they were married in the eyes of God? Was Rico right to leave without Poppy, and return to help his family in East Germany? Why or why not? Do you think he would have taken Poppy to Germany had they had a legal marriage certificate?

15. Though she tried, Emilia could not reciprocate her friend Matteo's romantic feelings. But when Poppy tells her love comes in many forms and that not all love is romantic love, she rethinks her relationship with Matt. Do you think feelings of deep friendship and respect are enough to sustain a happy marriage? Love plays many roles, according to Poppy. What are love's most important roles to you? Do you suspect the importance of these roles changes over time?

16. When Poppy sees Rico's gunshot wound and learns that he tried twice to escape East

Germany, she says, "I should have waited." Of course, waiting for him in Italy would have been futile; he was never able to successfully escape. Why does Poppy say this? What is she feeling in that moment? The Berlin Wall came down in 1989, yet Rico and Poppy remained separated. Why didn't Rico try to find Poppy then? Why didn't she reach out to him?

17. Star-crossed is defined as "of a person or plan, thwarted by bad luck." In what ways are Rosa and Poppy star-crossed? Could either sister have changed her fate had she tried harder? Poppy collects and distributes lucky coins. What significance does this have in the story? Does Poppy believe in luck? Would Poppy consider herself a lucky or unlucky person? Would you agree?

ABOUT THE AUTHOR

Lori Nelson Spielman is the *New York Times* bestselling author of *The Life List* and *Sweet Forgiveness.* She is a former speech pathologist, guidance counselor, and homebound teacher. She enjoys fitness running, traveling, and reading, though writing is her true passion. She lives in Michigan with her husband.

CONNECT ONLINE
LoriNelsonSpielman.com
@LNelsonSpielman

The employees of Thorndike Press hope you have enjoyed this Large Print book. All our Thorndike, Wheeler, and Kennebec Large Print titles are designed for easy reading, and all our books are made to last. Other Thorndike Press Large Print books are available at your library, through selected bookstores, or directly from us.

For information about titles, please call:
(800) 223-1244

or visit our website at:
gale.com/thorndike

To share your comments, please write:

Publisher
Thorndike Press
10 Water St., Suite 310
Waterville, ME 04901

577